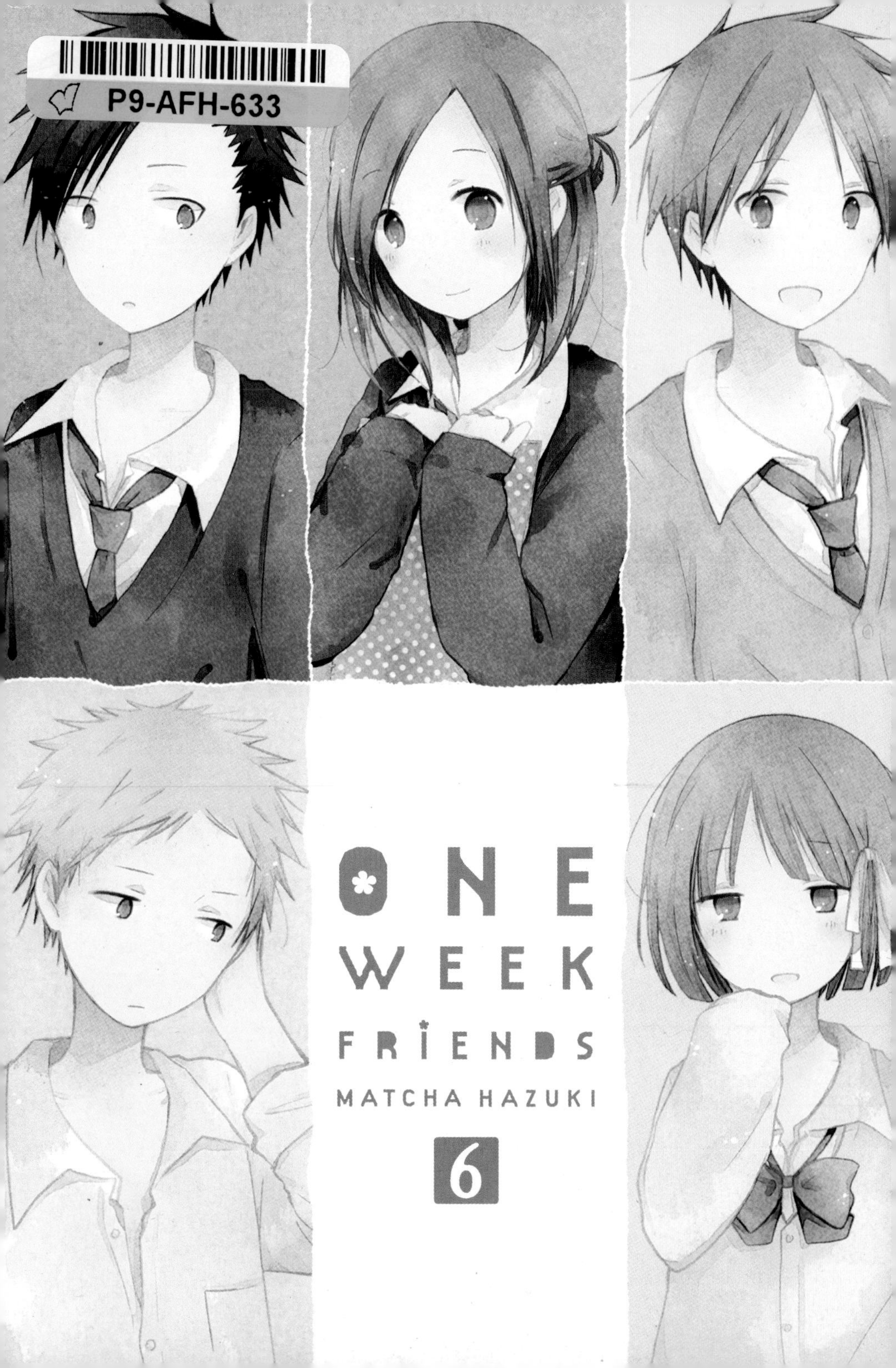
ONE WEEK FRIENDS
MATCHA HAZUKI
6
P9-AFH-633

ONE WEEK FRIENDS 6

Contents

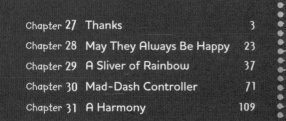

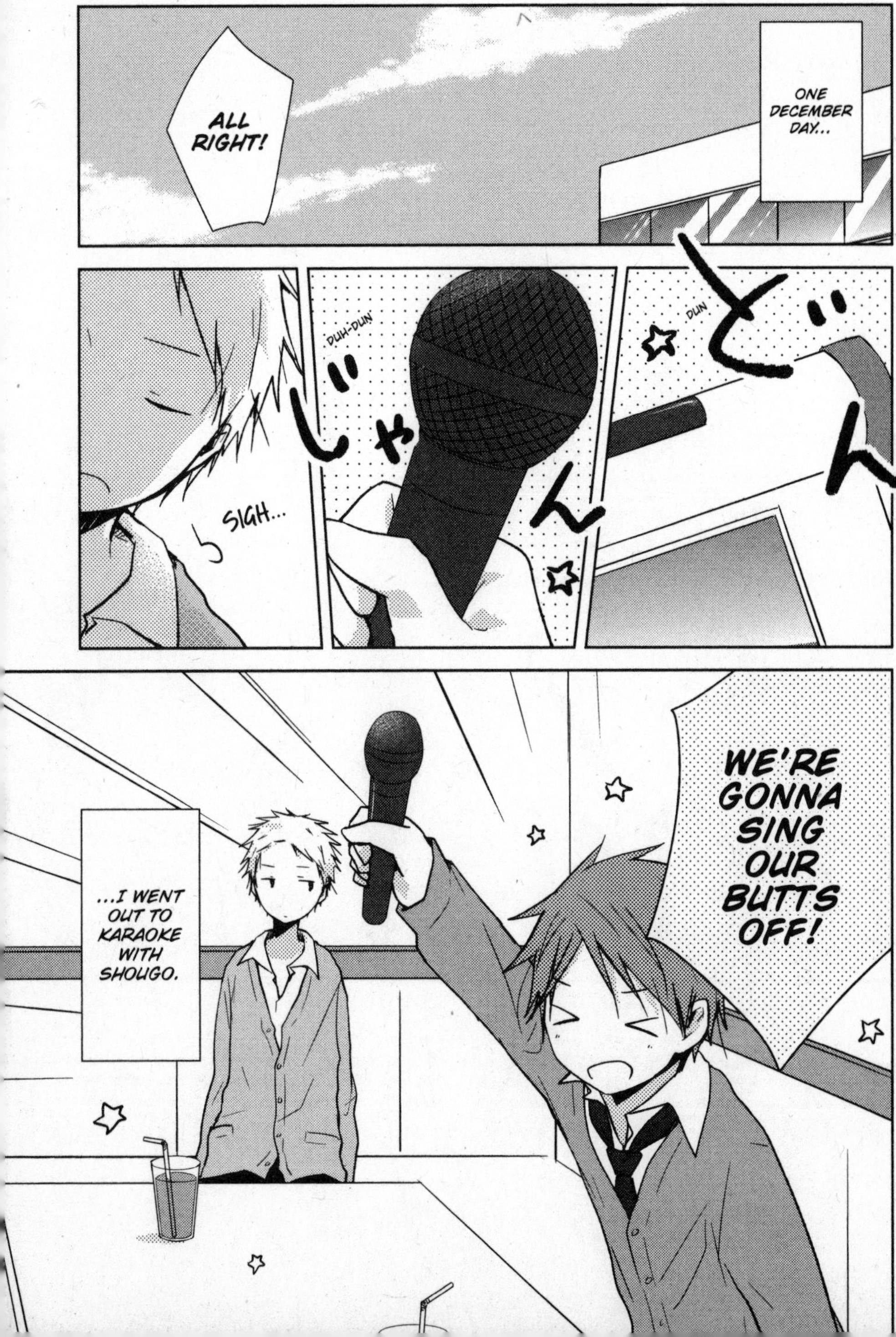
ONE DECEMBER DAY...
ALL RIGHT!
DUN
どん
DUH-DUN
じゃん
SIGH...
WE'RE GONNA SING OUR BUTTS OFF!
...I WENT OUT TO KARAOKE WITH SHOUGO.

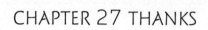

CHAPTER 27 THANKS

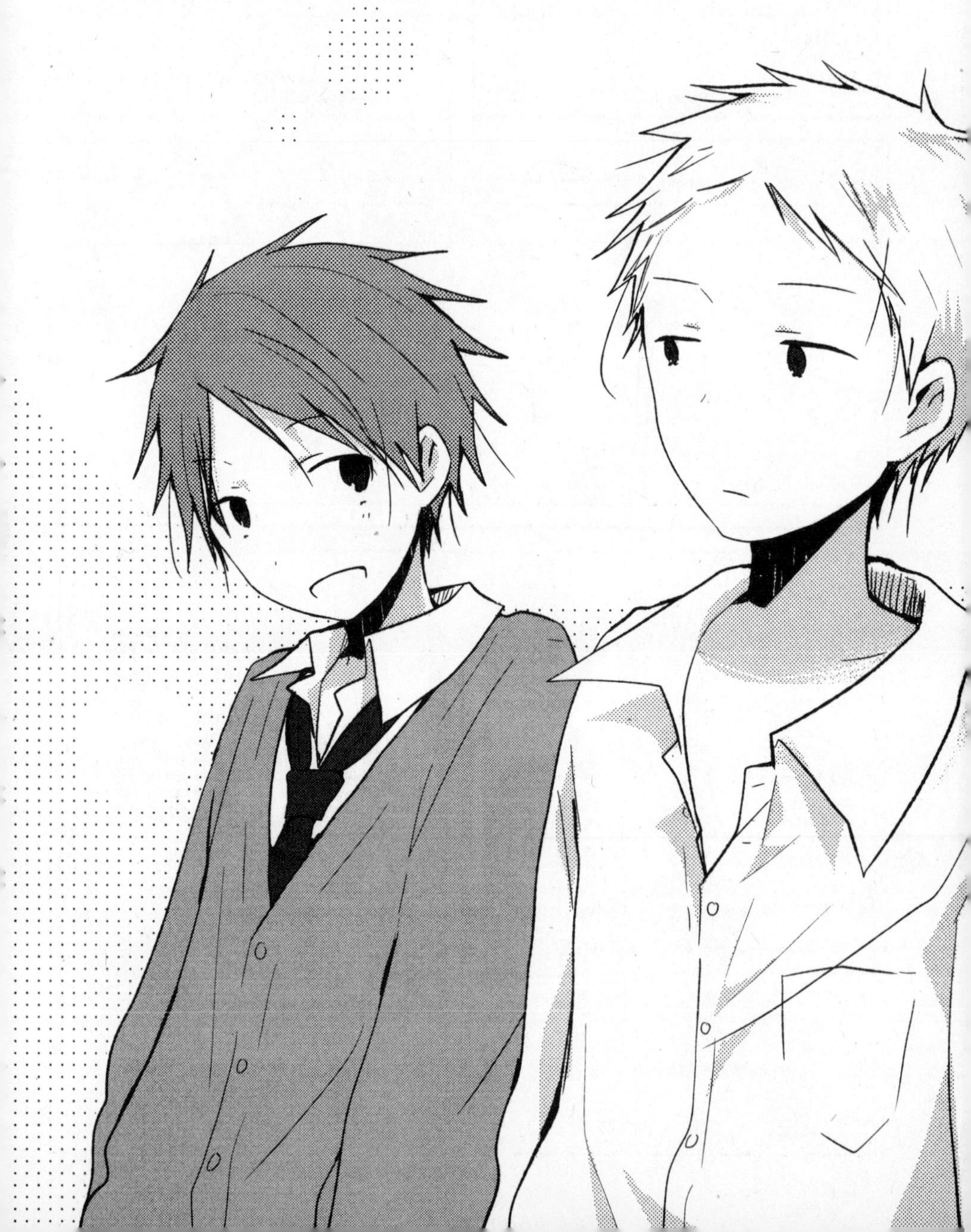

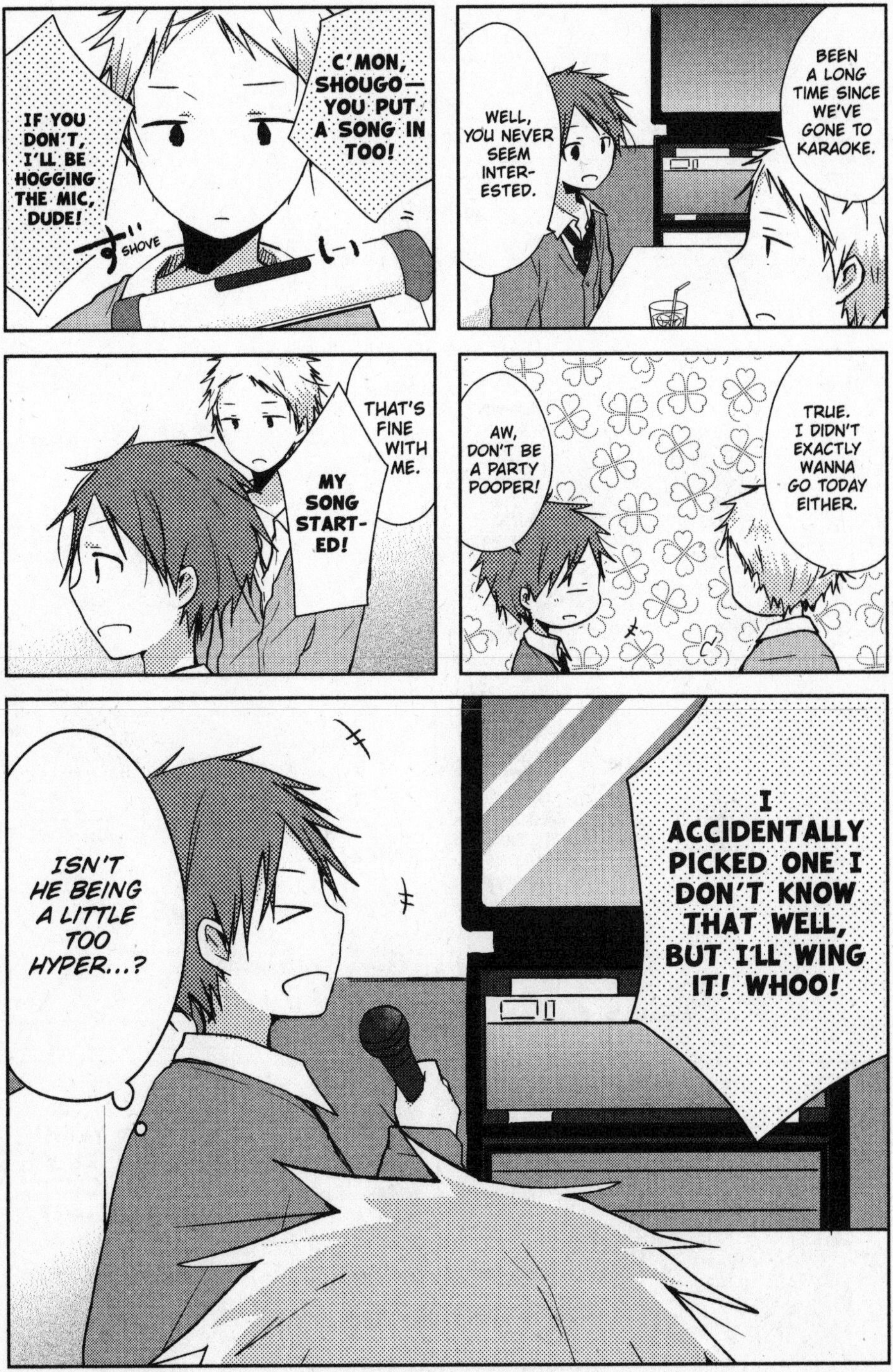
BEEN A LONG TIME SINCE WE'VE GONE TO KARAOKE.
WELL, YOU NEVER SEEM INTERESTED.
C'MON, SHOUGO— YOU PUT A SONG IN TOO!
IF YOU DON'T, I'LL BE HOGGING THE MIC, DUDE!
SHOVE
TRUE. I DIDN'T EXACTLY WANNA GO TODAY EITHER.
AW, DON'T BE A PARTY POOPER!
THAT'S FINE WITH ME.
MY SONG STARTED!
I ACCIDENTALLY PICKED ONE I DON'T KNOW THAT WELL, BUT I'LL WING IT! WHOO!
ISN'T HE BEING A LITTLE TOO HYPER...?

HYPED UP

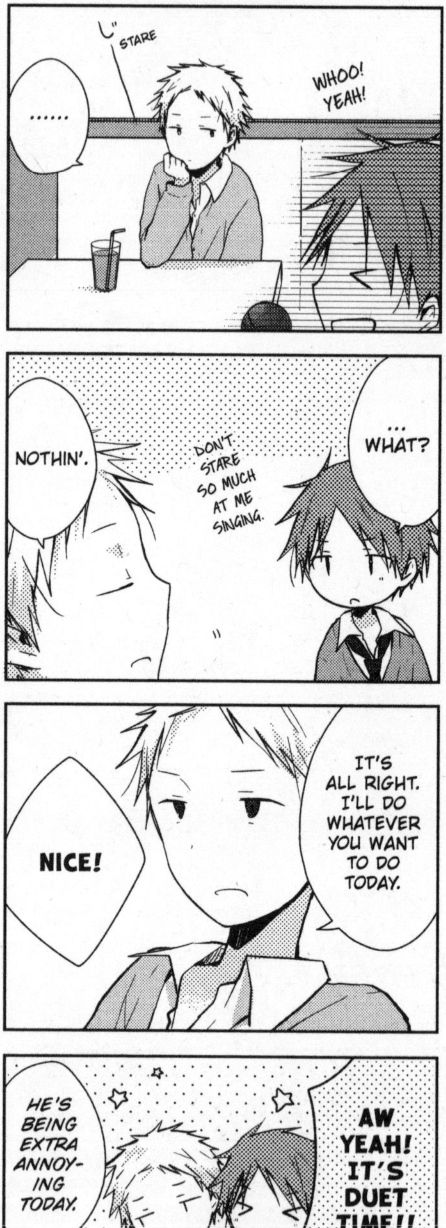
WHOO! YEAH!
じ" STARE
......
...WHAT?
DON'T STARE SO MUCH AT ME SINGING.
NOTHIN'.
IT'S ALL RIGHT. I'LL DO WHATEVER YOU WANT TO DO TODAY.
NICE!
AW YEAH! IT'S DUET TIME!!
HE'S BEING EXTRA ANNOYING TODAY.

ASKED FOR IT

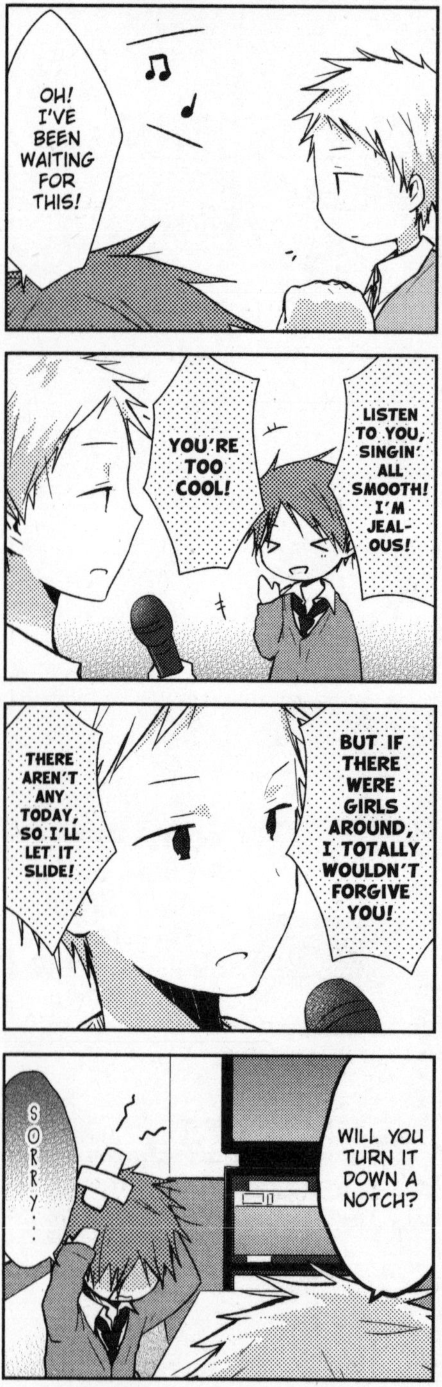
OH! I'VE BEEN WAITING FOR THIS!
LISTEN TO YOU, SINGIN' ALL SMOOTH! I'M JEALOUS!
YOU'RE TOO COOL!
BUT IF THERE WERE GIRLS AROUND, I TOTALLY WOULDN'T FORGIVE YOU!
THERE AREN'T ANY TODAY, SO I'LL LET IT SLIDE!
WILL YOU TURN IT DOWN A NOTCH?
SORRY...

REMINISCING

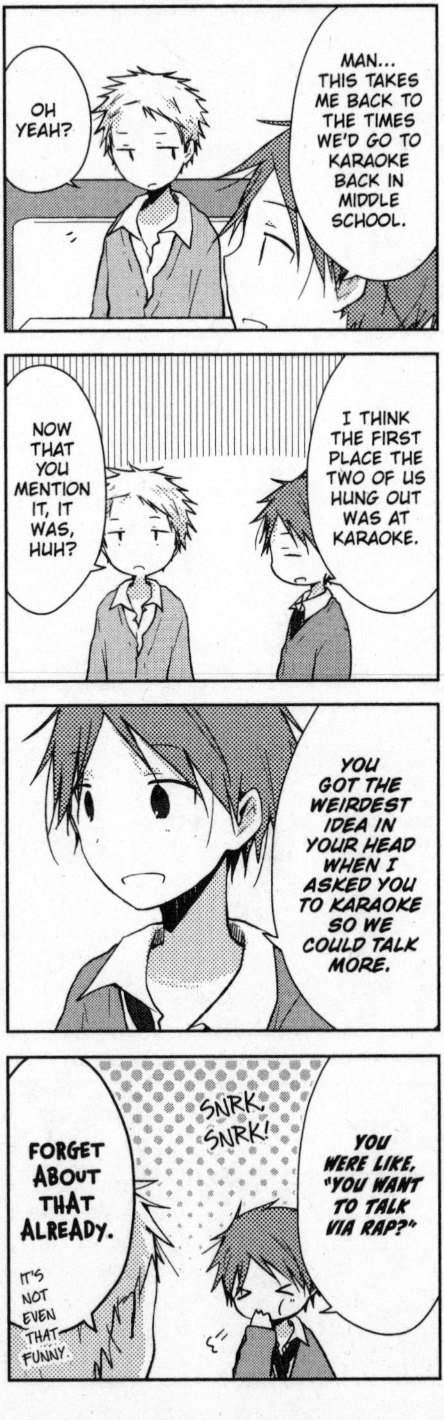
MAN... THIS TAKES ME BACK TO THE TIMES WE'D GO TO KARAOKE BACK IN MIDDLE SCHOOL.
OH YEAH?
I THINK THE FIRST PLACE THE TWO OF US HUNG OUT WAS AT KARAOKE.
NOW THAT YOU MENTION IT, IT WAS, HUH?
YOU GOT THE WEIRDEST IDEA IN YOUR HEAD WHEN I ASKED YOU TO KARAOKE SO WE COULD TALK MORE.
YOU WERE LIKE, "YOU WANT TO TALK VIA RAP?"
SNRK, SNRK!
FORGET ABOUT THAT ALREADY.
IT'S NOT EVEN THAT FUNNY.

GOING WITH THE FLOW

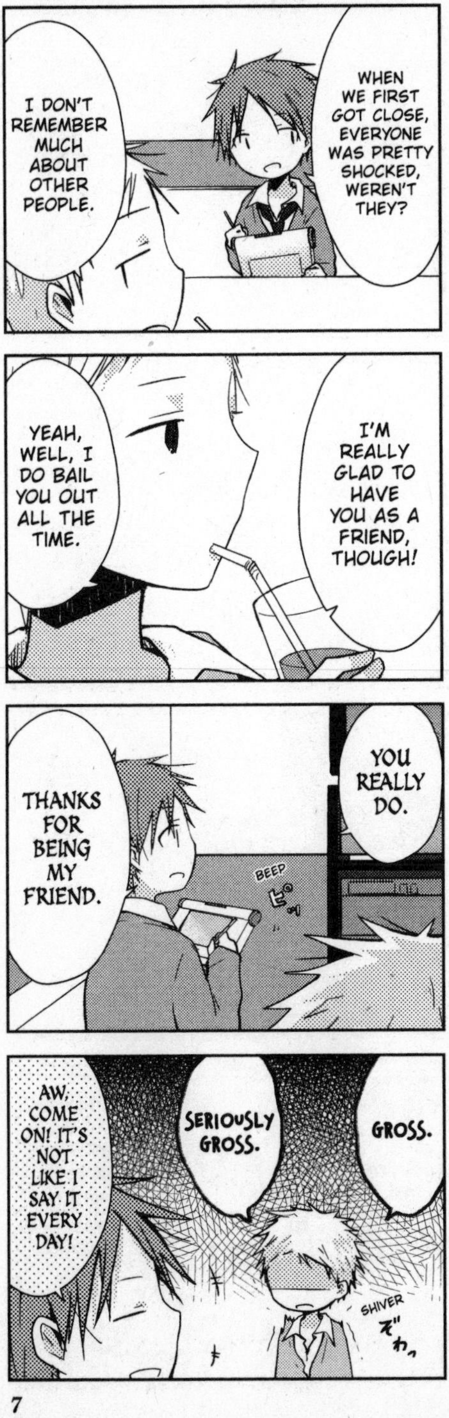
WHEN WE FIRST GOT CLOSE, EVERYONE WAS PRETTY SHOCKED, WEREN'T THEY?
I DON'T REMEMBER MUCH ABOUT OTHER PEOPLE.
I'M REALLY GLAD TO HAVE YOU AS A FRIEND, THOUGH!
YEAH, WELL, I DO BAIL YOU OUT ALL THE TIME.
YOU REALLY DO.
BEEP
THANKS FOR BEING MY FRIEND.
GROSS.
SERIOUSLY GROSS.
AW, COME ON! IT'S NOT LIKE I SAY IT EVERY DAY!
SHIVER

GETTING TOO HYPED

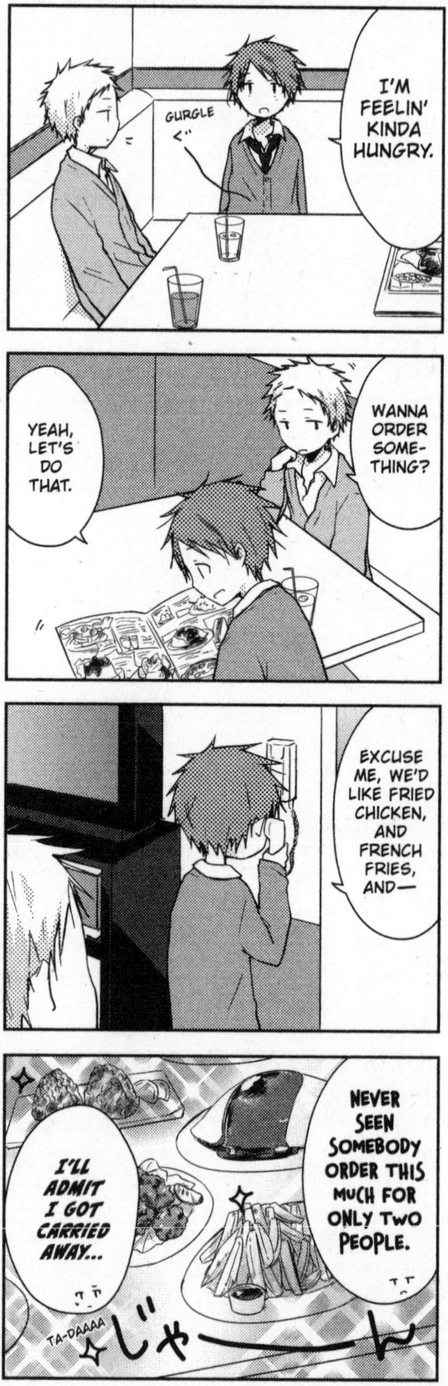

I'M FEELIN' KINDA HUNGRY.
GURGLE
WANNA ORDER SOMETHING?
YEAH, LET'S DO THAT.
EXCUSE ME, WE'D LIKE FRIED CHICKEN, AND FRENCH FRIES, AND—
NEVER SEEN SOMEBODY ORDER THIS MUCH FOR ONLY TWO PEOPLE.
I'LL ADMIT I GOT CARRIED AWAY...
TA-DAAAA
じゃーーん

SOMETHING'S WRONG

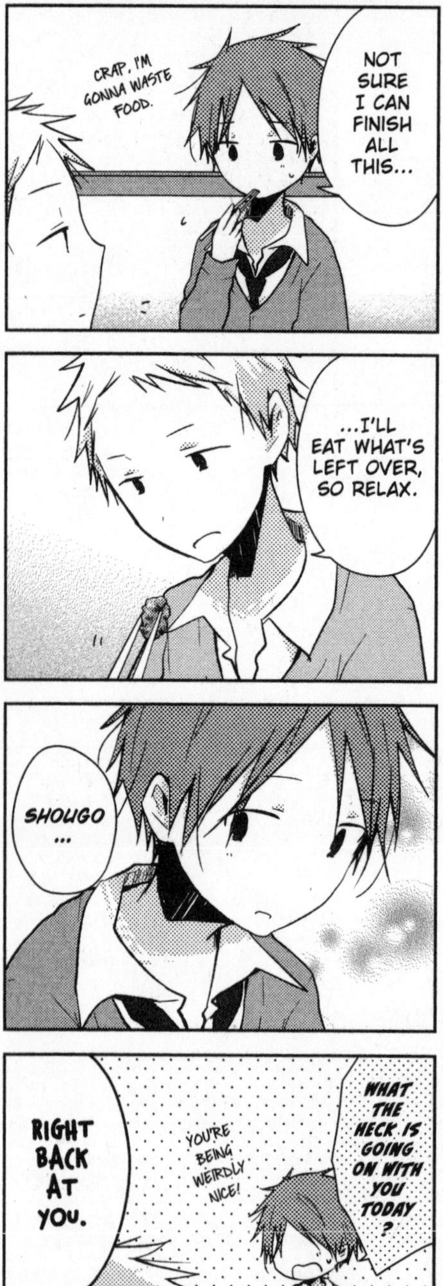

NOT SURE I CAN FINISH ALL THIS...
CRAP, I'M GONNA WASTE FOOD.
...I'LL EAT WHAT'S LEFT OVER, SO RELAX.
SHOUGO ...
WHAT THE HECK IS GOING ON WITH YOU TODAY?
YOU'RE BEING WEIRDLY NICE!
RIGHT BACK AT YOU.

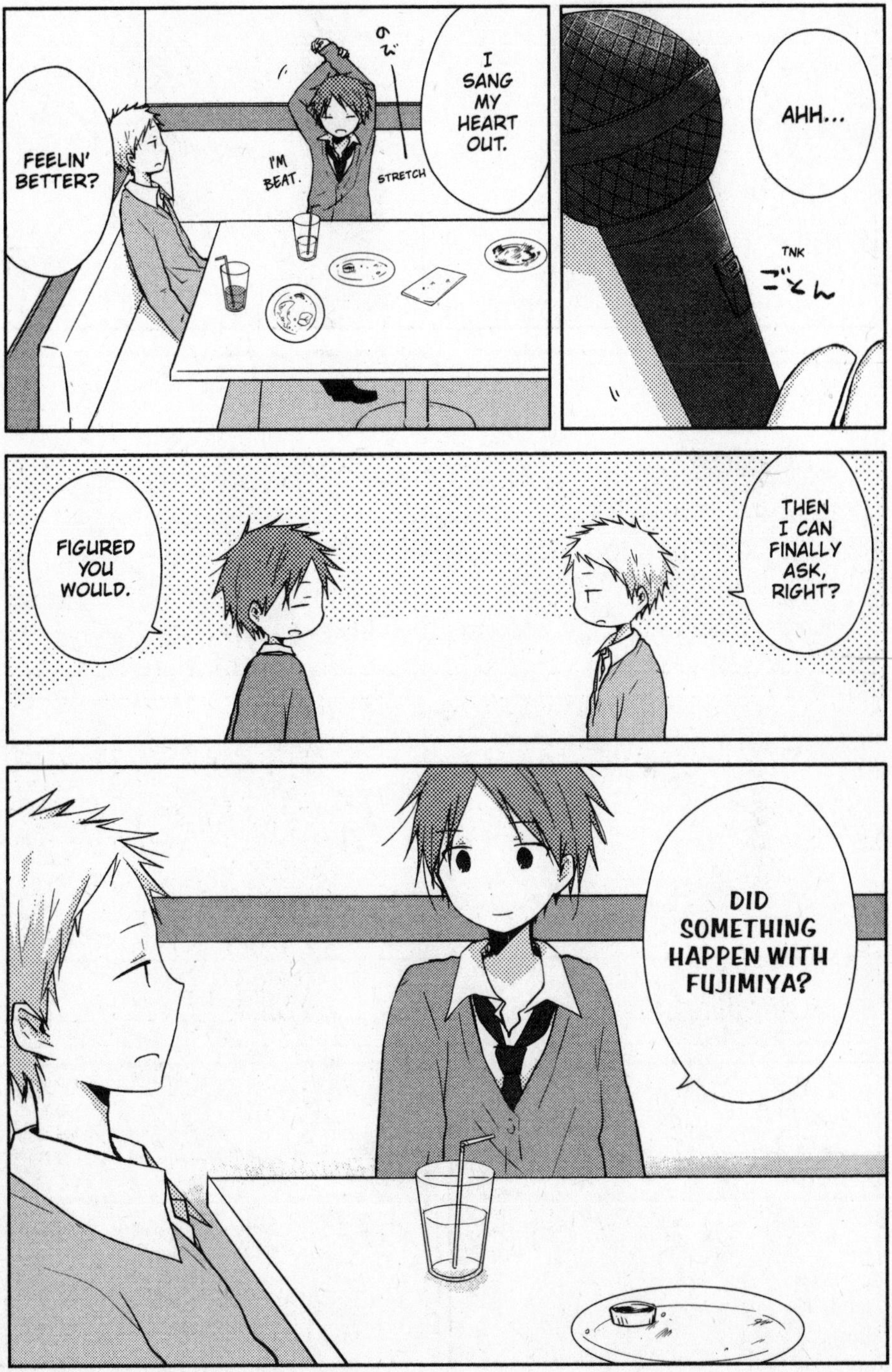
AHH...
TNK
ごとん
I SANG MY HEART OUT.
のび
STRETCH
I'M BEAT.
FEELIN' BETTER?
THEN I CAN FINALLY ASK, RIGHT?
FIGURED YOU WOULD.
DID SOMETHING HAPPEN WITH FUJIMIYA?

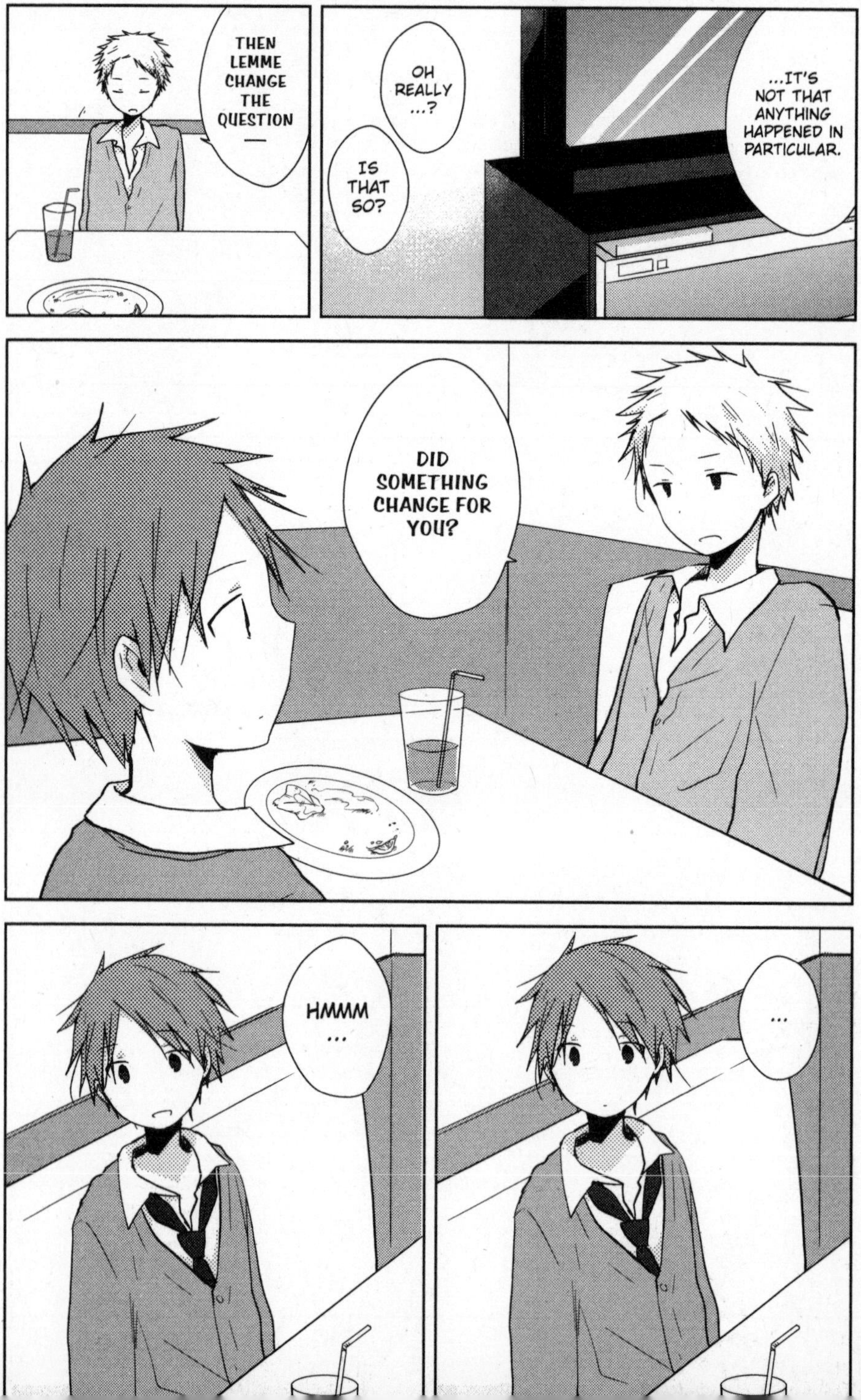
...IT'S NOT THAT ANYTHING HAPPENED IN PARTICULAR.
OH REALLY ...?
IS THAT SO?
THEN LEMME CHANGE THE QUESTION —
DID SOMETHING CHANGE FOR YOU?
...
HMMM ...

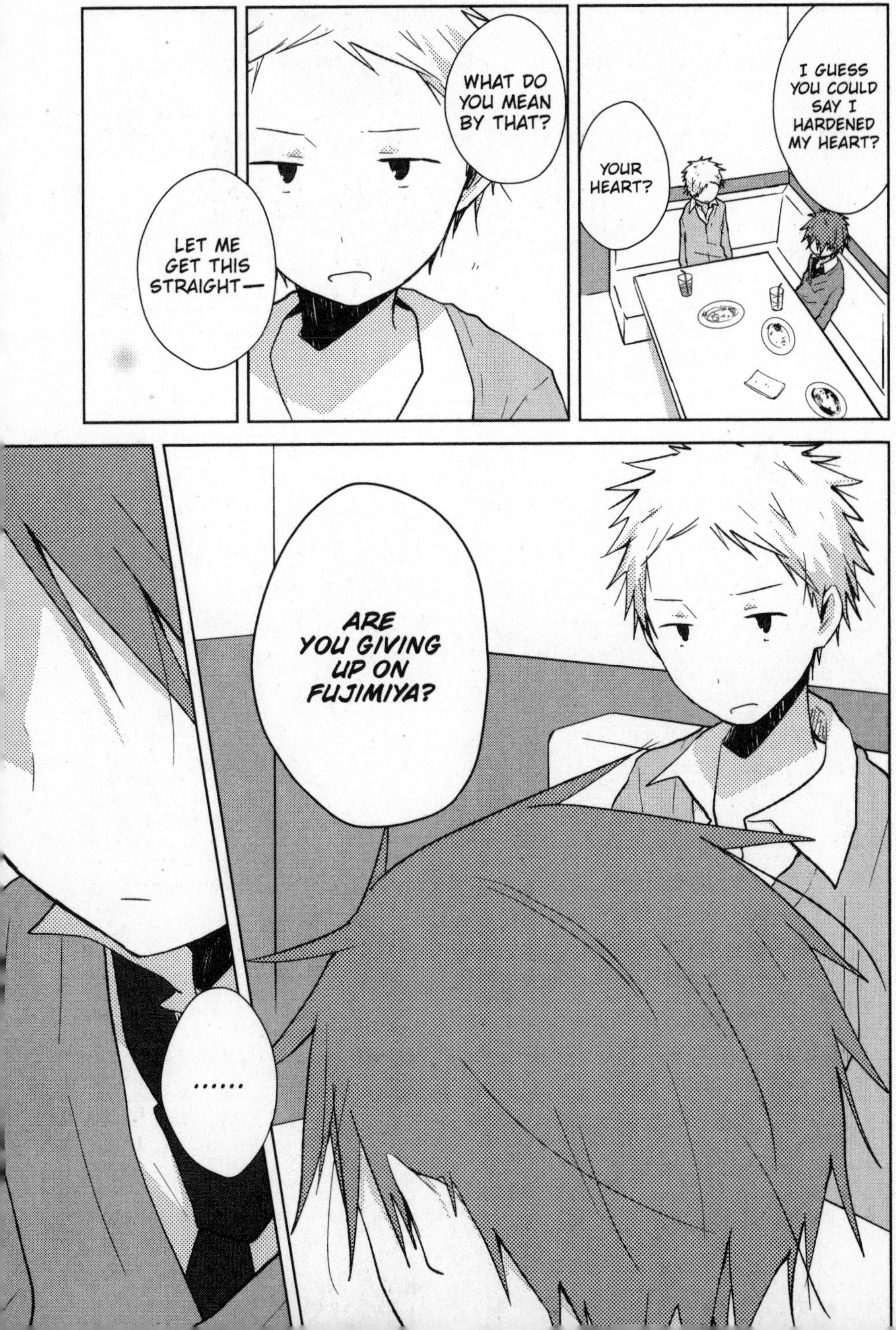
I GUESS YOU COULD SAY I HARDENED MY HEART?
YOUR HEART?
WHAT DO YOU MEAN BY THAT?
LET ME GET THIS STRAIGHT—
ARE YOU GIVING UP ON FUJIMIYA?
......

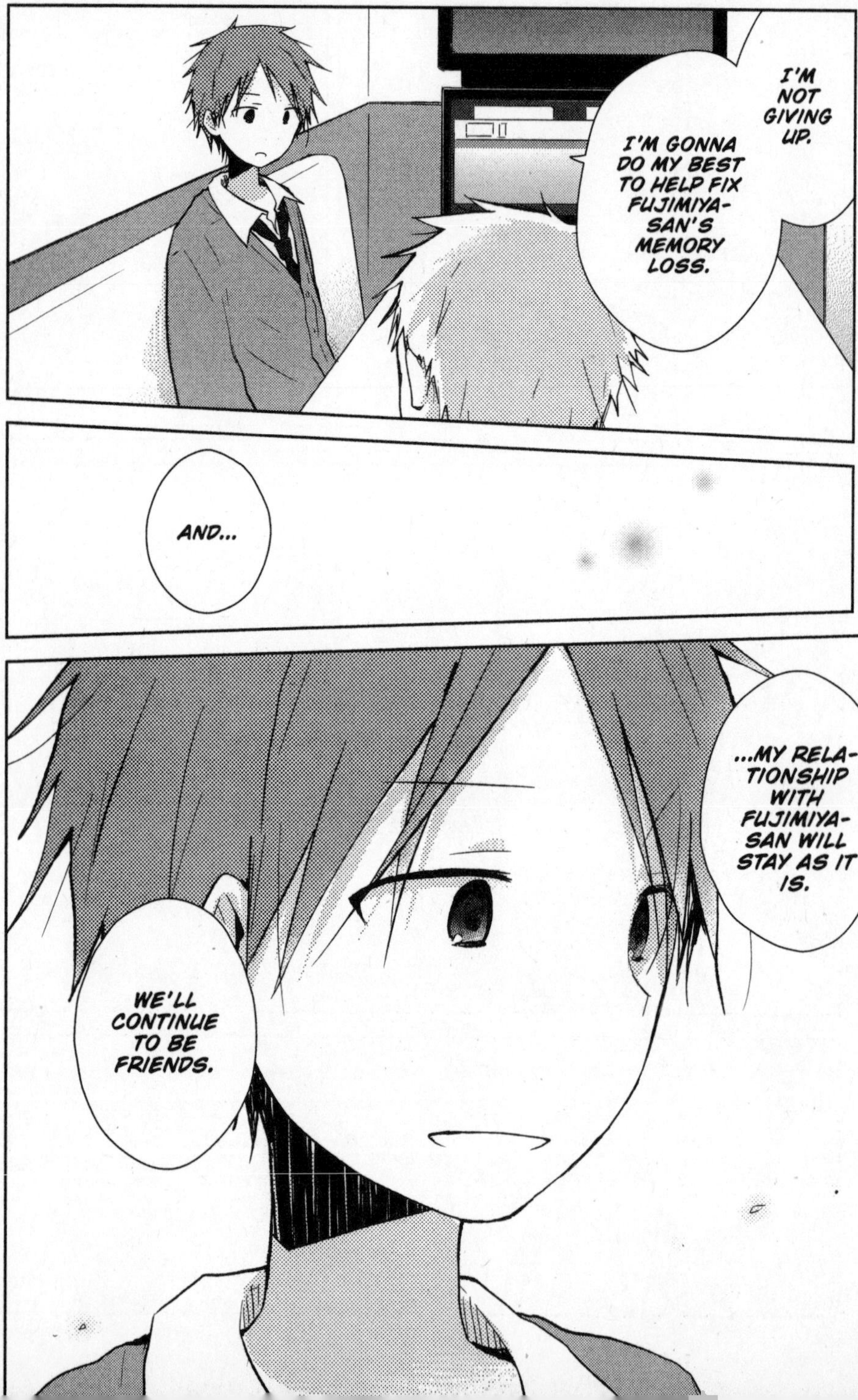
I'M NOT GIVING UP.
I'M GONNA DO MY BEST TO HELP FIX FUJIMIYA-SAN'S MEMORY LOSS.
AND...
...MY RELATIONSHIP WITH FUJIMIYA-SAN WILL STAY AS IT IS.
WE'LL CONTINUE TO BE FRIENDS.

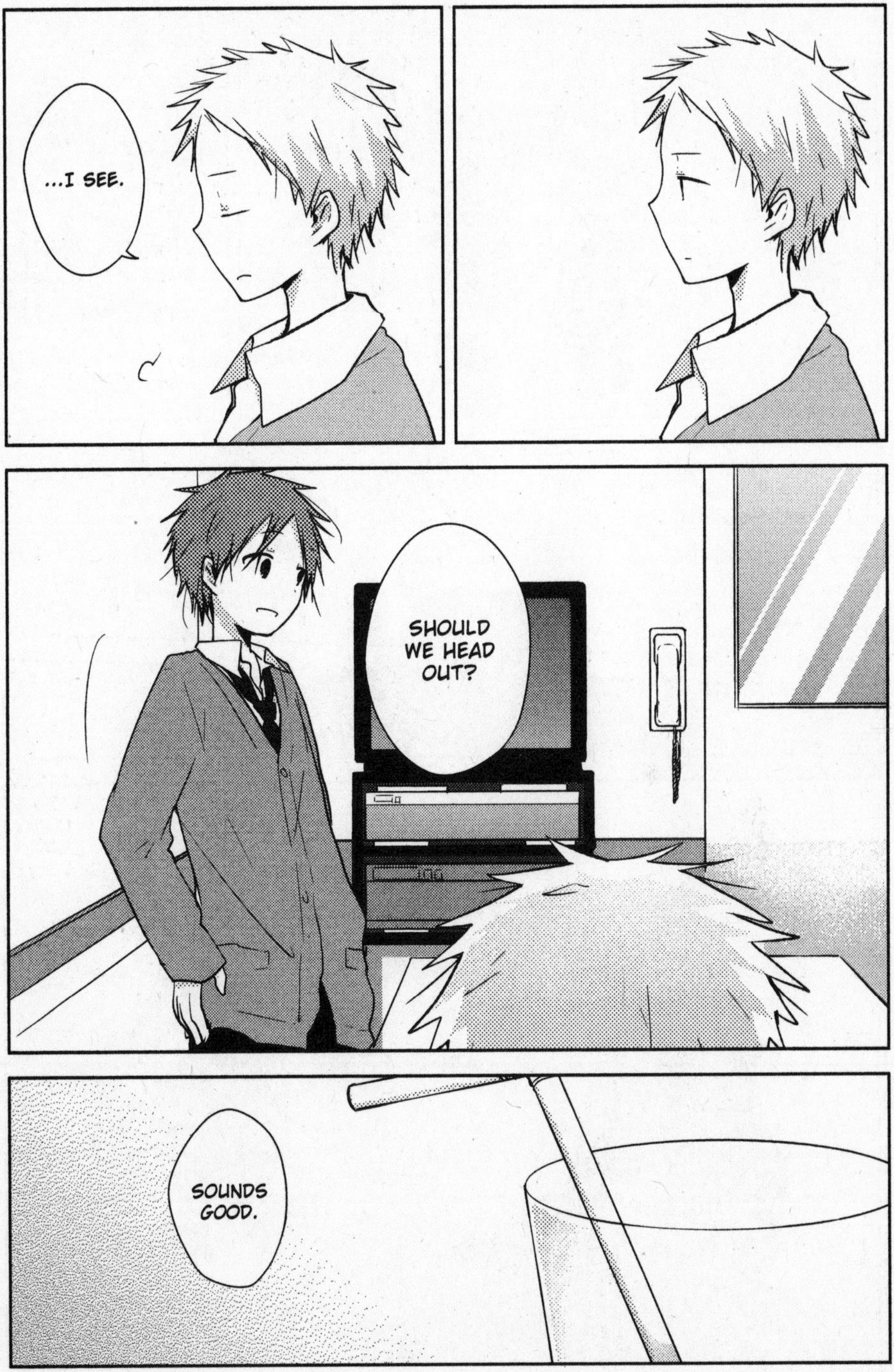
...I SEE.
SHOULD WE HEAD OUT?
SOUNDS GOOD.

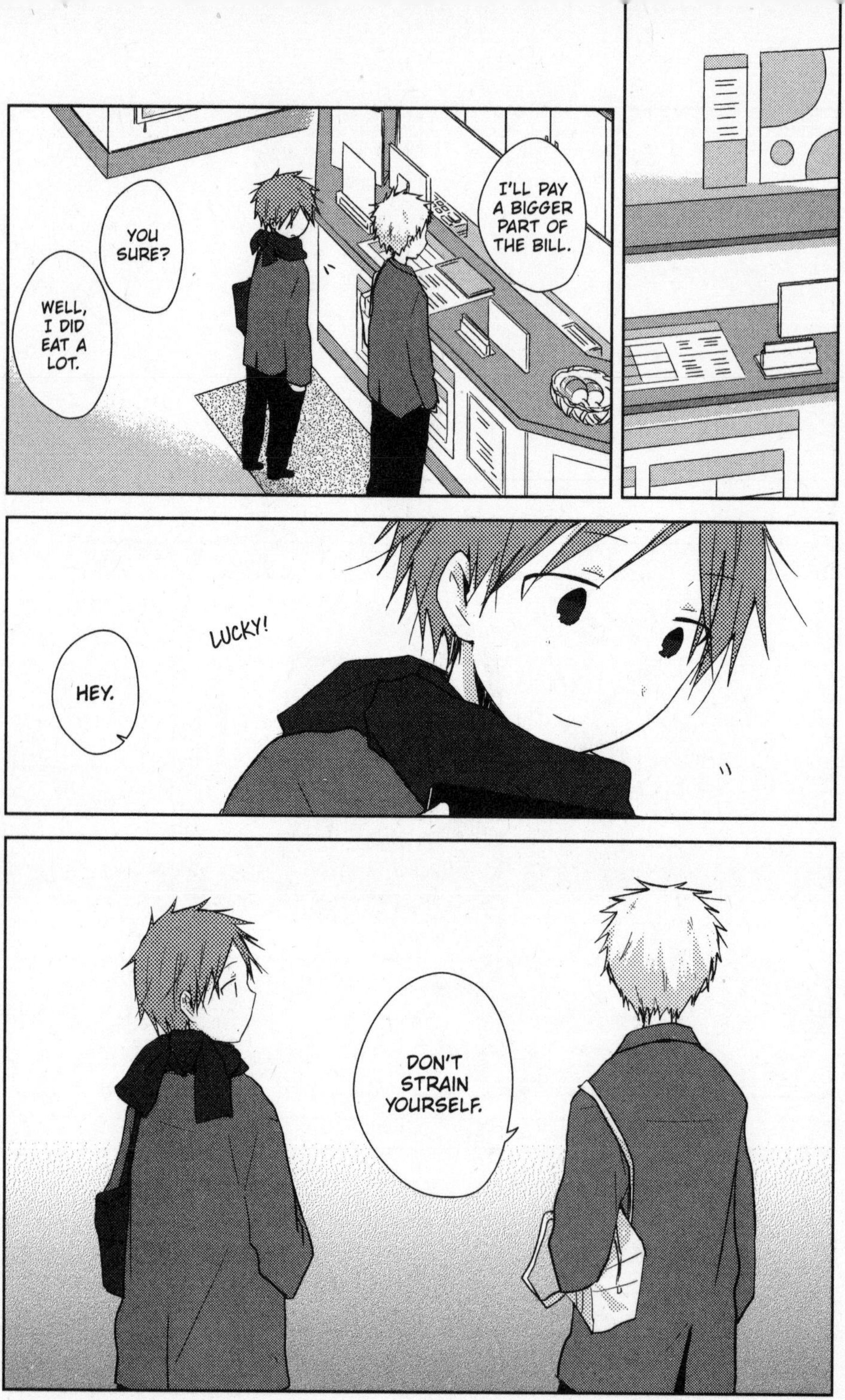
I'LL PAY A BIGGER PART OF THE BILL.
YOU SURE?
WELL, I DID EAT A LOT.
LUCKY!
HEY.
DON'T STRAIN YOURSELF.

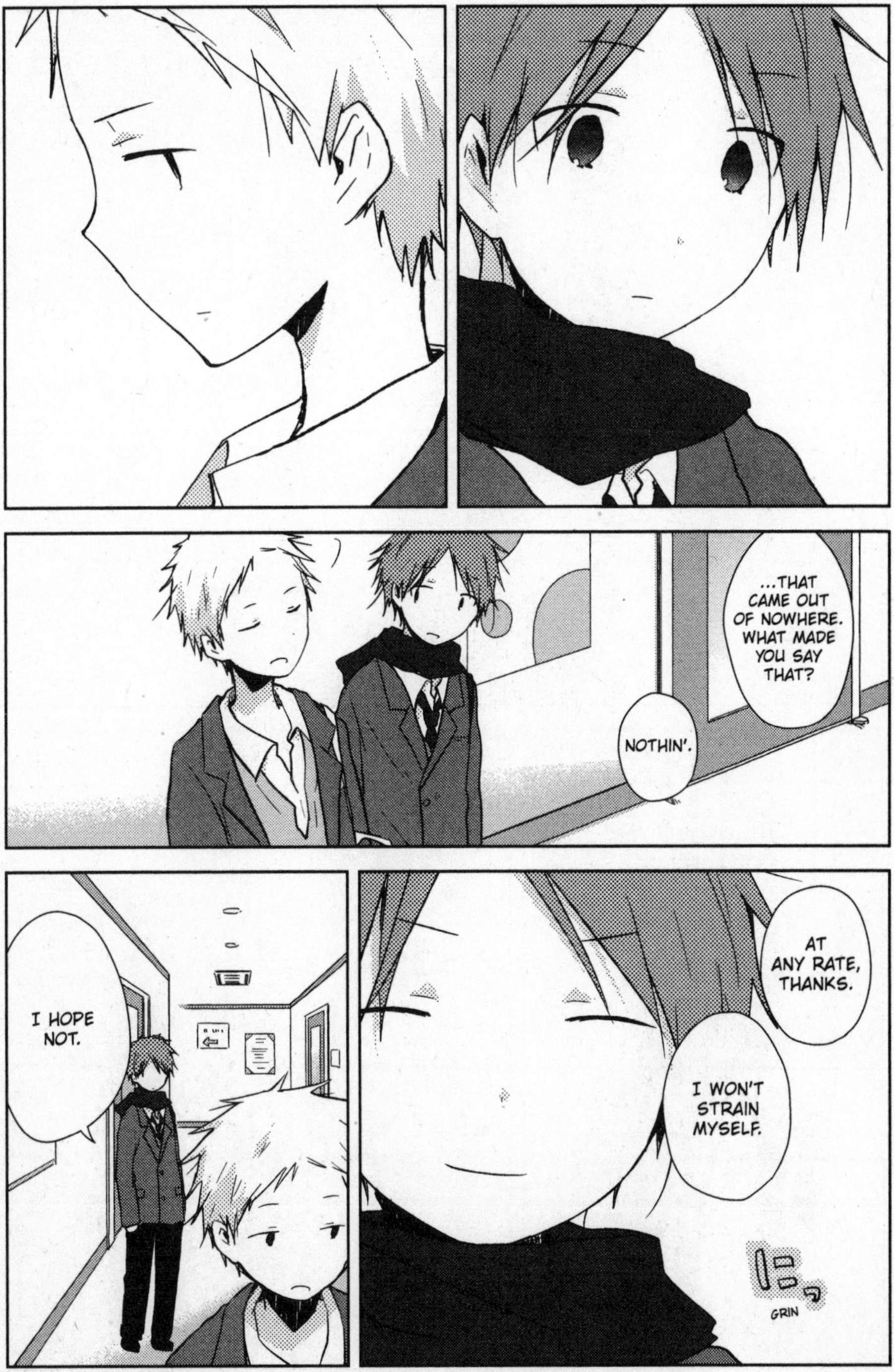
...THAT CAME OUT OF NOWHERE. WHAT MADE YOU SAY THAT?
NOTHIN'.
AT ANY RATE, THANKS.
I WON'T STRAIN MYSELF.
GRIN
I HOPE NOT.

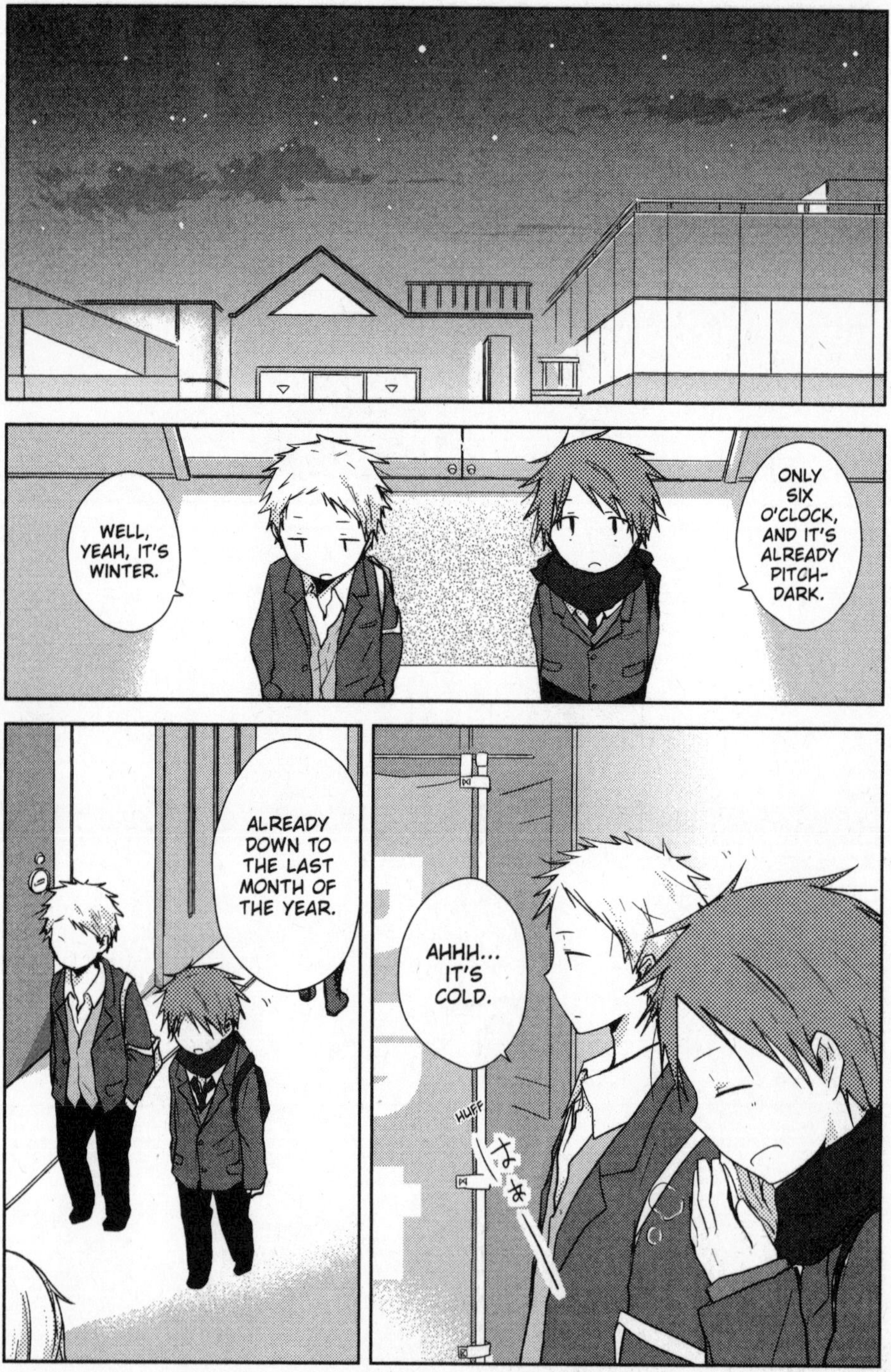
ONLY SIX O'CLOCK, AND IT'S ALREADY PITCH-DARK.
WELL, YEAH, IT'S WINTER.
AHHH... IT'S COLD.
HUFF
はぁ
ALREADY DOWN TO THE LAST MONTH OF THE YEAR.

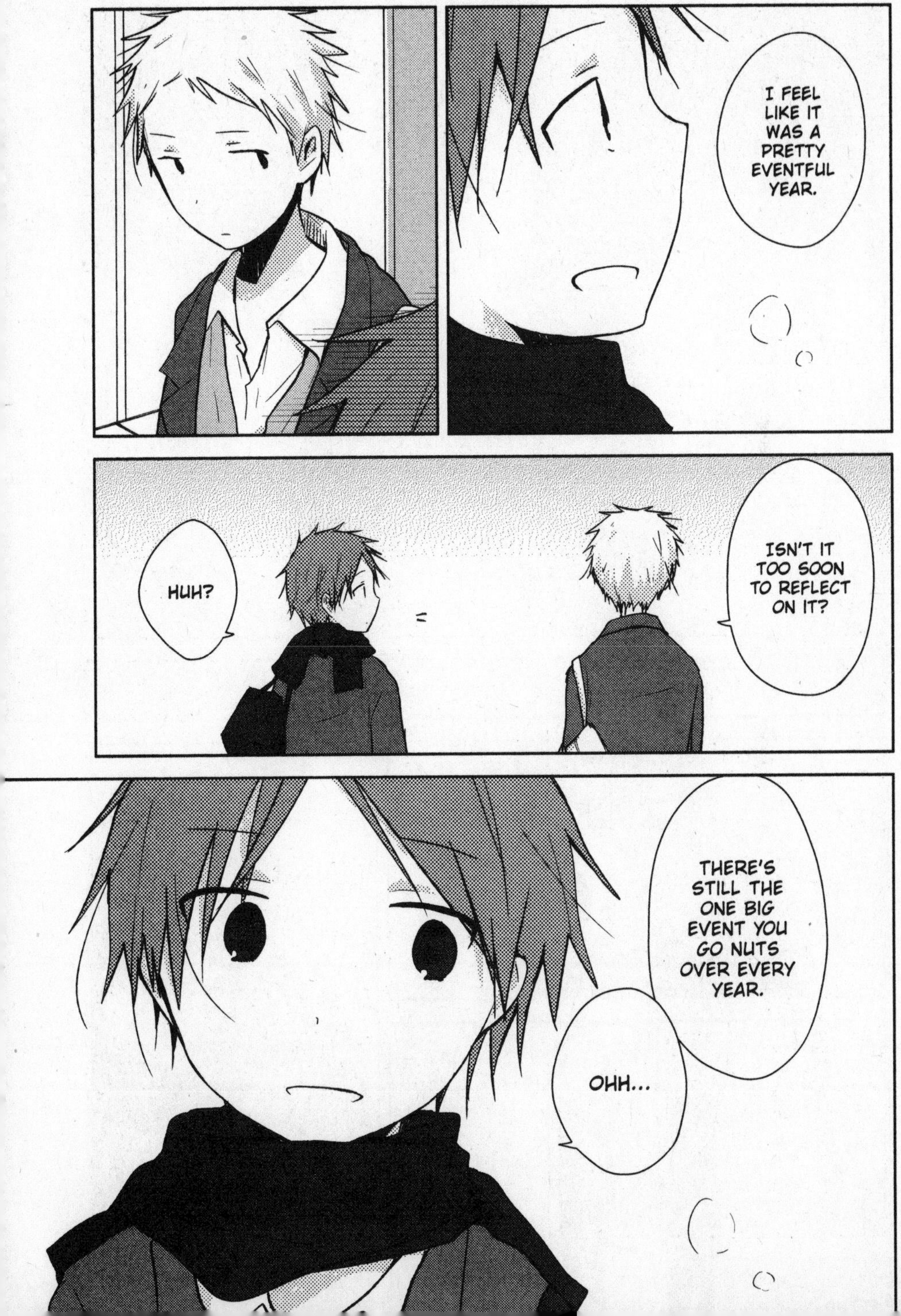
I FEEL LIKE IT WAS A PRETTY EVENTFUL YEAR.
ISN'T IT TOO SOON TO REFLECT ON IT?
HUH?
THERE'S STILL THE ONE BIG EVENT YOU GO NUTS OVER EVERY YEAR.
OHH...

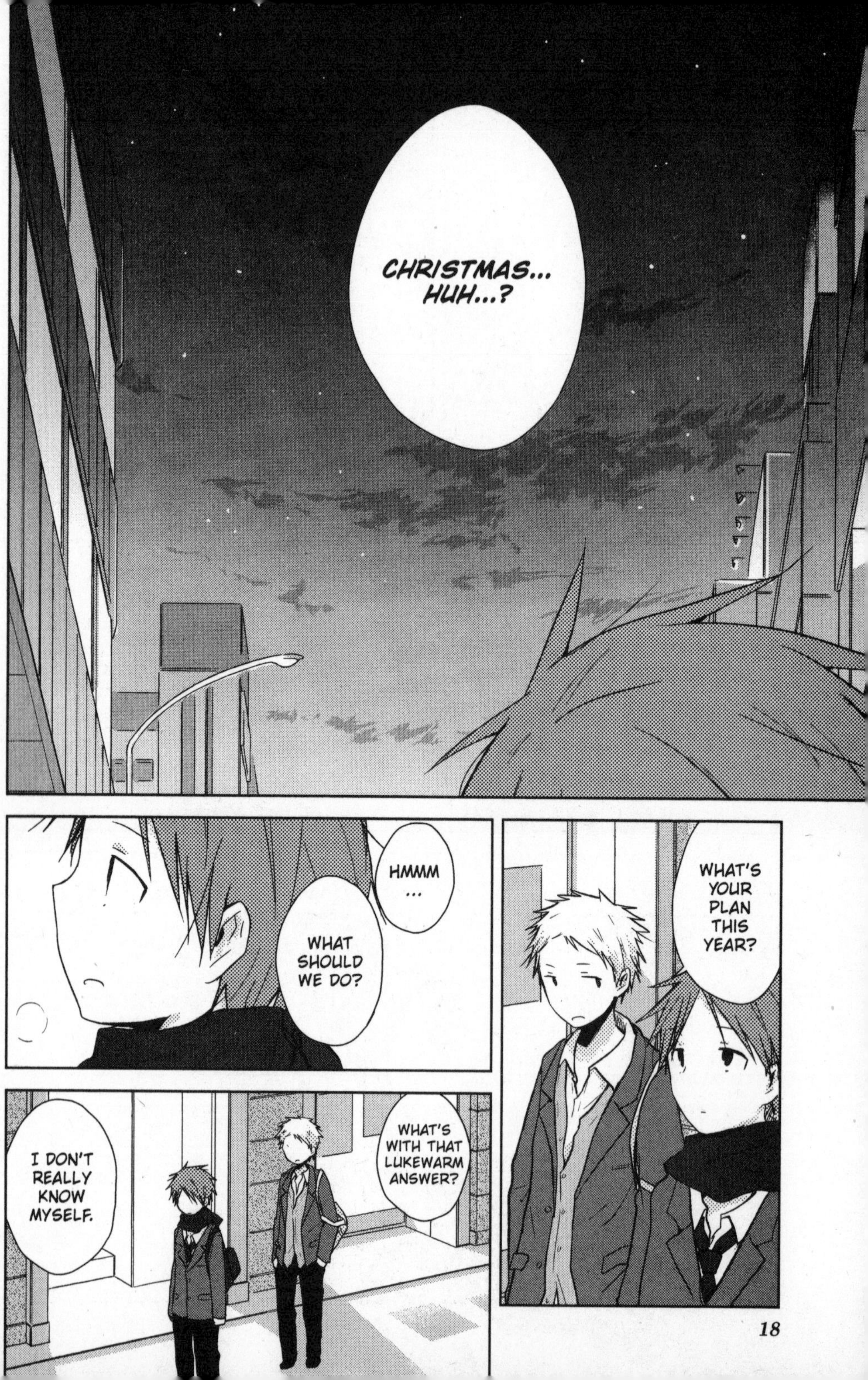
CHRISTMAS... HUH...?
WHAT'S YOUR PLAN THIS YEAR?
HMMM ...
WHAT SHOULD WE DO?
WHAT'S WITH THAT LUKEWARM ANSWER?
I DON'T REALLY KNOW MYSELF.

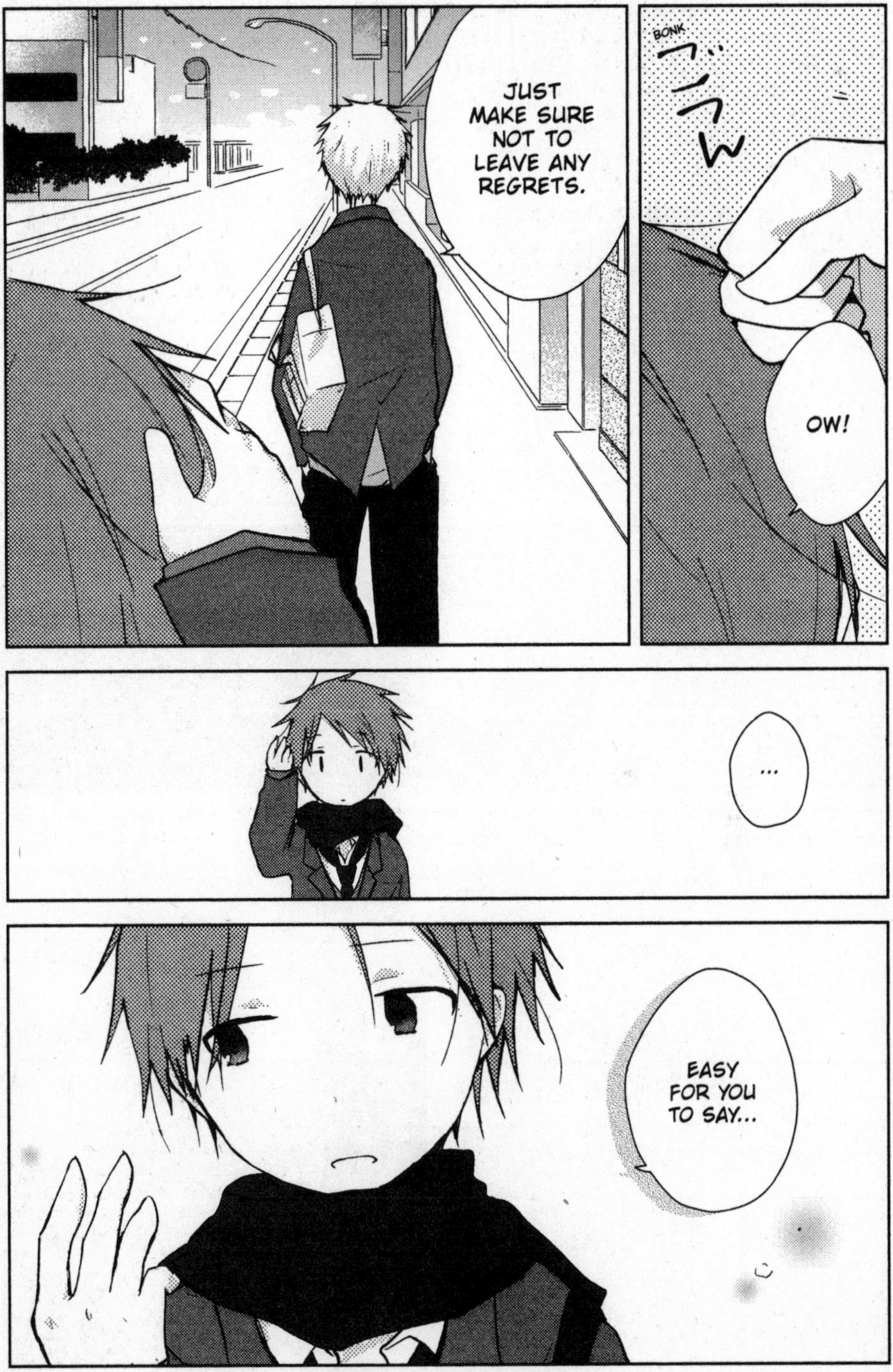
BONK
OW!
JUST MAKE SURE NOT TO LEAVE ANY REGRETS.
...
EASY FOR YOU TO SAY...

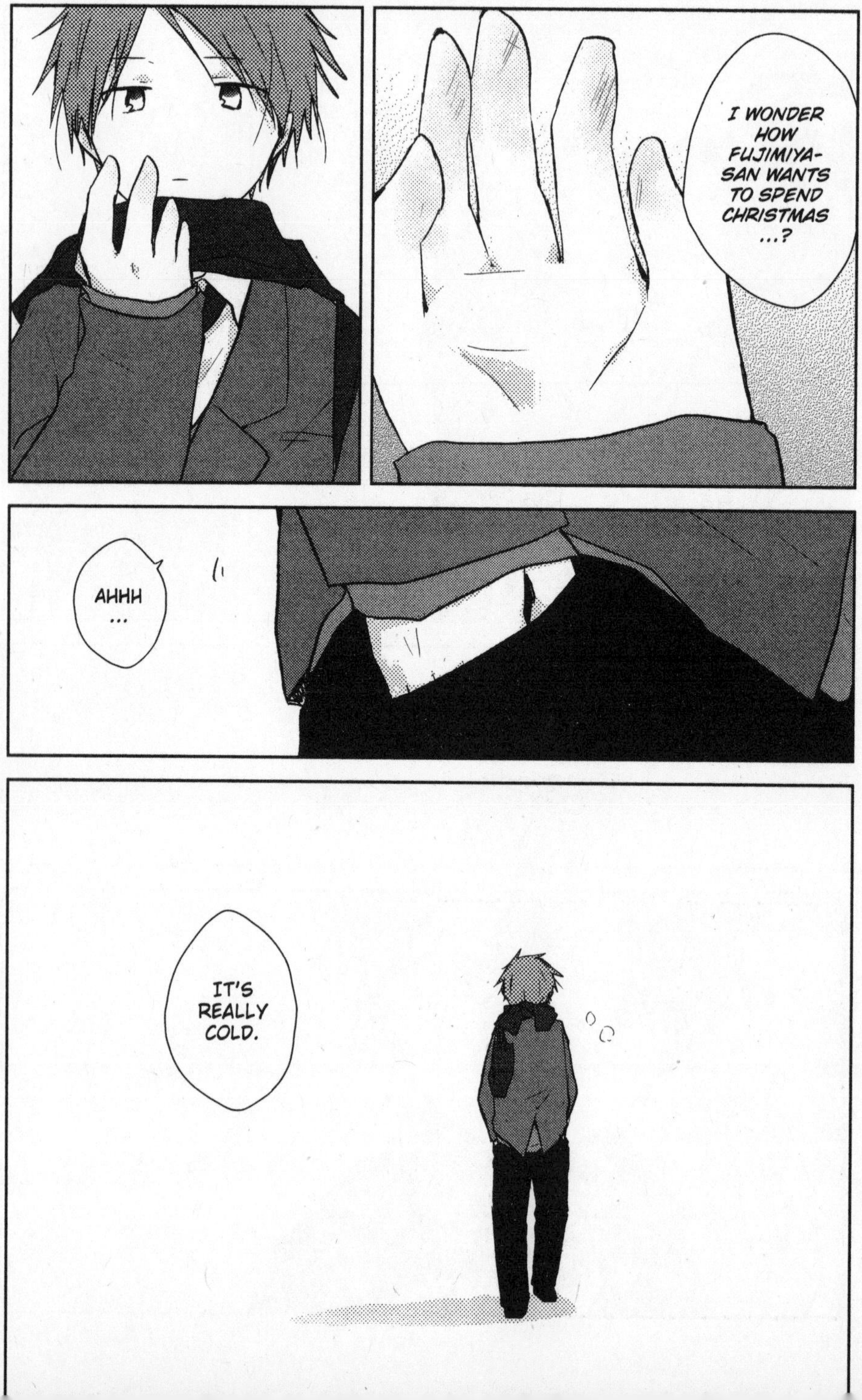
I WONDER HOW FUJIMIYA-SAN WANTS TO SPEND CHRISTMAS ...?
AHHH ...
IT'S REALLY COLD.

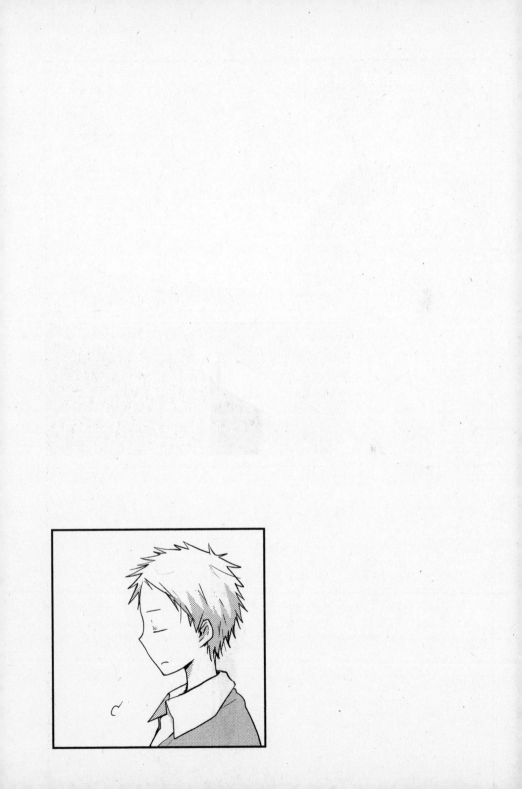

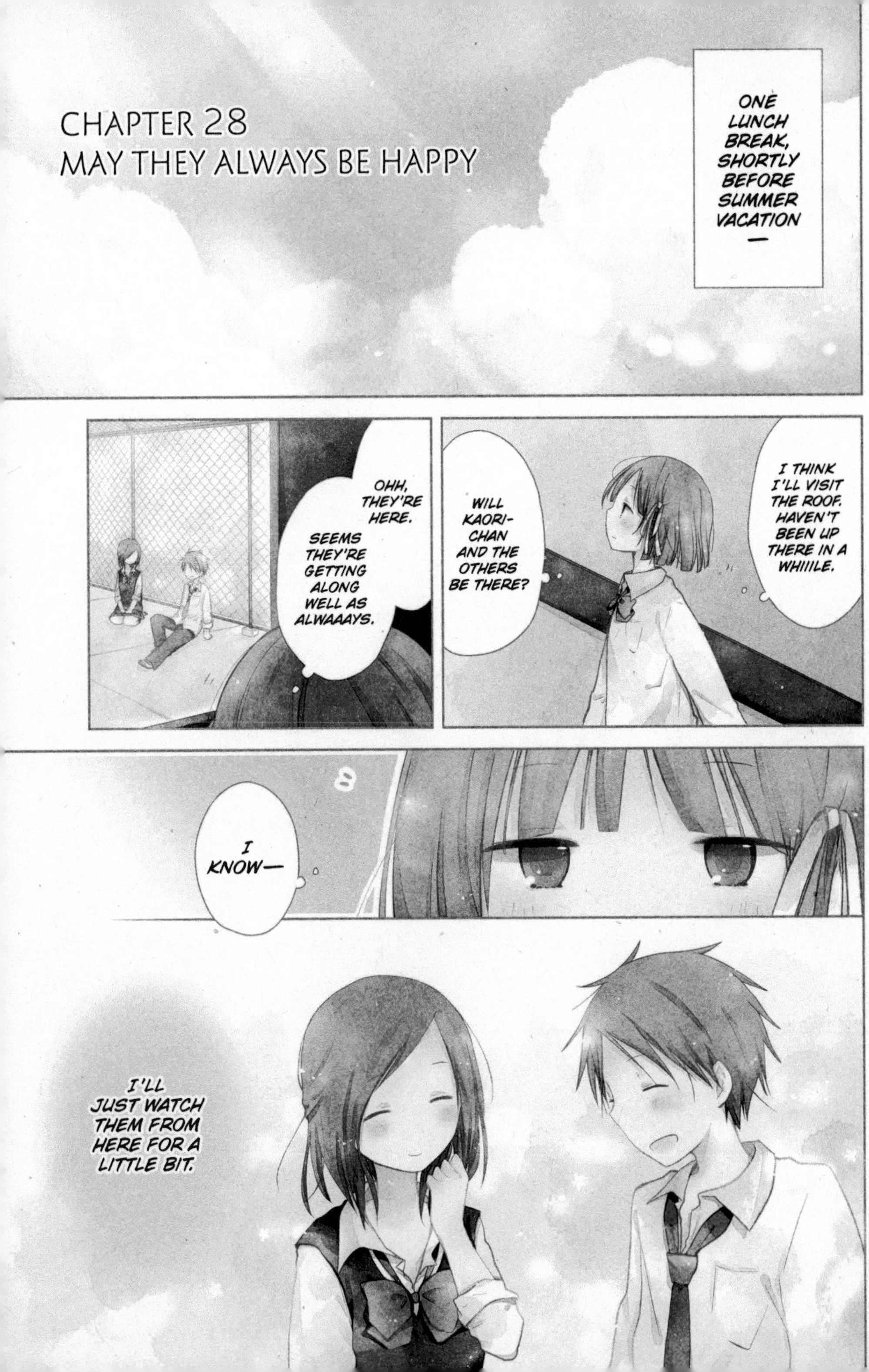
ONE LUNCH BREAK, SHORTLY BEFORE SUMMER VACATION —
CHAPTER 28
MAY THEY ALWAYS BE HAPPY
I THINK I'LL VISIT THE ROOF. HAVEN'T BEEN UP THERE IN A WHIIILE.
WILL KAORI-CHAN AND THE OTHERS BE THERE?
OHH, THEY'RE HERE.
SEEMS THEY'RE GETTING ALONG WELL AS ALWAAAYS.
I KNOW—
I'LL JUST WATCH THEM FROM HERE FOR A LITTLE BIT.

ONE
WEEK
FRIENDS

ONE MORE TIME

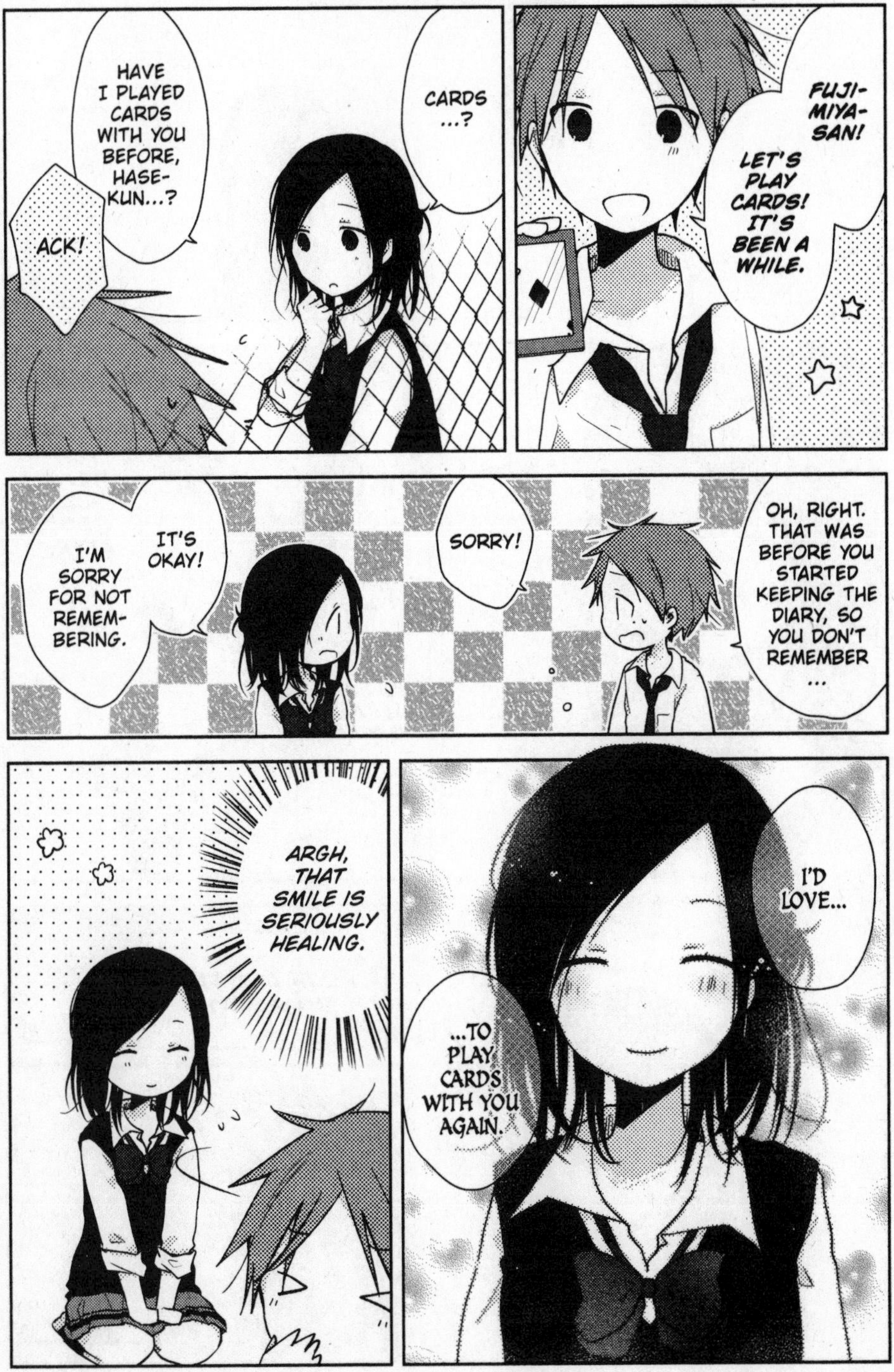
FUJI-MIYA-SAN!
LET'S PLAY CARDS! IT'S BEEN A WHILE.
CARDS ...?
HAVE I PLAYED CARDS WITH YOU BEFORE, HASE-KUN...?
ACK!
OH, RIGHT. THAT WAS BEFORE YOU STARTED KEEPING THE DIARY, SO YOU DON'T REMEMBER ...
SORRY!
IT'S OKAY!
I'M SORRY FOR NOT REMEM-BERING.
I'D LOVE...
...TO PLAY CARDS WITH YOU AGAIN.
ARGH, THAT SMILE IS SERIOUSLY HEALING.

SURE ENOUGH

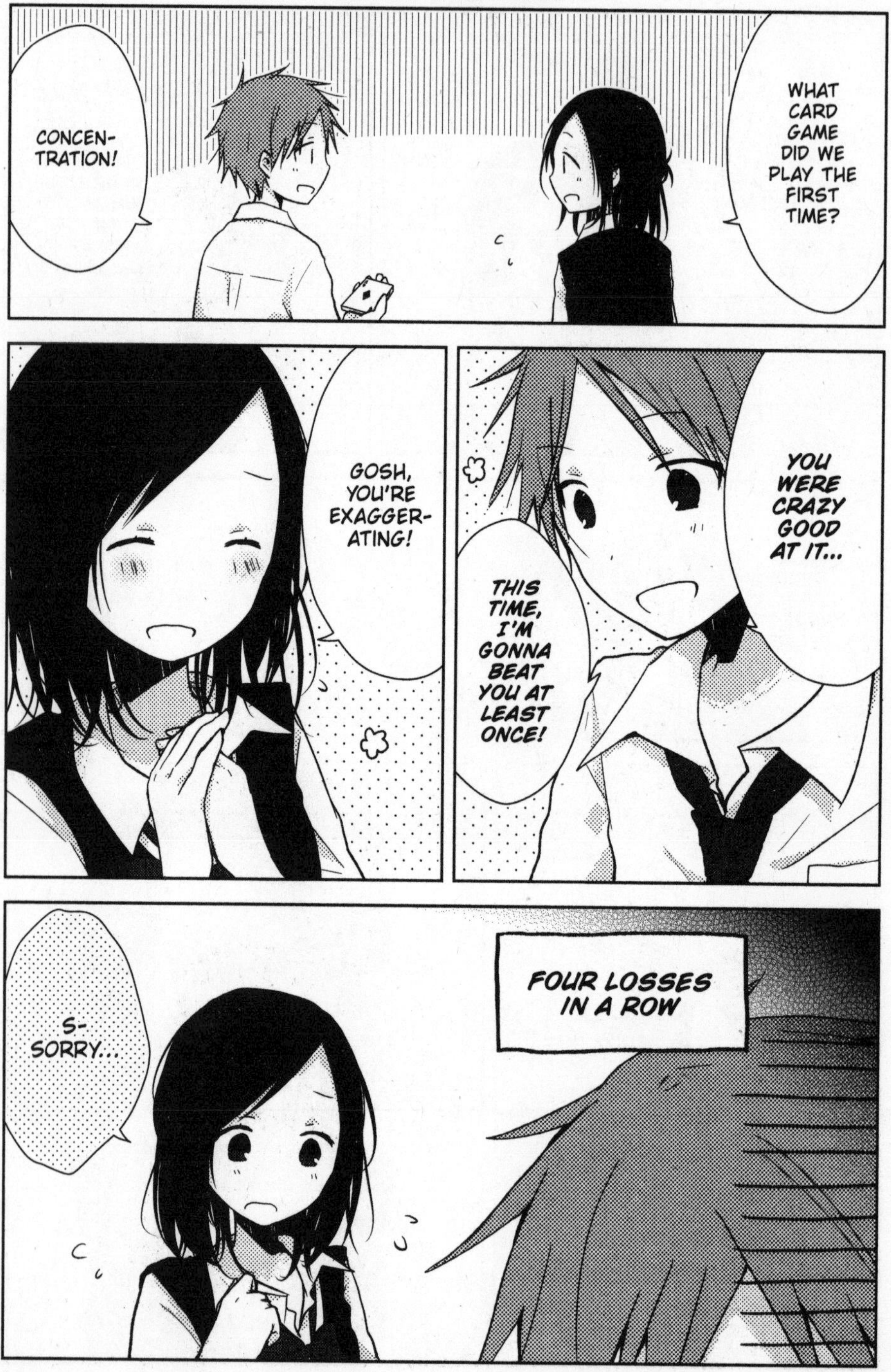
WHAT CARD GAME DID WE PLAY THE FIRST TIME?
CONCENTRATION!
YOU WERE CRAZY GOOD AT IT...
THIS TIME, I'M GONNA BEAT YOU AT LEAST ONCE!
GOSH, YOU'RE EXAGGERATING!
FOUR LOSSES IN A ROW
S-SORRY...

ORIGIN OF THE NAME

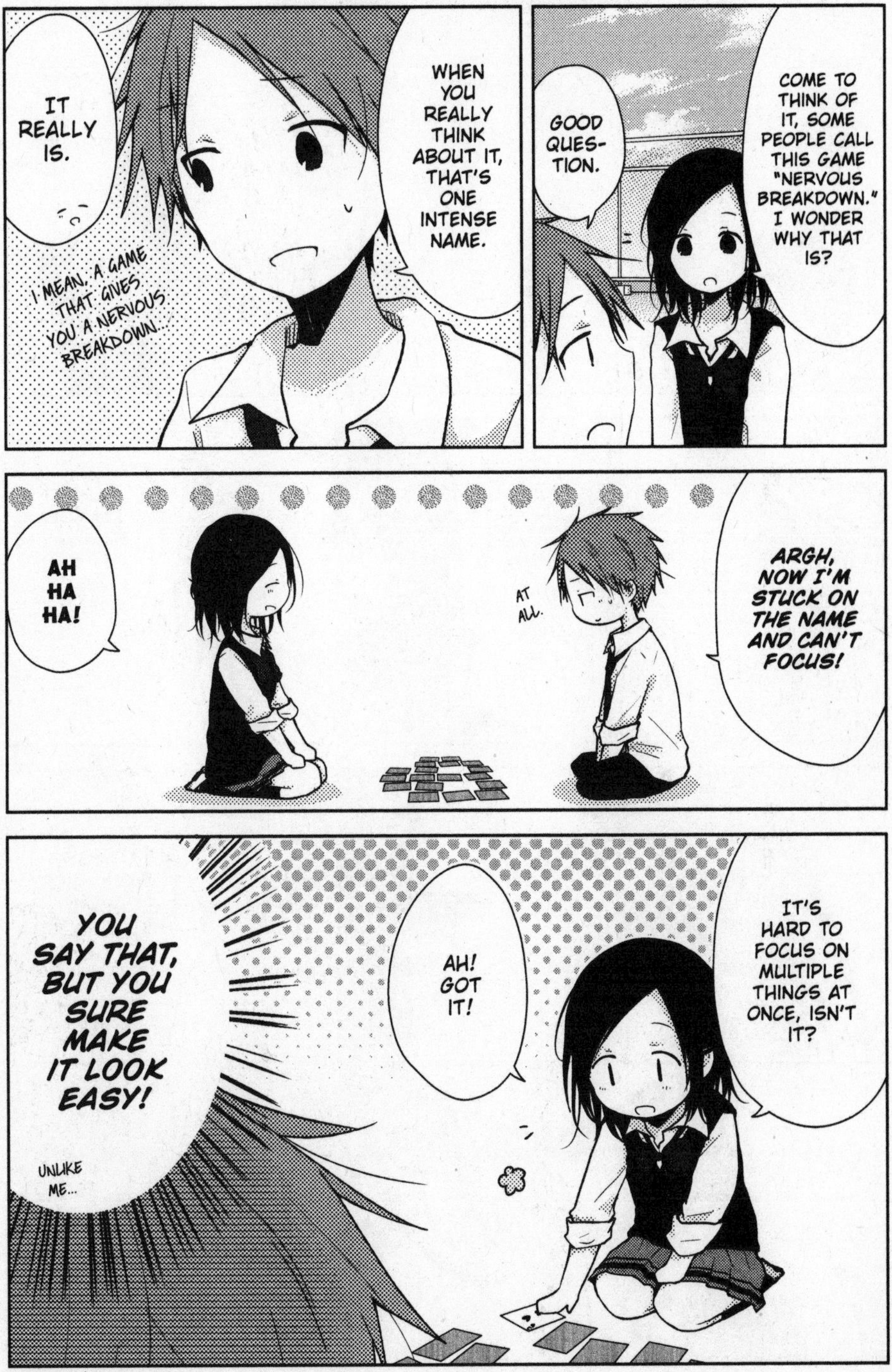
COME TO THINK OF IT, SOME PEOPLE CALL THIS GAME "NERVOUS BREAKDOWN." I WONDER WHY THAT IS?
GOOD QUESTION.
WHEN YOU REALLY THINK ABOUT IT, THAT'S ONE INTENSE NAME.
IT REALLY IS.
I MEAN, A GAME THAT GIVES YOU A NERVOUS BREAKDOWN...
ARGH, NOW I'M STUCK ON THE NAME AND CAN'T FOCUS!
AT ALL.
AH HA HA!
IT'S HARD TO FOCUS ON MULTIPLE THINGS AT ONCE, ISN'T IT?
AH! GOT IT!
YOU SAY THAT, BUT YOU SURE MAKE IT LOOK EASY!
UNLIKE ME...

THAT PART OF YOU

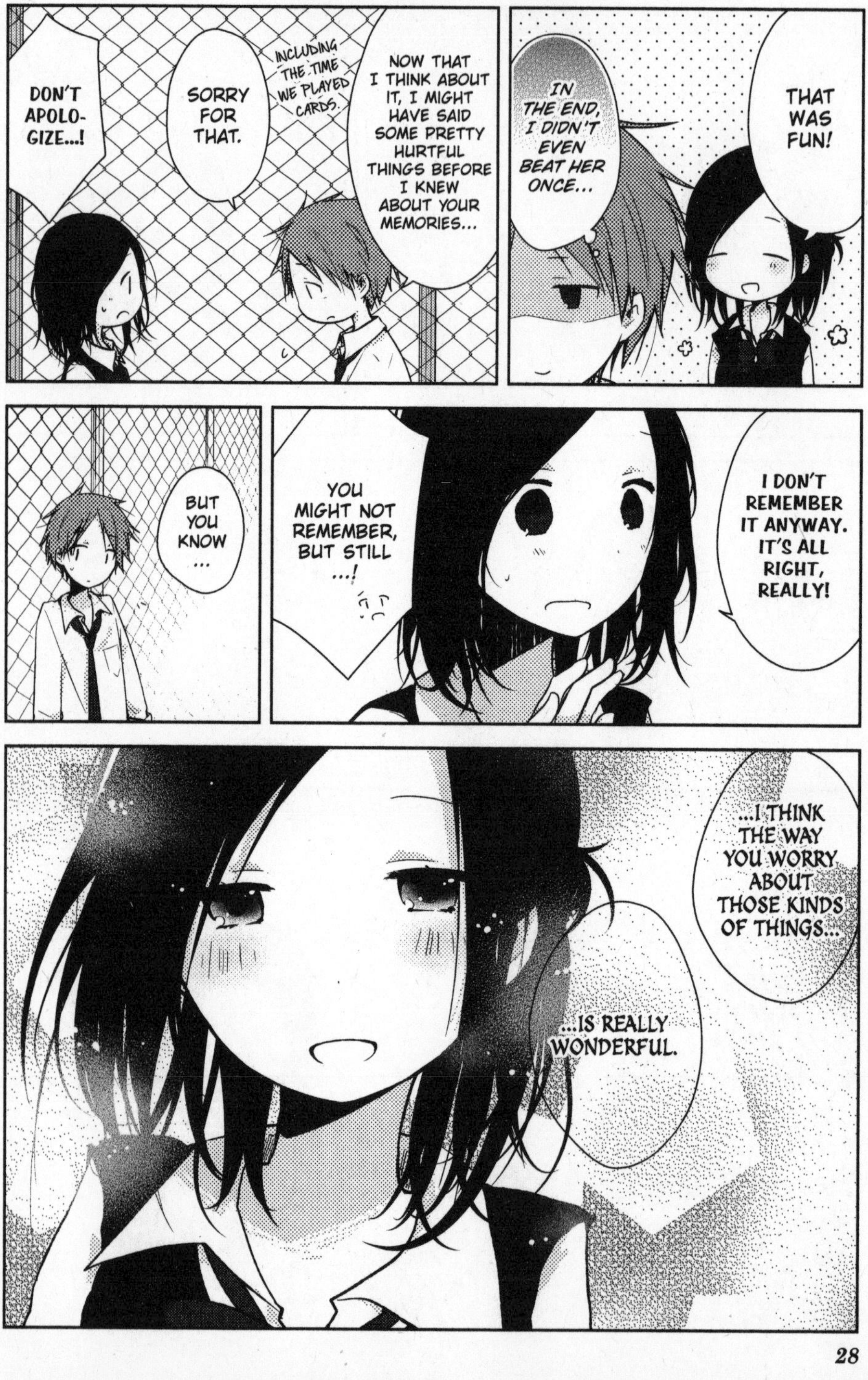
THAT WAS FUN!
IN THE END, I DIDN'T EVEN BEAT HER ONCE...
NOW THAT I THINK ABOUT IT, I MIGHT HAVE SAID SOME PRETTY HURTFUL THINGS BEFORE I KNEW ABOUT YOUR MEMORIES...
INCLUDING THE TIME WE PLAYED CARDS.
SORRY FOR THAT.
DON'T APOLO-GIZE...!
I DON'T REMEMBER IT ANYWAY. IT'S ALL RIGHT, REALLY!
YOU MIGHT NOT REMEMBER, BUT STILL ...!
BUT YOU KNOW ...
...I THINK THE WAY YOU WORRY ABOUT THOSE KINDS OF THINGS...
...IS REALLY WONDERFUL.

HUH?

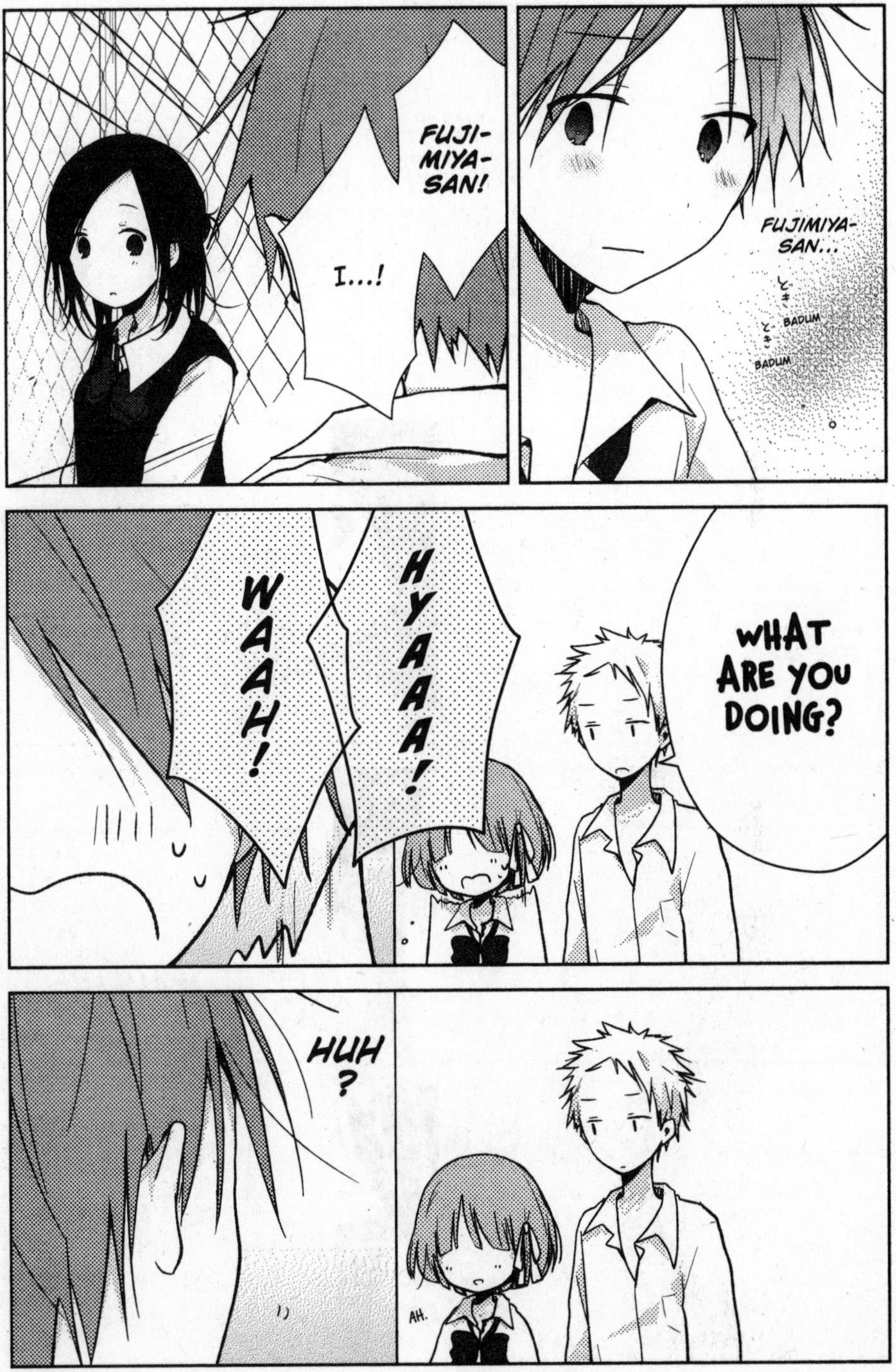

FUJIMIYA-SAN...
どき どき
BADUM BADUM
FUJI-MIYA-SAN!
I...!
WHAT ARE YOU DOING?
HYAAAA!
WAAAH!
AH.
HUH?

HOW LONG

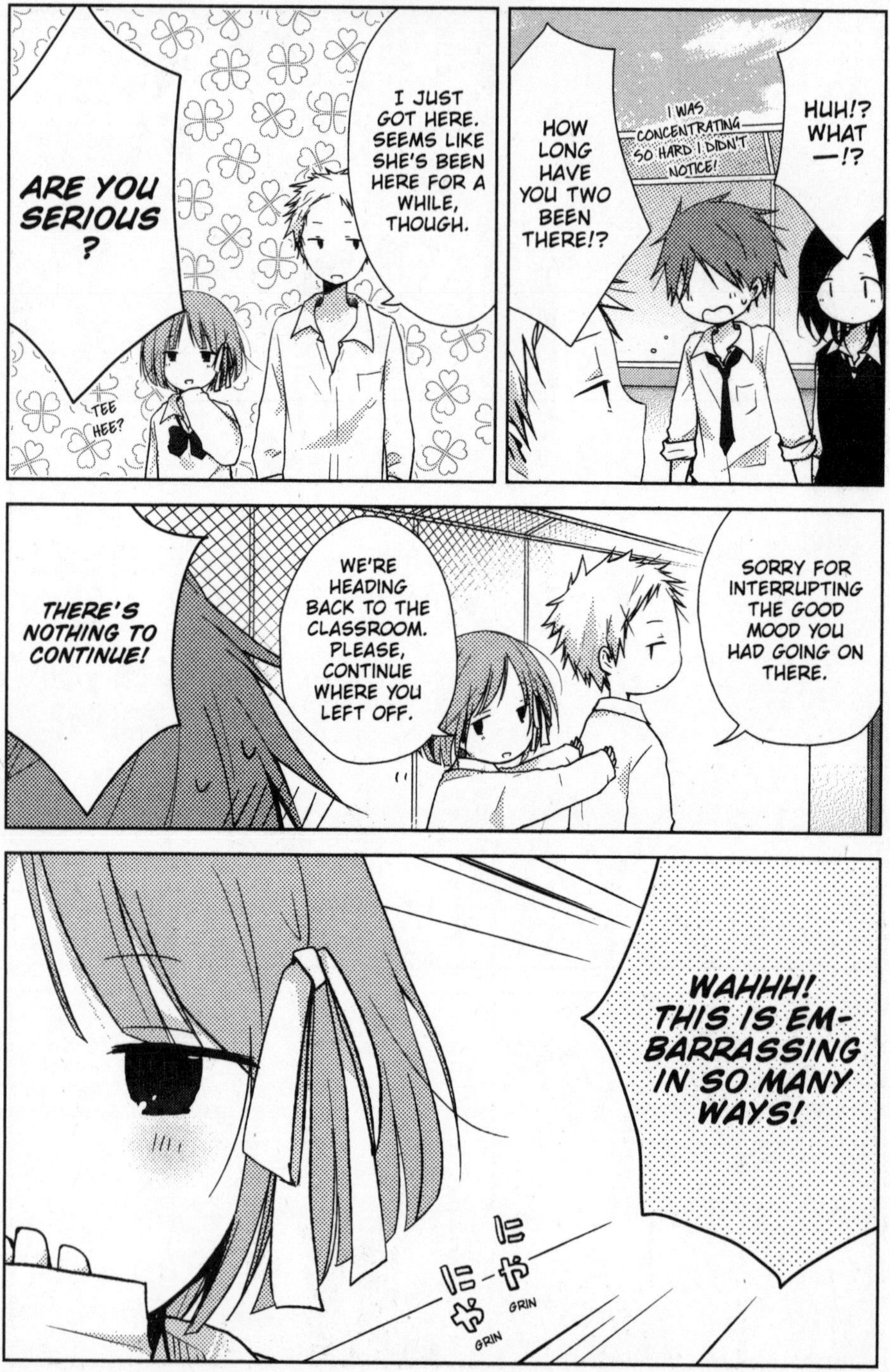
HUH!? WHAT—!?
I WAS CONCENTRATING SO HARD I DIDN'T NOTICE!
HOW LONG HAVE YOU TWO BEEN THERE!?
I JUST GOT HERE. SEEMS LIKE SHE'S BEEN HERE FOR A WHILE, THOUGH.
ARE YOU SERIOUS?
TEE HEE?
SORRY FOR INTERRUPTING THE GOOD MOOD YOU HAD GOING ON THERE.
WE'RE HEADING BACK TO THE CLASSROOM. PLEASE, CONTINUE WHERE YOU LEFT OFF.
THERE'S NOTHING TO CONTINUE!
WAHHH! THIS IS EM-BARRASSING IN SO MANY WAYS!
にや GRIN
にや GRIN

THIS CLOSE FOREVER

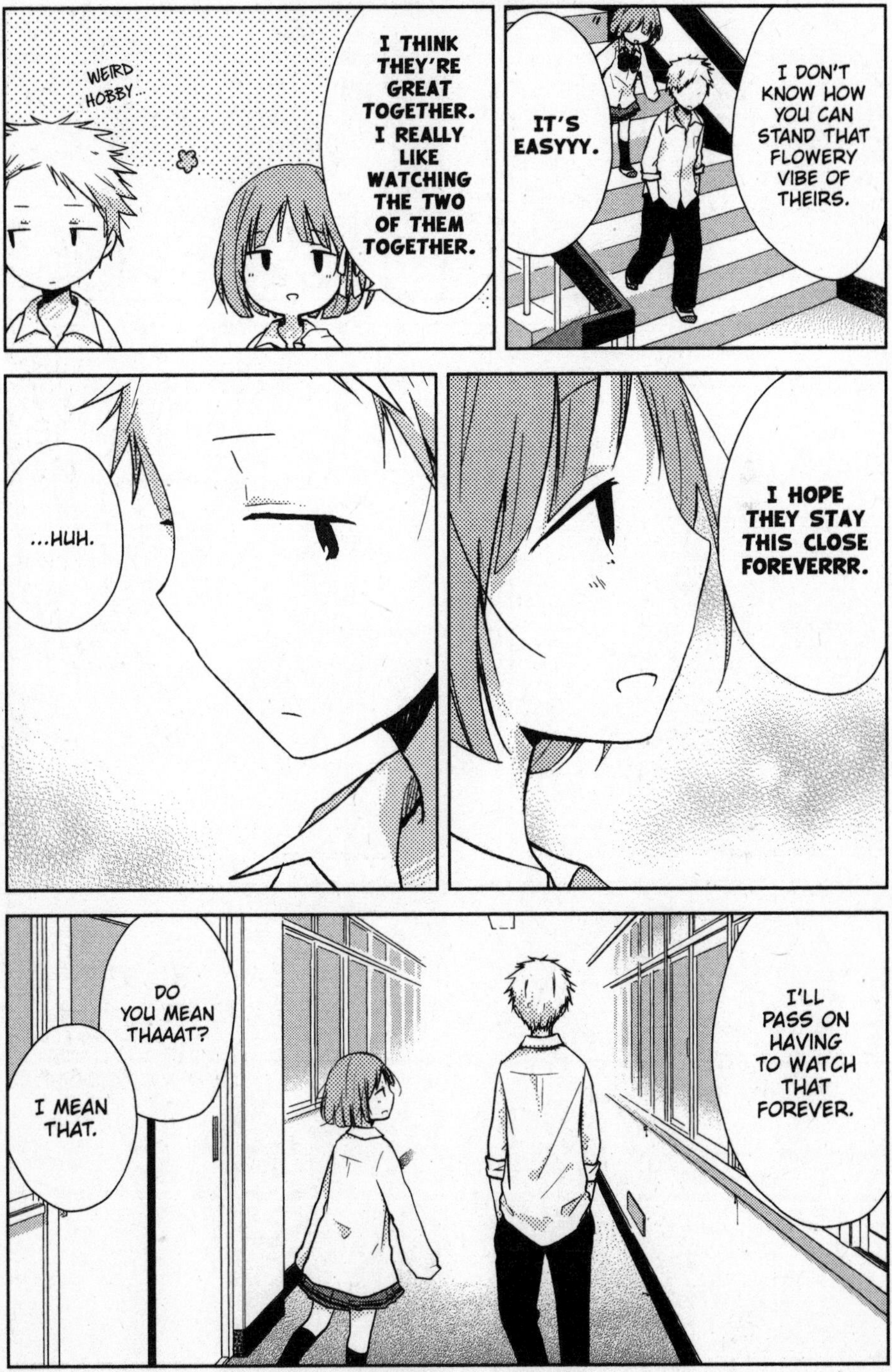
I DON'T KNOW HOW YOU CAN STAND THAT FLOWERY VIBE OF THEIRS.
IT'S EASYYY.
I THINK THEY'RE GREAT TOGETHER. I REALLY LIKE WATCHING THE TWO OF THEM TOGETHER.
WEIRD HOBBY...
I HOPE THEY STAY THIS CLOSE FOREVERRR.
...HUH.
I'LL PASS ON HAVING TO WATCH THAT FOREVER.
DO YOU MEAN THAAAT?
I MEAN THAT.

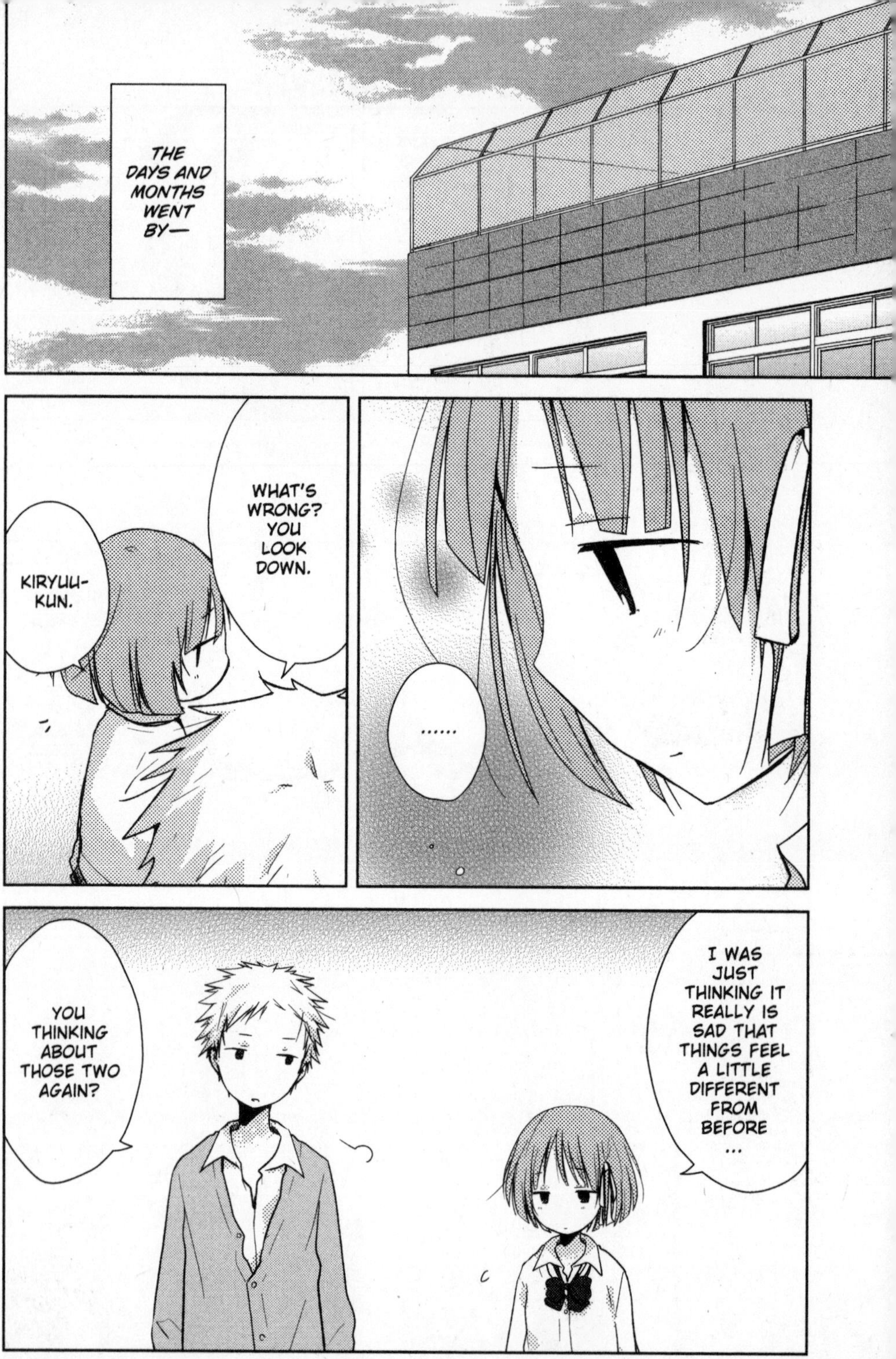
THE DAYS AND MONTHS WENT BY—
......
WHAT'S WRONG? YOU LOOK DOWN.
KIRYUU-KUN.
I WAS JUST THINKING IT REALLY IS SAD THAT THINGS FEEL A LITTLE DIFFERENT FROM BEFORE ...
YOU THINKING ABOUT THOSE TWO AGAIN?

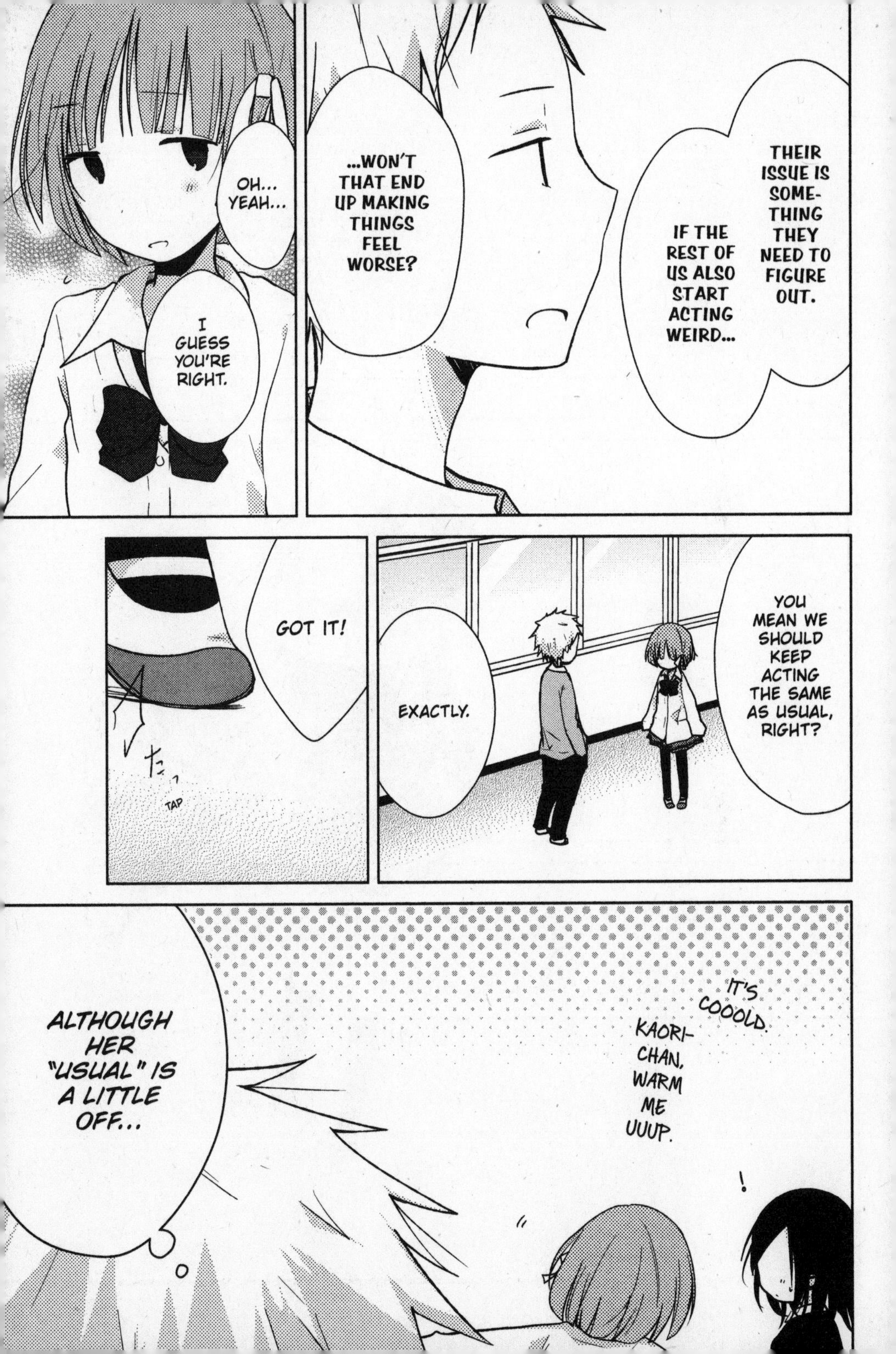
THEIR ISSUE IS SOMETHING THEY NEED TO FIGURE OUT.
IF THE REST OF US ALSO START ACTING WEIRD...
...WON'T THAT END UP MAKING THINGS FEEL WORSE?
OH... YEAH...
I GUESS YOU'RE RIGHT.
YOU MEAN WE SHOULD KEEP ACTING THE SAME AS USUAL, RIGHT?
EXACTLY.
GOT IT!
TAP
IT'S COOOLD.
KAORI-CHAN, WARM ME UUUP.
!
ALTHOUGH HER "USUAL" IS A LITTLE OFF...

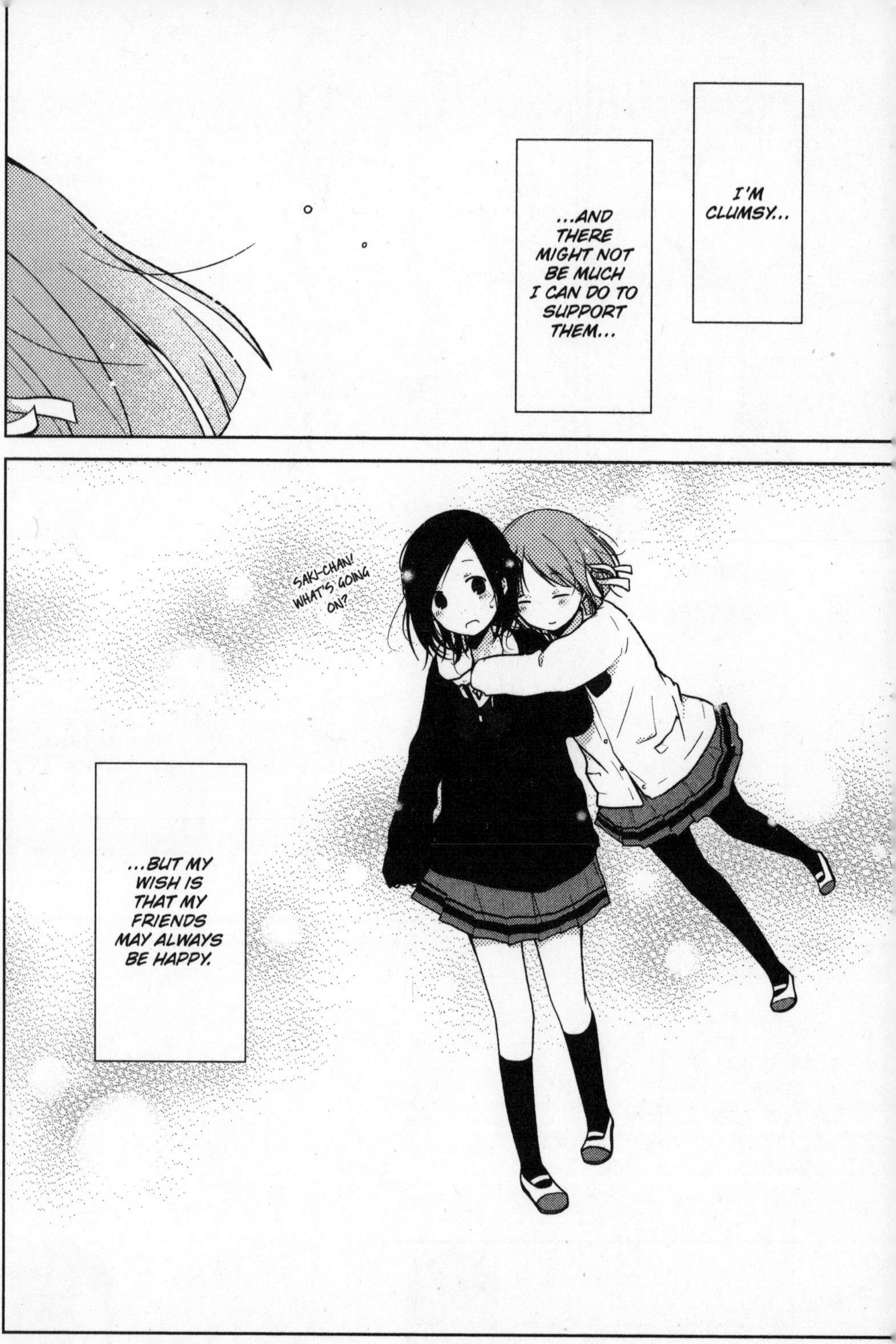
I'M CLUMSY...
...AND THERE MIGHT NOT BE MUCH I CAN DO TO SUPPORT THEM...
SAKI-CHAN! WHAT'S GOING ON?
...BUT MY WISH IS THAT MY FRIENDS MAY ALWAYS BE HAPPY.

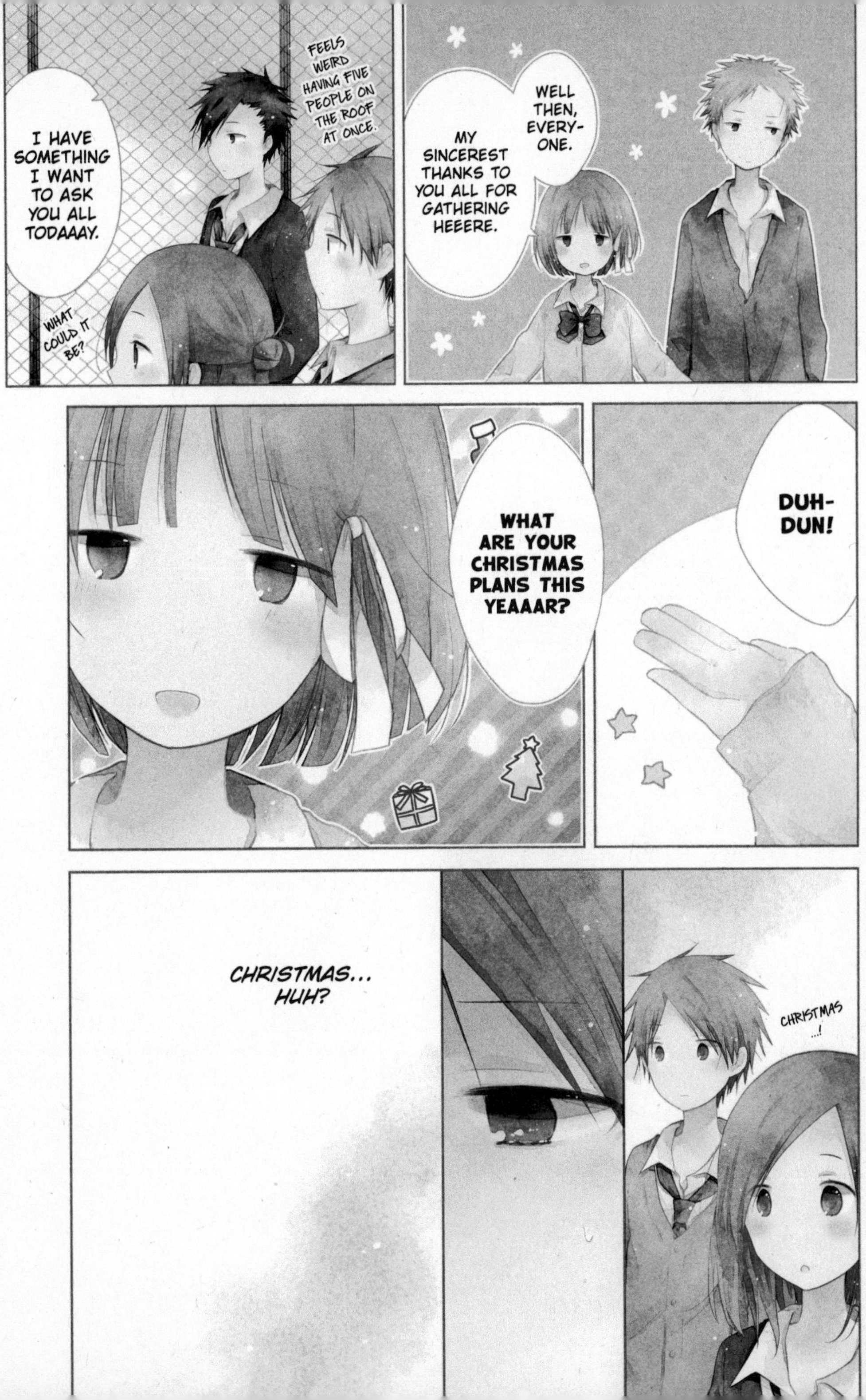
WELL THEN, EVERY-ONE.
MY SINCEREST THANKS TO YOU ALL FOR GATHERING HEEERE.
I HAVE SOMETHING I WANT TO ASK YOU ALL TODAAAY.
FEELS WEIRD HAVING FIVE PEOPLE ON THE ROOF AT ONCE.
WHAT COULD IT BE?
DUH-DUN!
WHAT ARE YOUR CHRISTMAS PLANS THIS YEAAAR?
CHRISTMAS ...!
CHRISTMAS... HUH?

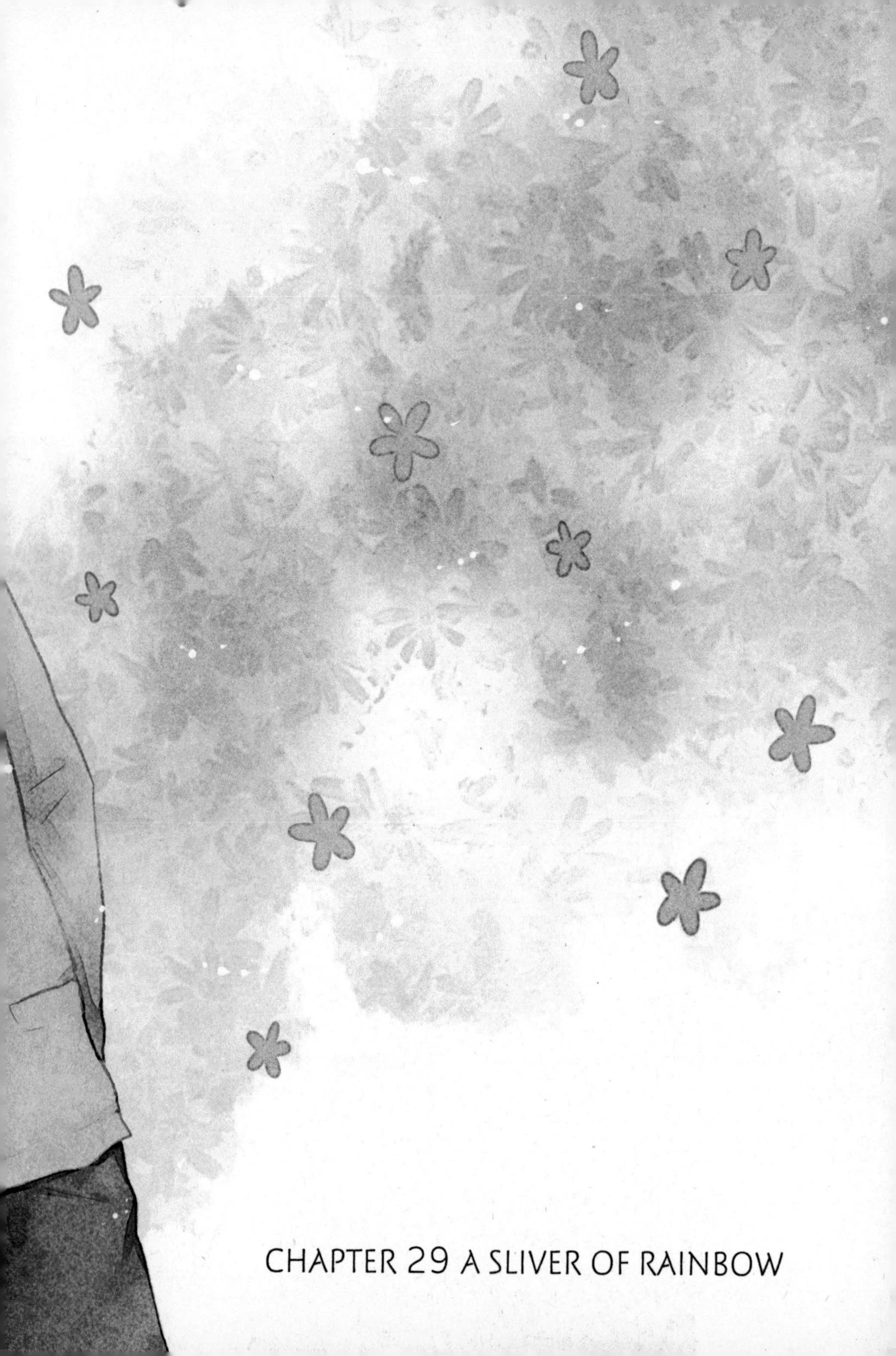

CHAPTER 29 A SLIVER OF RAINBOW

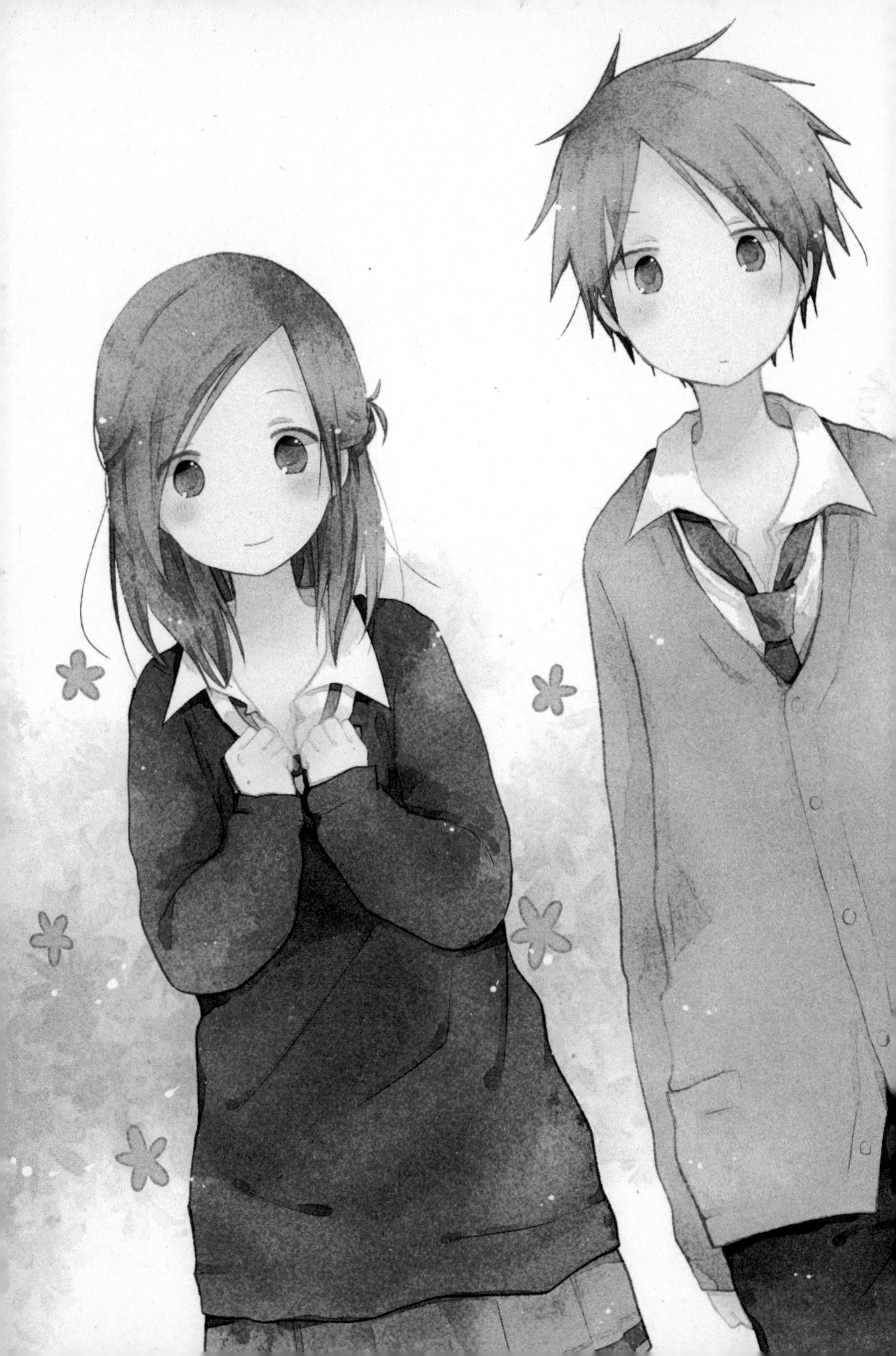

ONE
WEEK
FRIENDS

CHRISTMAS PARTY

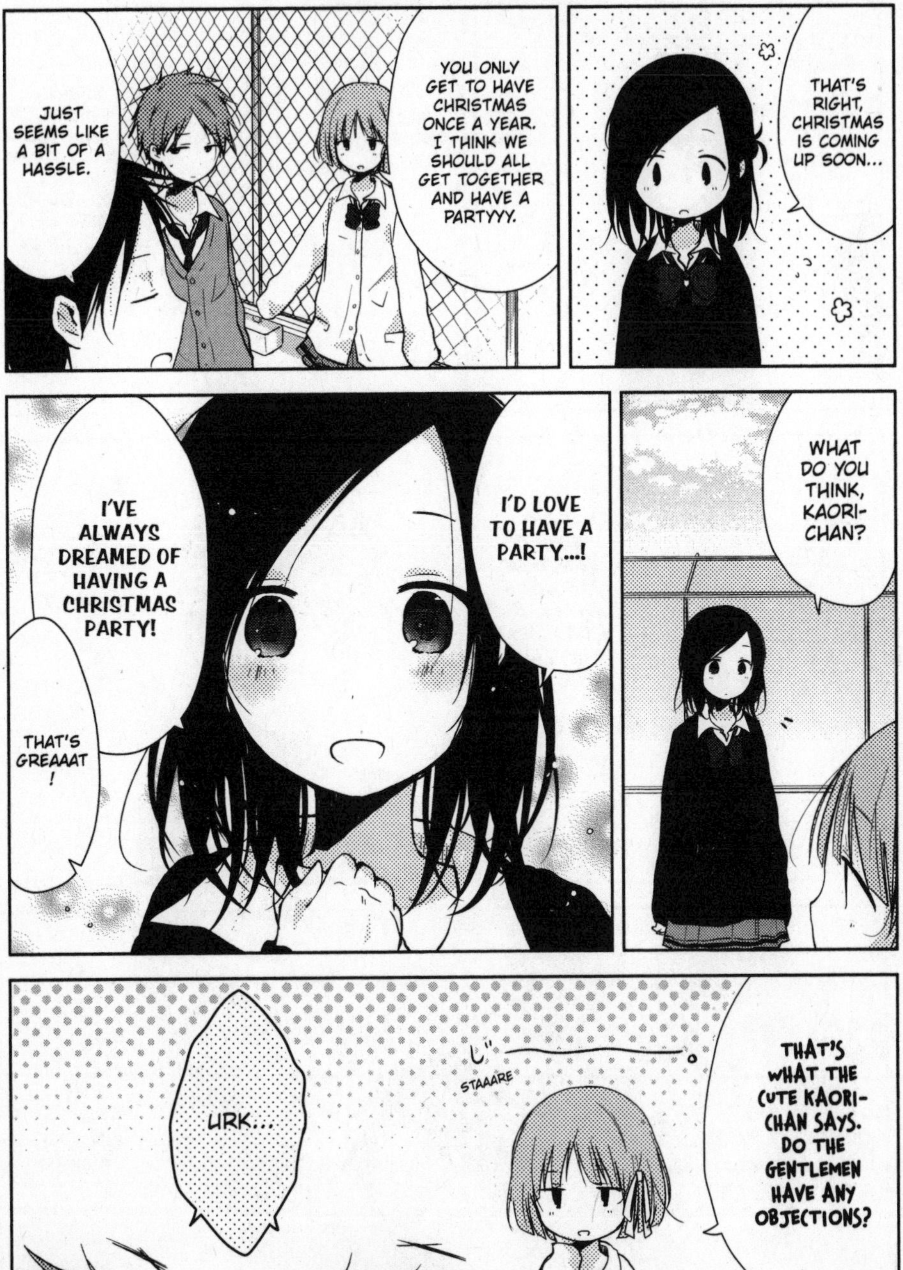
THAT'S RIGHT, CHRISTMAS IS COMING UP SOON...
YOU ONLY GET TO HAVE CHRISTMAS ONCE A YEAR. I THINK WE SHOULD ALL GET TOGETHER AND HAVE A PARTYYY.
JUST SEEMS LIKE A BIT OF A HASSLE.
WHAT DO YOU THINK, KAORI-CHAN?
I'D LOVE TO HAVE A PARTY...!
I'VE ALWAYS DREAMED OF HAVING A CHRISTMAS PARTY!
THAT'S GREAAAT!
THAT'S WHAT THE CUTE KAORI-CHAN SAYS. DO THE GENTLEMEN HAVE ANY OBJECTIONS?
じ————。
STAAARE
URK...

PLANS?

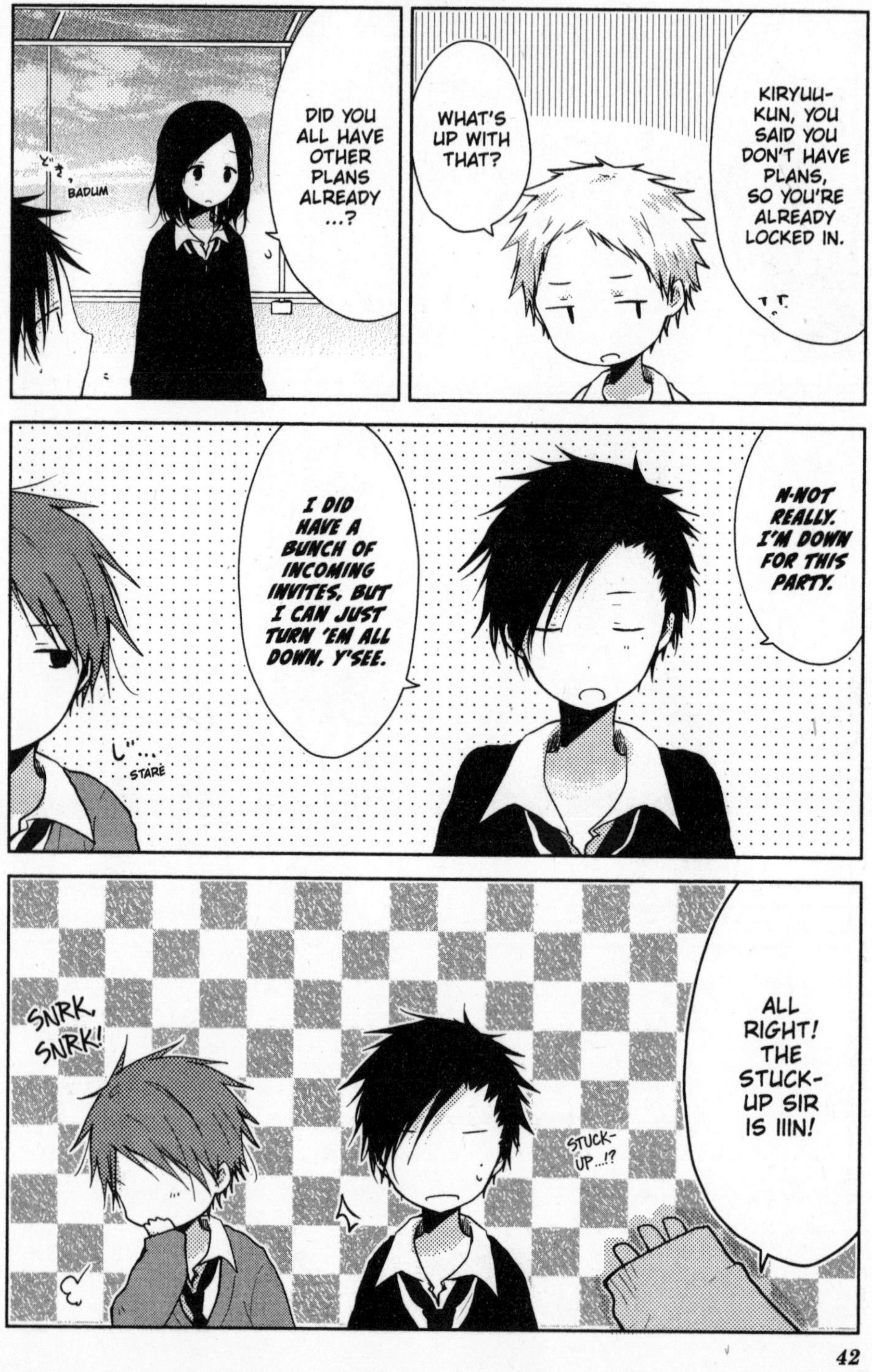

KIRYUU-KUN, YOU SAID YOU DON'T HAVE PLANS, SO YOU'RE ALREADY LOCKED IN.
WHAT'S UP WITH THAT?
DID YOU ALL HAVE OTHER PLANS ALREADY ...?
どき, BADUM
N-NOT REALLY. I'M DOWN FOR THIS PARTY.
I DID HAVE A BUNCH OF INCOMING INVITES, BUT I CAN JUST TURN 'EM ALL DOWN, Y'SEE.
じ… STARE
ALL RIGHT! THE STUCK-UP SIR IS IIIN!
STUCK-UP...!?
SNRK, SNRK!

THE LAST HOLDOUT

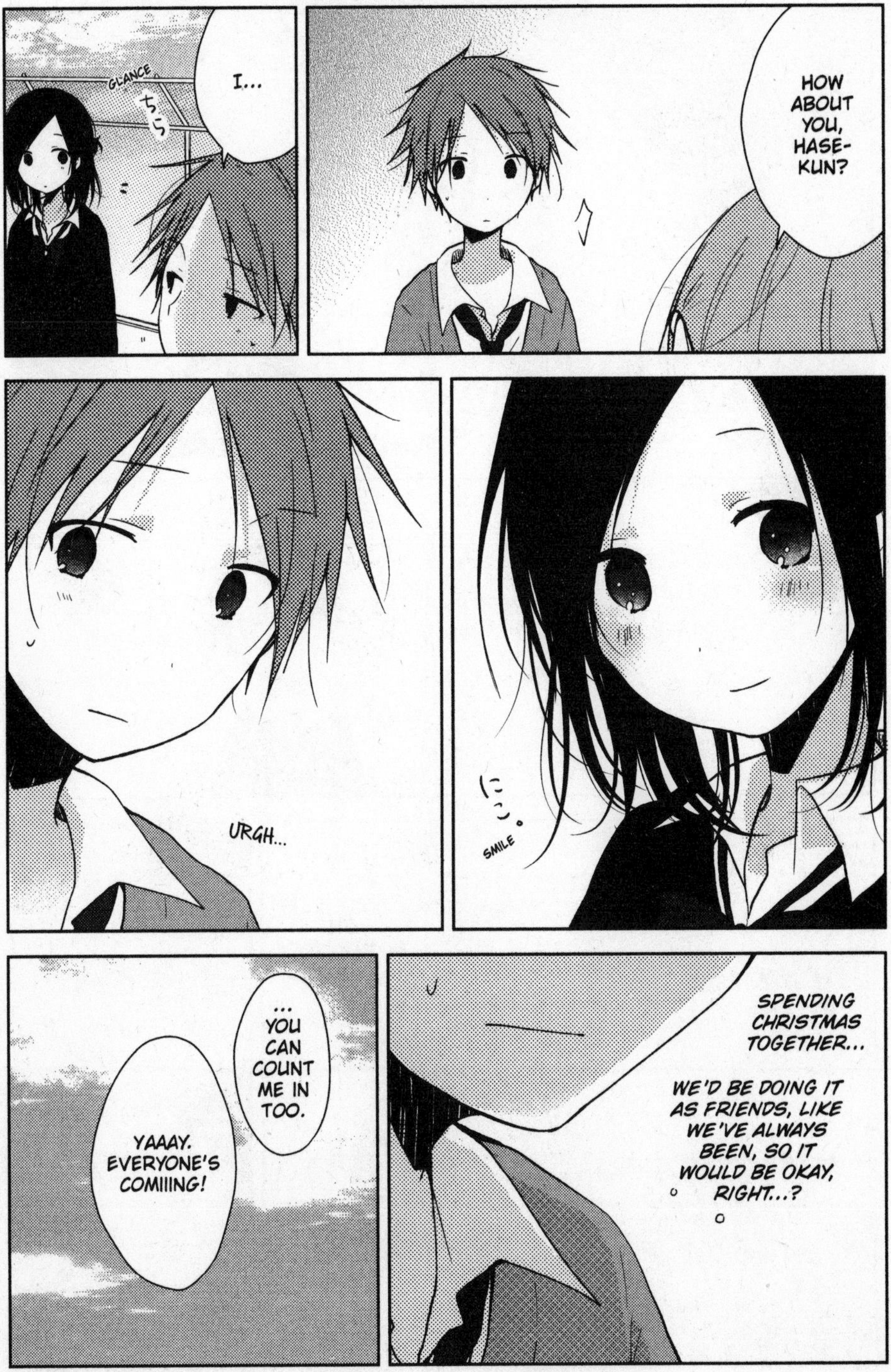
HOW ABOUT YOU, HASE-KUN?
I...
GLANCE
SMILE
URGH...
SPENDING CHRISTMAS TOGETHER...
WE'D BE DOING IT AS FRIENDS, LIKE WE'VE ALWAYS BEEN, SO IT WOULD BE OKAY, RIGHT...?
...YOU CAN COUNT ME IN TOO.
YAAAY. EVERYONE'S COMIIING!

KAORI'S HOUSE

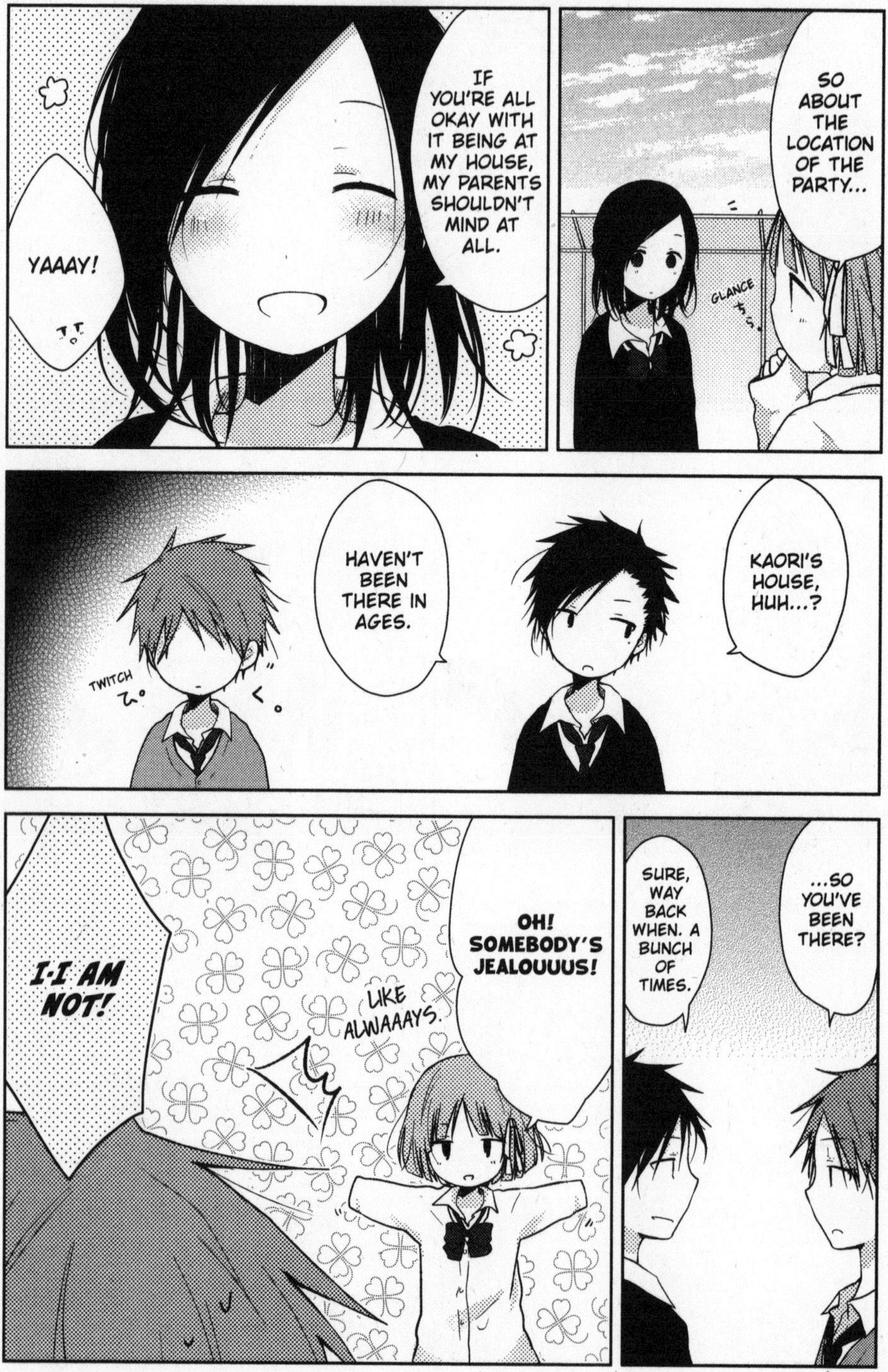
SO ABOUT THE LOCATION OF THE PARTY...
GLANCE
IF YOU'RE ALL OKAY WITH IT BEING AT MY HOUSE, MY PARENTS SHOULDN'T MIND AT ALL.
YAAAY!
KAORI'S HOUSE, HUH...?
HAVEN'T BEEN THERE IN AGES.
TWITCH
...SO YOU'VE BEEN THERE?
SURE, WAY BACK WHEN. A BUNCH OF TIMES.
OH! SOMEBODY'S JEALOUUUS!
LIKE ALWAAAYS.
I-I AM NOT!

TRYING & FAILING

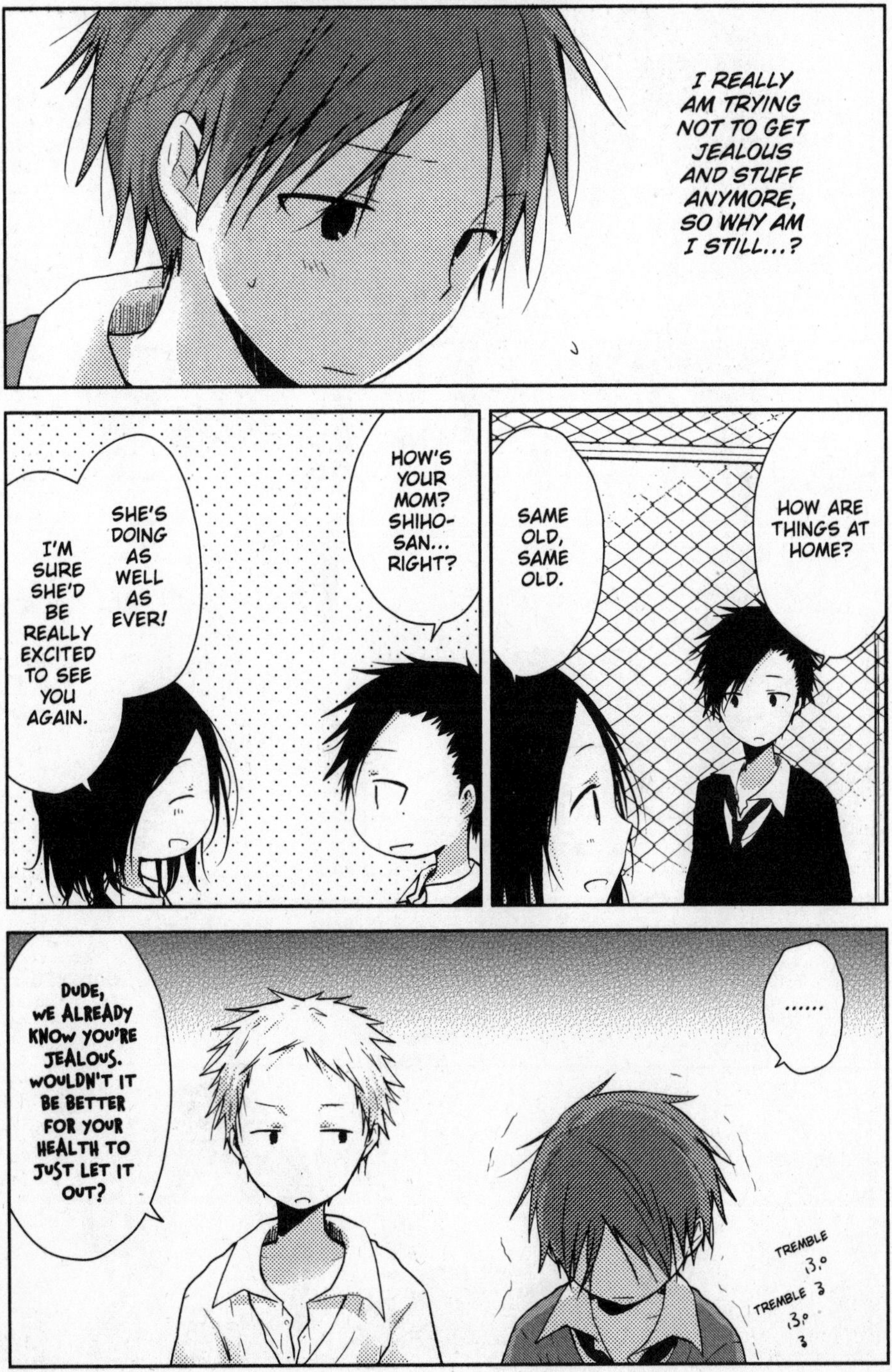
I REALLY AM TRYING NOT TO GET JEALOUS AND STUFF ANYMORE, SO WHY AM I STILL...?
HOW ARE THINGS AT HOME?
SAME OLD, SAME OLD.
HOW'S YOUR MOM? SHIHO-SAN... RIGHT?
SHE'S DOING AS WELL AS EVER!
I'M SURE SHE'D BE REALLY EXCITED TO SEE YOU AGAIN.
......
DUDE, WE ALREADY KNOW YOU'RE JEALOUS. WOULDN'T IT BE BETTER FOR YOUR HEALTH TO JUST LET IT OUT?
TREMBLE
TREMBLE

OH MY GOODNESS

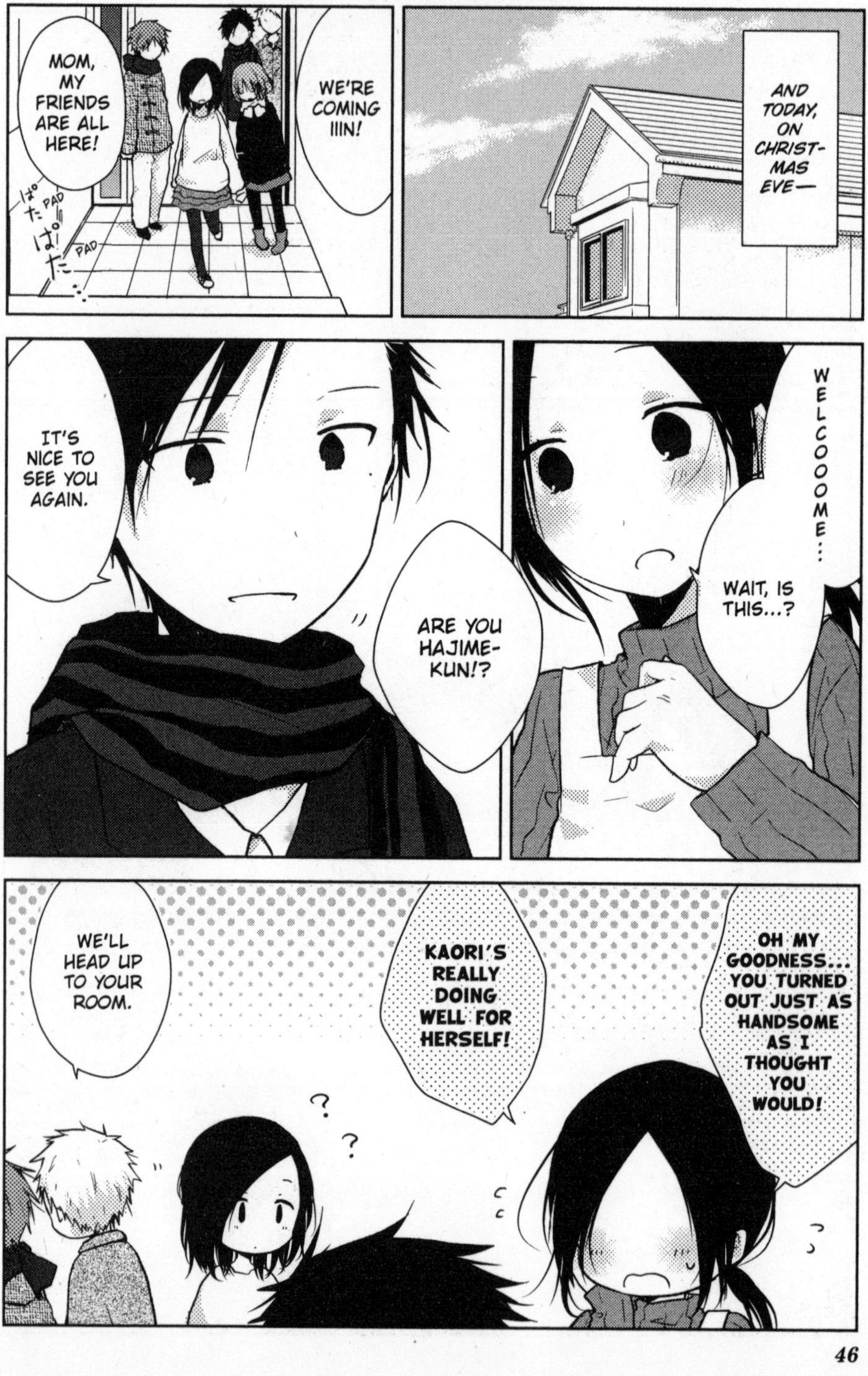
AND TODAY, ON CHRISTMAS EVE—
WE'RE COMING IIIN!
MOM, MY FRIENDS ARE ALL HERE!
ぱた PAD
ぱた PAD
WELCOOOOME...
WAIT, IS THIS...?
ARE YOU HAJIME-KUN!?
IT'S NICE TO SEE YOU AGAIN.
OH MY GOODNESS... YOU TURNED OUT JUST AS HANDSOME AS I THOUGHT YOU WOULD!
KAORI'S REALLY DOING WELL FOR HERSELF!
WE'LL HEAD UP TO YOUR ROOM.

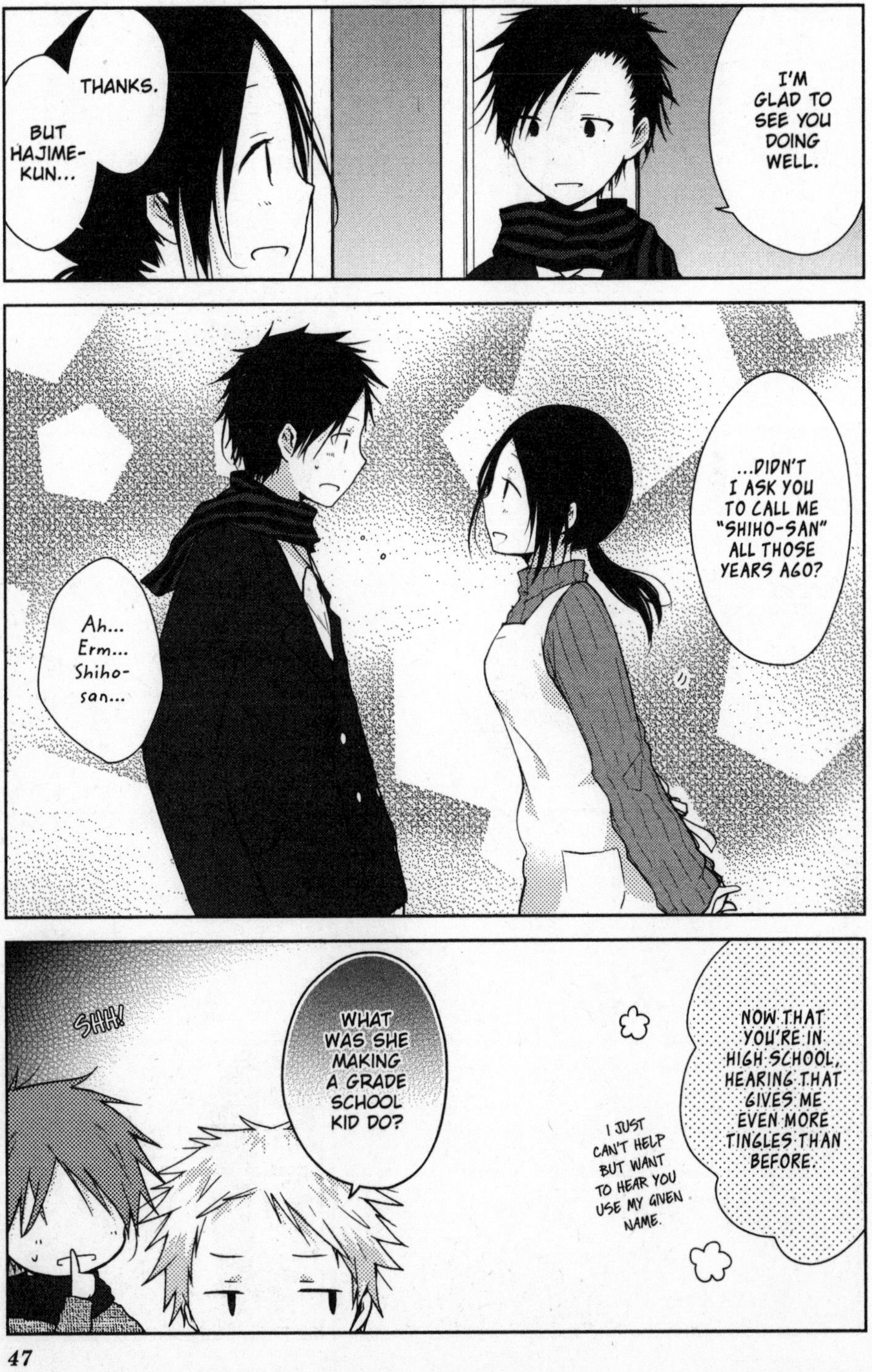
I'M GLAD TO SEE YOU DOING WELL.
THANKS.
BUT HAJIME-KUN...
...DIDN'T I ASK YOU TO CALL ME "SHIHO-SAN" ALL THOSE YEARS AGO?
Ah... Erm... Shiho-san...
NOW THAT YOU'RE IN HIGH SCHOOL, HEARING THAT GIVES ME EVEN MORE TINGLES THAN BEFORE.
I JUST CAN'T HELP BUT WANT TO HEAR YOU USE MY GIVEN NAME.
WHAT WAS SHE MAKING A GRADE SCHOOL KID DO?
SHH!

PARTY KICKOFF

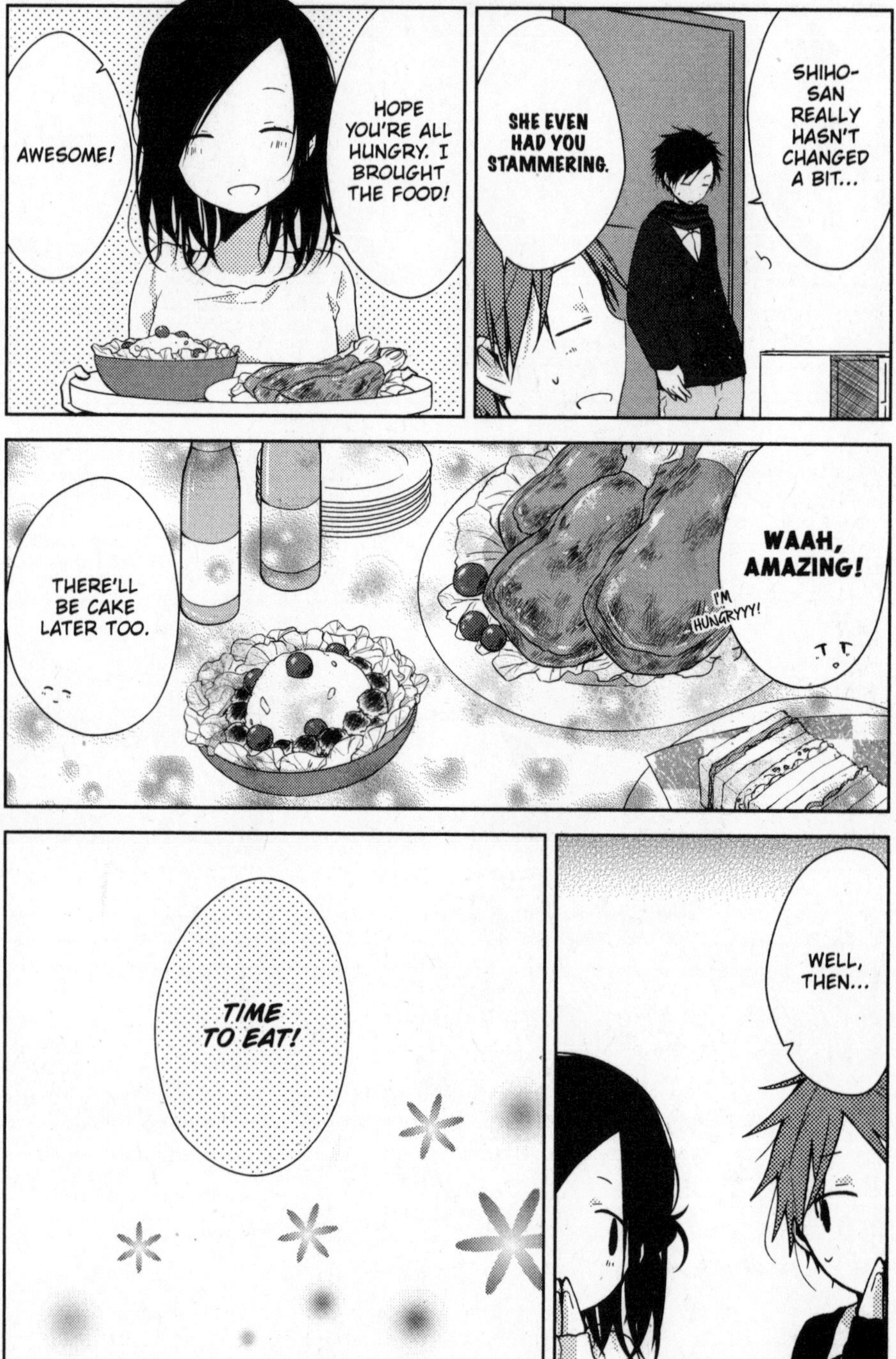
SHIHO-SAN REALLY HASN'T CHANGED A BIT...
SHE EVEN HAD YOU STAMMERING.
HOPE YOU'RE ALL HUNGRY. I BROUGHT THE FOOD!
AWESOME!
WAAH, AMAZING!
I'M HUNGRYYY!
THERE'LL BE CAKE LATER TOO.
WELL, THEN...
TIME TO EAT!

SURPRISE ATTACK

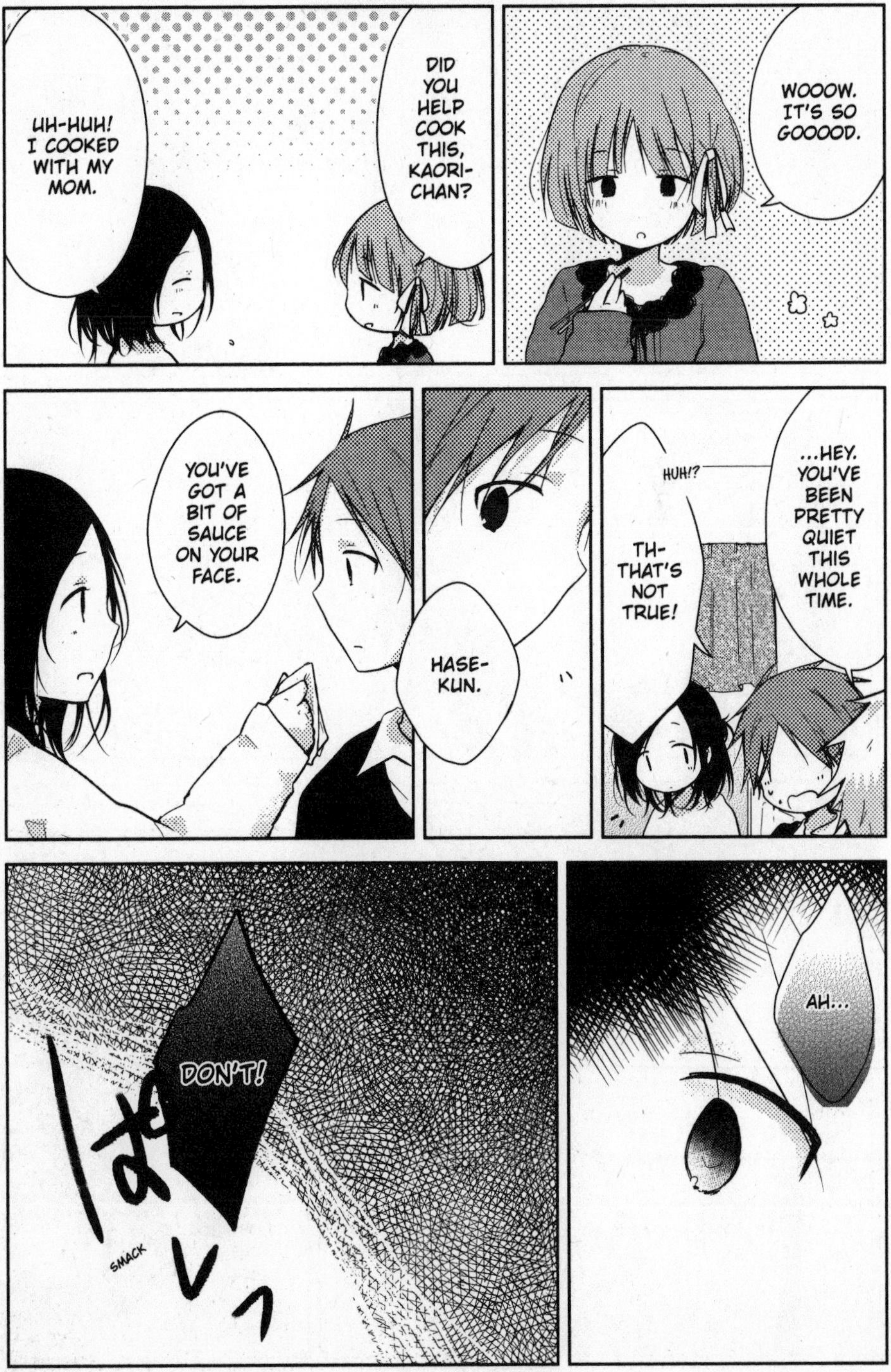
WOOOW. IT'S SO GOOOOD.
DID YOU HELP COOK THIS, KAORI-CHAN?
UH-HUH! I COOKED WITH MY MOM.
...HEY. YOU'VE BEEN PRETTY QUIET THIS WHOLE TIME.
HUH!?
TH-THAT'S NOT TRUE!
HASE-KUN.
YOU'VE GOT A BIT OF SAUCE ON YOUR FACE.
AH...
DON'T!
SMACK

AWKWARD ATMOSPHERE

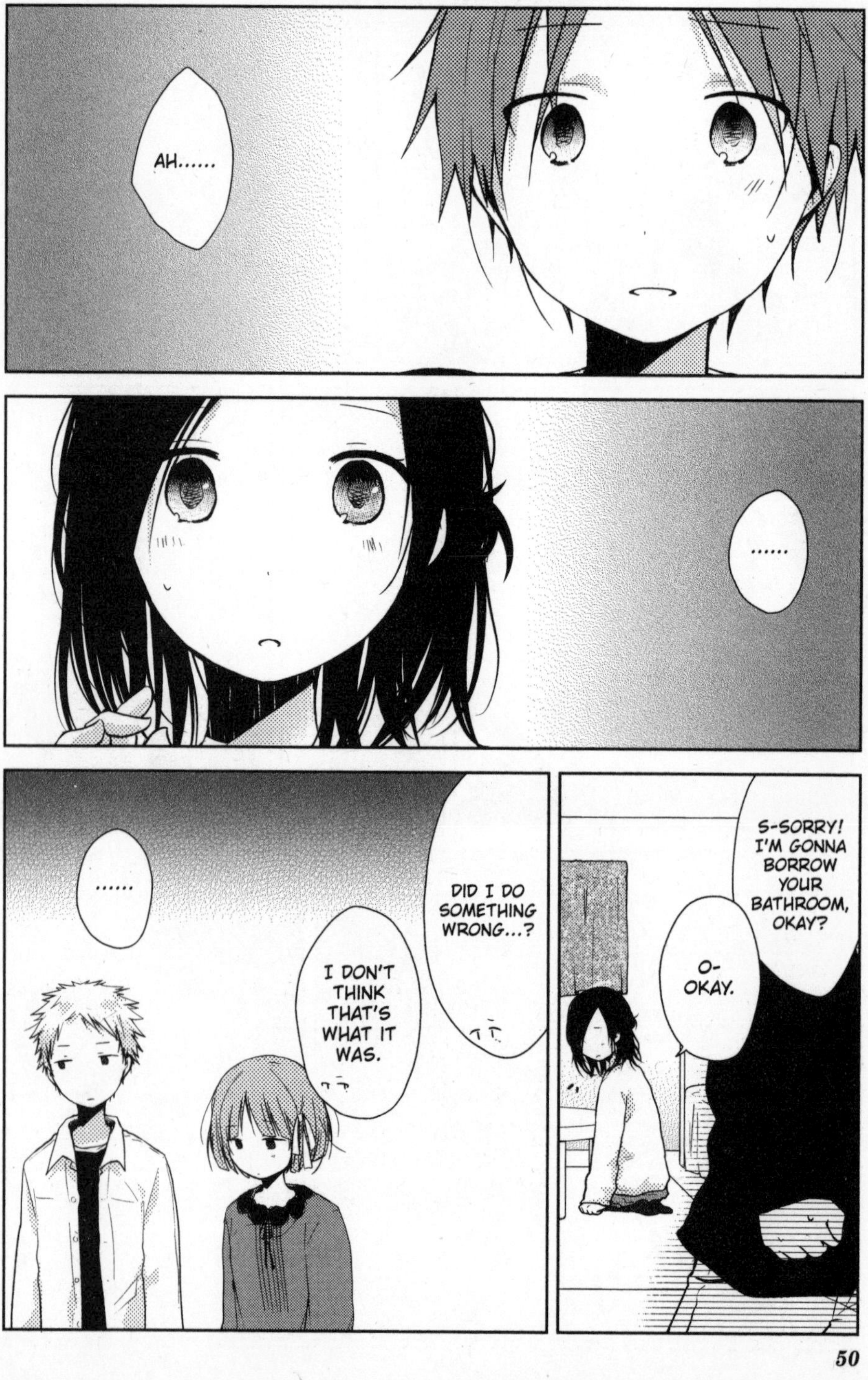
AH......
......
S-SORRY! I'M GONNA BORROW YOUR BATHROOM, OKAY?
O-OKAY.
DID I DO SOMETHING WRONG...?
......
I DON'T THINK THAT'S WHAT IT WAS.

GOING AWRY

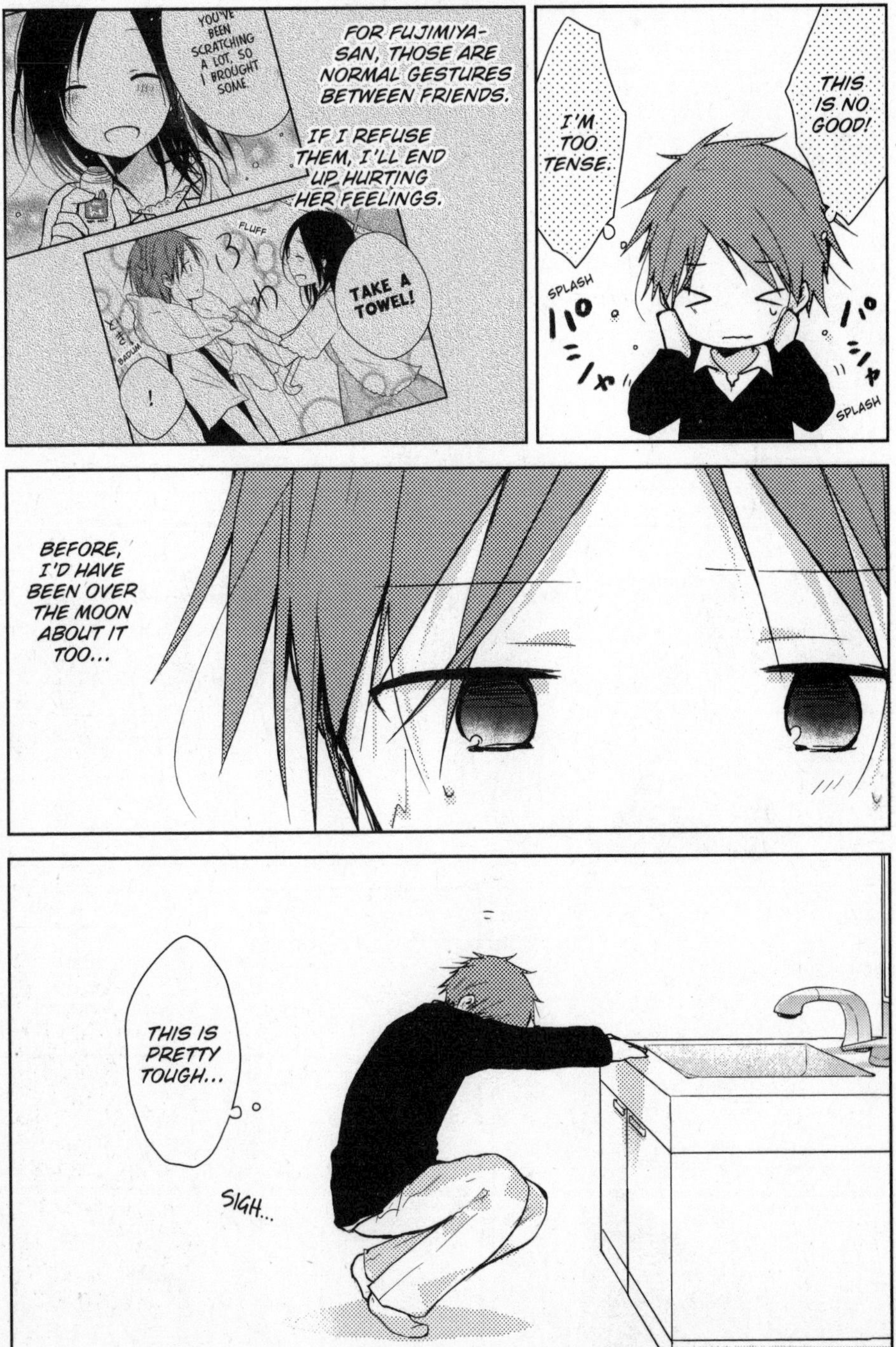

THIS IS NO GOOD!
I'M TOO TENSE.
SPLASH
SPLASH
FOR FUJIMIYA-SAN, THOSE ARE NORMAL GESTURES BETWEEN FRIENDS.
YOU'VE BEEN SCRATCHING A LOT, SO I BROUGHT SOME.
IF I REFUSE THEM, I'LL END UP HURTING HER FEELINGS.
TAKE A TOWEL!
FLUFF
BADUM
!
BEFORE, I'D HAVE BEEN OVER THE MOON ABOUT IT TOO...
THIS IS PRETTY TOUGH...
SIGH...

THOUGH I KNOW

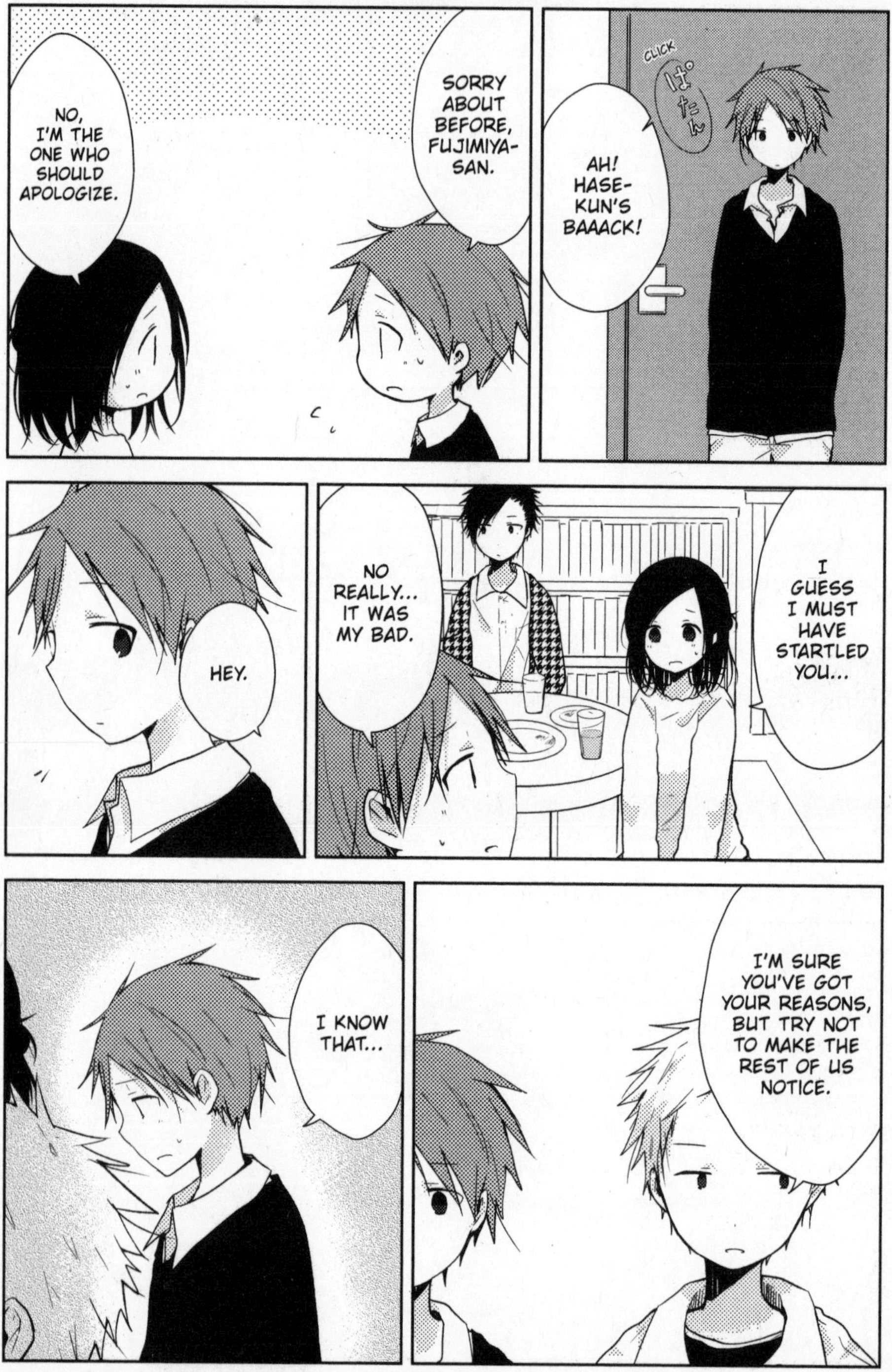
CLICK
ぱたん
AH! HASE-KUN'S BAAACK!
SORRY ABOUT BEFORE, FUJIMIYA-SAN.
NO, I'M THE ONE WHO SHOULD APOLOGIZE.
I GUESS I MUST HAVE STARTLED YOU...
NO REALLY... IT WAS MY BAD.
HEY.
I'M SURE YOU'VE GOT YOUR REASONS, BUT TRY NOT TO MAKE THE REST OF US NOTICE.
I KNOW THAT...

I WANTED TO

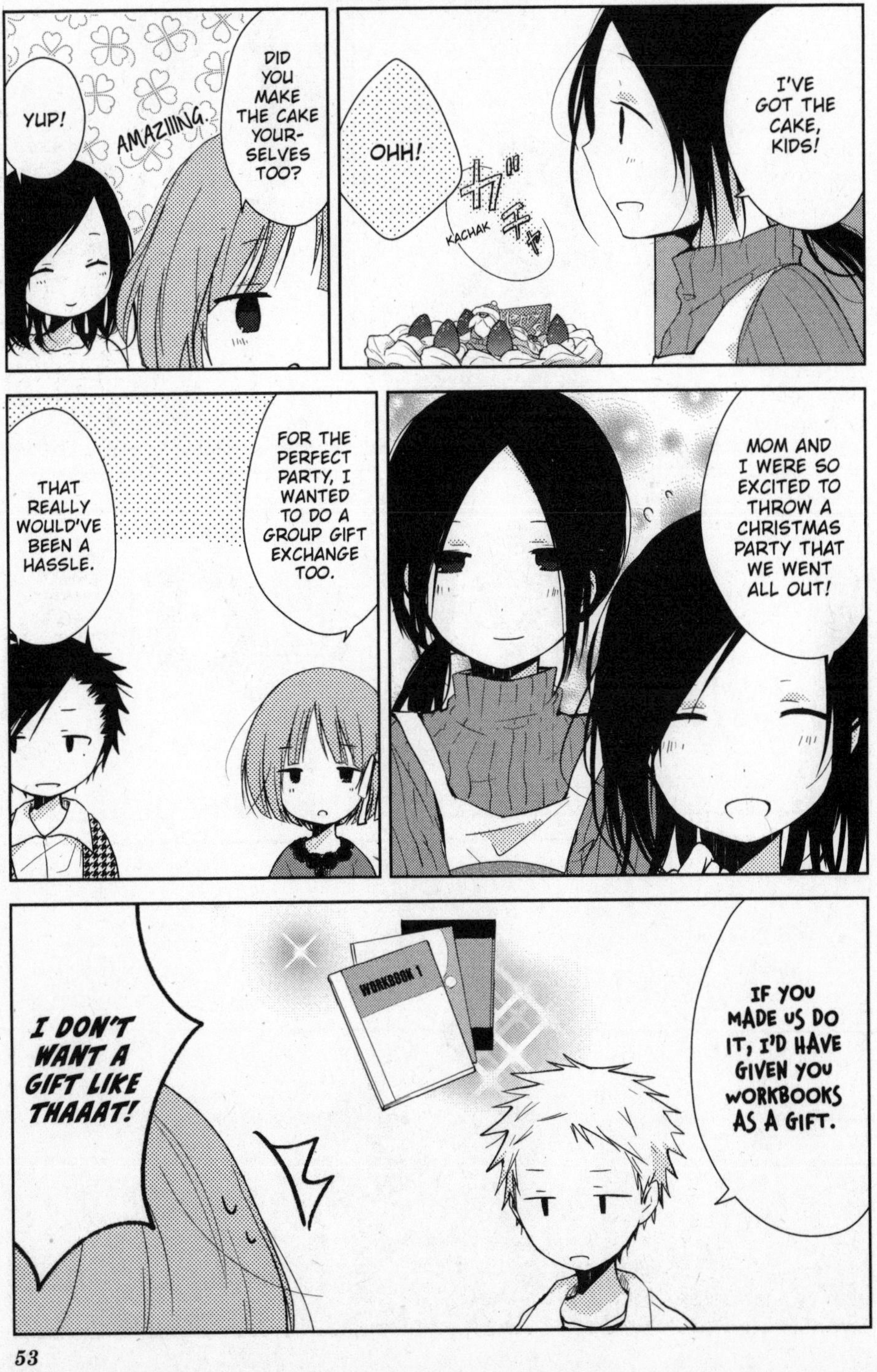

I'VE GOT THE CAKE, KIDS!
OHH!
KACHAK
DID YOU MAKE THE CAKE YOURSELVES TOO?
AMAZIIING.
YUP!
MOM AND I WERE SO EXCITED TO THROW A CHRISTMAS PARTY THAT WE WENT ALL OUT!
FOR THE PERFECT PARTY, I WANTED TO DO A GROUP GIFT EXCHANGE TOO.
THAT REALLY WOULD'VE BEEN A HASSLE.
IF YOU MADE US DO IT, I'D HAVE GIVEN YOU WORKBOOKS AS A GIFT.
WORKBOOK 1
I DON'T WANT A GIFT LIKE THAAAT!

ACTUALLY

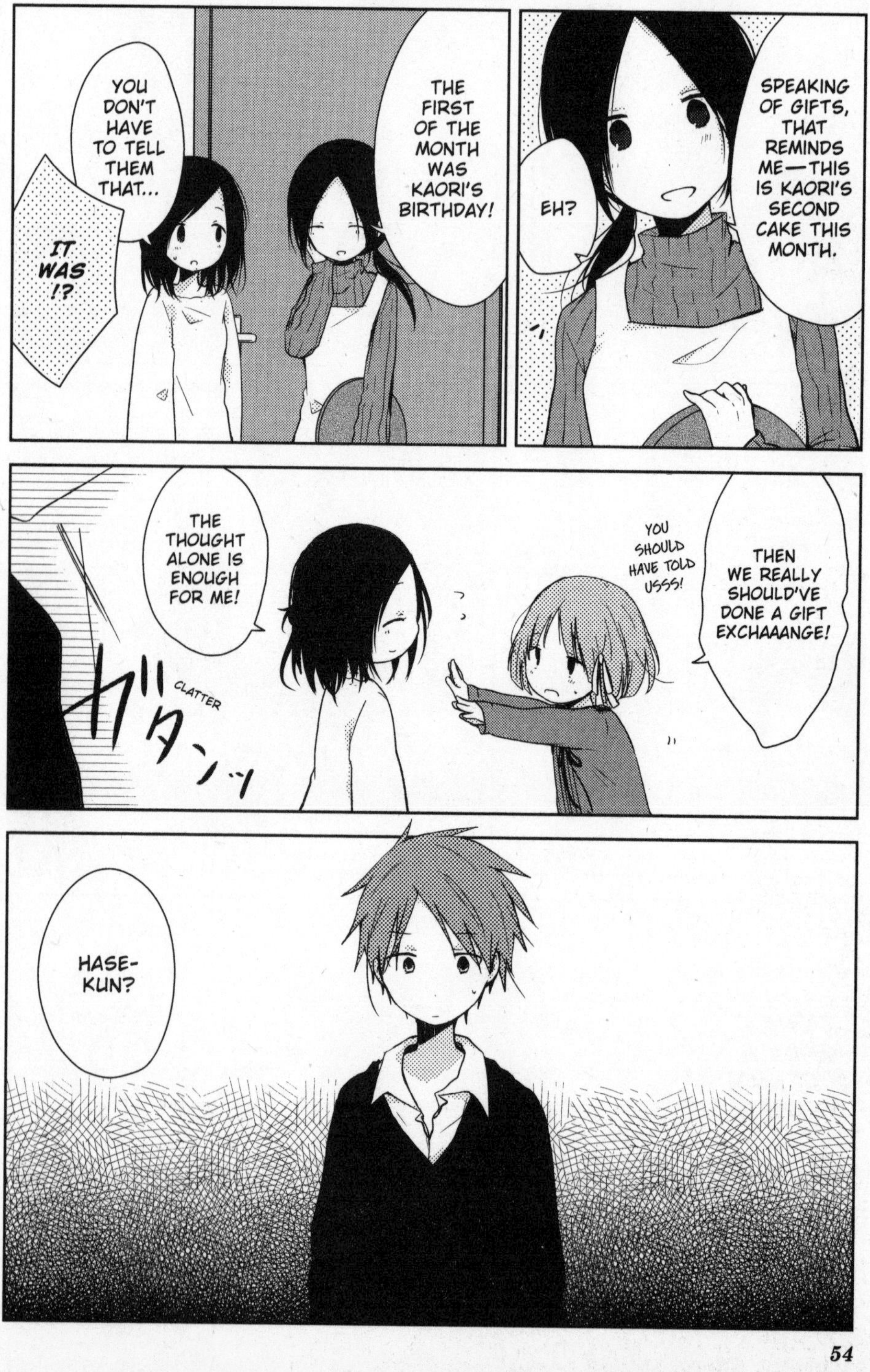
SPEAKING OF GIFTS, THAT REMINDS ME—THIS IS KAORI'S SECOND CAKE THIS MONTH.
EH?
THE FIRST OF THE MONTH WAS KAORI'S BIRTHDAY!
YOU DON'T HAVE TO TELL THEM THAT...
IT WAS!?
THEN WE REALLY SHOULD'VE DONE A GIFT EXCHAAANGE!
YOU SHOULD HAVE TOLD USSS!
THE THOUGHT ALONE IS ENOUGH FOR ME!
ガタンッ
CLATTER
HASE-KUN?

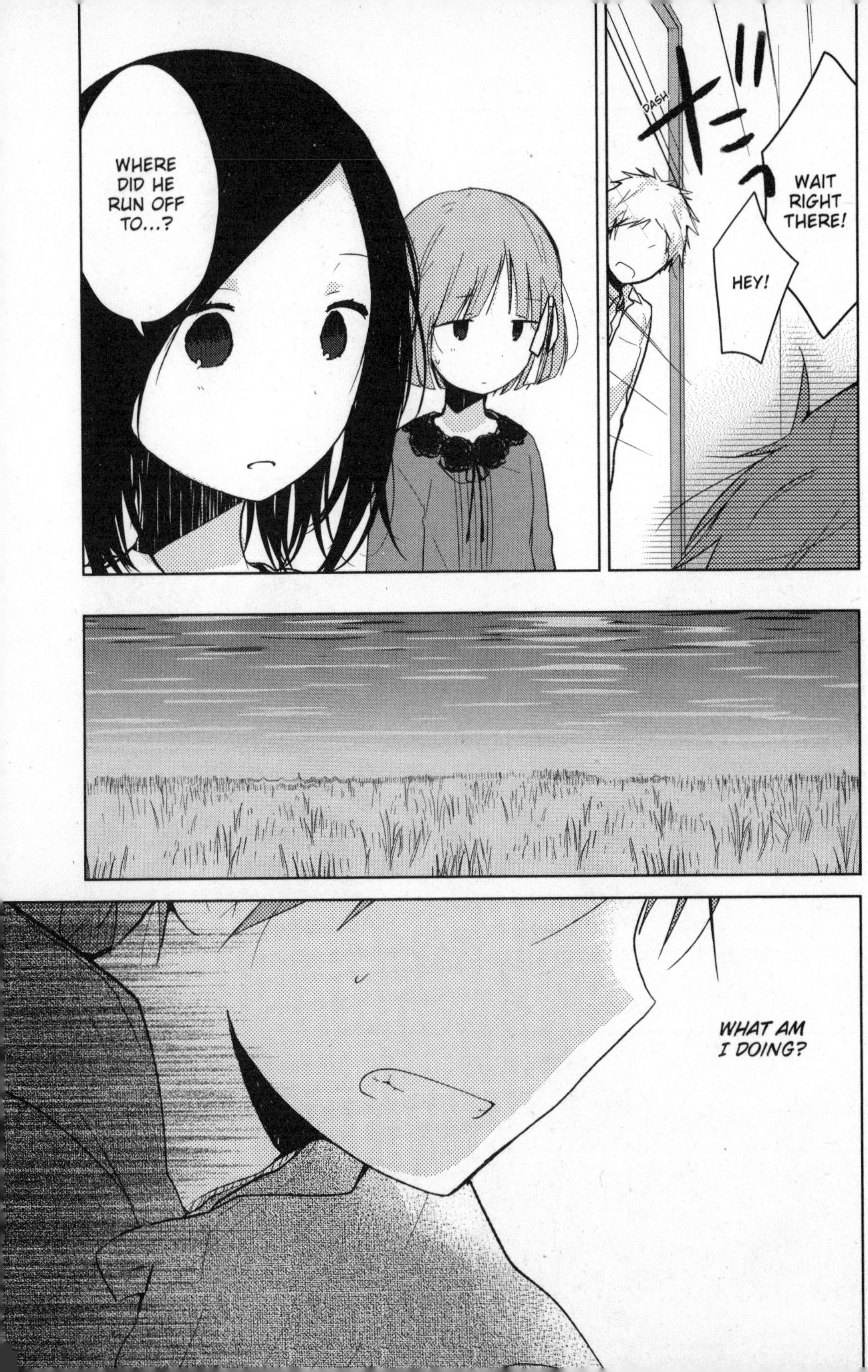
DASH
WAIT RIGHT THERE!
HEY!
WHERE DID HE RUN OFF TO...?
WHAT AM I DOING?

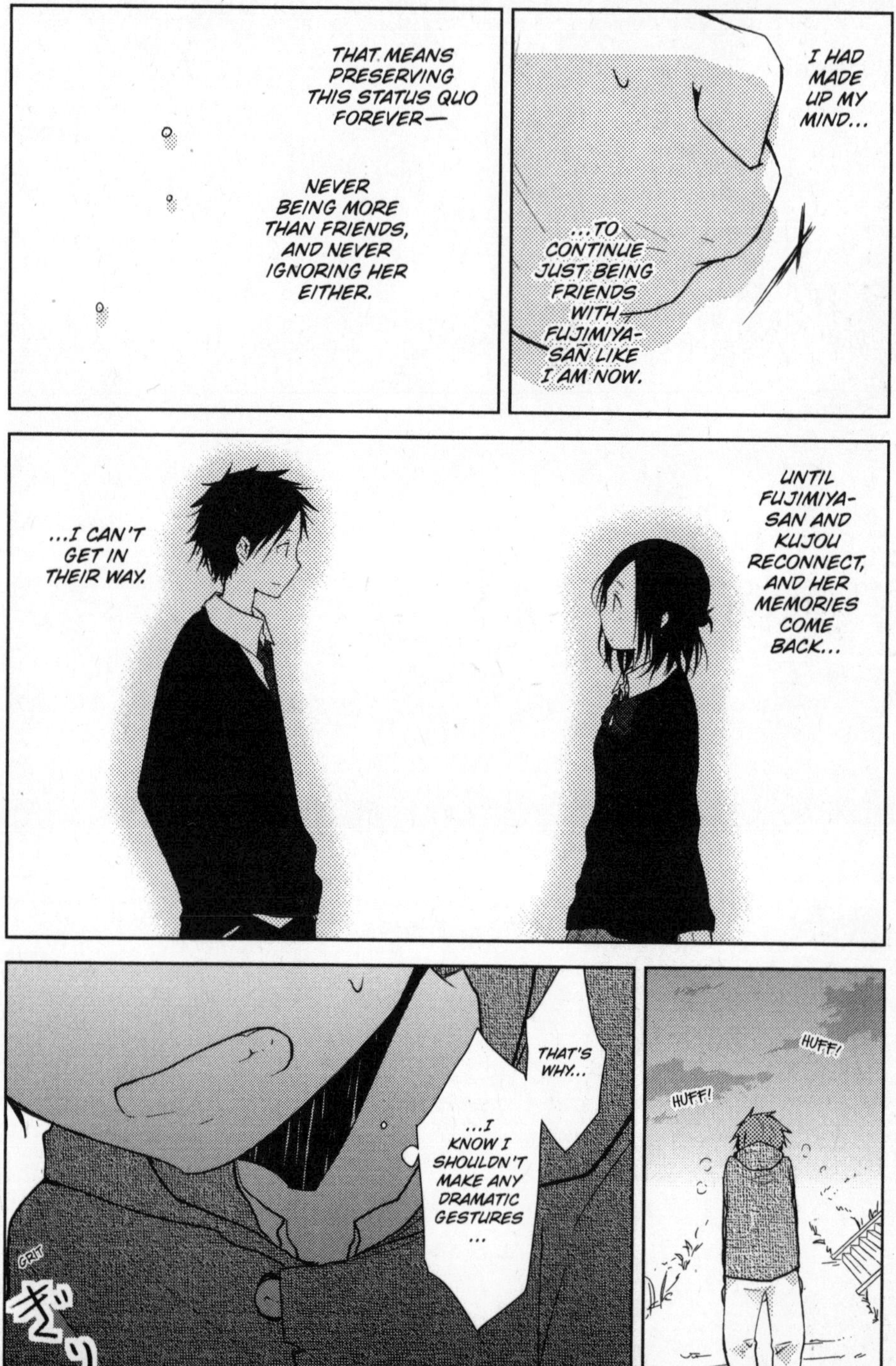
I HAD MADE UP MY MIND...
...TO CONTINUE JUST BEING FRIENDS WITH FUJIMIYA-SAN LIKE I AM NOW.
THAT MEANS PRESERVING THIS STATUS QUO FOREVER—
NEVER BEING MORE THAN FRIENDS, AND NEVER IGNORING HER EITHER.
UNTIL FUJIMIYA-SAN AND KUJOU RECONNECT, AND HER MEMORIES COME BACK...
...I CAN'T GET IN THEIR WAY.
HUFF!
HUFF!
THAT'S WHY...
...I KNOW I SHOULDN'T MAKE ANY DRAMATIC GESTURES...
GRIT
ぎり

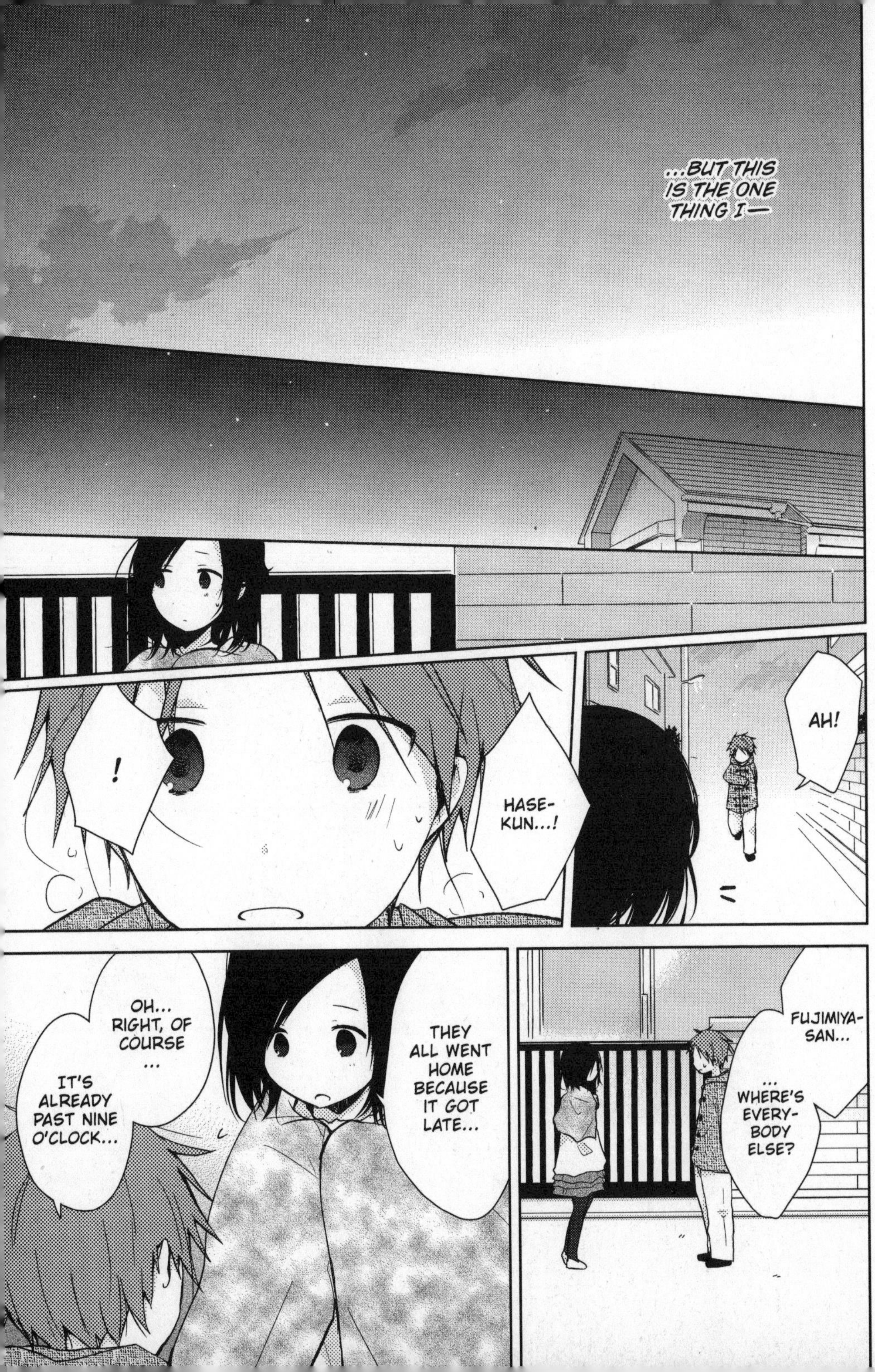
...BUT THIS IS THE ONE THING I—
AH!
!
HASE-KUN...!
FUJIMIYA-SAN...
...WHERE'S EVERYBODY ELSE?
THEY ALL WENT HOME BECAUSE IT GOT LATE...
OH... RIGHT, OF COURSE...
IT'S ALREADY PAST NINE O'CLOCK...

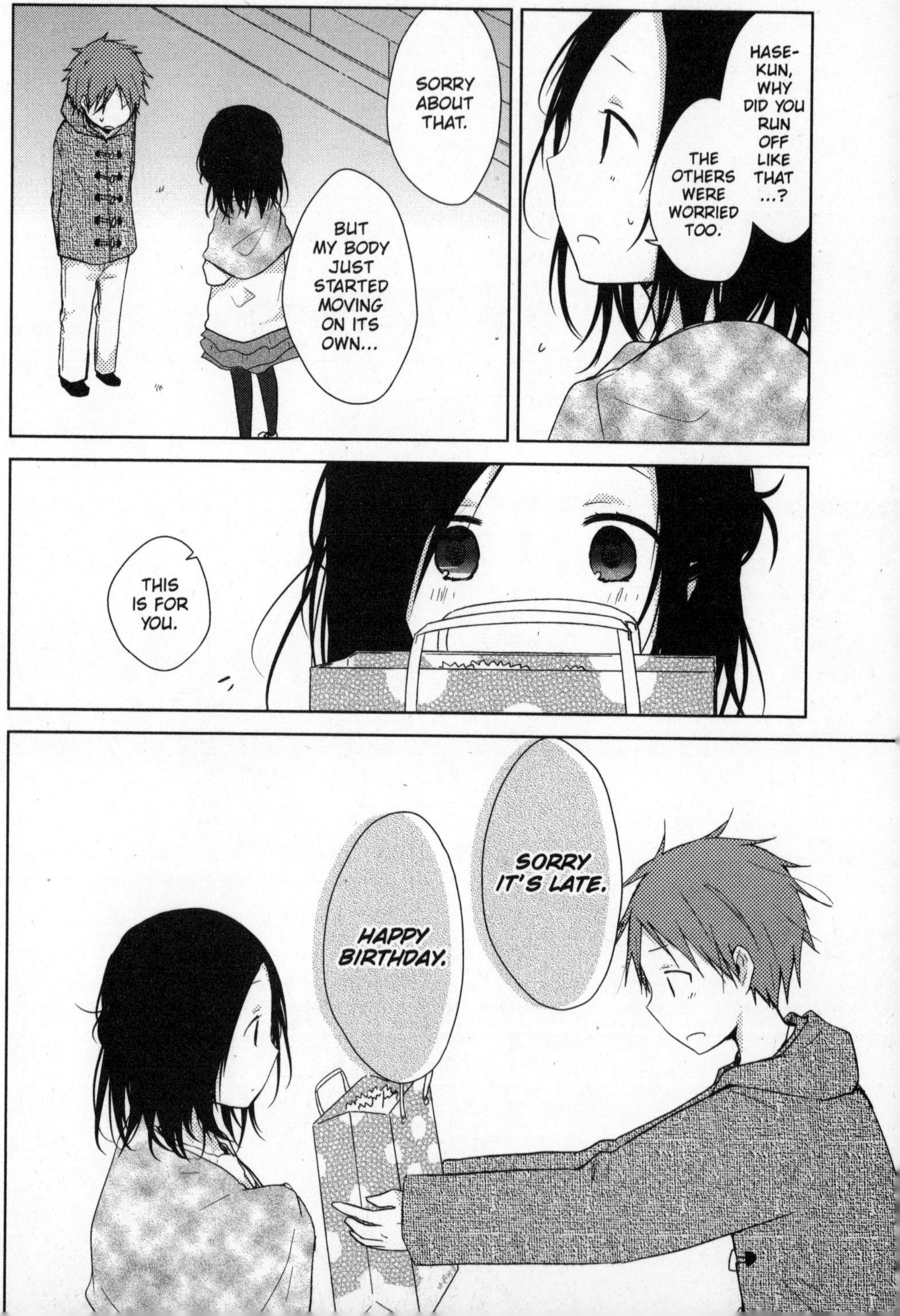
HASE-KUN, WHY DID YOU RUN OFF LIKE THAT ...?
THE OTHERS WERE WORRIED TOO.
SORRY ABOUT THAT.
BUT MY BODY JUST STARTED MOVING ON ITS OWN...
THIS IS FOR YOU.
SORRY IT'S LATE.
HAPPY BIRTHDAY.

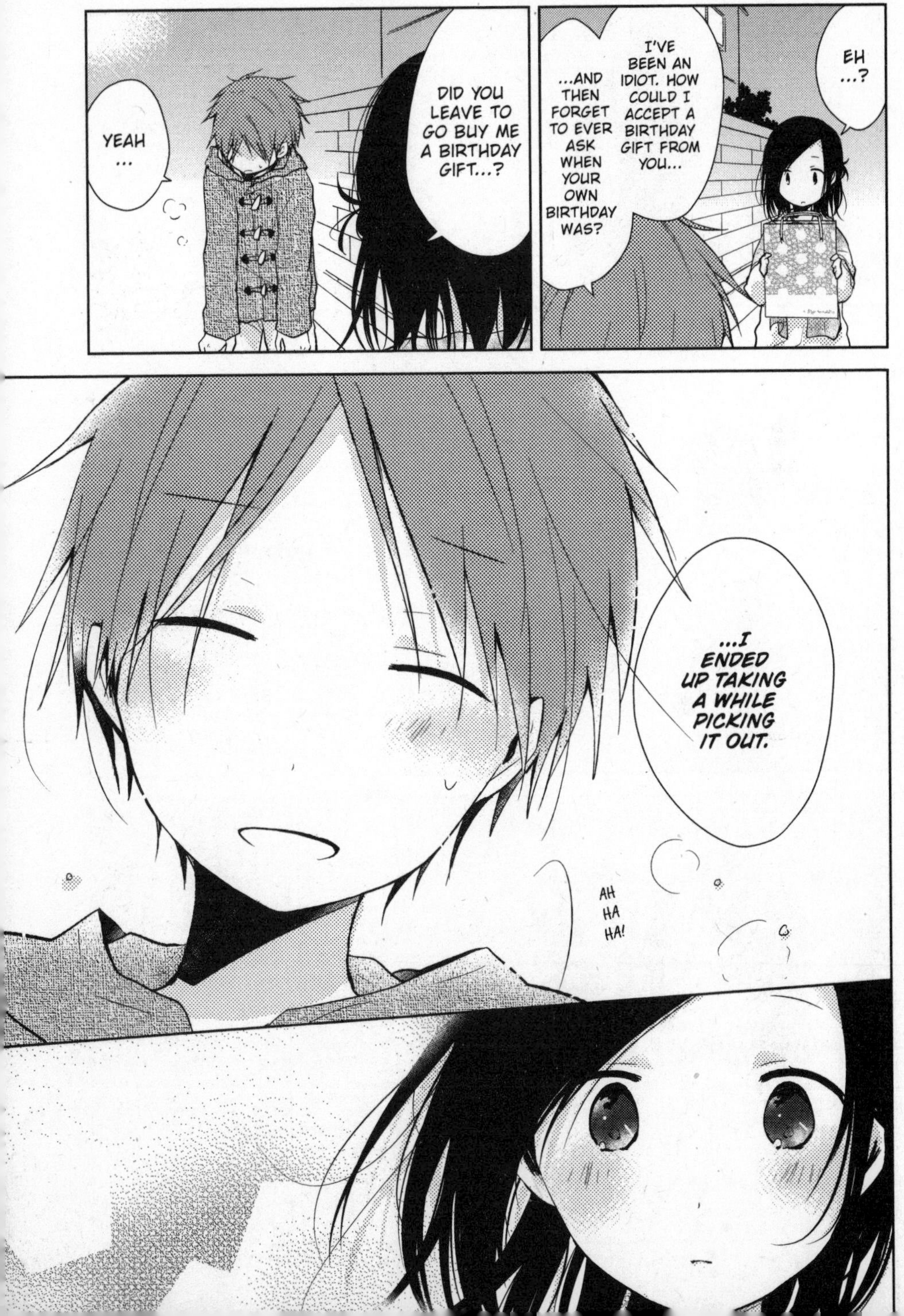
EH ...?
I'VE BEEN AN IDIOT. HOW COULD I ACCEPT A BIRTHDAY GIFT FROM YOU...
...AND THEN FORGET TO EVER ASK WHEN YOUR OWN BIRTHDAY WAS?
DID YOU LEAVE TO GO BUY ME A BIRTHDAY GIFT...?
YEAH ...
...I ENDED UP TAKING A WHILE PICKING IT OUT.
AH HA HA!

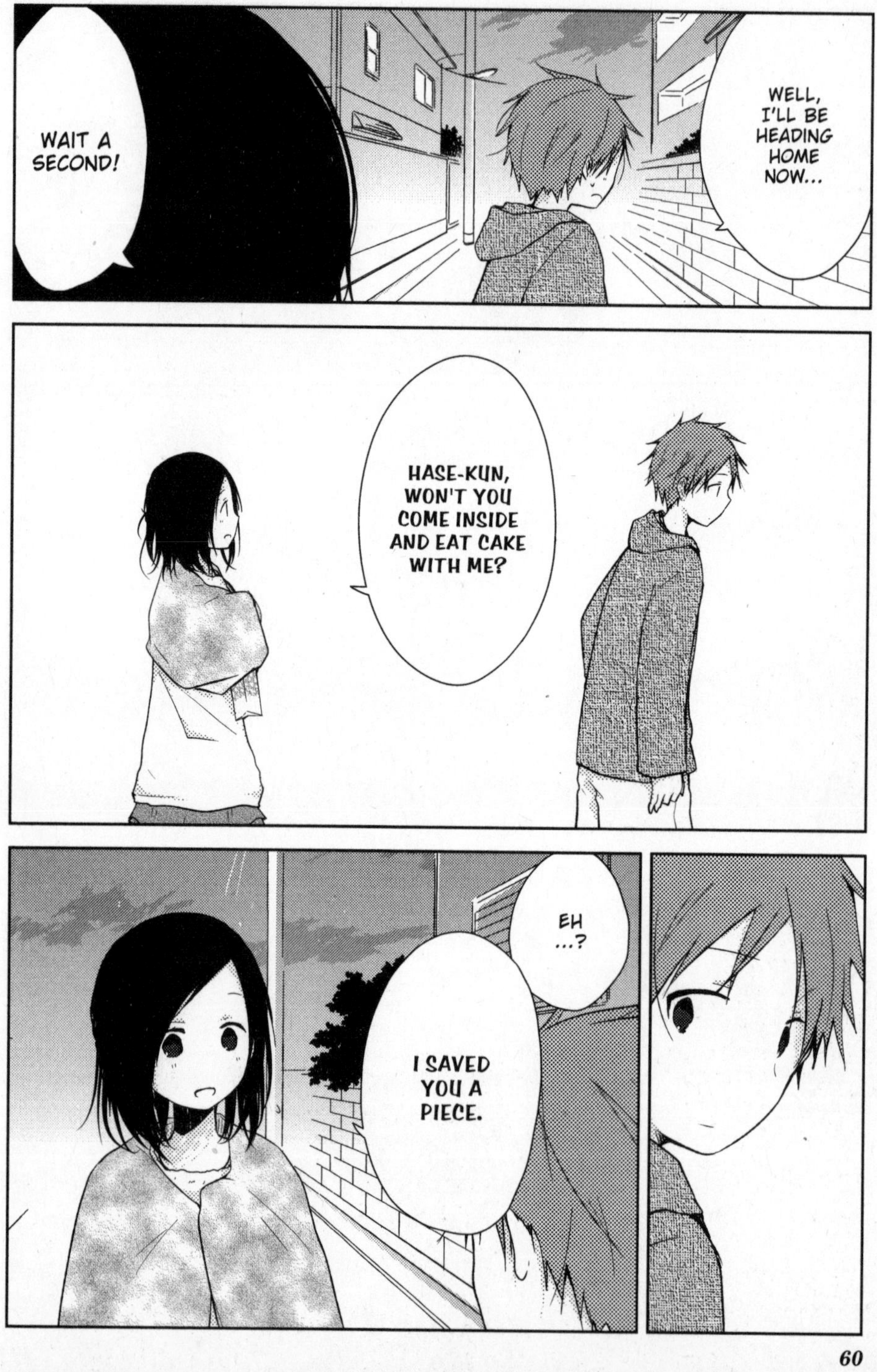
WELL, I'LL BE HEADING HOME NOW...
WAIT A SECOND!
HASE-KUN, WON'T YOU COME INSIDE AND EAT CAKE WITH ME?
EH ...?
I SAVED YOU A PIECE.

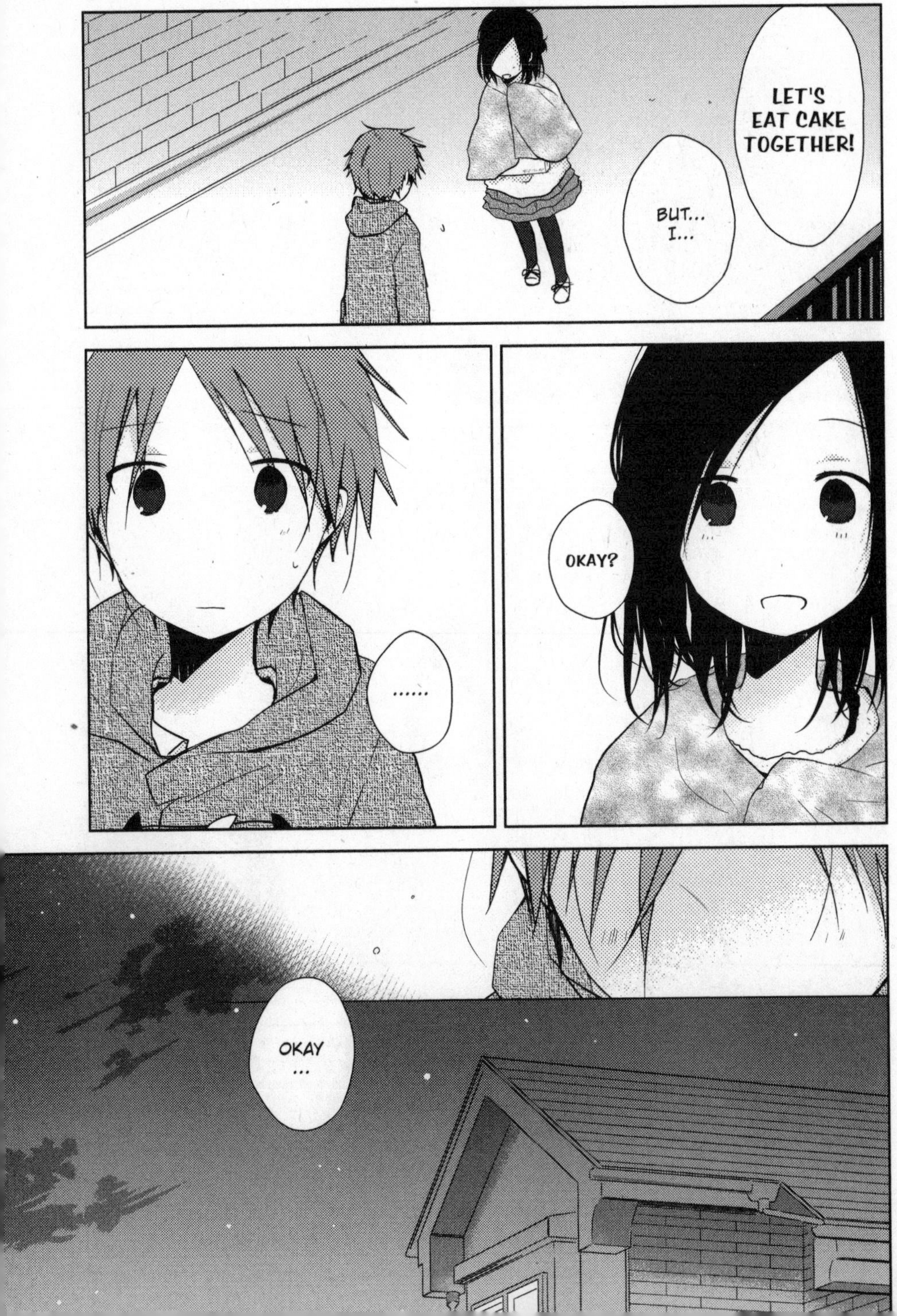
LET'S EAT CAKE TOGETHER!
BUT... I...
OKAY?
......
OKAY ...

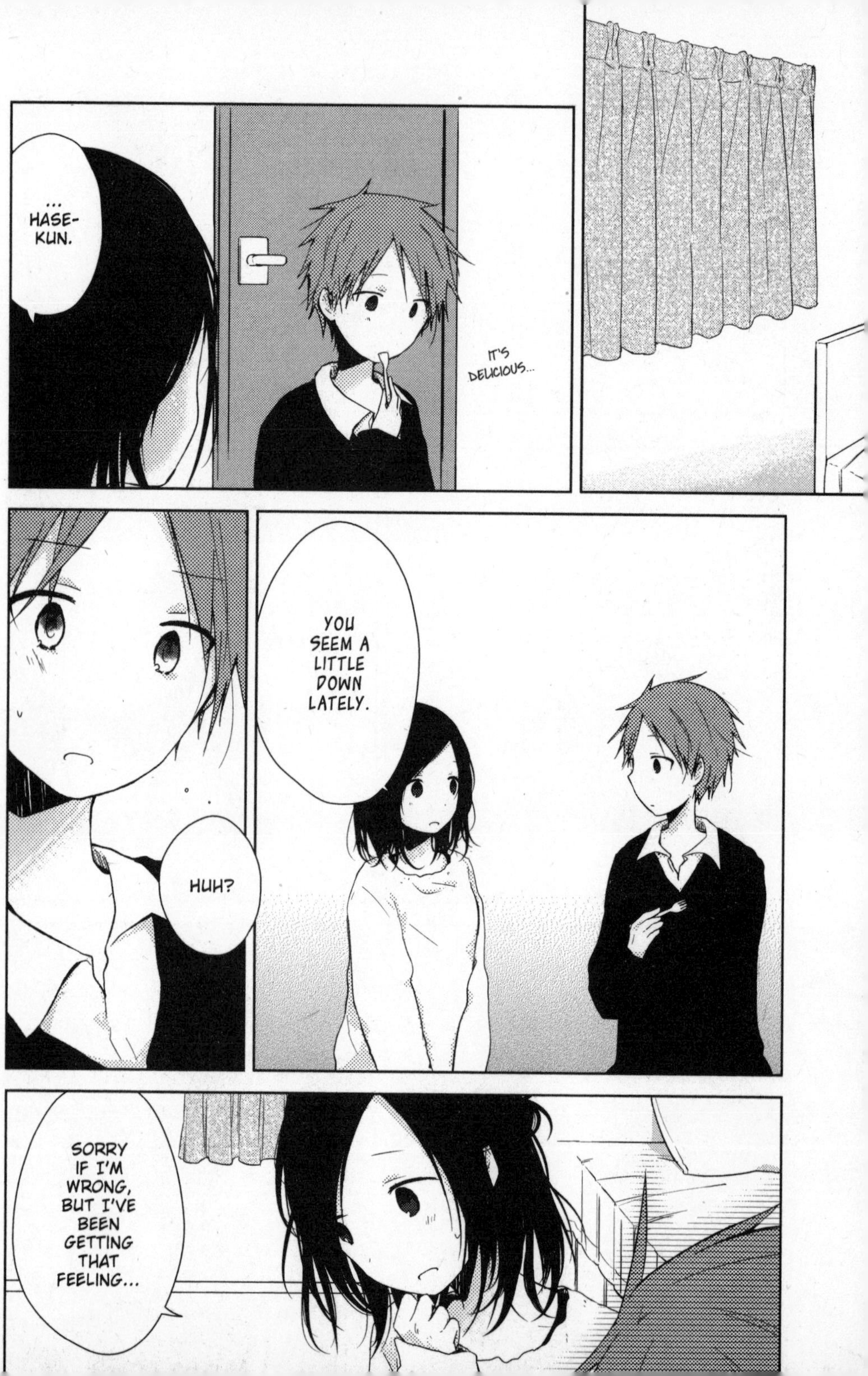
IT'S DELICIOUS...
... HASE-KUN.
YOU SEEM A LITTLE DOWN LATELY.
HUH?
SORRY IF I'M WRONG, BUT I'VE BEEN GETTING THAT FEELING...

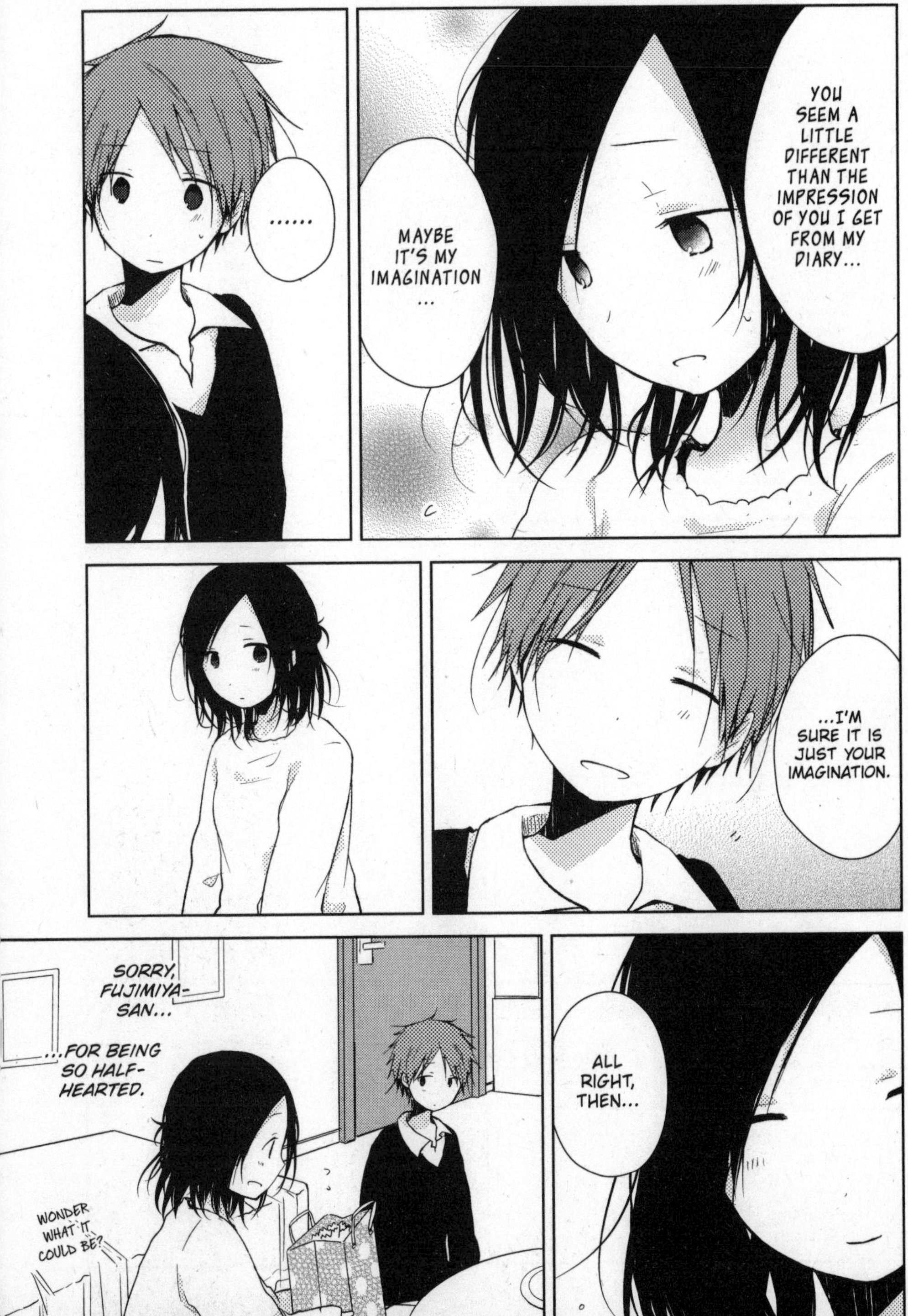
YOU SEEM A LITTLE DIFFERENT THAN THE IMPRESSION OF YOU I GET FROM MY DIARY...
MAYBE IT'S MY IMAGINATION ...
......
...I'M SURE IT IS JUST YOUR IMAGINATION.
ALL RIGHT, THEN...
SORRY, FUJIMIYA-SAN...
...FOR BEING SO HALF-HEARTED.
WONDER WHAT IT COULD BE?

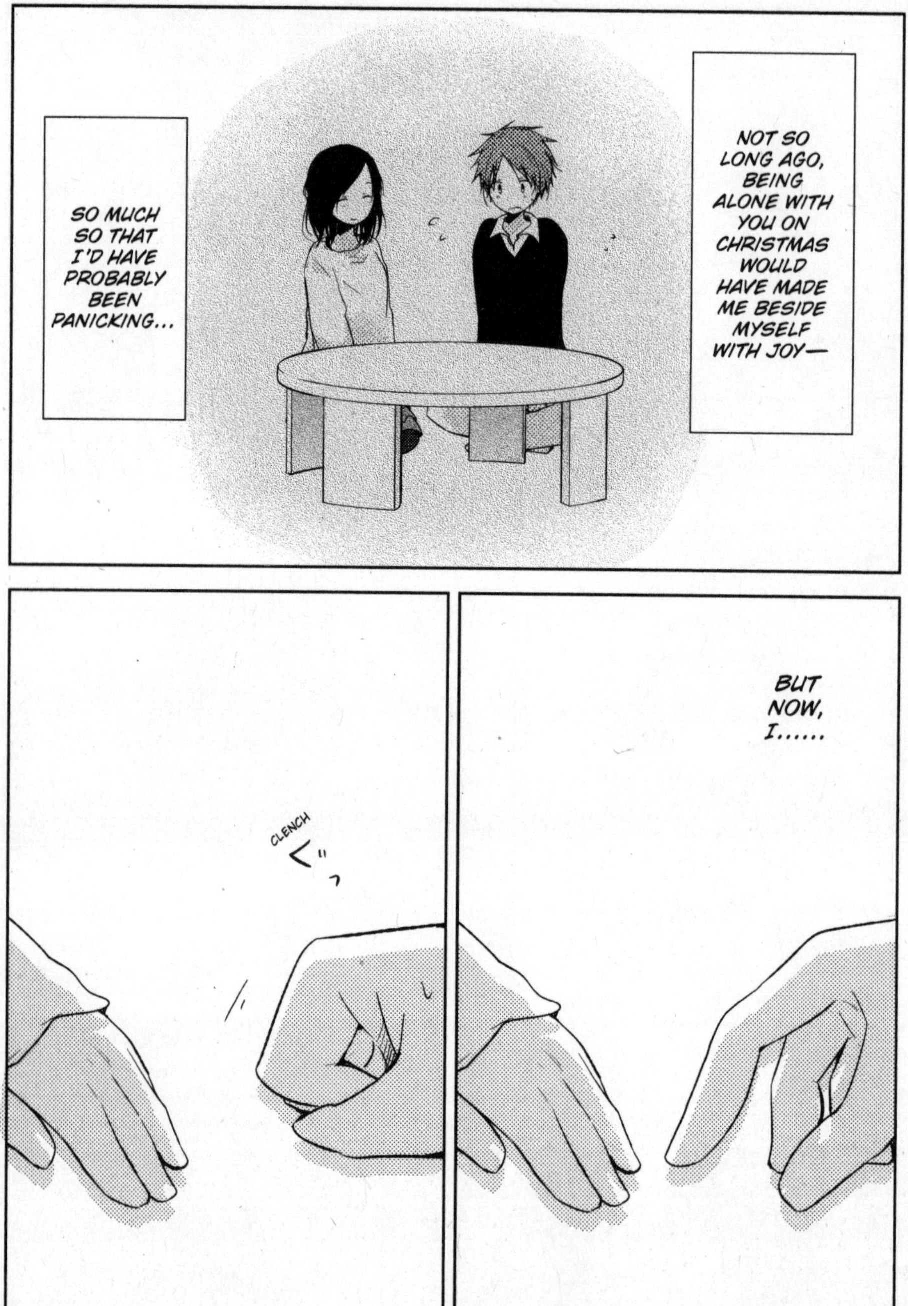
NOT SO LONG AGO, BEING ALONE WITH YOU ON CHRISTMAS WOULD HAVE MADE ME BESIDE MYSELF WITH JOY—
SO MUCH SO THAT I'D HAVE PROBABLY BEEN PANICKING...
BUT NOW, I......
CLENCH

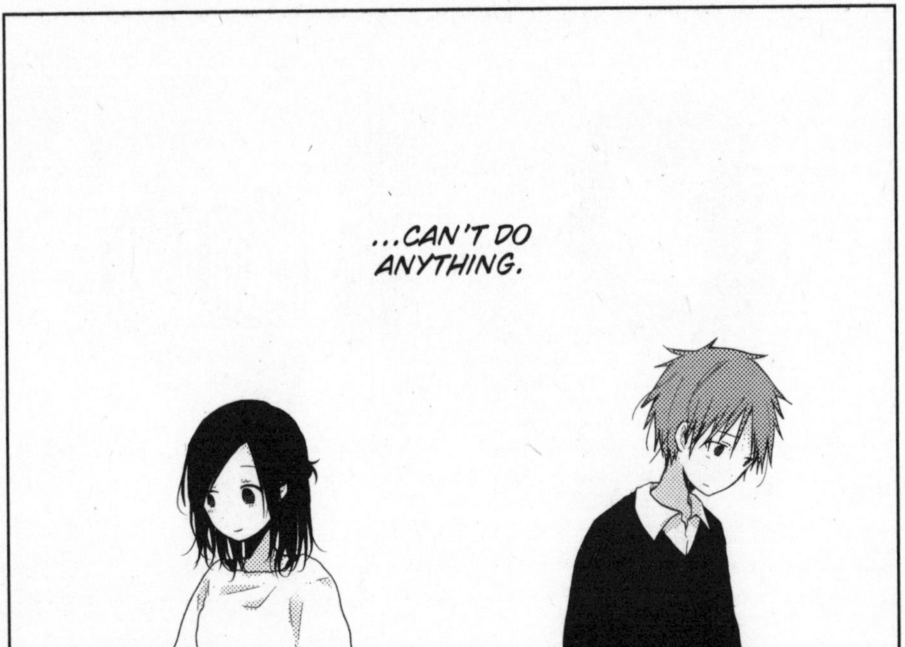
...CAN'T DO ANYTHING.
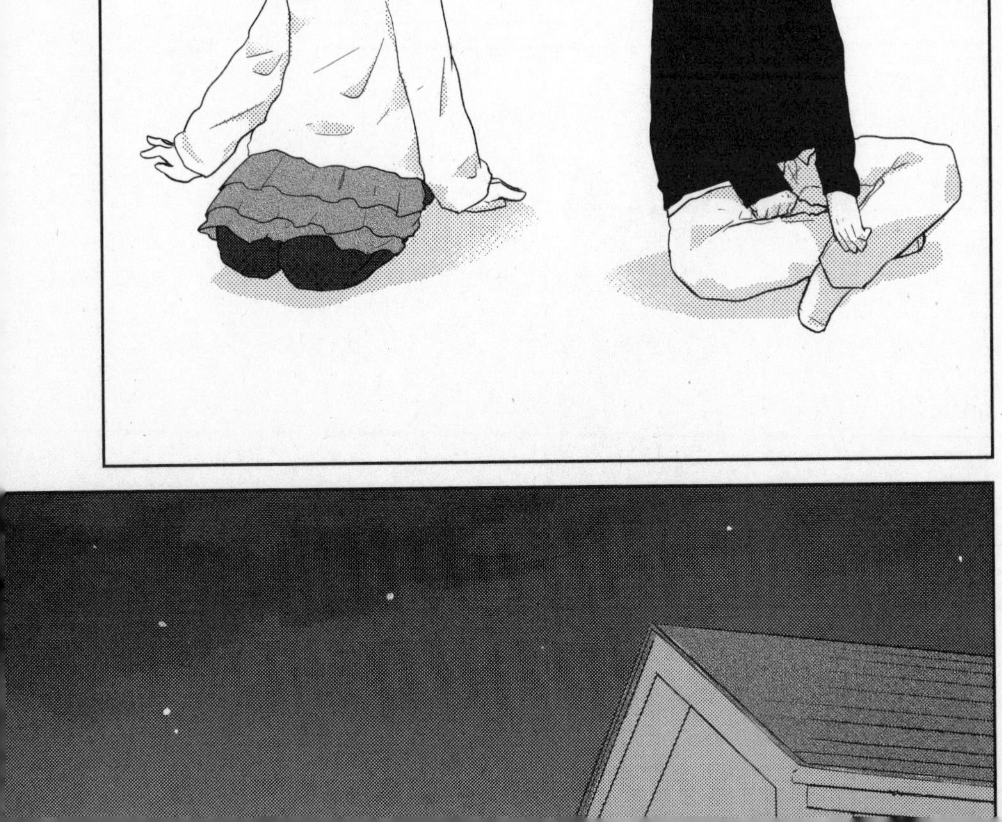

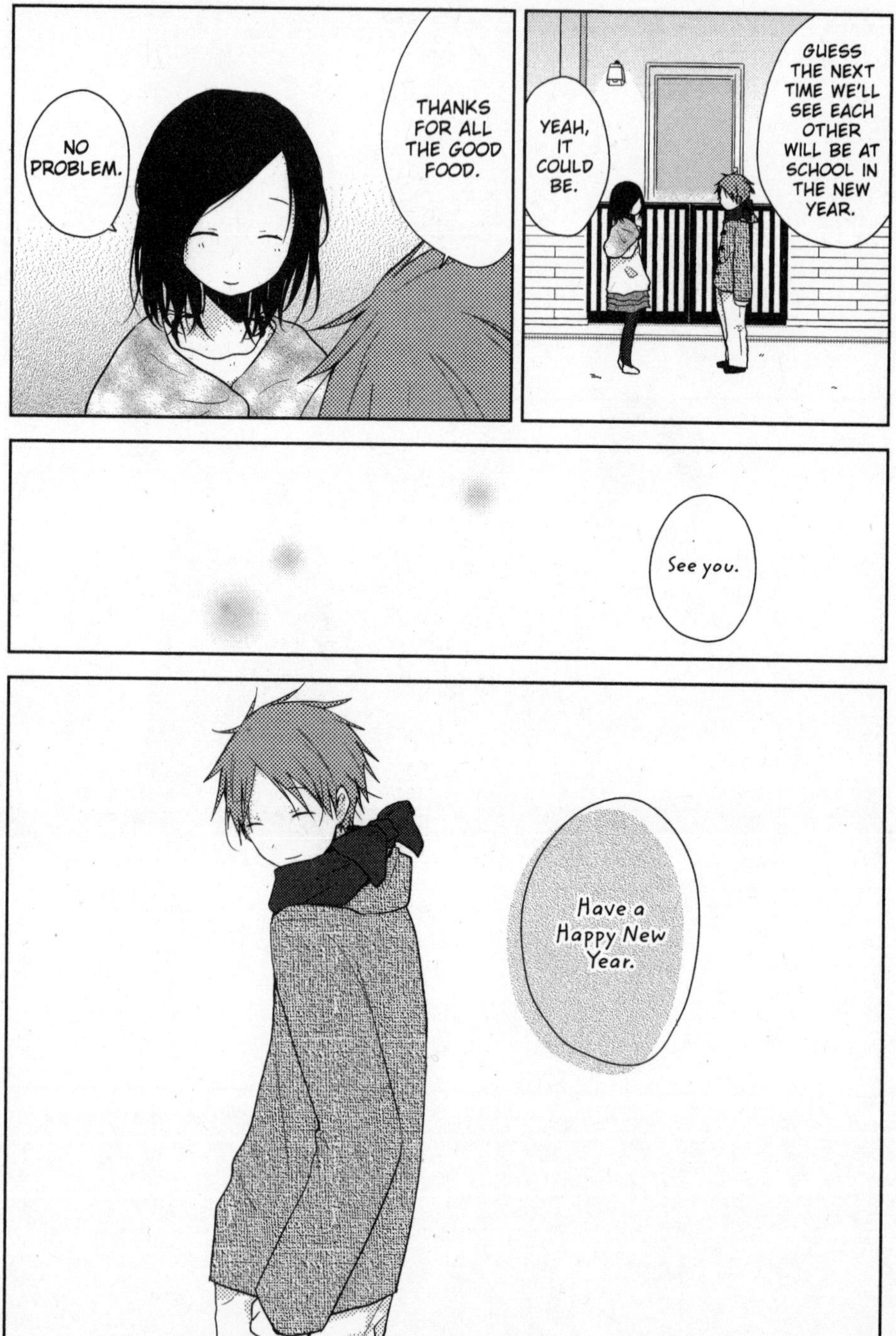
GUESS THE NEXT TIME WE'LL SEE EACH OTHER WILL BE AT SCHOOL IN THE NEW YEAR.
YEAH, IT COULD BE.
THANKS FOR ALL THE GOOD FOOD.
NO PROBLEM.
See you.
Have a Happy New Year.

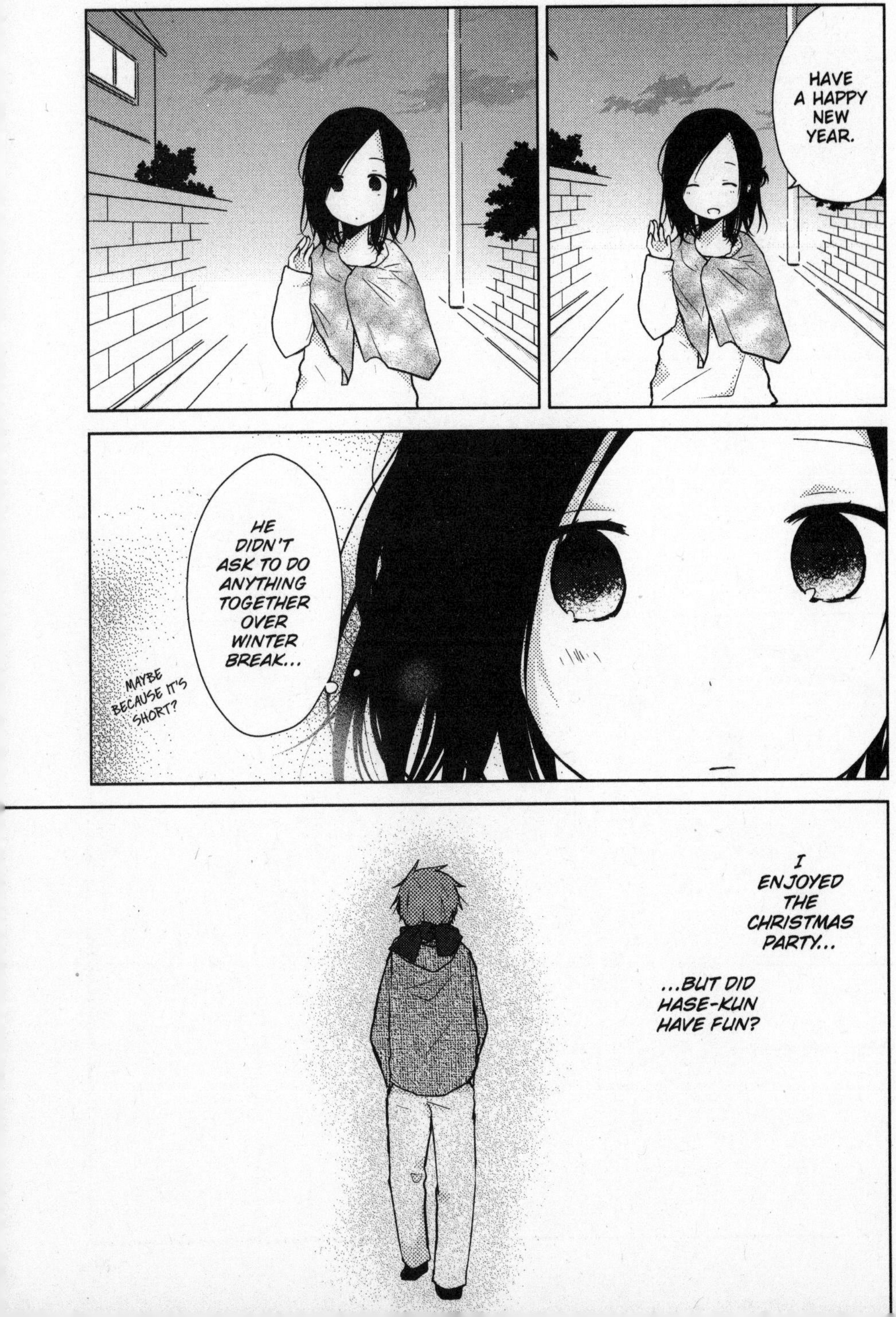
HAVE A HAPPY NEW YEAR.
HE DIDN'T ASK TO DO ANYTHING TOGETHER OVER WINTER BREAK...
MAYBE BECAUSE IT'S SHORT?
I ENJOYED THE CHRISTMAS PARTY...
...BUT DID HASE-KUN HAVE FUN?

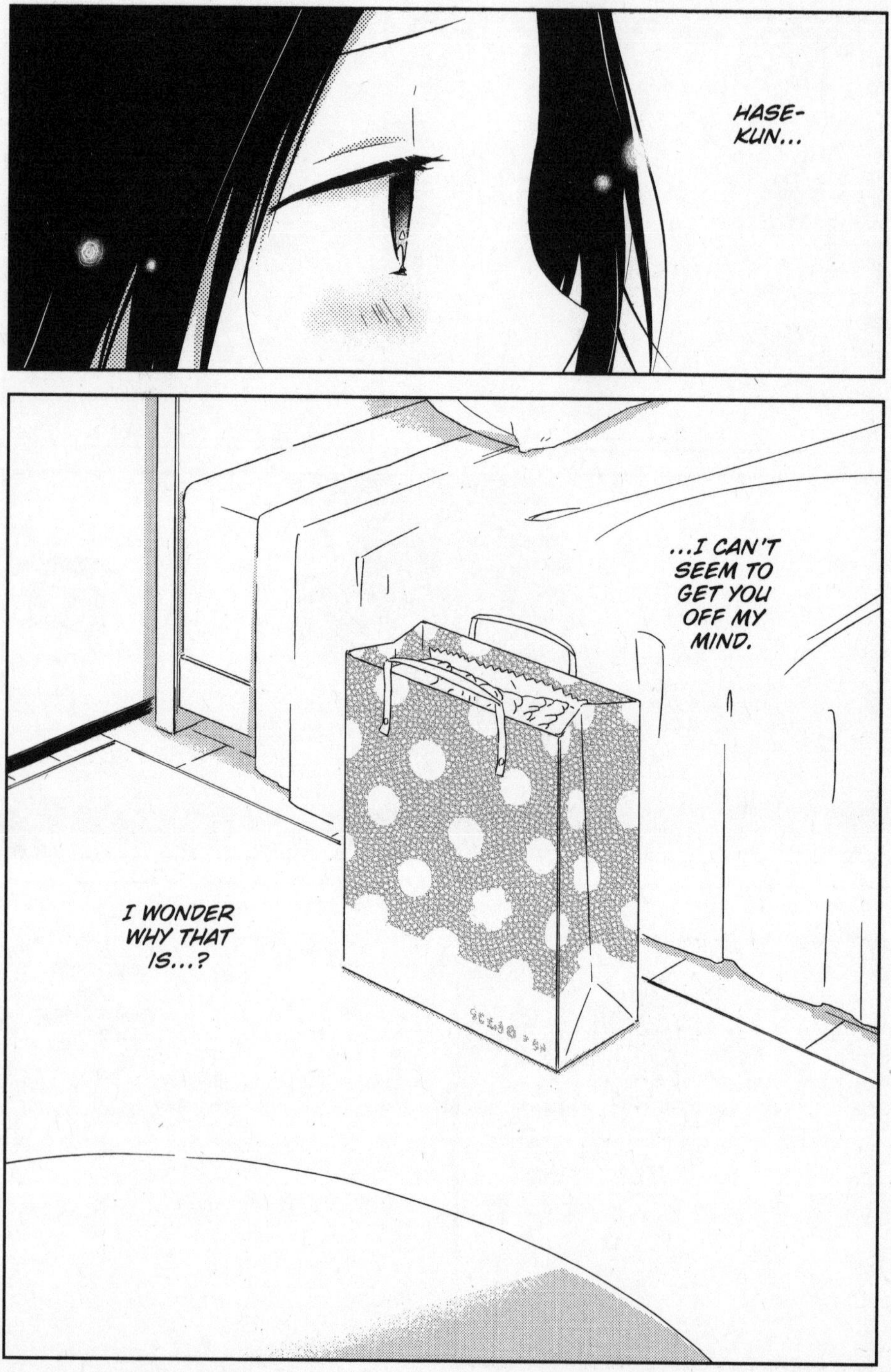
HASE-KUN...
...I CAN'T SEEM TO GET YOU OFF MY MIND.
I WONDER WHY THAT IS...?

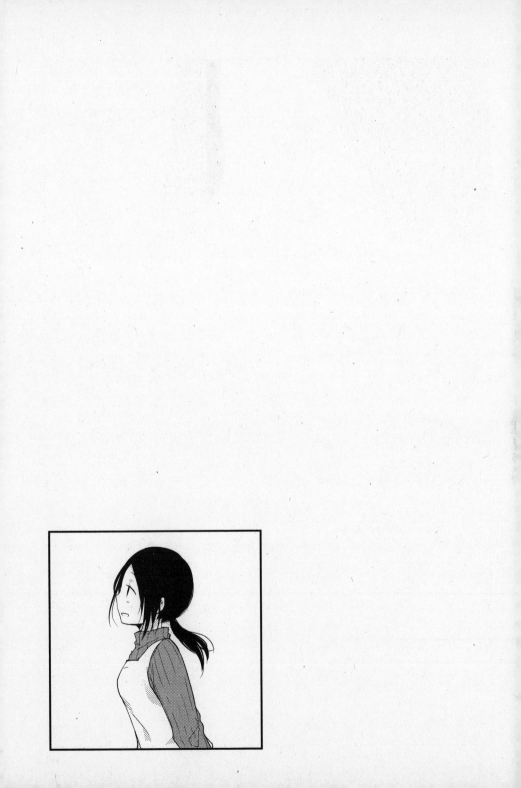

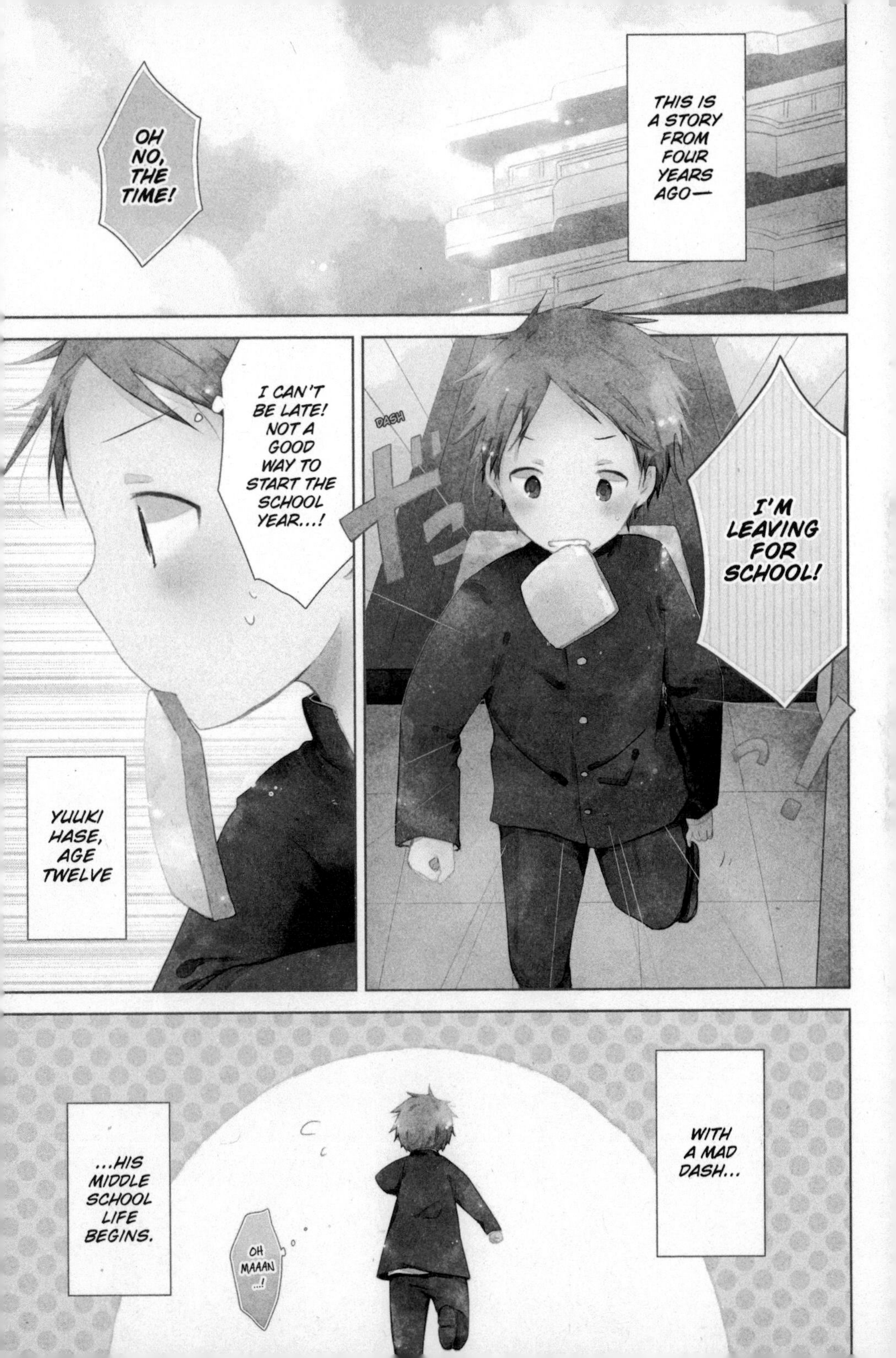
THIS IS A STORY FROM FOUR YEARS AGO—
OH NO, THE TIME!
I'M LEAVING FOR SCHOOL!
DASH
I CAN'T BE LATE! NOT A GOOD WAY TO START THE SCHOOL YEAR...!
YUUKI HASE, AGE TWELVE
WITH A MAD DASH...
...HIS MIDDLE SCHOOL LIFE BEGINS.
OH MAAAN ...!

CHAPTER 30 MAD-DASH CONTROLLER

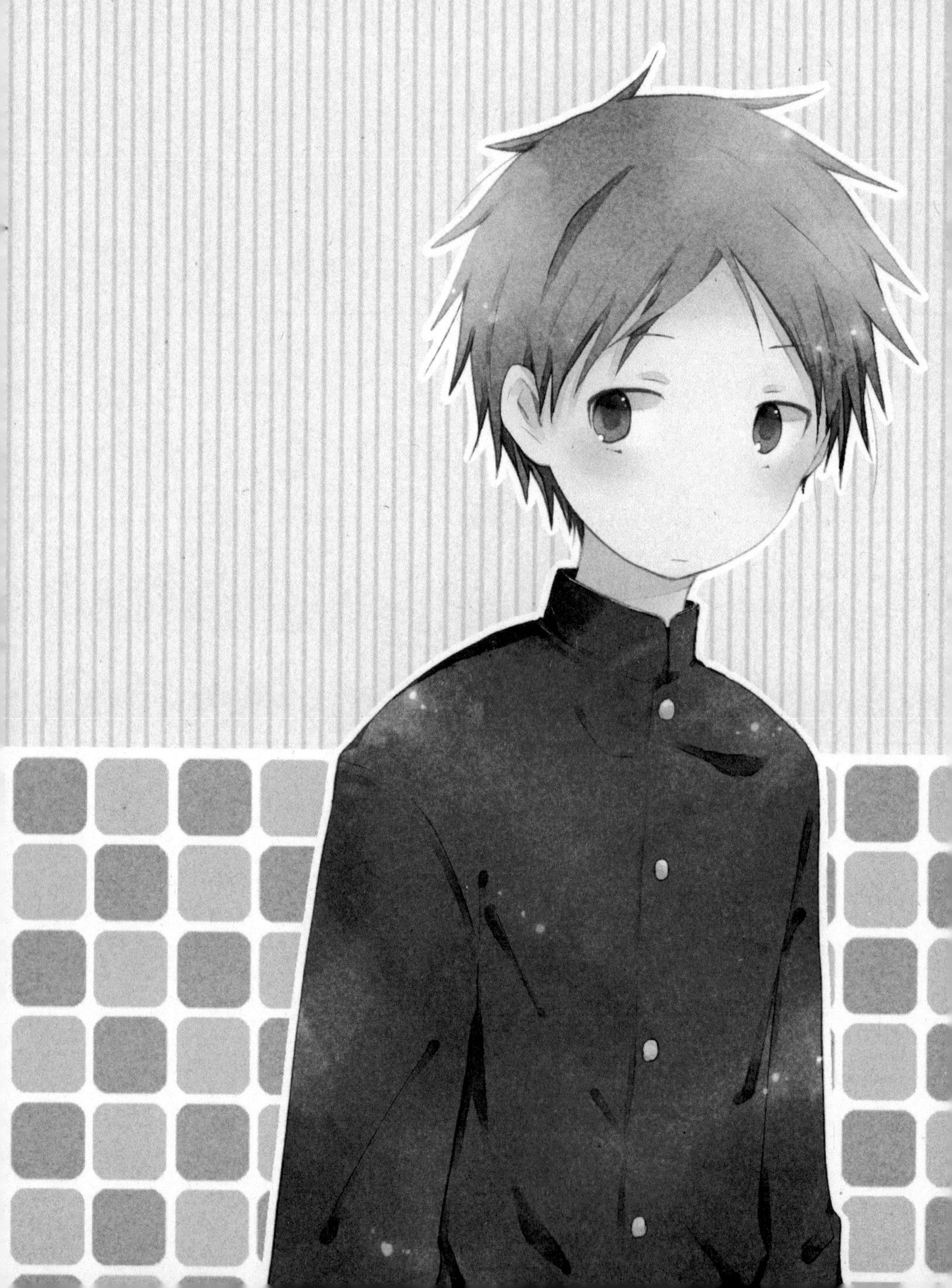

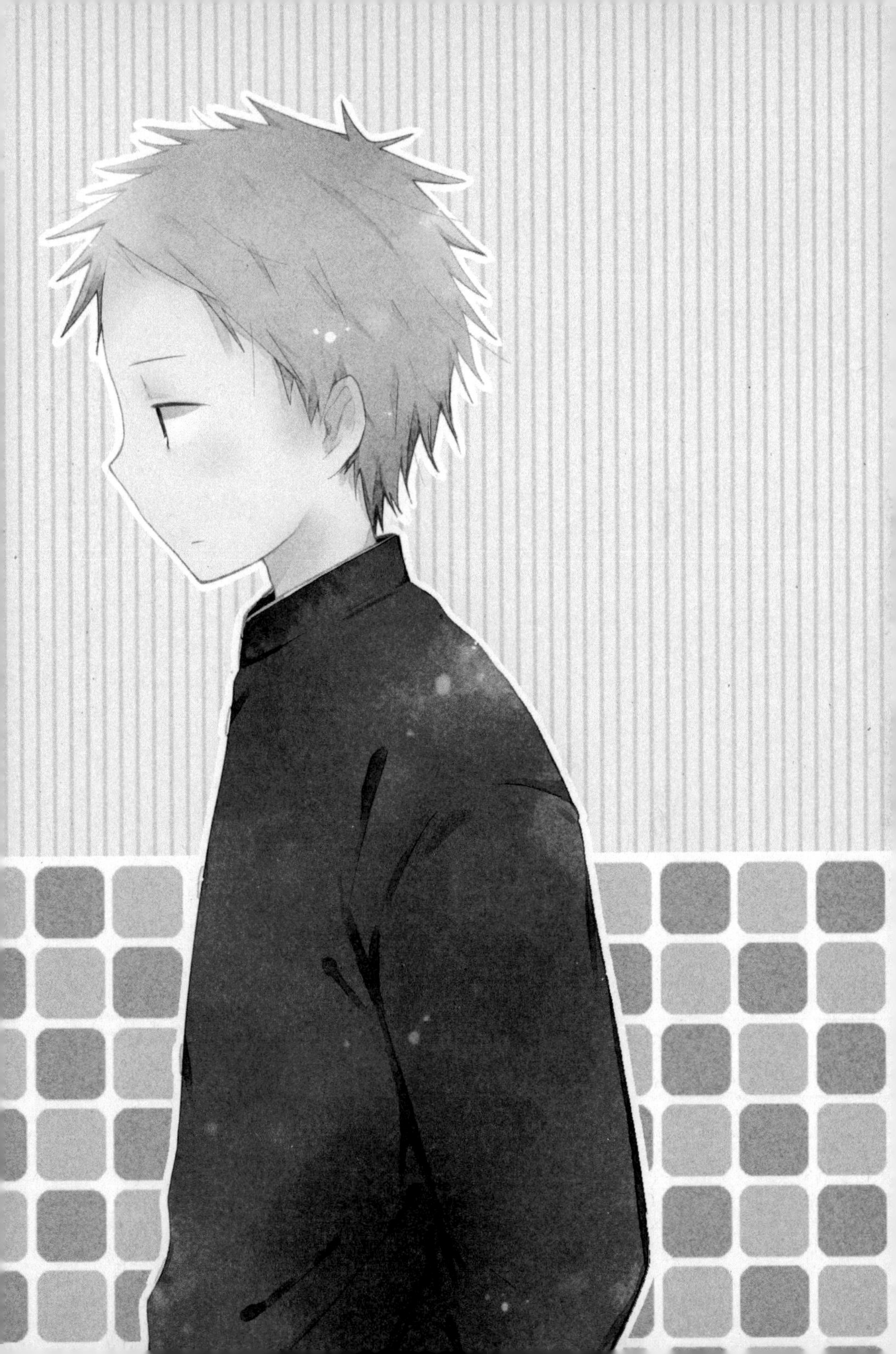

ONE WEEK FRIENDS

BRAND-NEW

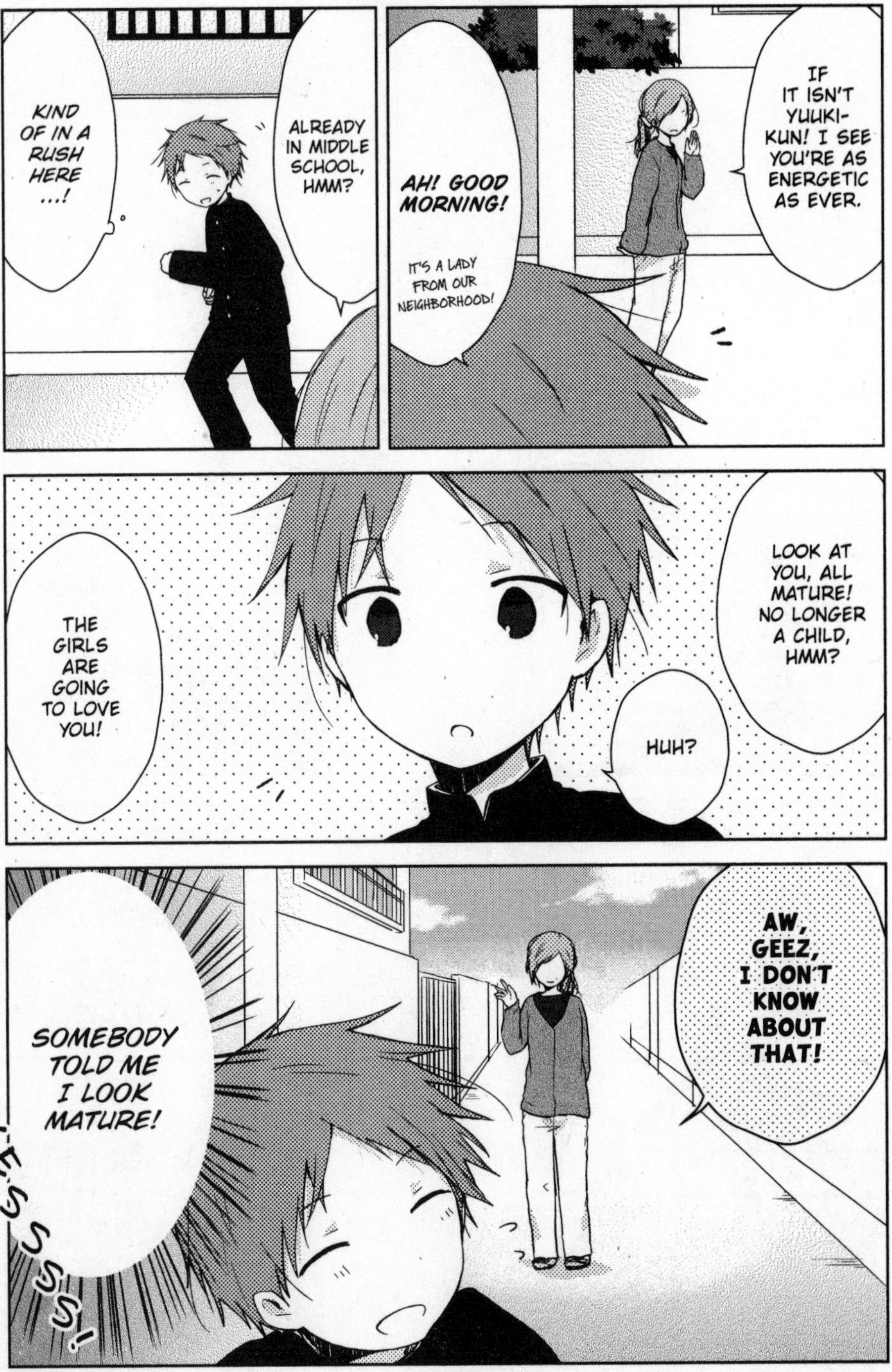
IF IT ISN'T YUUKI-KUN! I SEE YOU'RE AS ENERGETIC AS EVER.
AH! GOOD MORNING!
IT'S A LADY FROM OUR NEIGHBORHOOD!
ALREADY IN MIDDLE SCHOOL, HMM?
KIND OF IN A RUSH HERE ...!
LOOK AT YOU, ALL MATURE! NO LONGER A CHILD, HMM?
HUH?
THE GIRLS ARE GOING TO LOVE YOU!
AW, GEEZ, I DON'T KNOW ABOUT THAT!
SOMEBODY TOLD ME I LOOK MATURE!
YESSSS!

THIS GUY

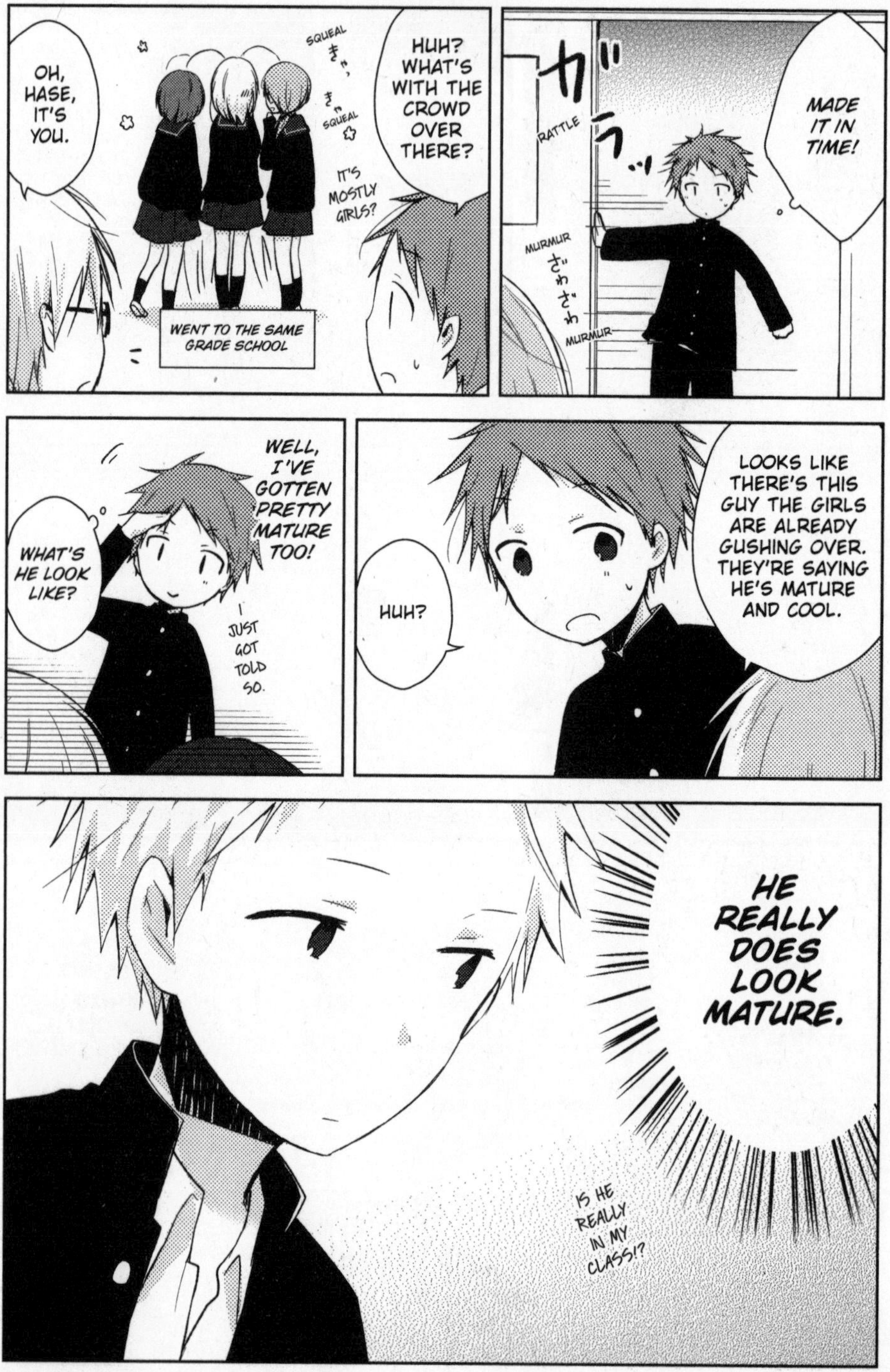

MADE IT IN TIME!
ガラッ
RATTLE
ざわざわ
MURMUR
MURMUR
HUH? WHAT'S WITH THE CROWD OVER THERE?
IT'S MOSTLY GIRLS?
きゃ
SQUEAL
きゃ
SQUEAL
OH, HASE, IT'S YOU.
WENT TO THE SAME GRADE SCHOOL
LOOKS LIKE THERE'S THIS GUY THE GIRLS ARE ALREADY GUSHING OVER. THEY'RE SAYING HE'S MATURE AND COOL.
HUH?
WELL, I'VE GOTTEN PRETTY MATURE TOO!
I JUST GOT TOLD SO.
WHAT'S HE LOOK LIKE?
HE REALLY DOES LOOK MATURE.
IS HE REALLY IN MY CLASS!?

EVEN BACK THEN

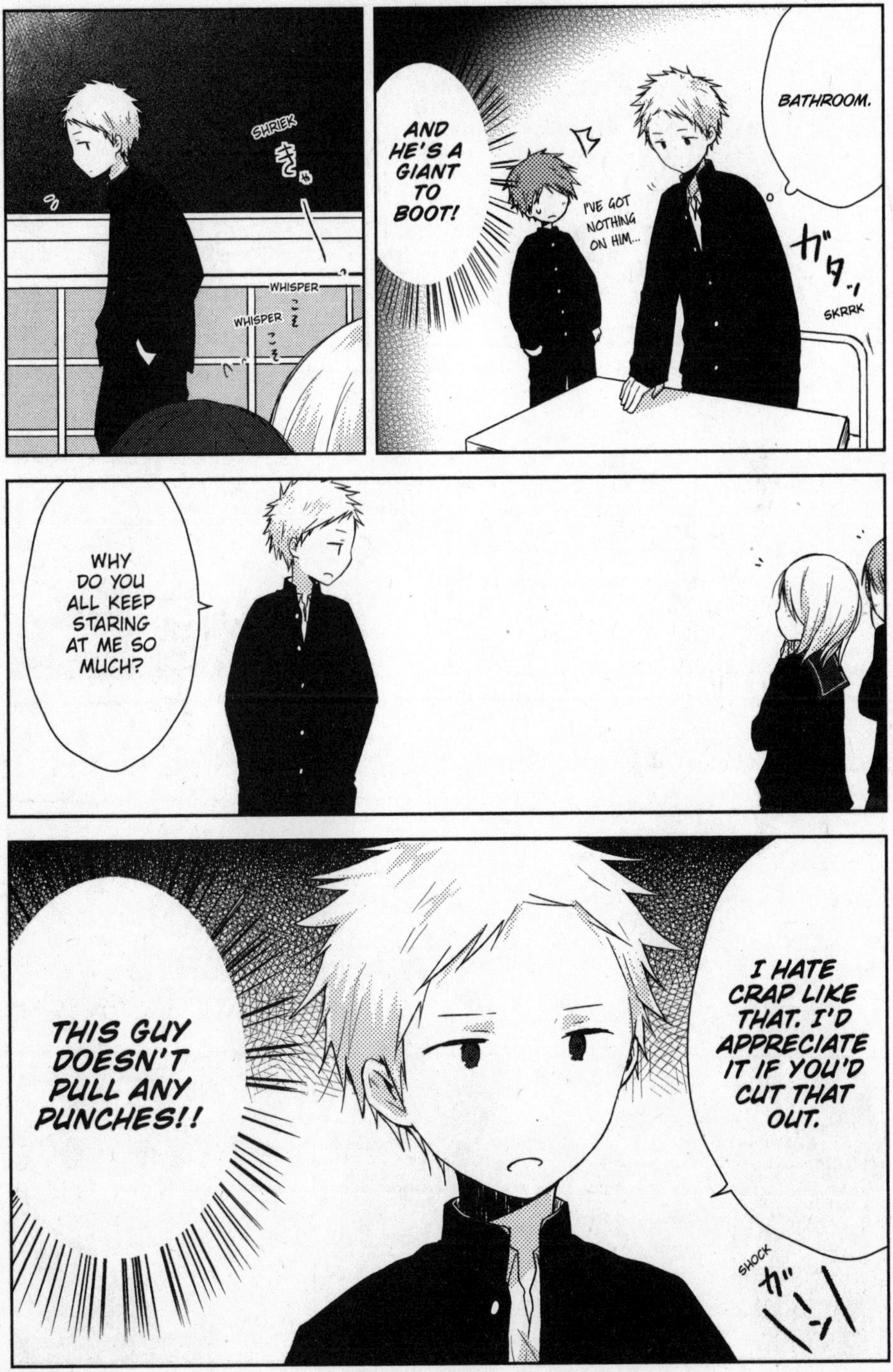
BATHROOM.
ガタッ
SKRRK
I'VE GOT NOTHING ON HIM...
AND HE'S A GIANT TO BOOT!
SHRIEK
きゃー
WHISPER
こそ
WHISPER
こそ
WHY DO YOU ALL KEEP STARING AT ME SO MUCH?
I HATE CRAP LIKE THAT. I'D APPRECIATE IT IF YOU'D CUT THAT OUT.
SHOCK
ガーン
THIS GUY DOESN'T PULL ANY PUNCHES!!

BLUNT

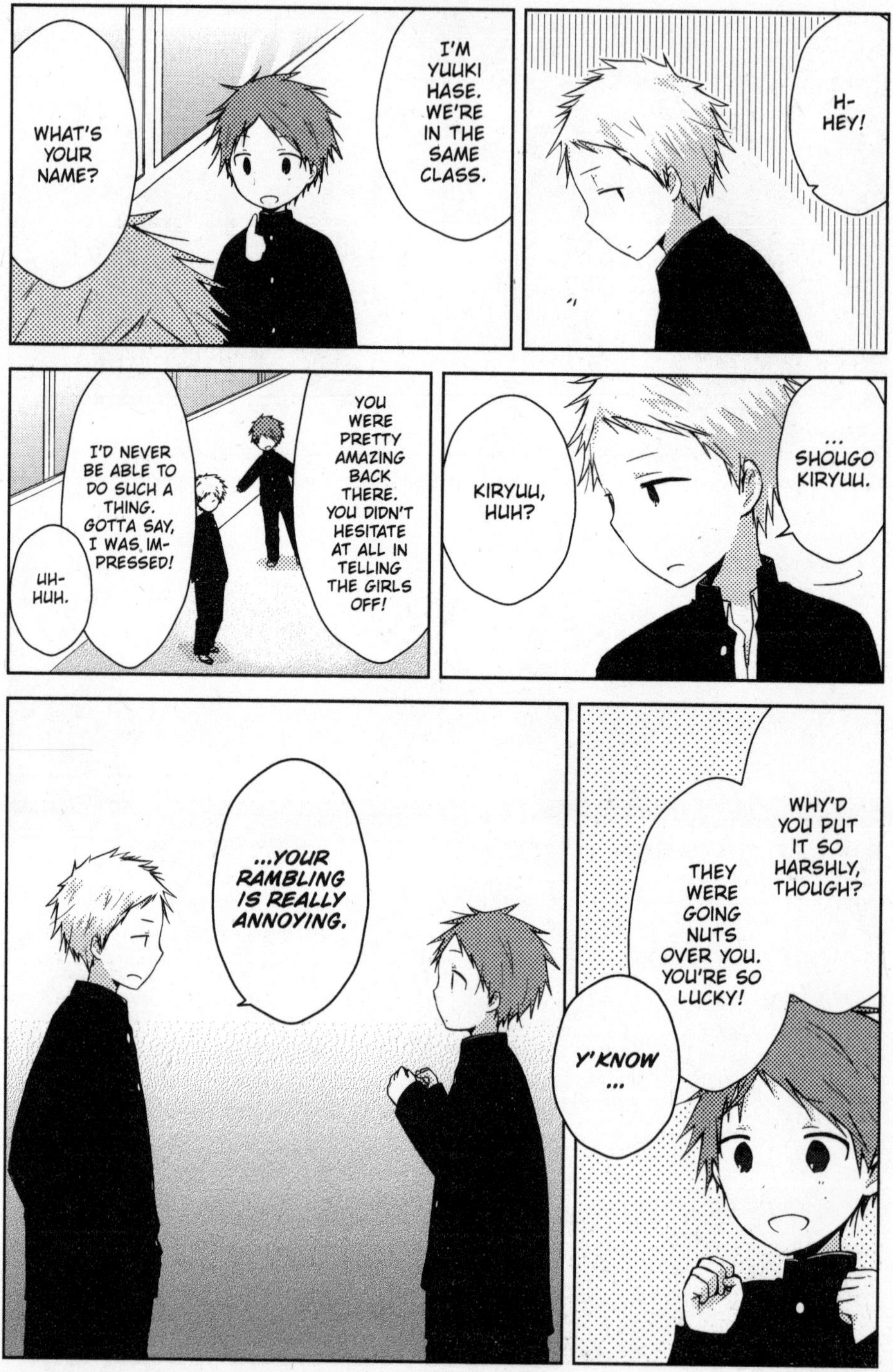
H- HEY!
I'M YUUKI HASE. WE'RE IN THE SAME CLASS.
WHAT'S YOUR NAME?
...SHOUGO KIRYUU.
KIRYUU, HUH?
YOU WERE PRETTY AMAZING BACK THERE. YOU DIDN'T HESITATE AT ALL IN TELLING THE GIRLS OFF!
I'D NEVER BE ABLE TO DO SUCH A THING. GOTTA SAY, I WAS IMPRESSED!
UH-HUH.
WHY'D YOU PUT IT SO HARSHLY, THOUGH?
THEY WERE GOING NUTS OVER YOU. YOU'RE SO LUCKY!
Y'KNOW...
...YOUR RAMBLING IS REALLY ANNOYING.

WORST POSSIBLE FIRST IMPRESSION

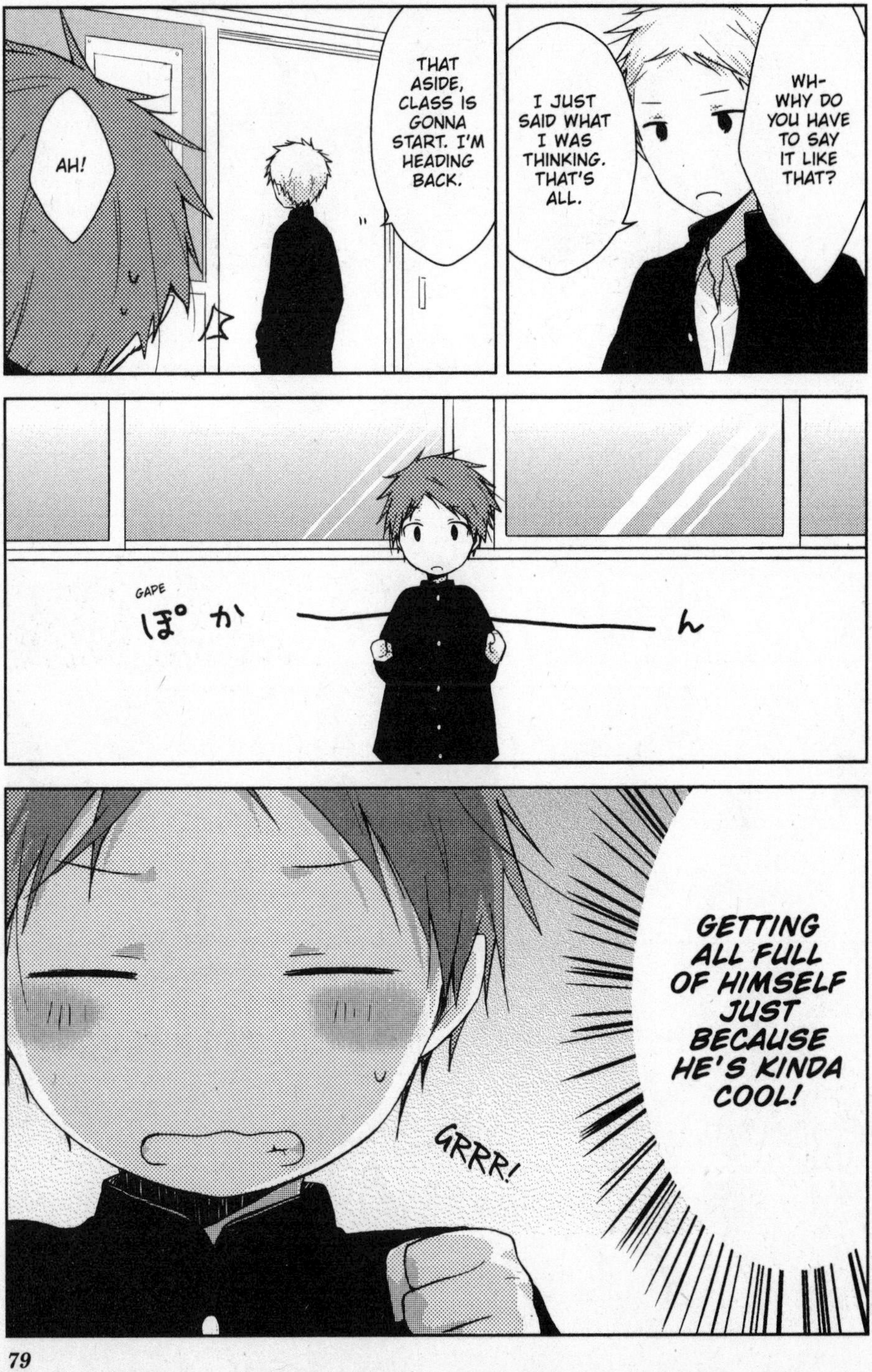
WH-WHY DO YOU HAVE TO SAY IT LIKE THAT?
I JUST SAID WHAT I WAS THINKING. THAT'S ALL.
THAT ASIDE, CLASS IS GONNA START. I'M HEADING BACK.
AH!
GAPE
ぽか――ん
GETTING ALL FULL OF HIMSELF JUST BECAUSE HE'S KINDA COOL!
GRRR!

LATE REALIZATION

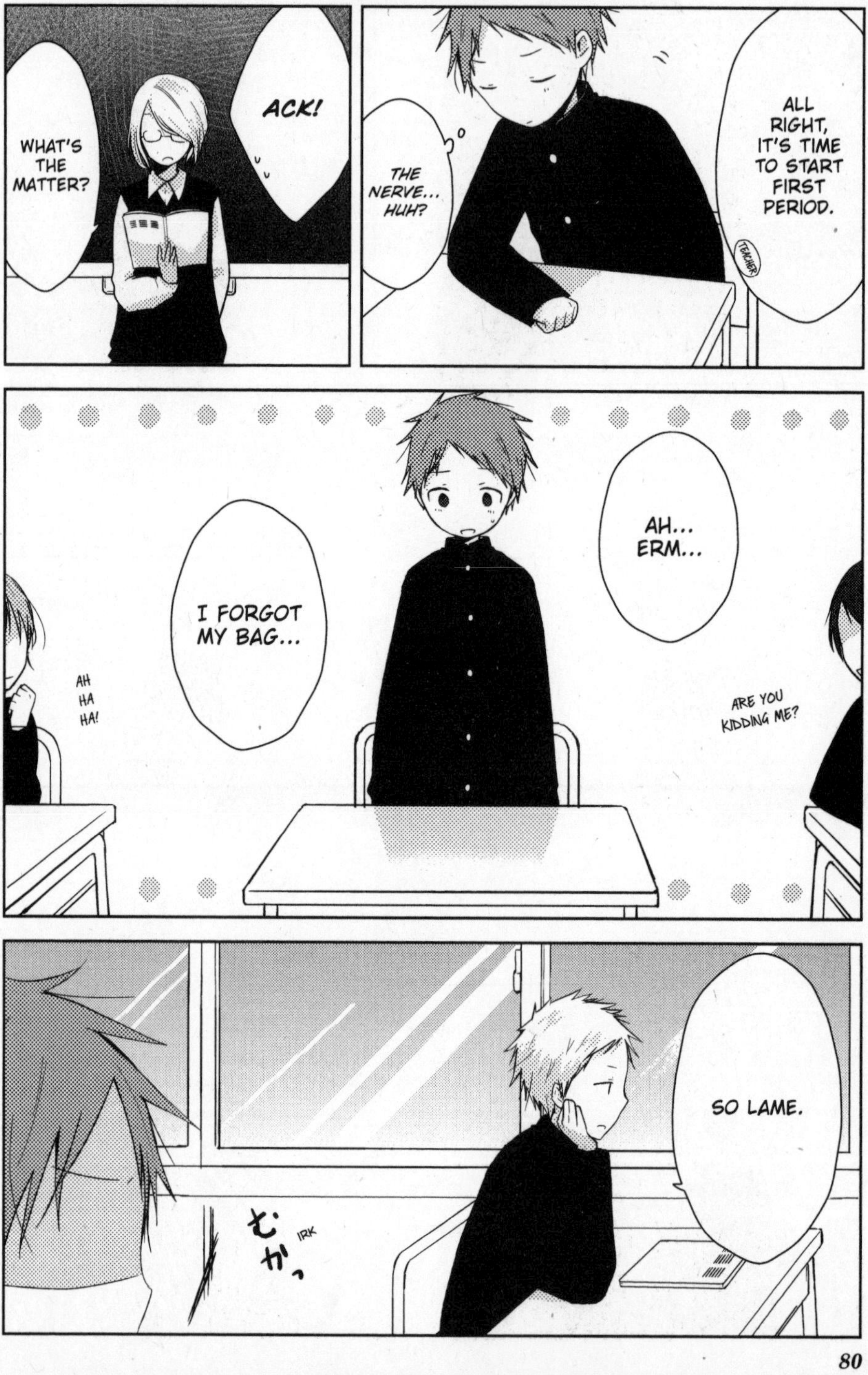

TEACHER
ALL RIGHT, IT'S TIME TO START FIRST PERIOD.
THE NERVE... HUH?
ACK!
WHAT'S THE MATTER?
AH... ERM...
ARE YOU KIDDING ME?
I FORGOT MY BAG...
AH HA HA!
SO LAME.
むかっ
IRK

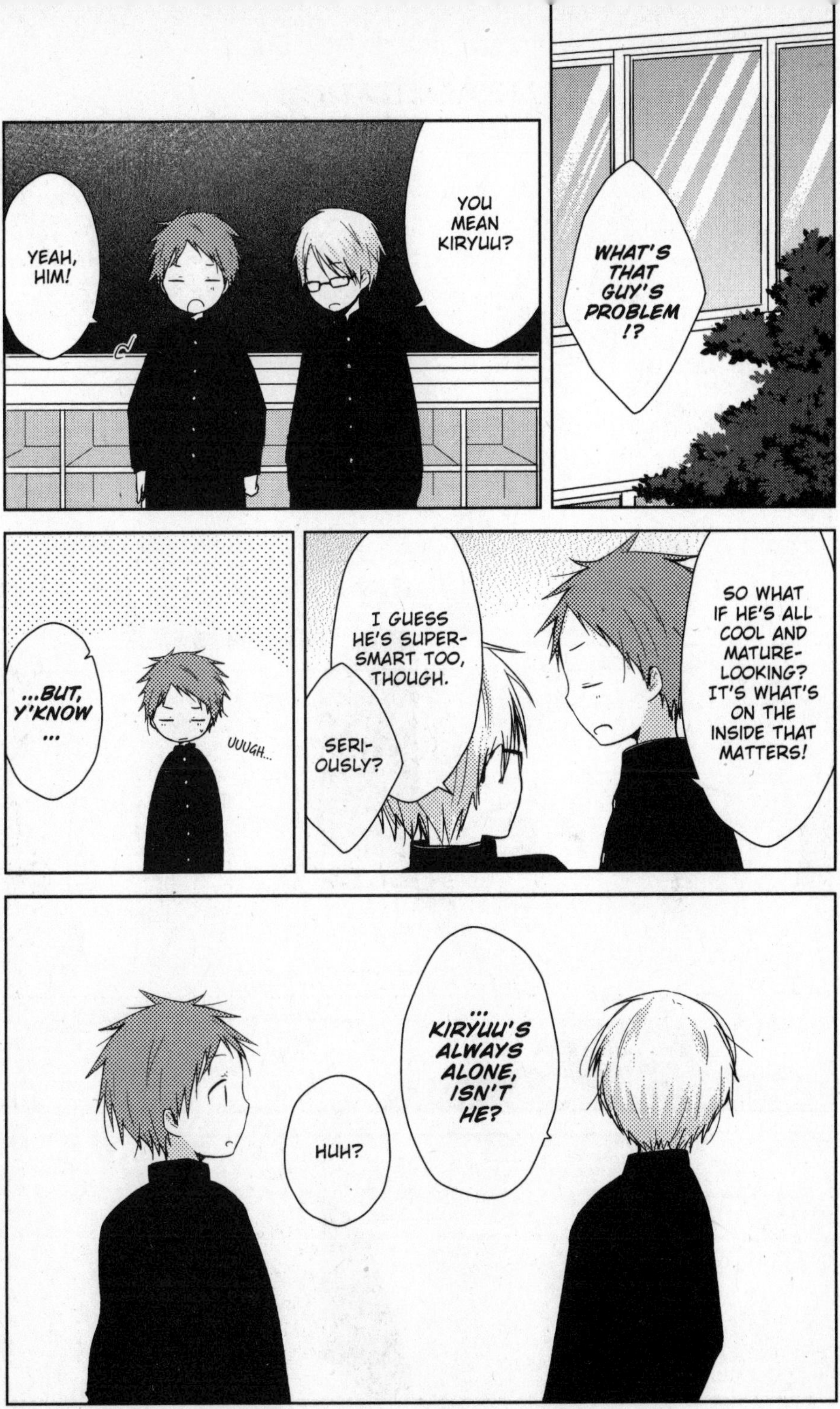
WHAT'S THAT GUY'S PROBLEM!?
YOU MEAN KIRYUU?
YEAH, HIM!
SO WHAT IF HE'S ALL COOL AND MATURE-LOOKING? IT'S WHAT'S ON THE INSIDE THAT MATTERS!
I GUESS HE'S SUPER-SMART TOO, THOUGH.
SERI-OUSLY?
...BUT, Y'KNOW...
UUUGH...
...KIRYUU'S ALWAYS ALONE, ISN'T HE?
HUH?

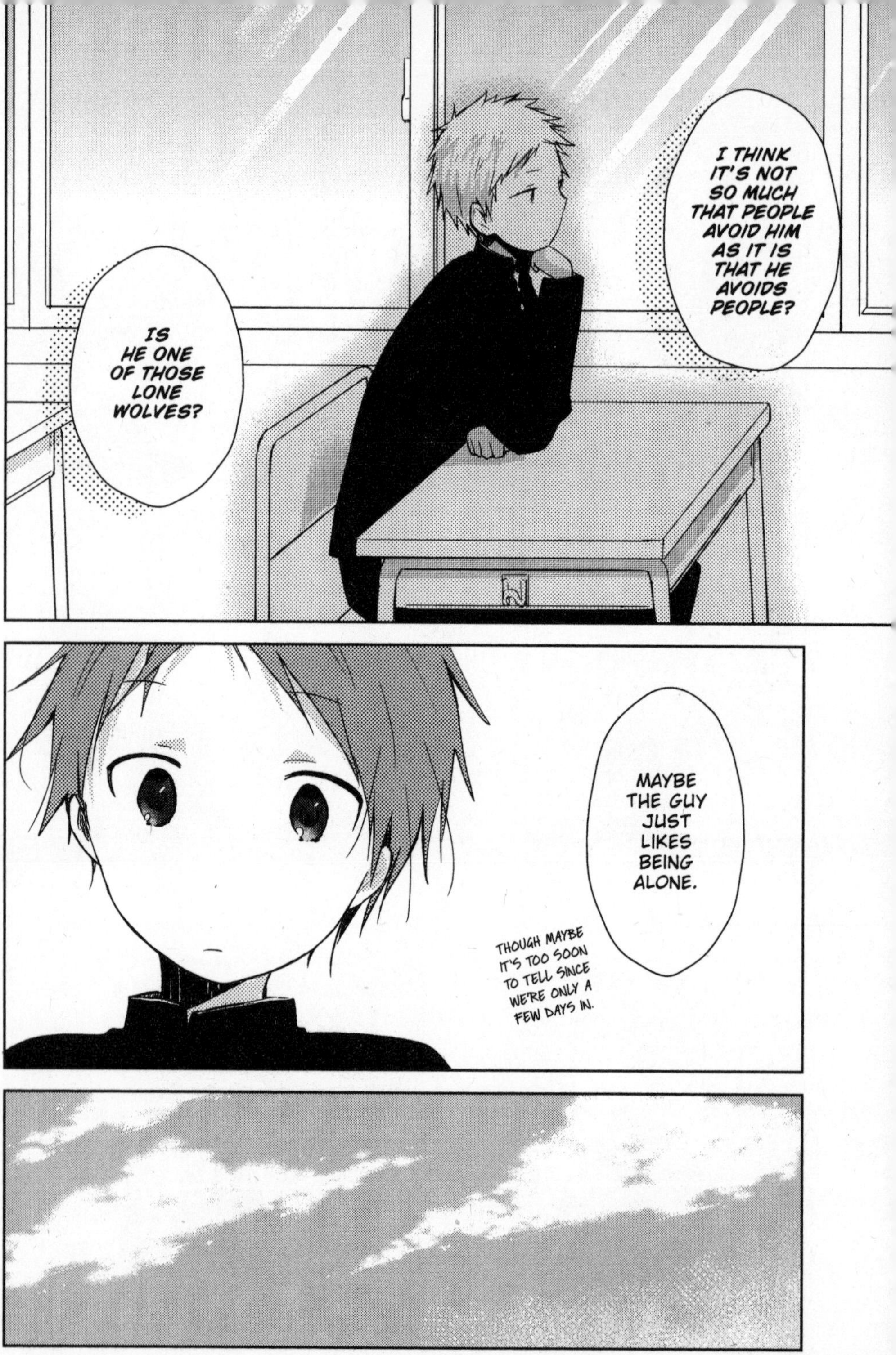
I THINK IT'S NOT SO MUCH THAT PEOPLE AVOID HIM AS IT IS THAT HE AVOIDS PEOPLE?
IS HE ONE OF THOSE LONE WOLVES?
MAYBE THE GUY JUST LIKES BEING ALONE.
THOUGH MAYBE IT'S TOO SOON TO TELL SINCE WE'RE ONLY A FEW DAYS IN.

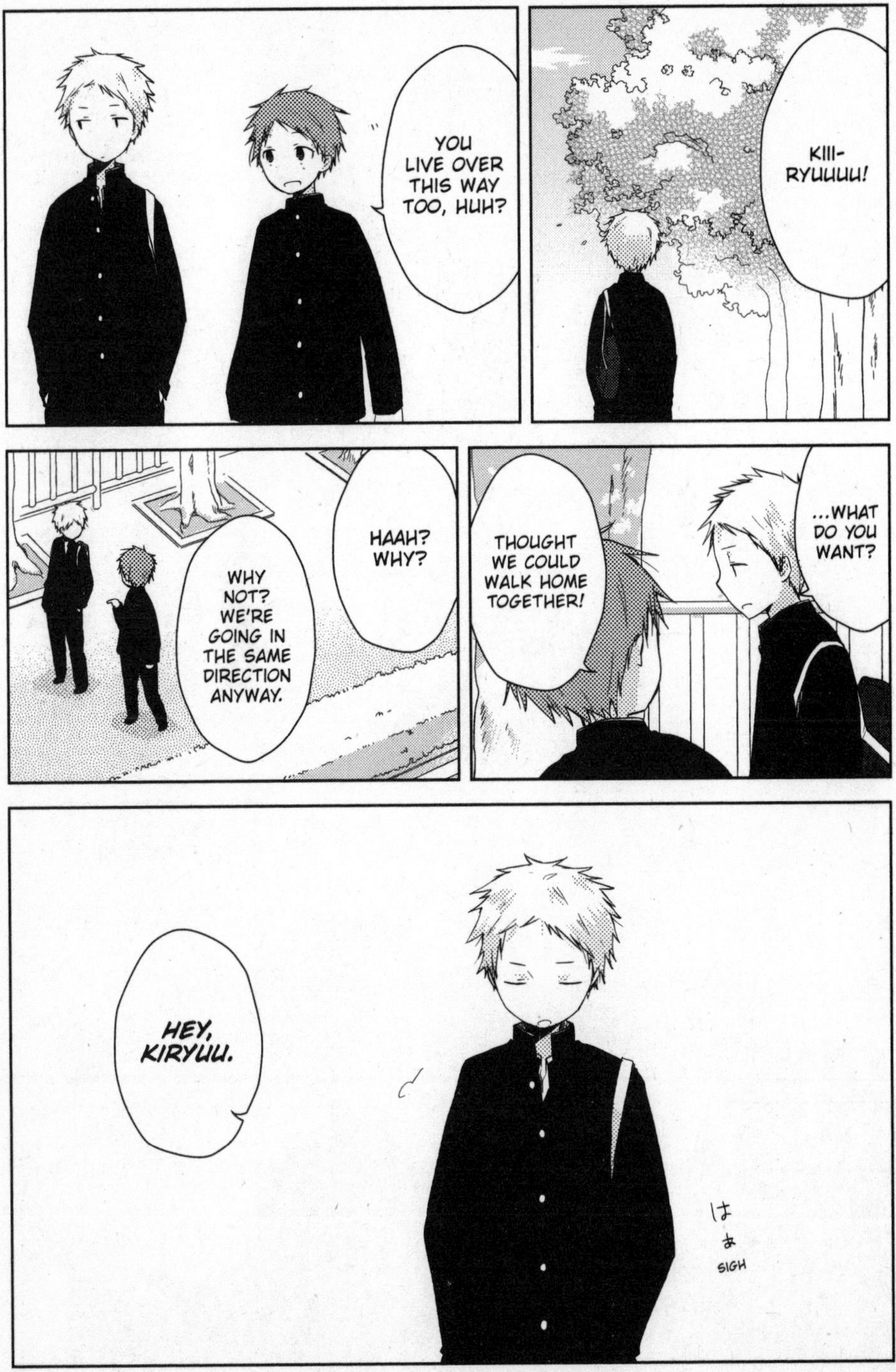
KIII-RYUUUU!
YOU LIVE OVER THIS WAY TOO, HUH?
...WHAT DO YOU WANT?
THOUGHT WE COULD WALK HOME TOGETHER!
HAAH? WHY?
WHY NOT? WE'RE GOING IN THE SAME DIRECTION ANYWAY.
HEY, KIRYUU.
はぁ
SIGH

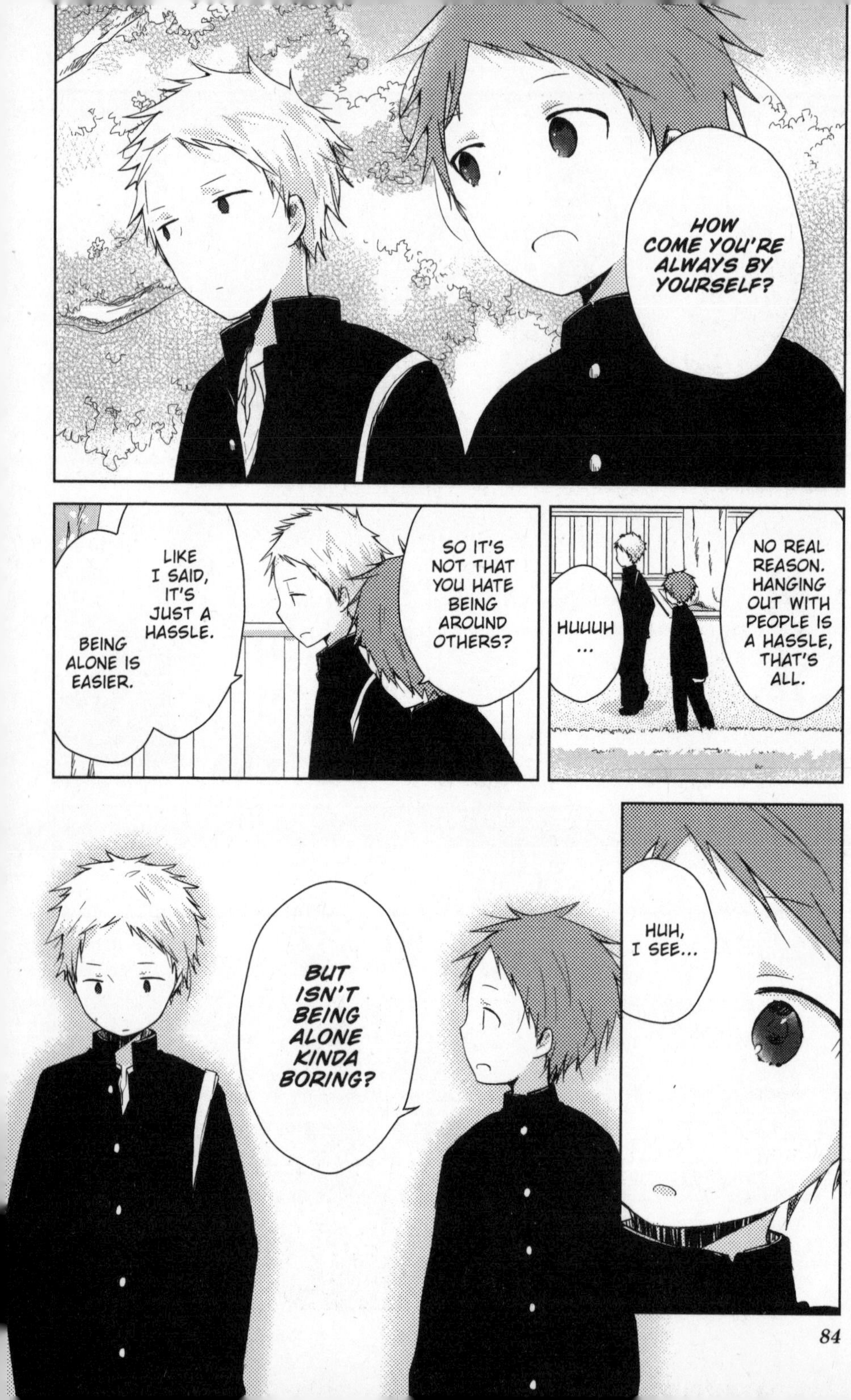
HOW COME YOU'RE ALWAYS BY YOURSELF?
NO REAL REASON. HANGING OUT WITH PEOPLE IS A HASSLE, THAT'S ALL.
HUUUH ...
SO IT'S NOT THAT YOU HATE BEING AROUND OTHERS?
LIKE I SAID, IT'S JUST A HASSLE.
BEING ALONE IS EASIER.
HUH, I SEE...
BUT ISN'T BEING ALONE KINDA BORING?

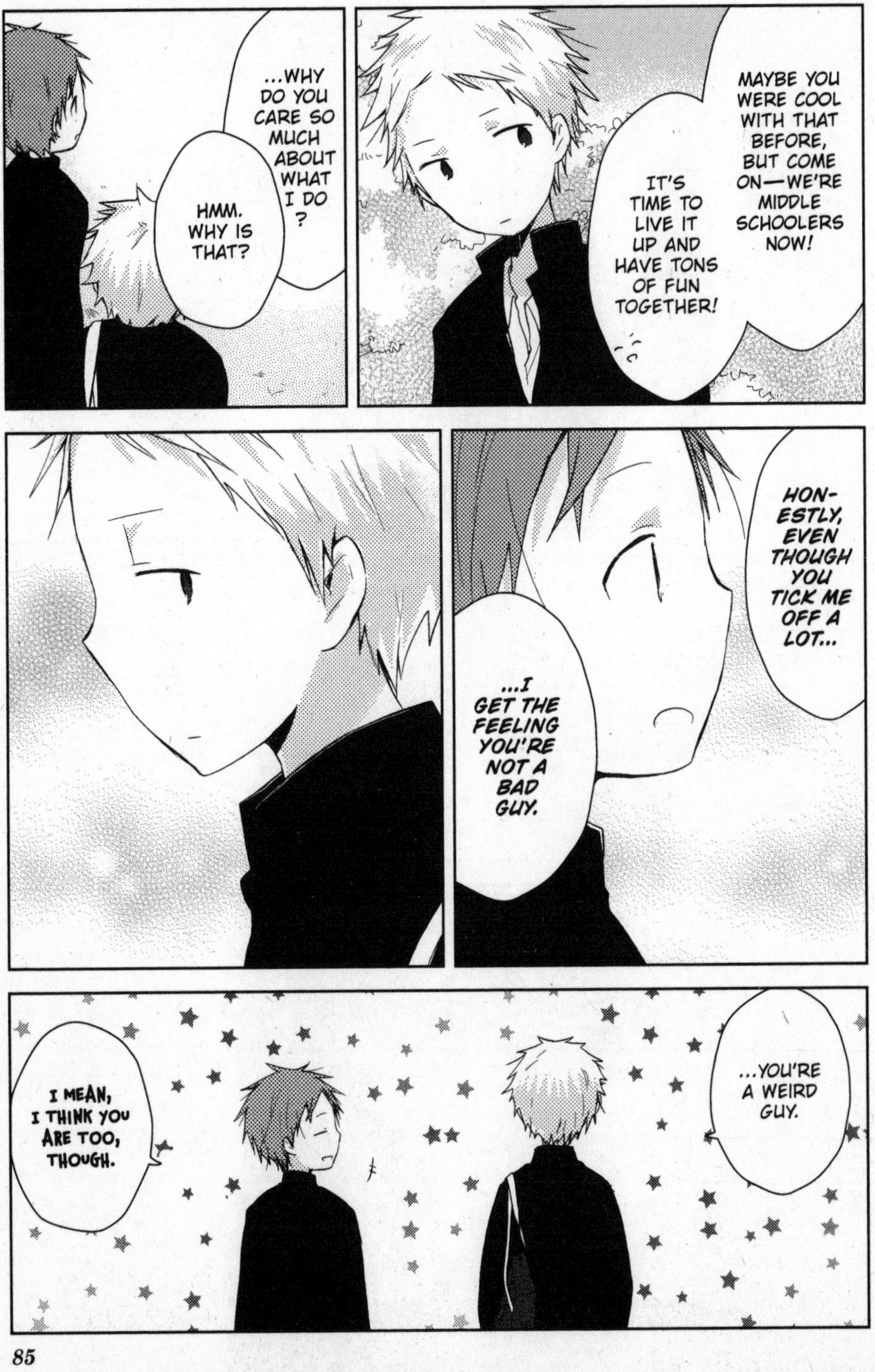
MAYBE YOU WERE COOL WITH THAT BEFORE, BUT COME ON—WE'RE MIDDLE SCHOOLERS NOW!
IT'S TIME TO LIVE IT UP AND HAVE TONS OF FUN TOGETHER!
...WHY DO YOU CARE SO MUCH ABOUT WHAT I DO?
HMM. WHY IS THAT?
HONESTLY, EVEN THOUGH YOU TICK ME OFF A LOT...
...I GET THE FEELING YOU'RE NOT A BAD GUY.
...YOU'RE A WEIRD GUY.
I MEAN, I THINK YOU ARE TOO, THOUGH.

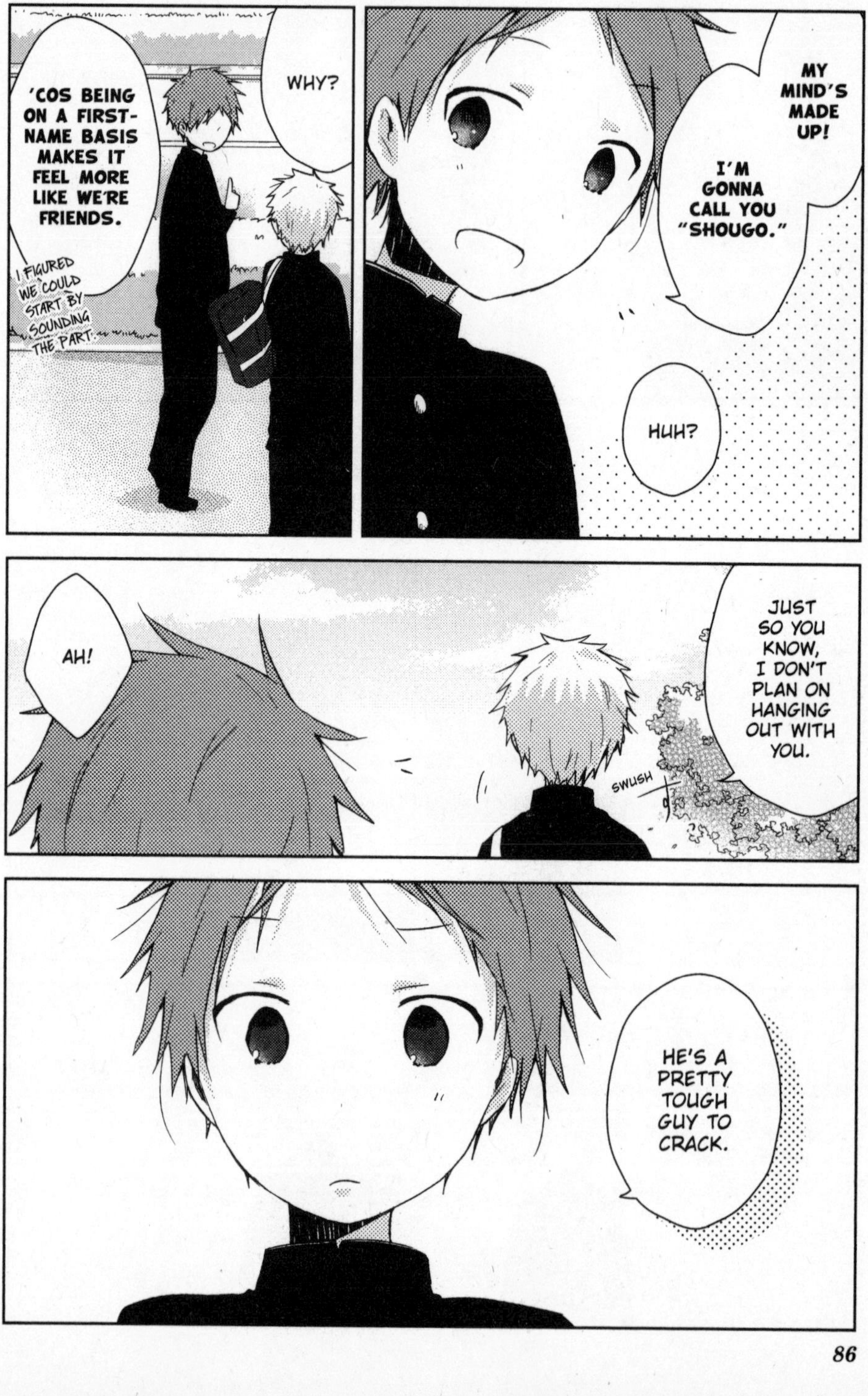
MY MIND'S MADE UP!
I'M GONNA CALL YOU "SHOUGO."
HUH?
WHY?
'COS BEING ON A FIRST-NAME BASIS MAKES IT FEEL MORE LIKE WE'RE FRIENDS.
I FIGURED WE COULD START BY SOUNDING THE PART.
JUST SO YOU KNOW, I DON'T PLAN ON HANGING OUT WITH YOU.
SWUSH
AH!
HE'S A PRETTY TOUGH GUY TO CRACK.

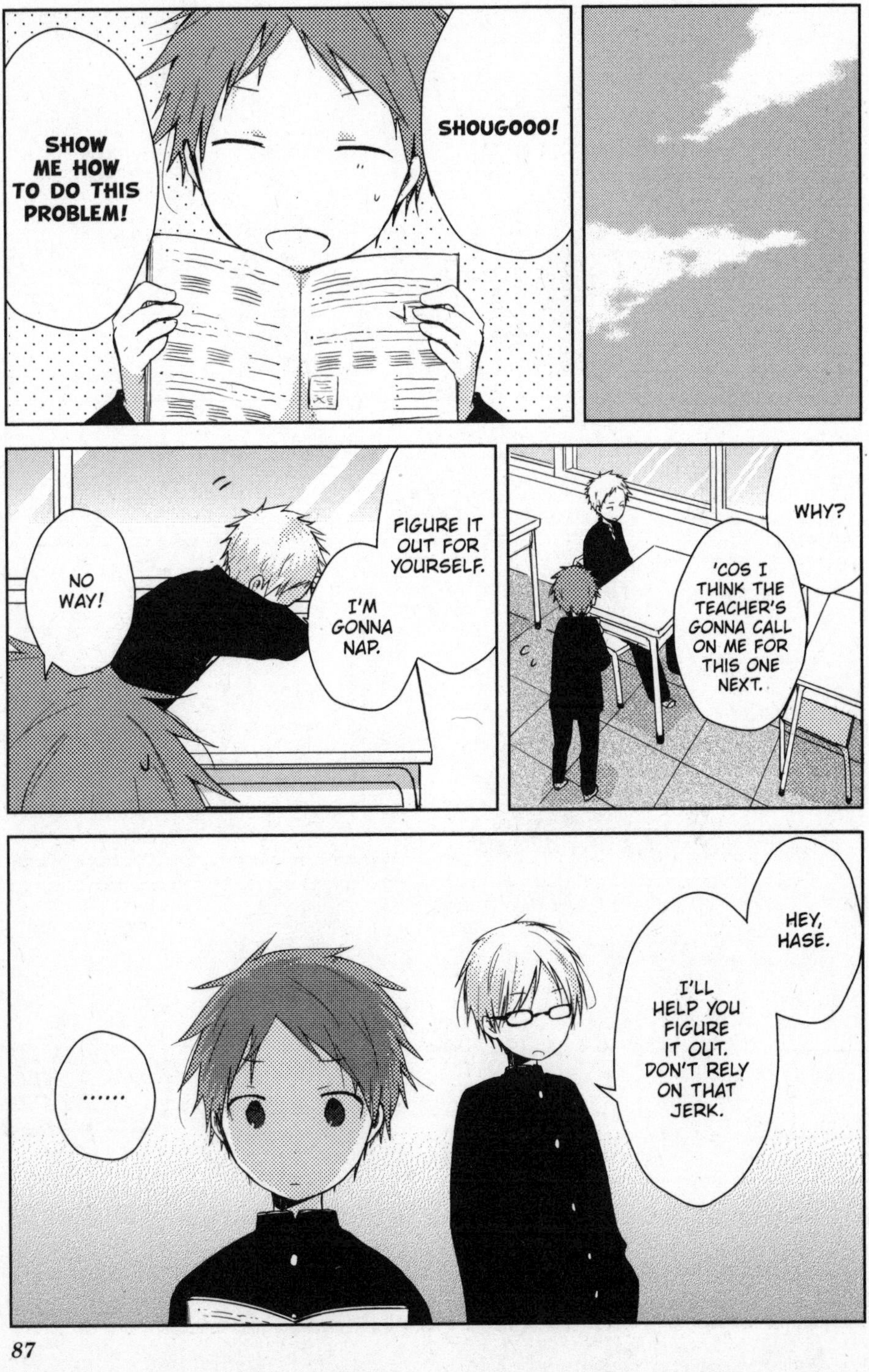
SHOUGOOO!
SHOW ME HOW TO DO THIS PROBLEM!
WHY?
'COS I THINK THE TEACHER'S GONNA CALL ON ME FOR THIS ONE NEXT.
FIGURE IT OUT FOR YOURSELF.
I'M GONNA NAP.
NO WAY!
HEY, HASE.
I'LL HELP YOU FIGURE IT OUT. DON'T RELY ON THAT JERK.
......

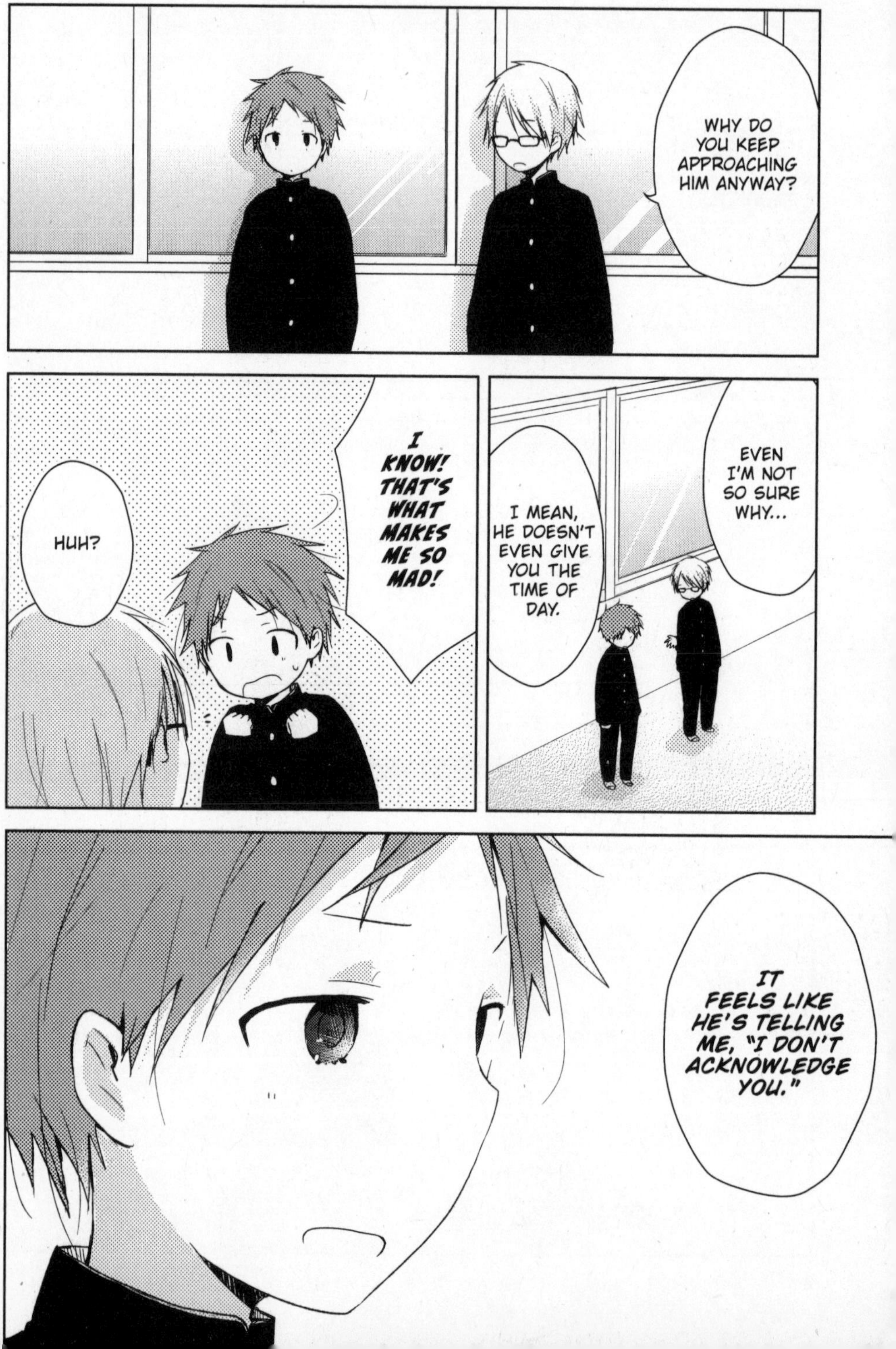
WHY DO YOU KEEP APPROACHING HIM ANYWAY?
EVEN I'M NOT SO SURE WHY...
I MEAN, HE DOESN'T EVEN GIVE YOU THE TIME OF DAY.
I KNOW! THAT'S WHAT MAKES ME SO MAD!
HUH?
IT FEELS LIKE HE'S TELLING ME, "I DON'T ACKNOWLEDGE YOU."

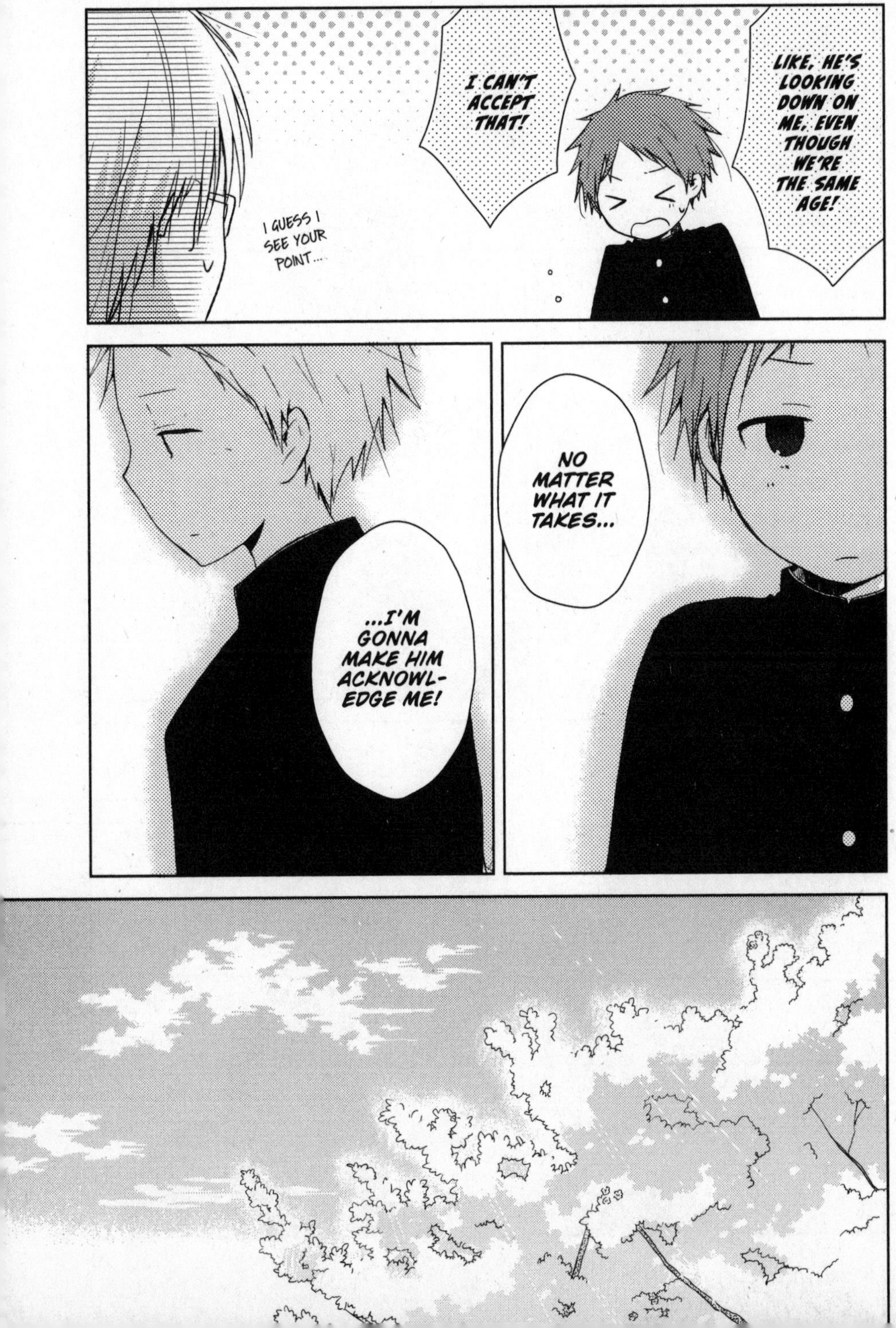
LIKE, HE'S LOOKING DOWN ON ME, EVEN THOUGH WE'RE THE SAME AGE!
I CAN'T ACCEPT THAT!
I GUESS I SEE YOUR POINT...
NO MATTER WHAT IT TAKES...
...I'M GONNA MAKE HIM ACKNOWLEDGE ME!

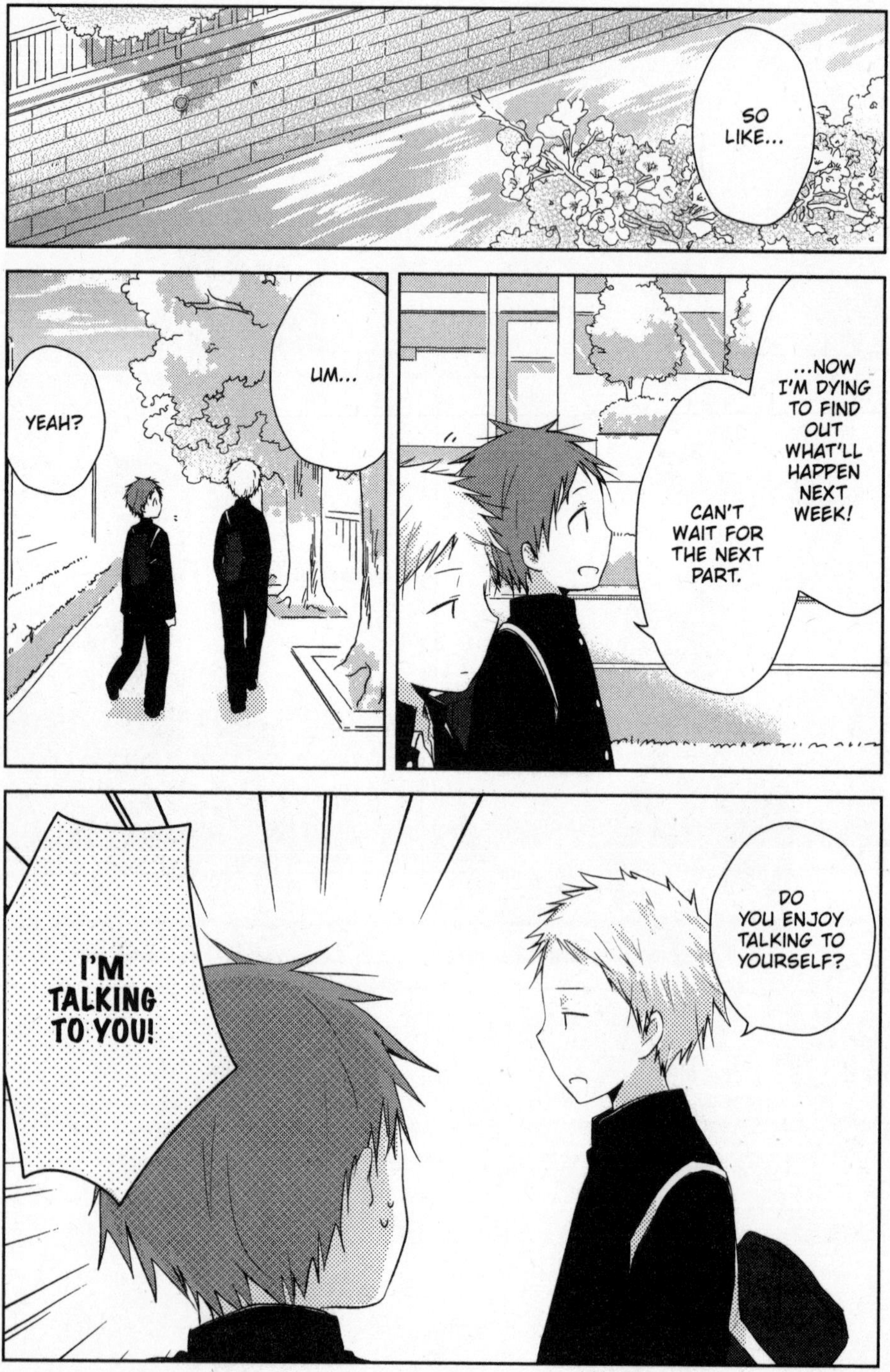
SO LIKE...
...NOW I'M DYING TO FIND OUT WHAT'LL HAPPEN NEXT WEEK!
CAN'T WAIT FOR THE NEXT PART.
UM...
YEAH?
DO YOU ENJOY TALKING TO YOURSELF?
I'M TALKING TO YOU!

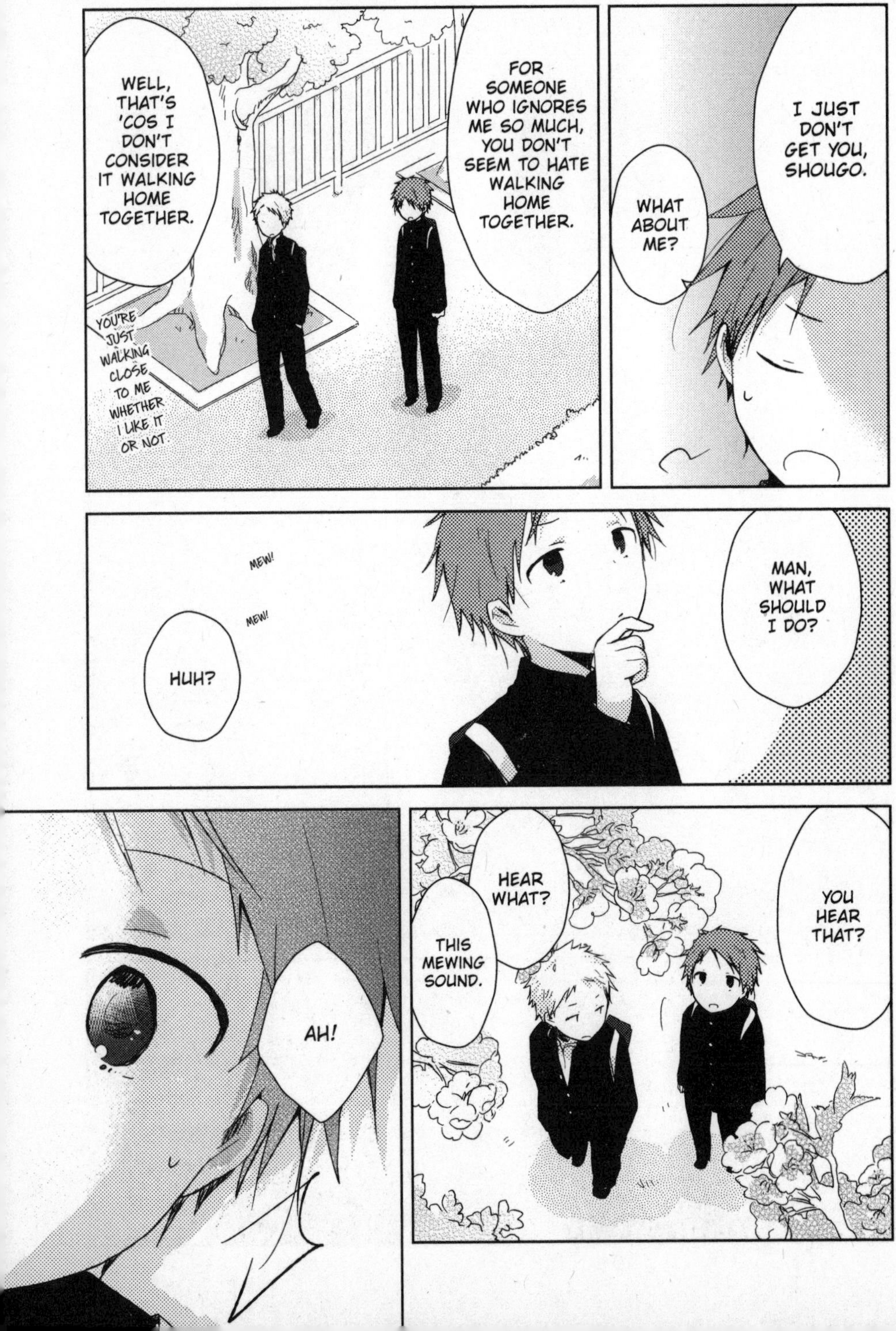
I JUST DON'T GET YOU, SHOUGO.
WHAT ABOUT ME?
FOR SOMEONE WHO IGNORES ME SO MUCH, YOU DON'T SEEM TO HATE WALKING HOME TOGETHER.
WELL, THAT'S 'COS I DON'T CONSIDER IT WALKING HOME TOGETHER.
YOU'RE JUST WALKING CLOSE TO ME WHETHER I LIKE IT OR NOT.
MAN, WHAT SHOULD I DO?
MEW!
MEW!
HUH?
YOU HEAR THAT?
HEAR WHAT?
THIS MEWING SOUND.
AH!

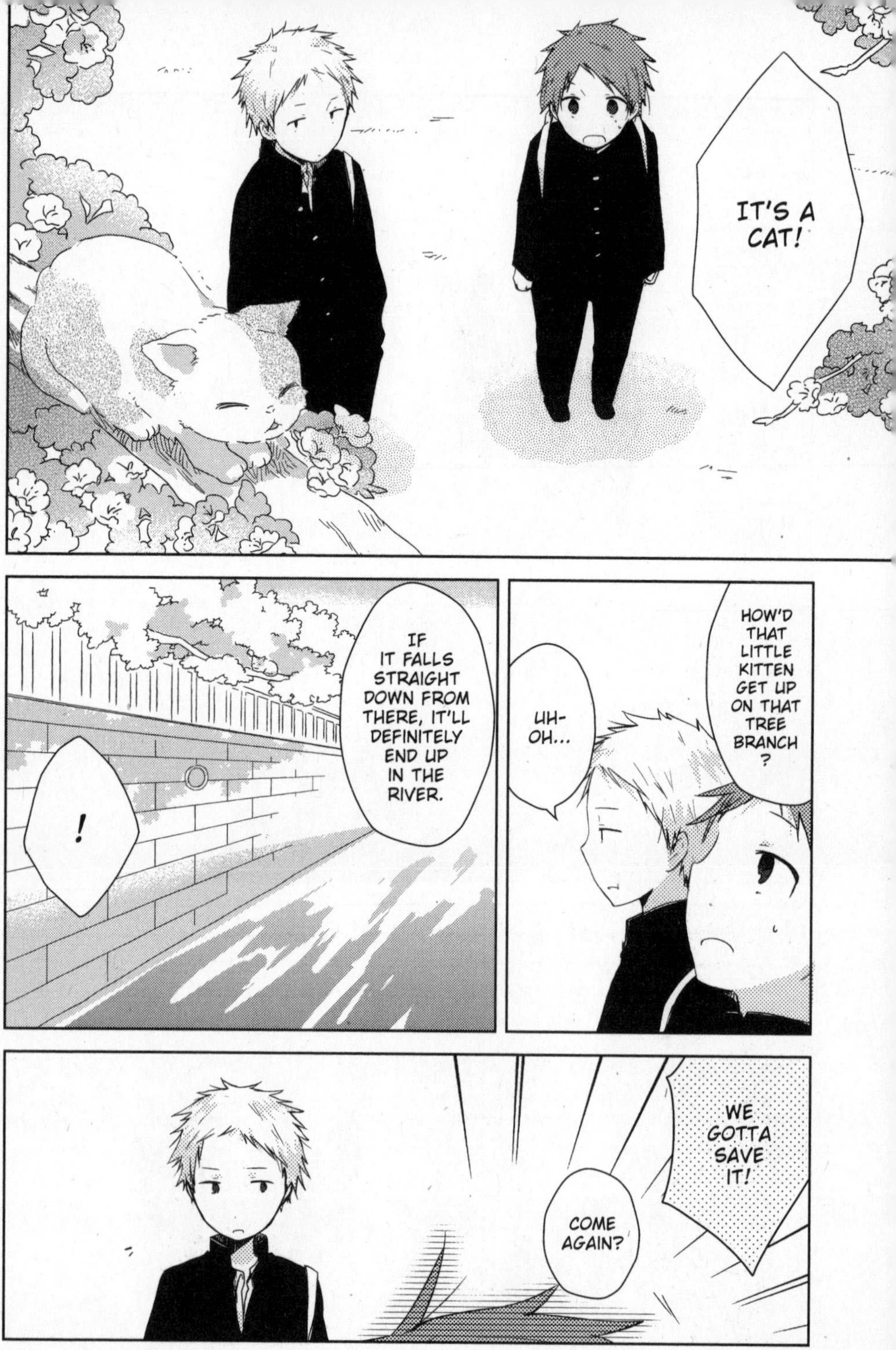
IT'S A CAT!
HOW'D THAT LITTLE KITTEN GET UP ON THAT TREE BRANCH?
UH-OH...
IF IT FALLS STRAIGHT DOWN FROM THERE, IT'LL DEFINITELY END UP IN THE RIVER.
!
WE GOTTA SAVE IT!
COME AGAIN?

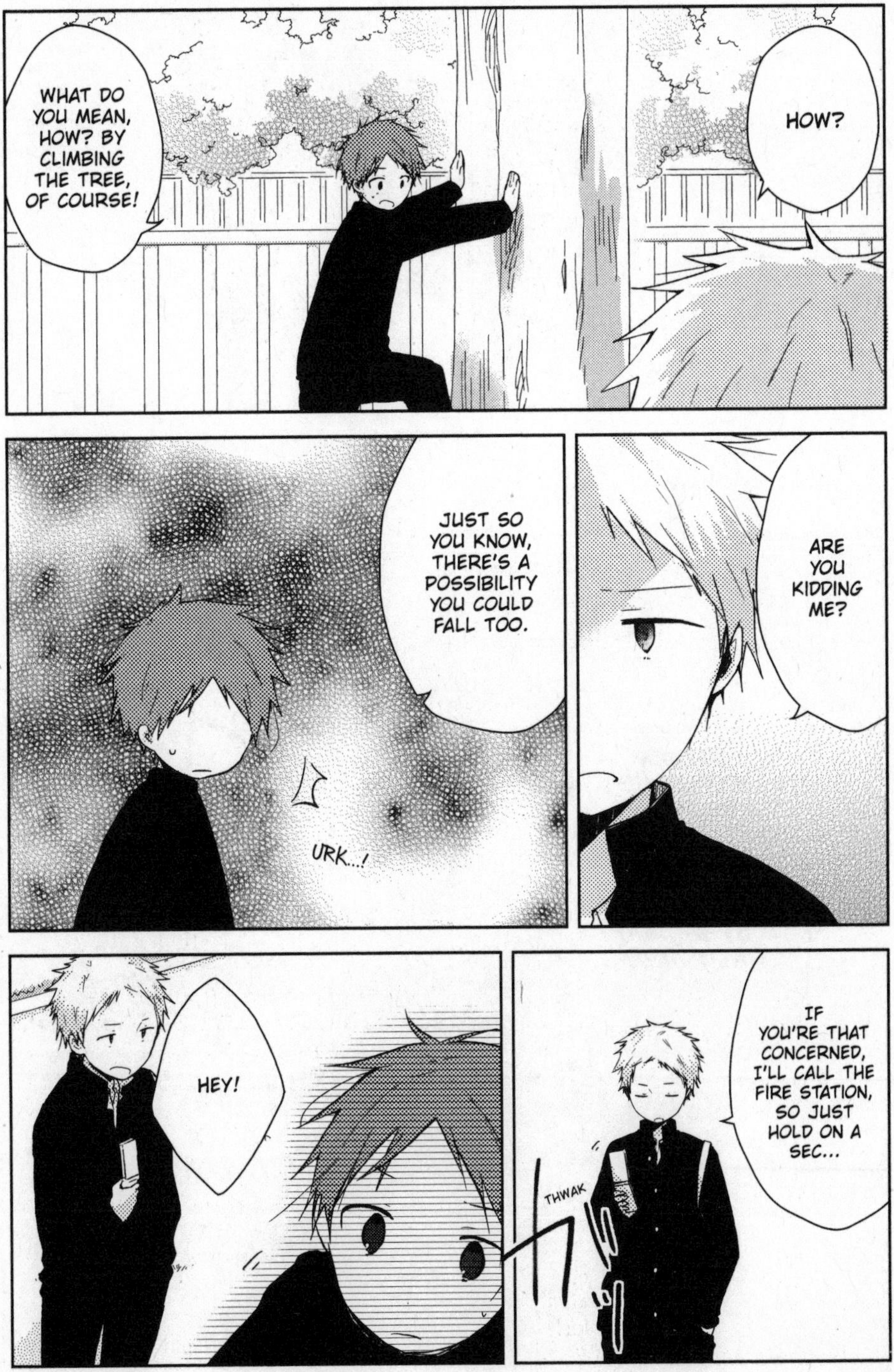
HOW?
WHAT DO YOU MEAN, HOW? BY CLIMBING THE TREE, OF COURSE!
ARE YOU KIDDING ME?
JUST SO YOU KNOW, THERE'S A POSSIBILITY YOU COULD FALL TOO.
URK...!
IF YOU'RE THAT CONCERNED, I'LL CALL THE FIRE STATION, SO JUST HOLD ON A SEC...
THWAK
HEY!

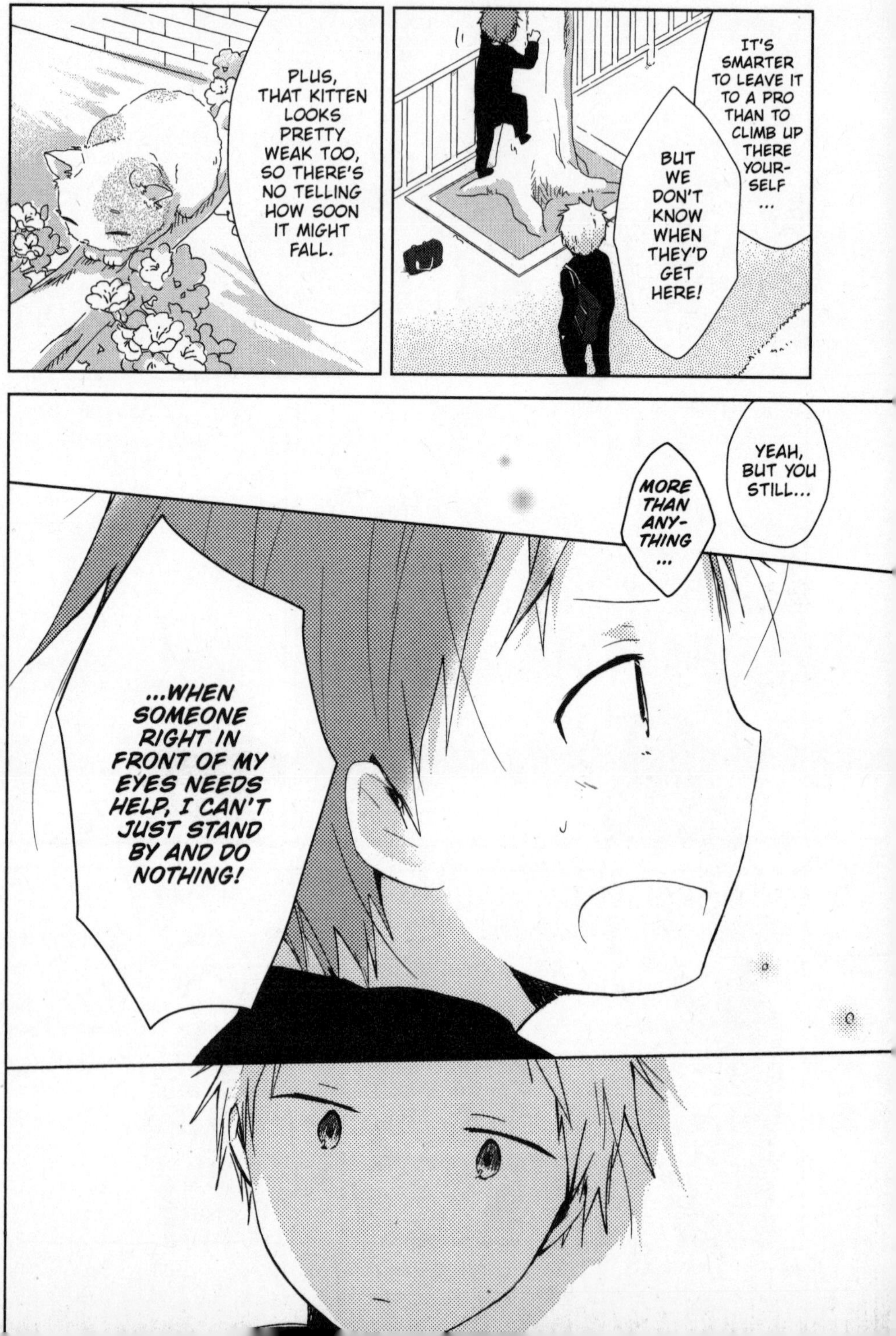
IT'S SMARTER TO LEAVE IT TO A PRO THAN TO CLIMB UP THERE YOUR-SELF...
BUT WE DON'T KNOW WHEN THEY'D GET HERE!
PLUS, THAT KITTEN LOOKS PRETTY WEAK TOO, SO THERE'S NO TELLING HOW SOON IT MIGHT FALL.
YEAH, BUT YOU STILL...
MORE THAN ANY-THING...
...WHEN SOMEONE RIGHT IN FRONT OF MY EYES NEEDS HELP, I CAN'T JUST STAND BY AND DO NOTHING!

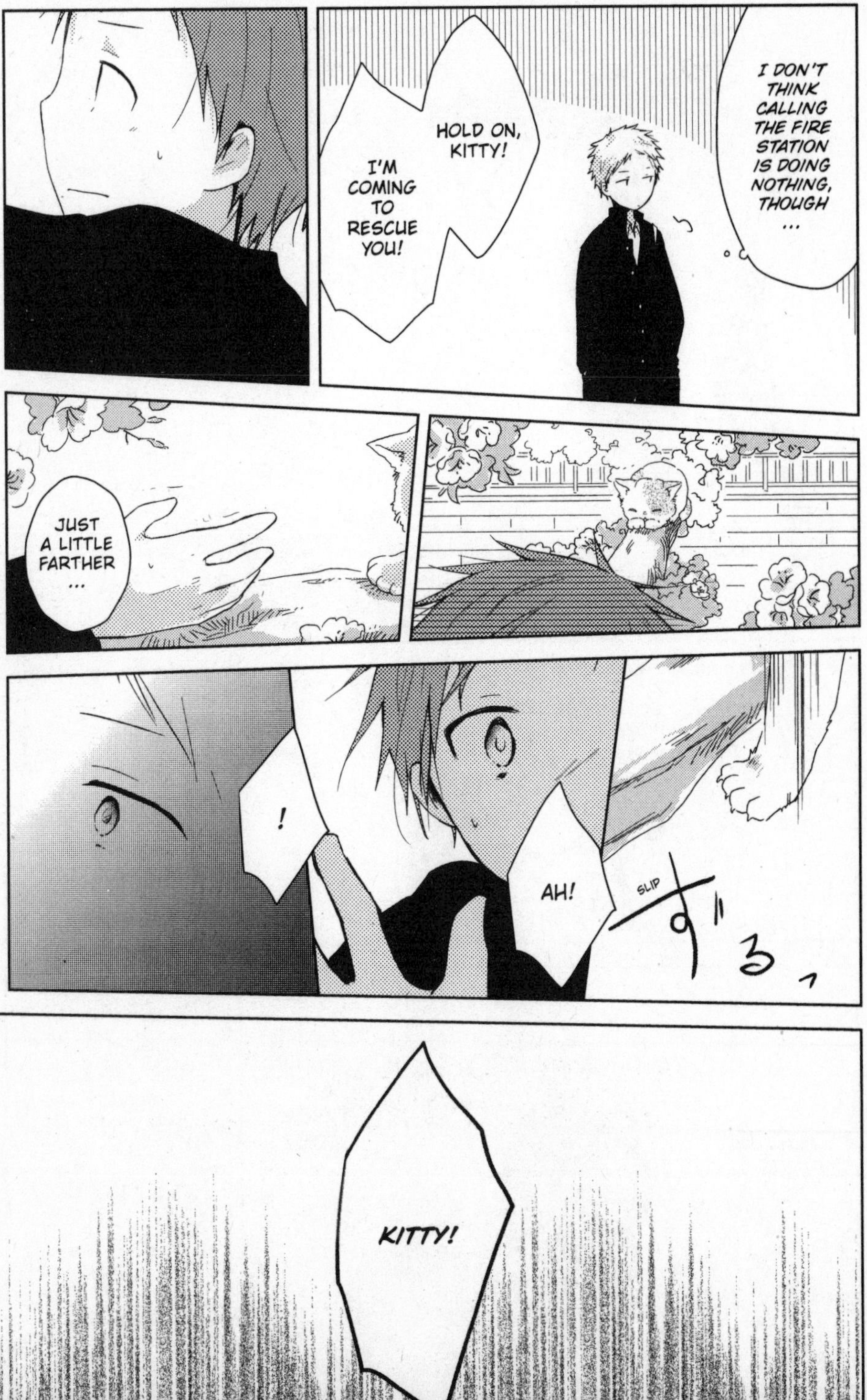
I DON'T THINK CALLING THE FIRE STATION IS DOING NOTHING, THOUGH ...
HOLD ON, KITTY!
I'M COMING TO RESCUE YOU!
JUST A LITTLE FARTHER ...
SLIP
AH!
!
KITTY!

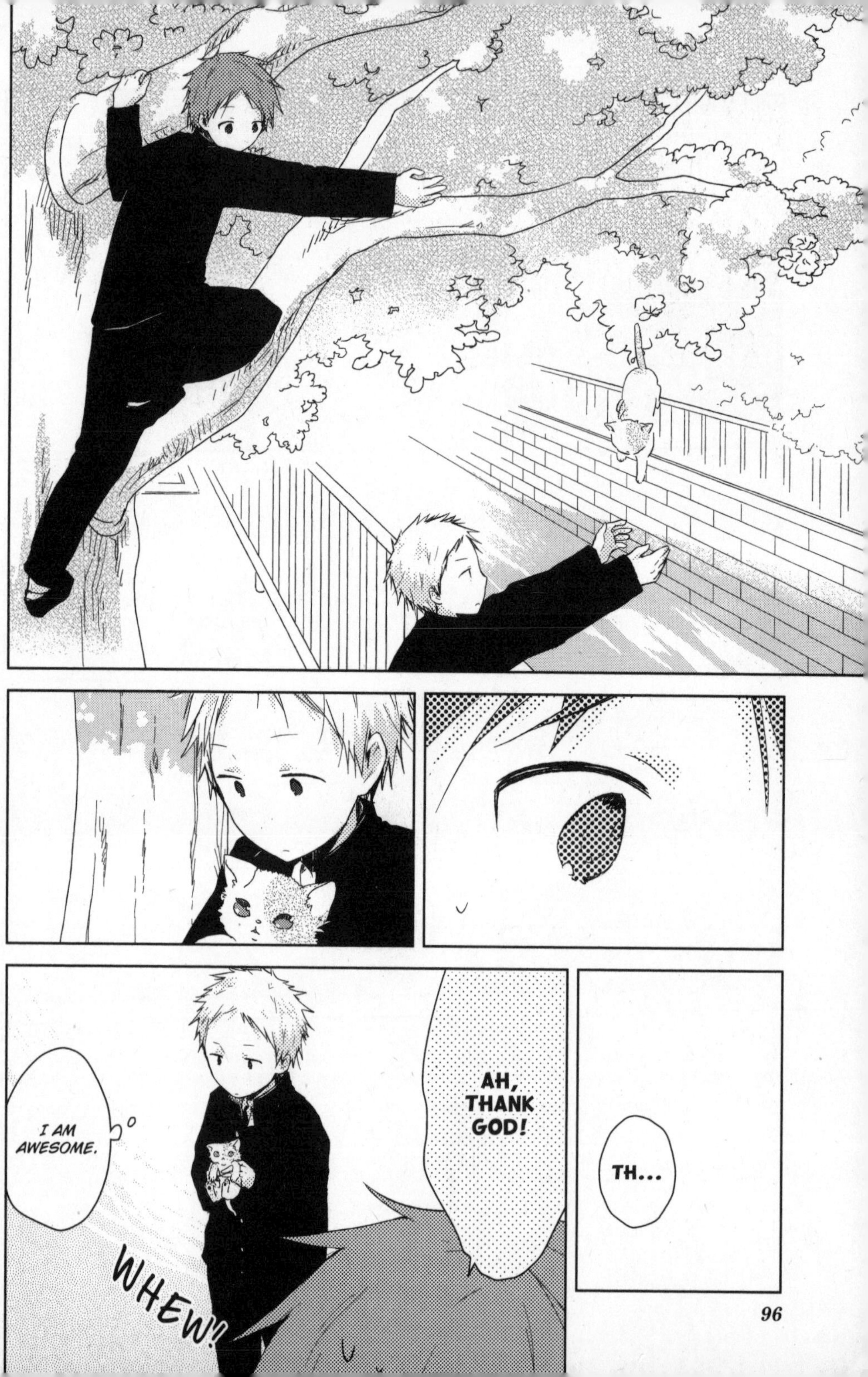

TH...
AH, THANK GOD!
I AM AWESOME.
WHEW!

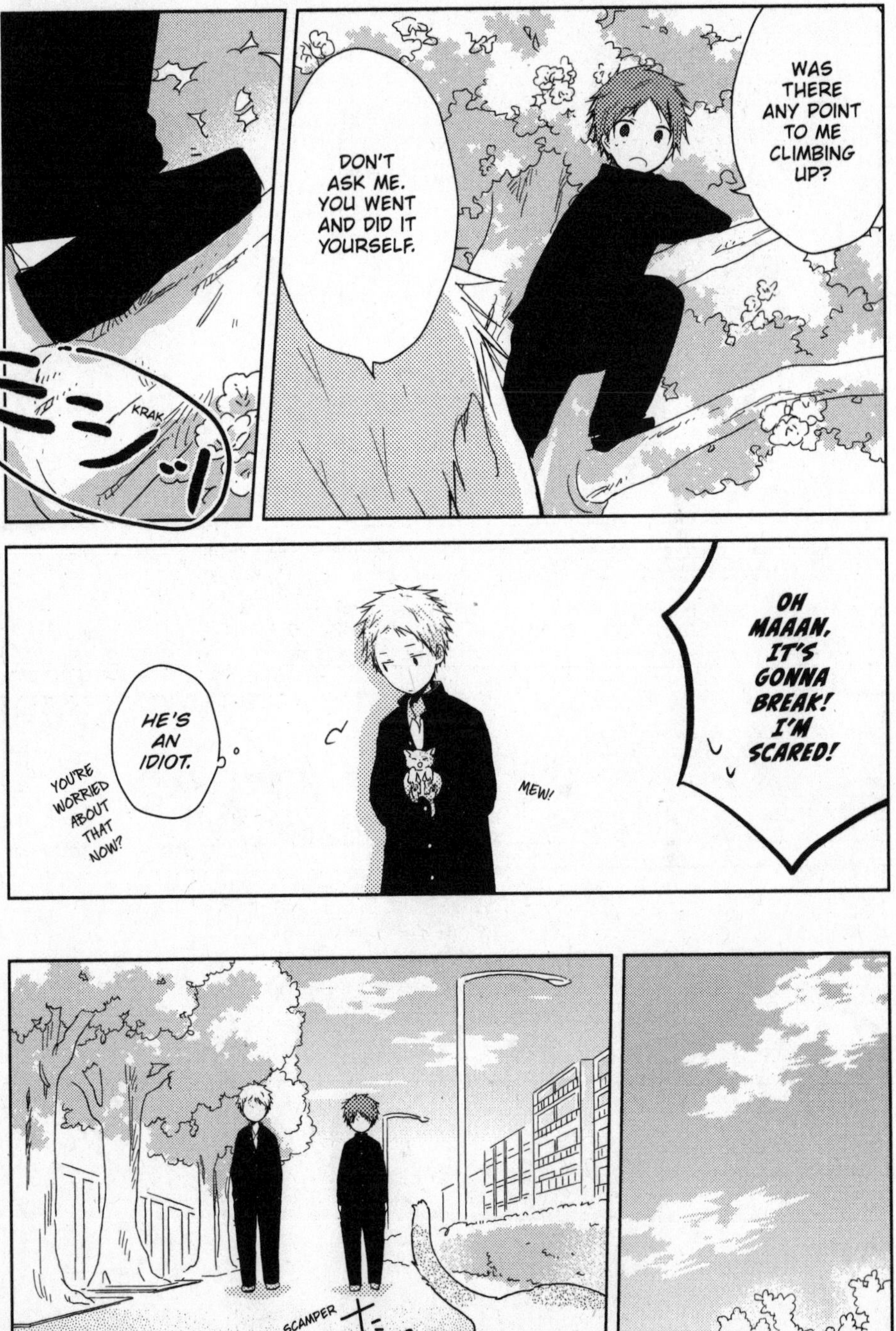
WAS THERE ANY POINT TO ME CLIMBING UP?
DON'T ASK ME. YOU WENT AND DID IT YOURSELF.
KRAK
OH MAAAN. IT'S GONNA BREAK! I'M SCARED!
MEW!
HE'S AN IDIOT.
YOU'RE WORRIED ABOUT THAT NOW?
SCAMPER

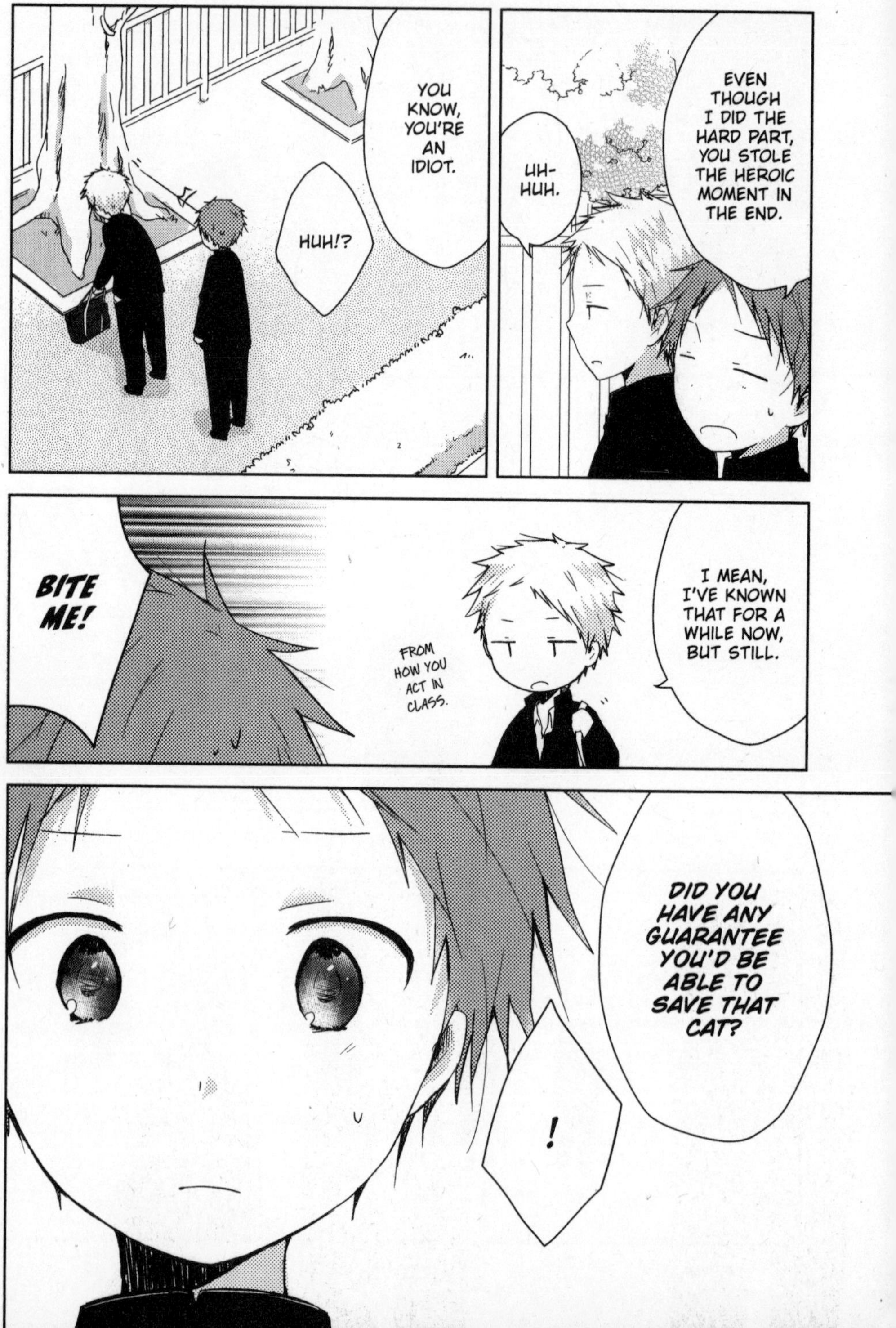
EVEN THOUGH I DID THE HARD PART, YOU STOLE THE HEROIC MOMENT IN THE END.
UH-HUH.
YOU KNOW, YOU'RE AN IDIOT.
HUH!?
I MEAN, I'VE KNOWN THAT FOR A WHILE NOW, BUT STILL.
FROM HOW YOU ACT IN CLASS.
BITE ME!
DID YOU HAVE ANY GUARANTEE YOU'D BE ABLE TO SAVE THAT CAT?
!

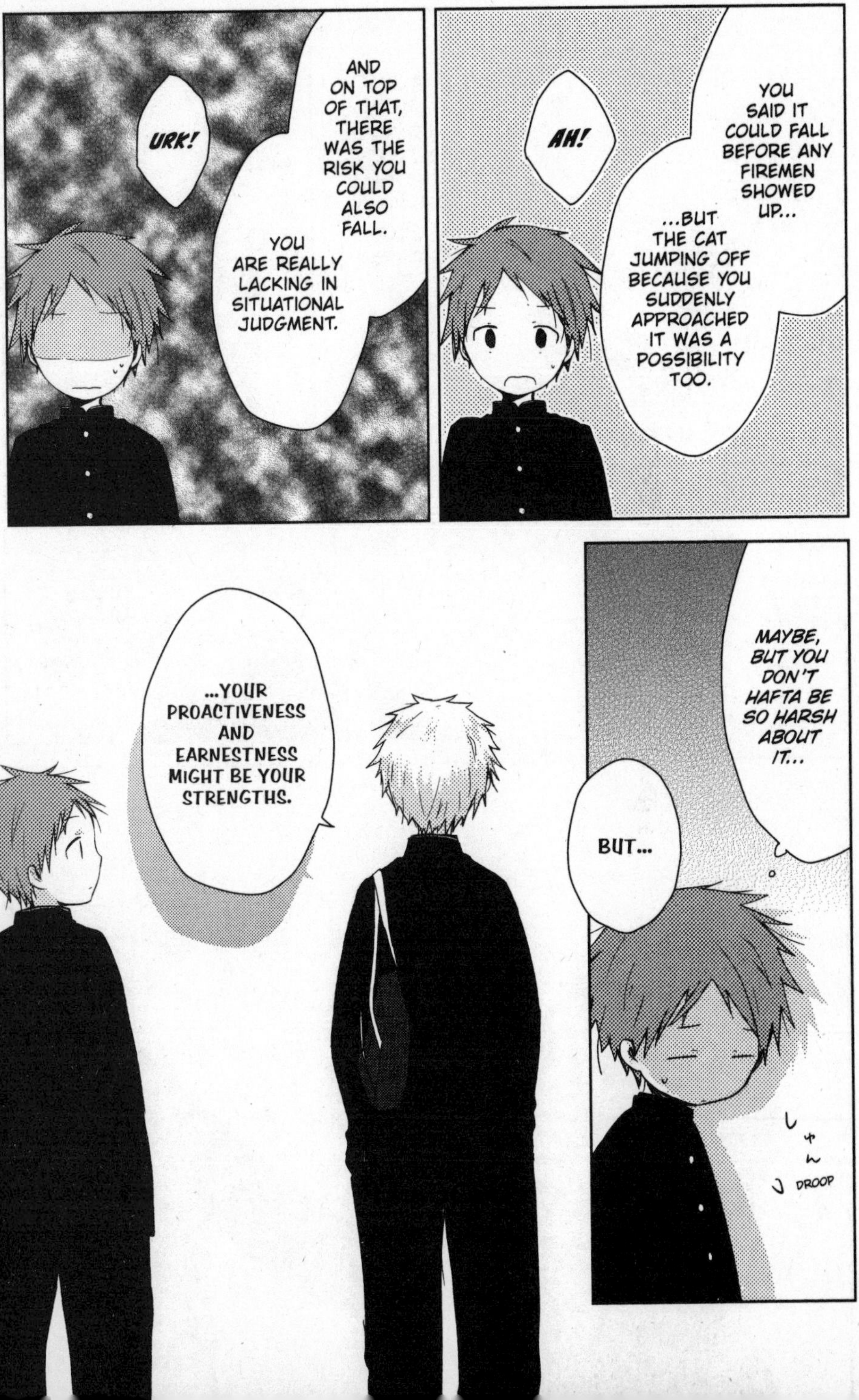

YOU SAID IT COULD FALL BEFORE ANY FIREMEN SHOWED UP...
...BUT THE CAT JUMPING OFF BECAUSE YOU SUDDENLY APPROACHED IT WAS A POSSIBILITY TOO.
AH!
AND ON TOP OF THAT, THERE WAS THE RISK YOU COULD ALSO FALL.
YOU ARE REALLY LACKING IN SITUATIONAL JUDGMENT.
URK!
MAYBE, BUT YOU DON'T HAFTA BE SO HARSH ABOUT IT...
BUT...
しゅん
DROOP
...YOUR PROACTIVENESS AND EARNESTNESS MIGHT BE YOUR STRENGTHS.

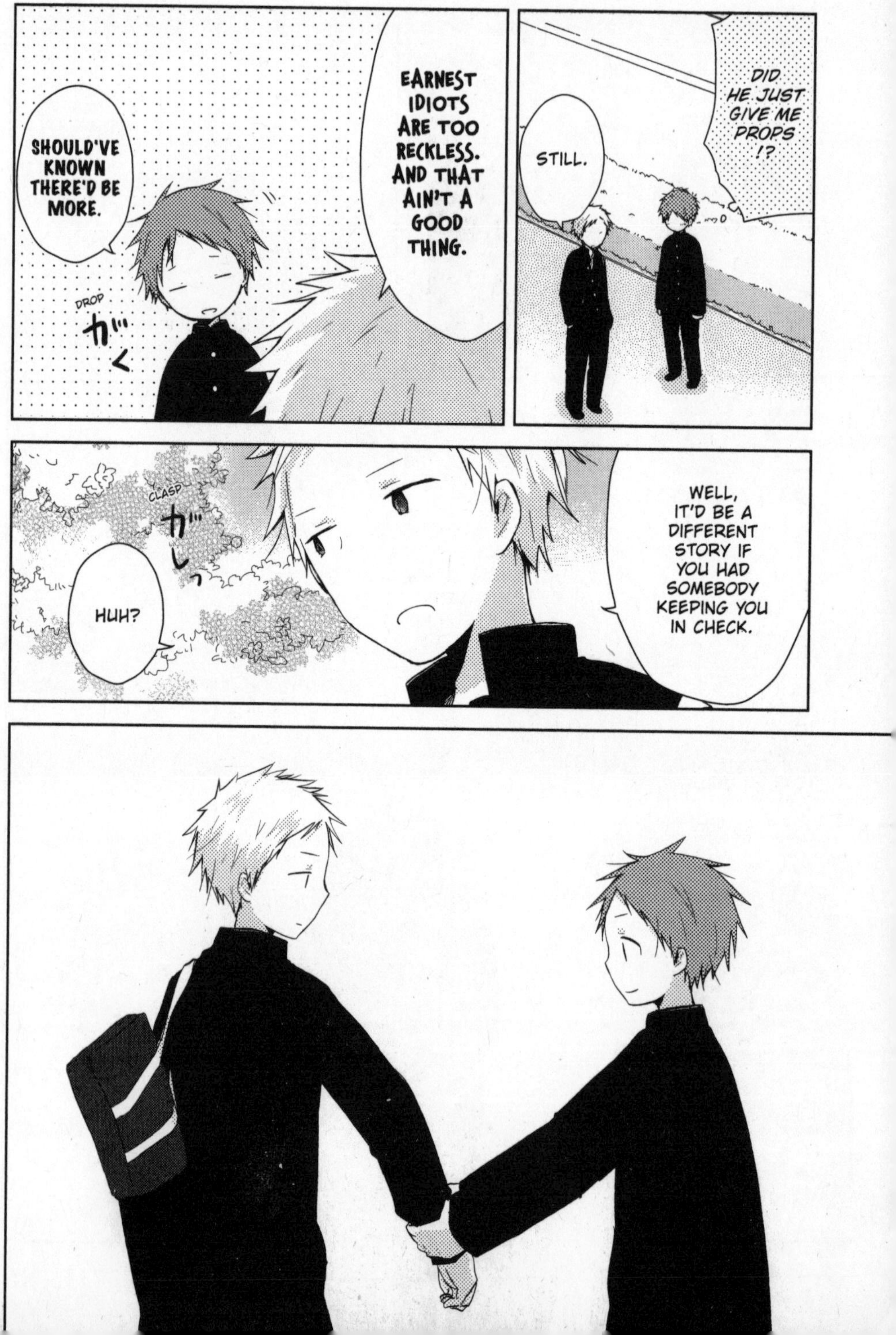
DID HE JUST GIVE ME PROPS!?
STILL.
EARNEST IDIOTS ARE TOO RECKLESS. AND THAT AIN'T A GOOD THING.
SHOULD'VE KNOWN THERE'D BE MORE.
DROP
ガく
WELL, IT'D BE A DIFFERENT STORY IF YOU HAD SOMEBODY KEEPING YOU IN CHECK.
CLASP
ガしっ
HUH?

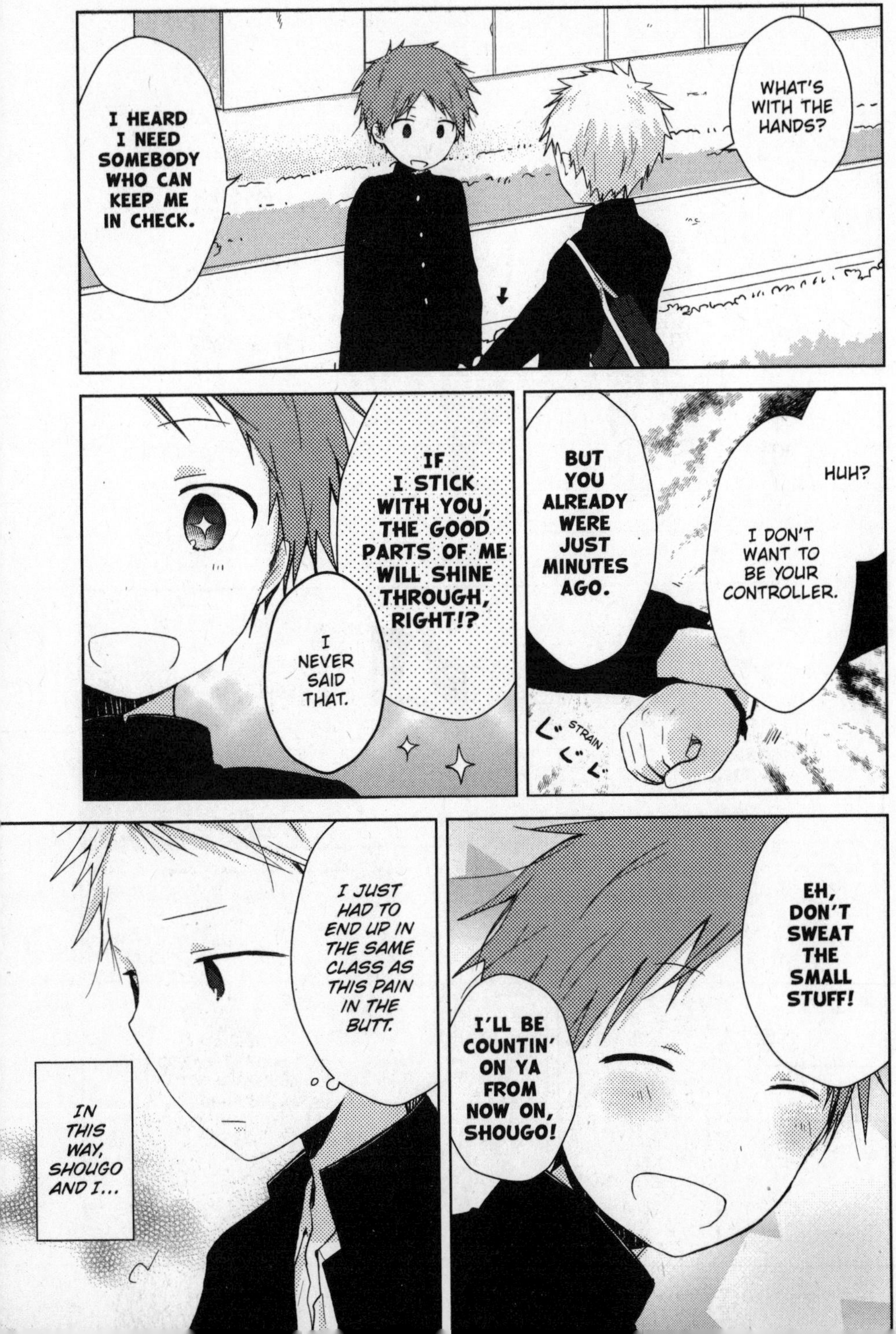
WHAT'S WITH THE HANDS?
I HEARD I NEED SOMEBODY WHO CAN KEEP ME IN CHECK.
HUH?
I DON'T WANT TO BE YOUR CONTROLLER.
BUT YOU ALREADY WERE JUST MINUTES AGO.
STRAIN
IF I STICK WITH YOU, THE GOOD PARTS OF ME WILL SHINE THROUGH, RIGHT!?
I NEVER SAID THAT.
EH, DON'T SWEAT THE SMALL STUFF!
I'LL BE COUNTIN' ON YA FROM NOW ON, SHOUGO!
I JUST HAD TO END UP IN THE SAME CLASS AS THIS PAIN IN THE BUTT.
IN THIS WAY, SHOUGO AND I...

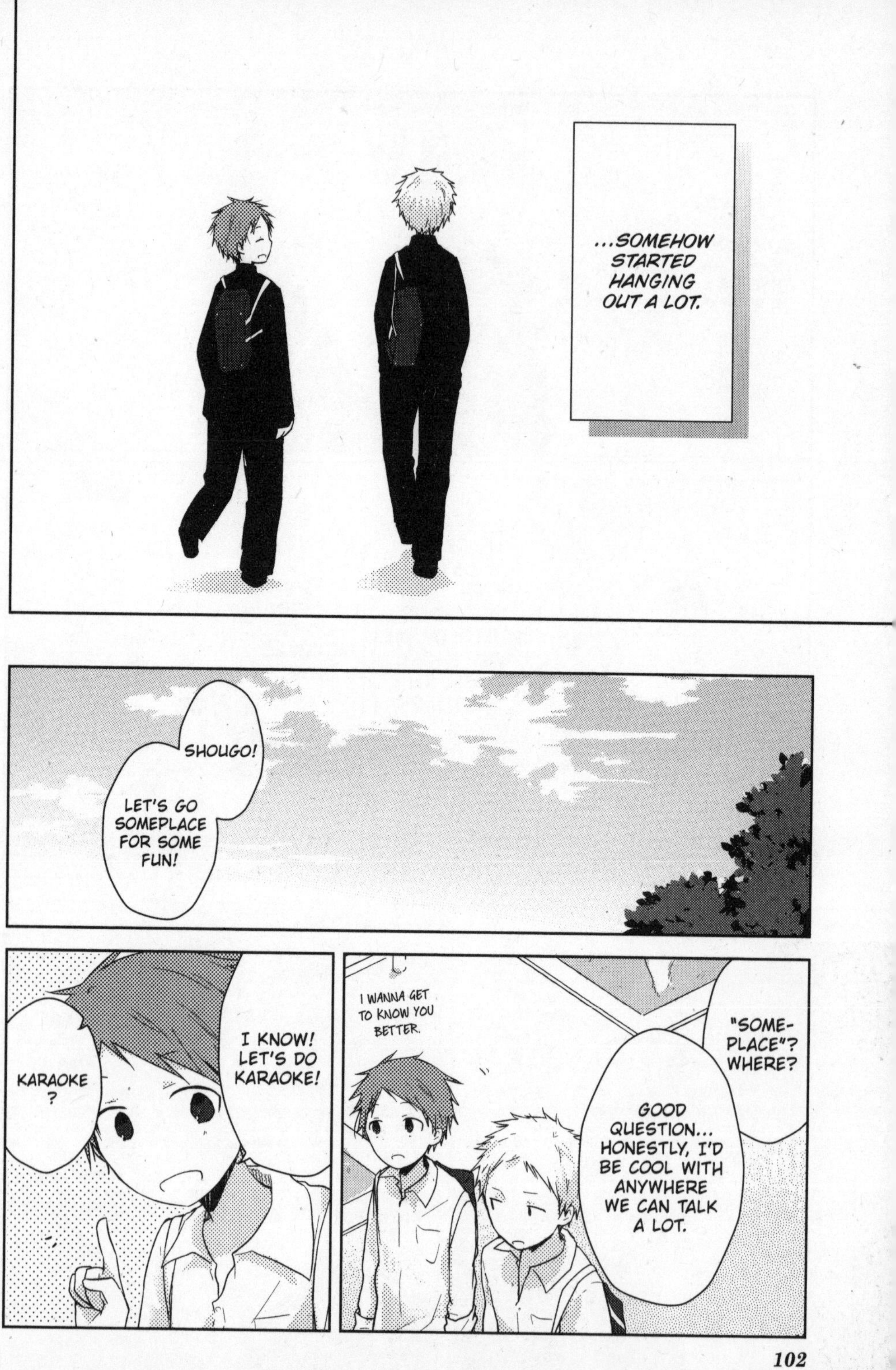
...SOMEHOW STARTED HANGING OUT A LOT.
SHOUGO!
LET'S GO SOMEPLACE FOR SOME FUN!
"SOME-PLACE"? WHERE?
GOOD QUESTION... HONESTLY, I'D BE COOL WITH ANYWHERE WE CAN TALK A LOT.
I WANNA GET TO KNOW YOU BETTER.
I KNOW! LET'S DO KARAOKE!
KARAOKE?

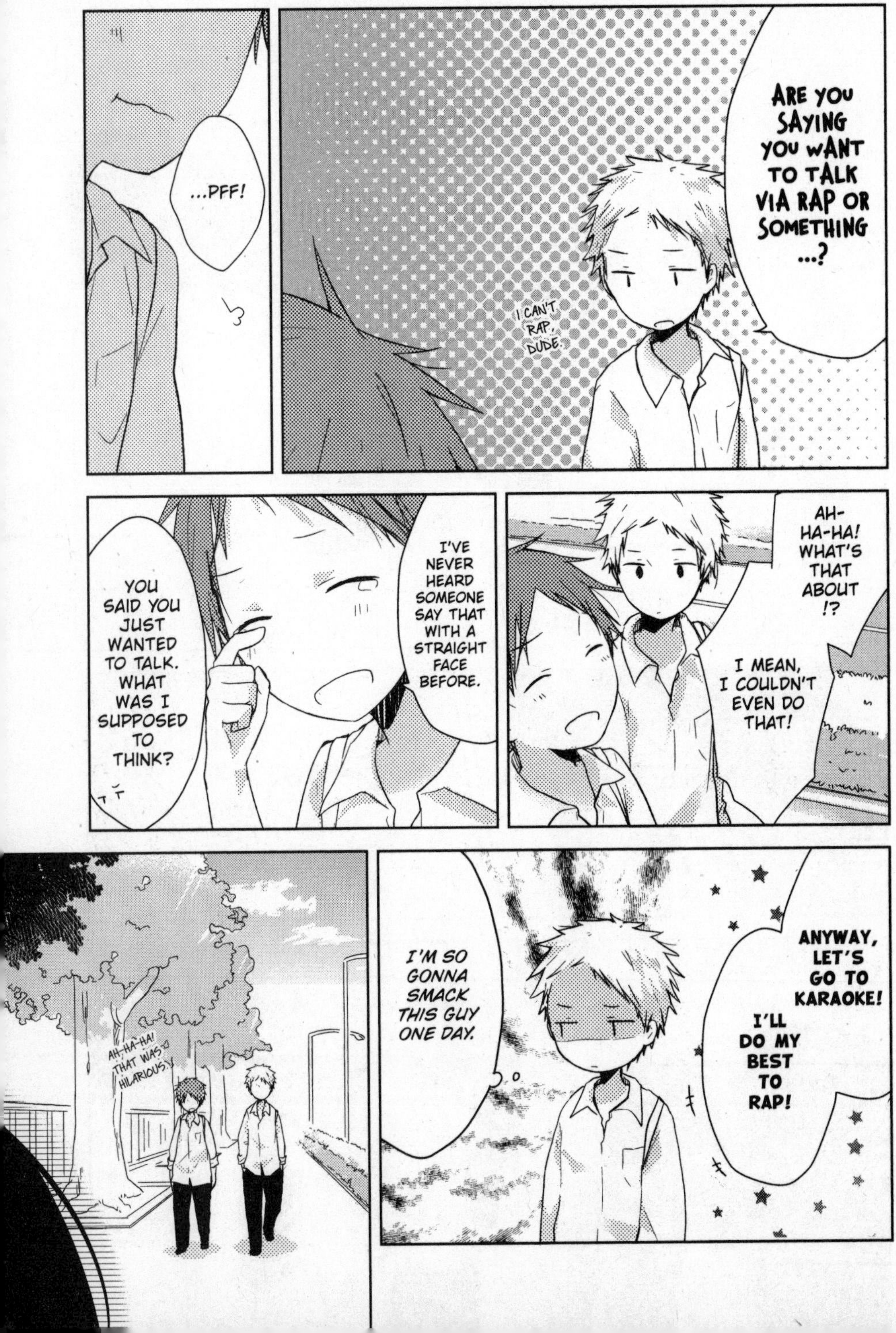
ARE YOU SAYING YOU WANT TO TALK VIA RAP OR SOMETHING ...?
I CAN'T RAP, DUDE.
...PFF!
AH-HA-HA! WHAT'S THAT ABOUT !?
I MEAN, I COULDN'T EVEN DO THAT!
I'VE NEVER HEARD SOMEONE SAY THAT WITH A STRAIGHT FACE BEFORE.
YOU SAID YOU JUST WANTED TO TALK. WHAT WAS I SUPPOSED TO THINK?
ANYWAY, LET'S GO TO KARAOKE!
I'LL DO MY BEST TO RAP!
I'M SO GONNA SMACK THIS GUY ONE DAY.
AH-HA-HA! THAT WAS HILARIOUS.

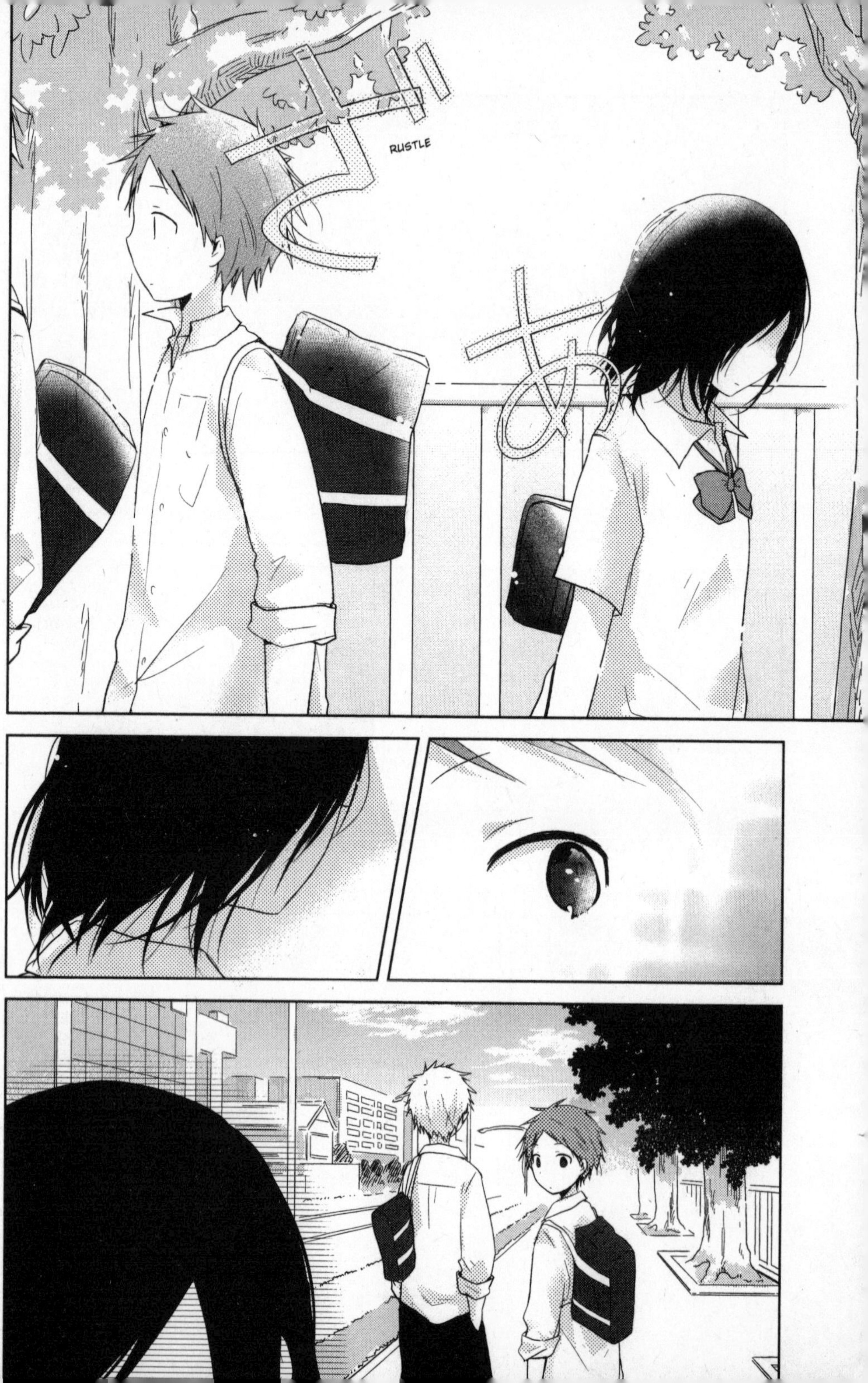
RUSTLE

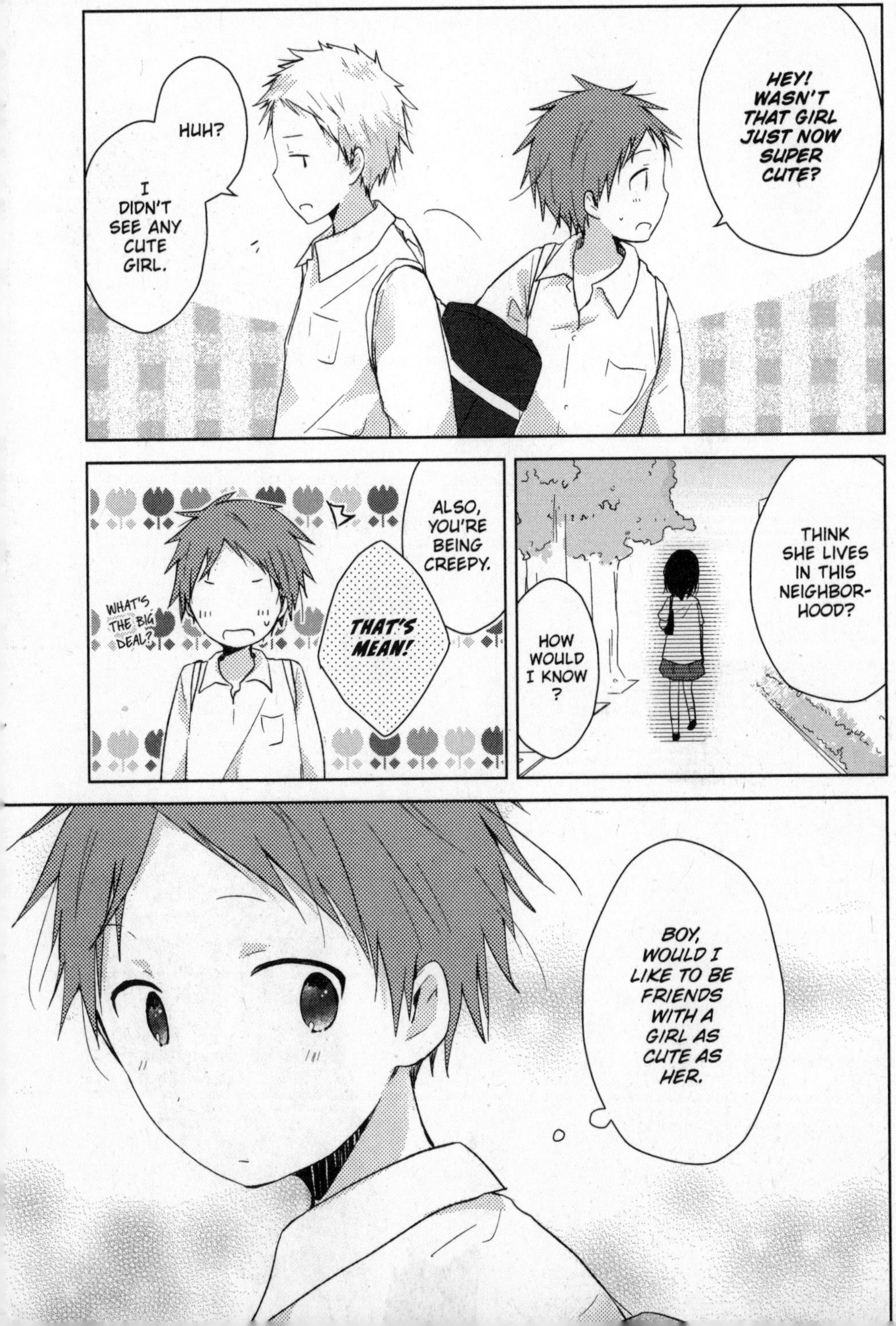
HEY! WASN'T THAT GIRL JUST NOW SUPER CUTE?
HUH?
I DIDN'T SEE ANY CUTE GIRL.
THINK SHE LIVES IN THIS NEIGHBOR-HOOD?
HOW WOULD I KNOW?
ALSO, YOU'RE BEING CREEPY.
THAT'S MEAN!
WHAT'S THE BIG DEAL?
BOY, WOULD I LIKE TO BE FRIENDS WITH A GIRL AS CUTE AS HER.

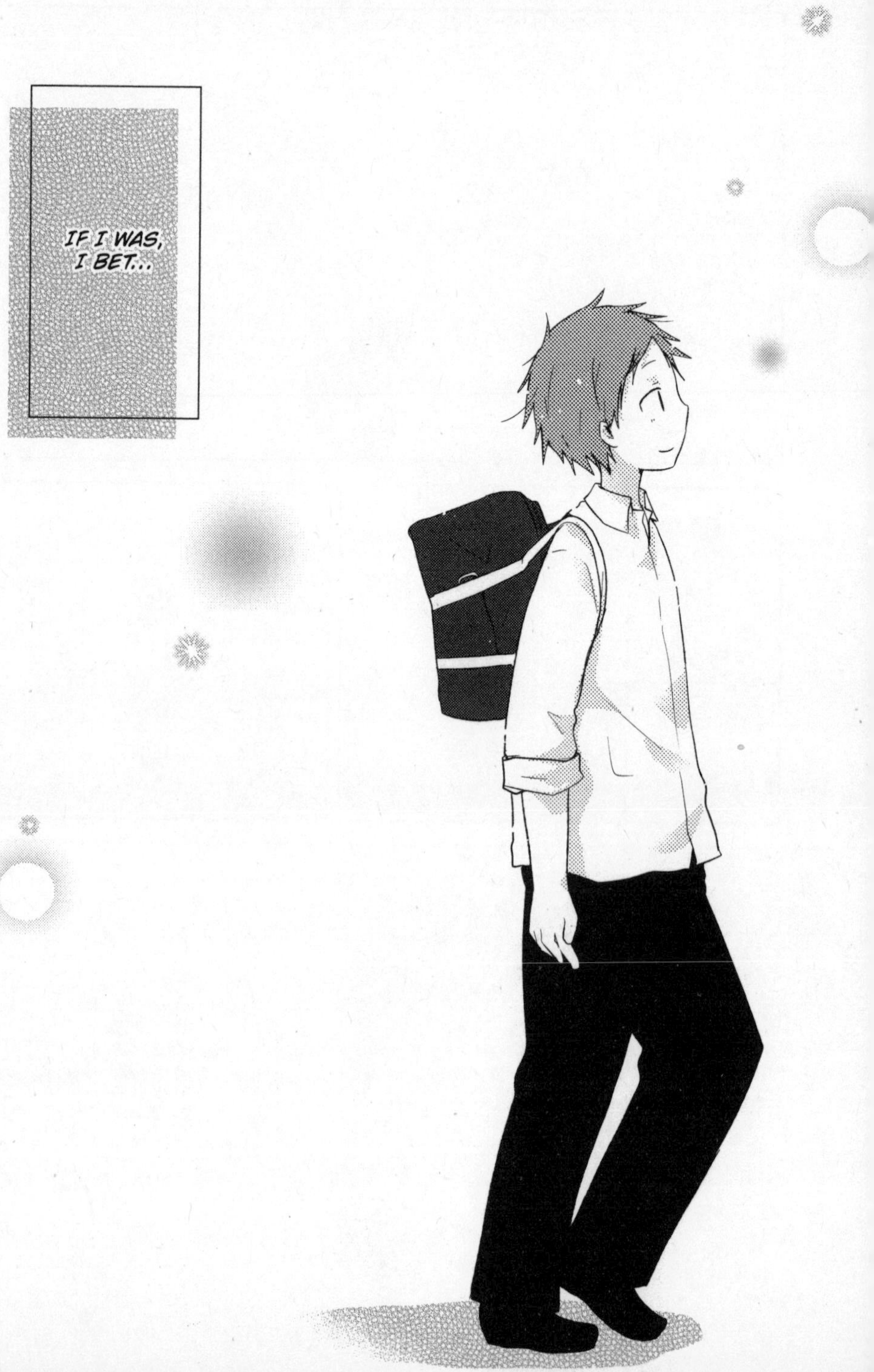
IF I WAS, I BET...

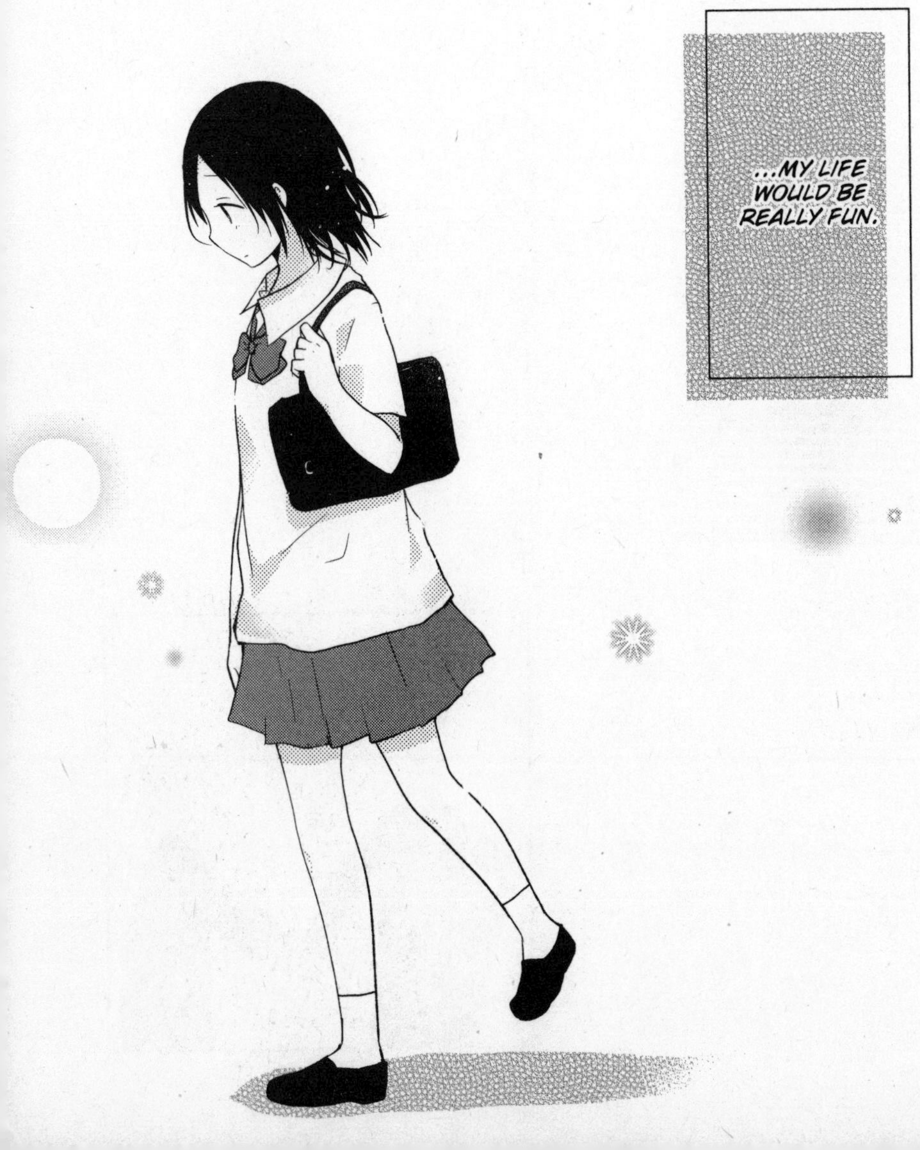
...MY LIFE WOULD BE REALLY FUN.

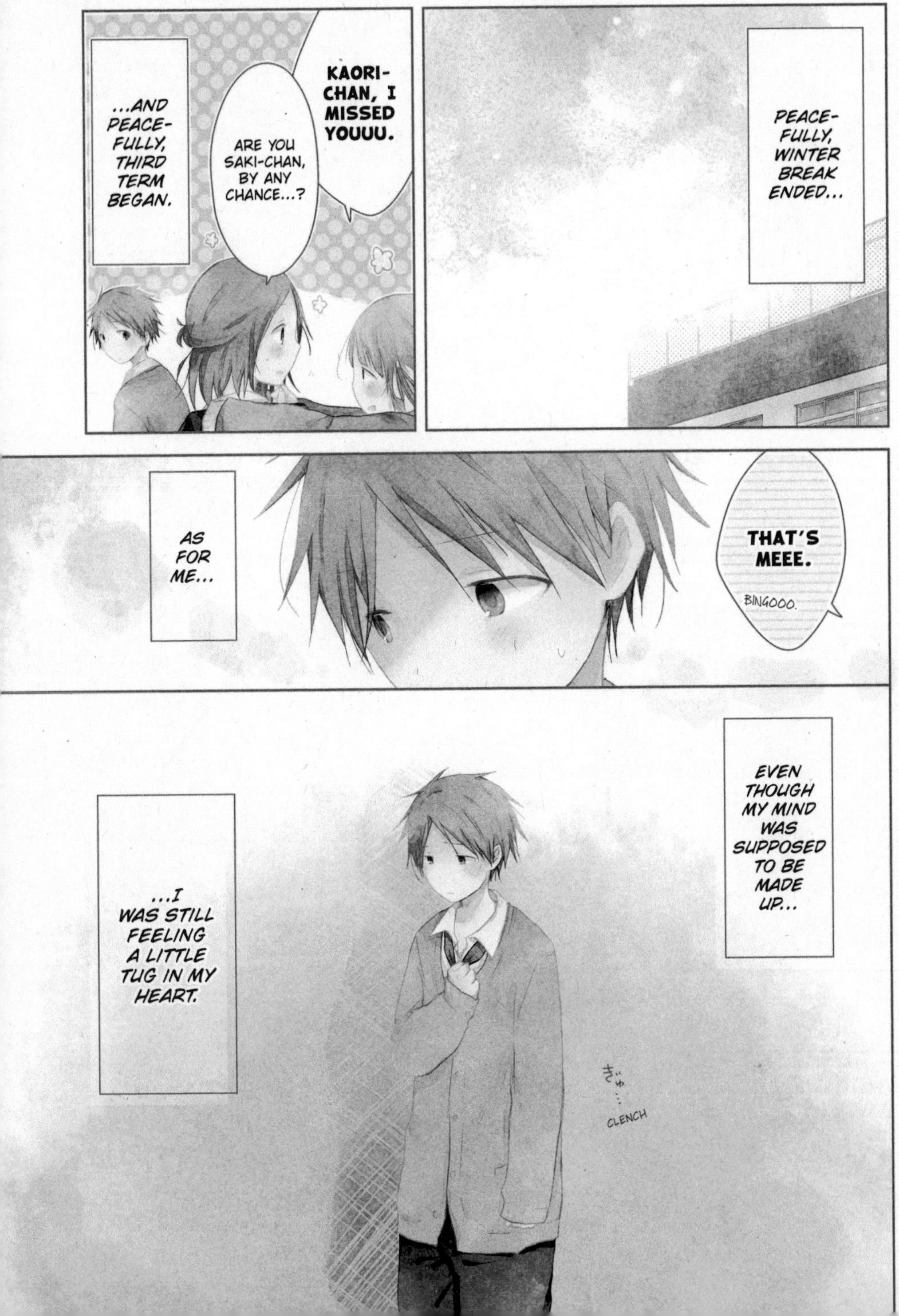
PEACE-FULLY, WINTER BREAK ENDED...
KAORI-CHAN, I MISSED YOUUU.
ARE YOU SAKI-CHAN, BY ANY CHANCE...?
...AND PEACE-FULLY, THIRD TERM BEGAN.
THAT'S MEEE.
BINGOOO.
AS FOR ME...
EVEN THOUGH MY MIND WAS SUPPOSED TO BE MADE UP...
ぎゅ…
CLENCH
...I WAS STILL FEELING A LITTLE TUG IN MY HEART.

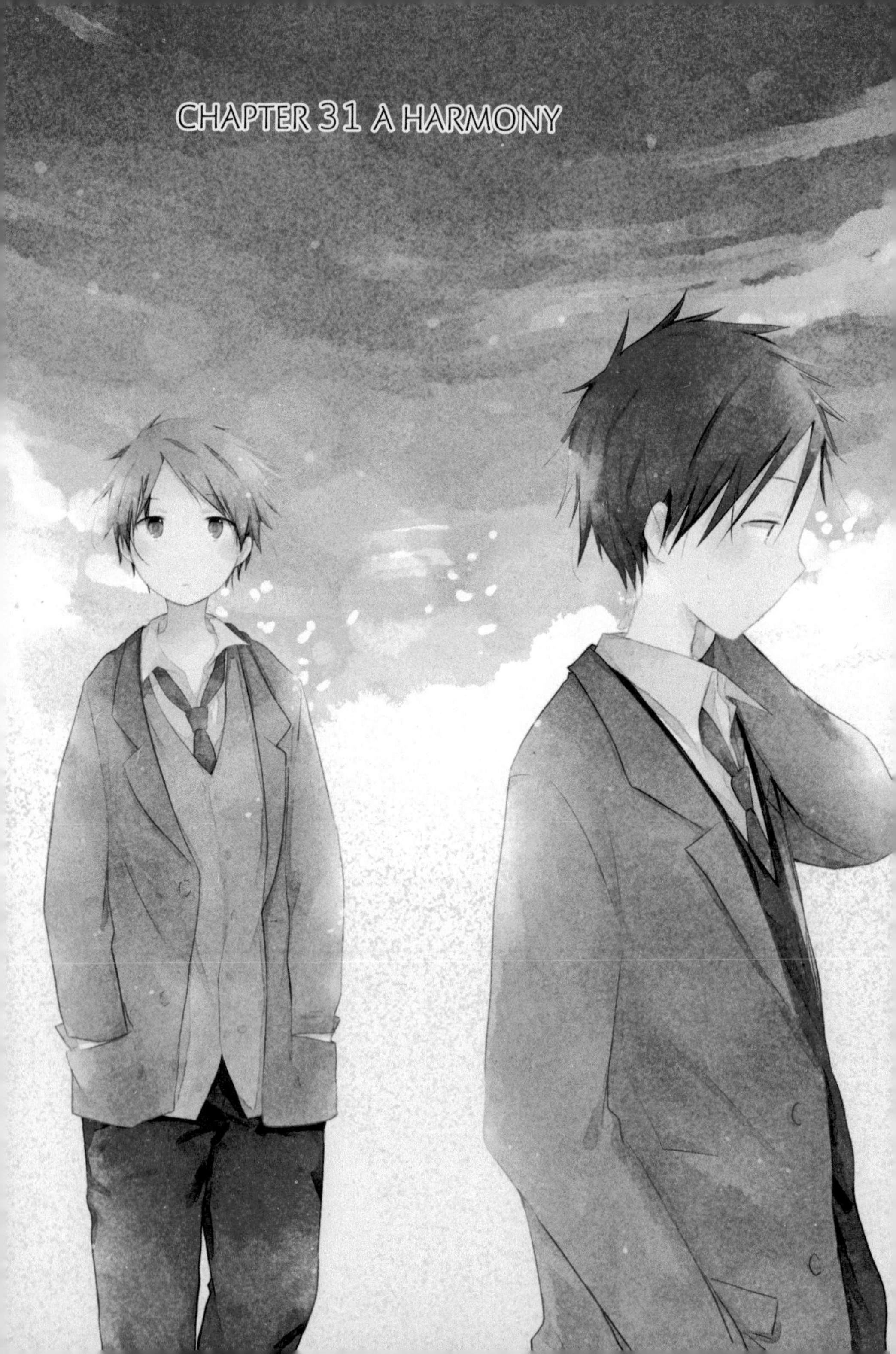
CHAPTER 31 A HARMONY

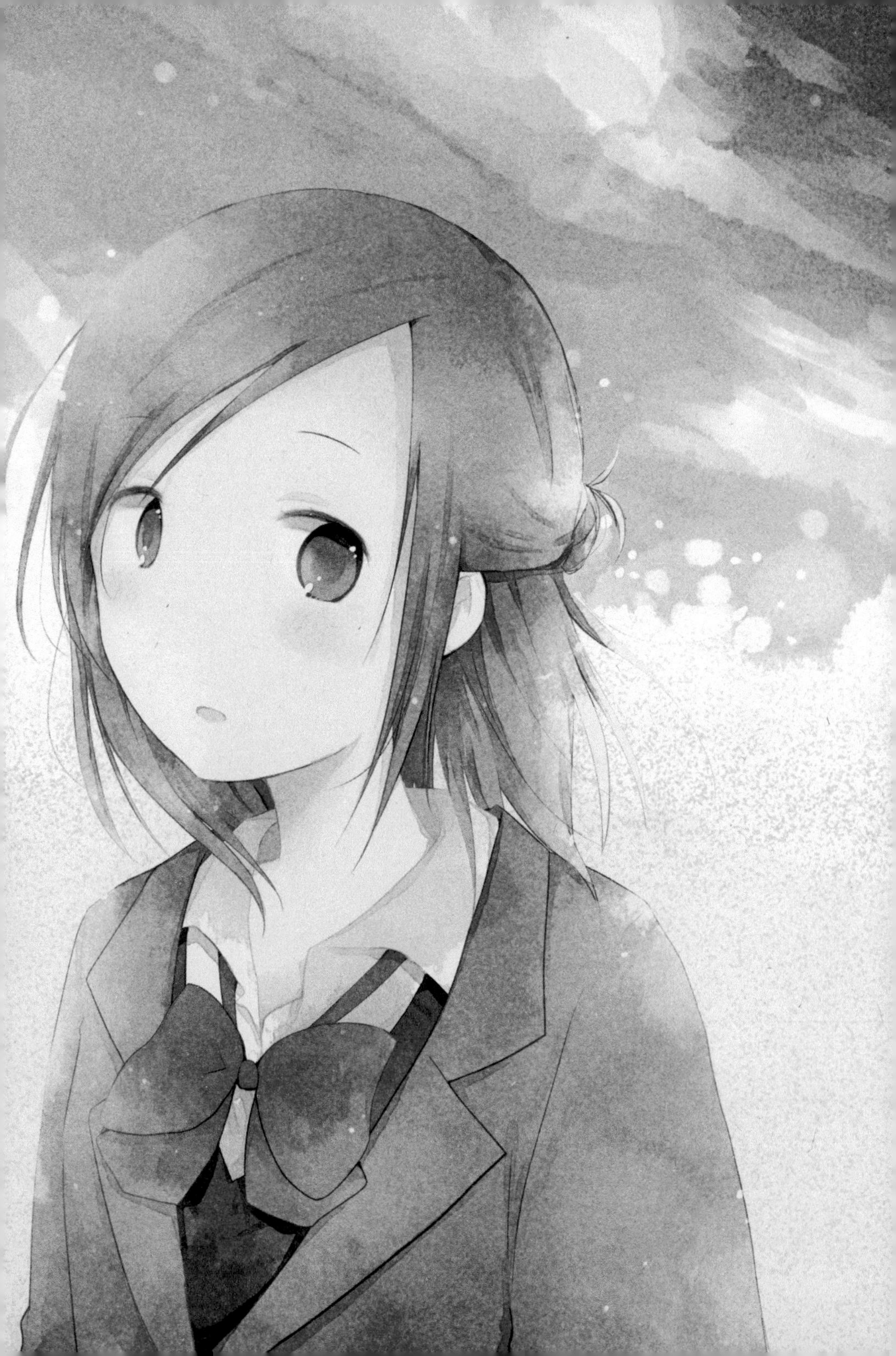

ONE
WEEK
FRIENDS

SCARF

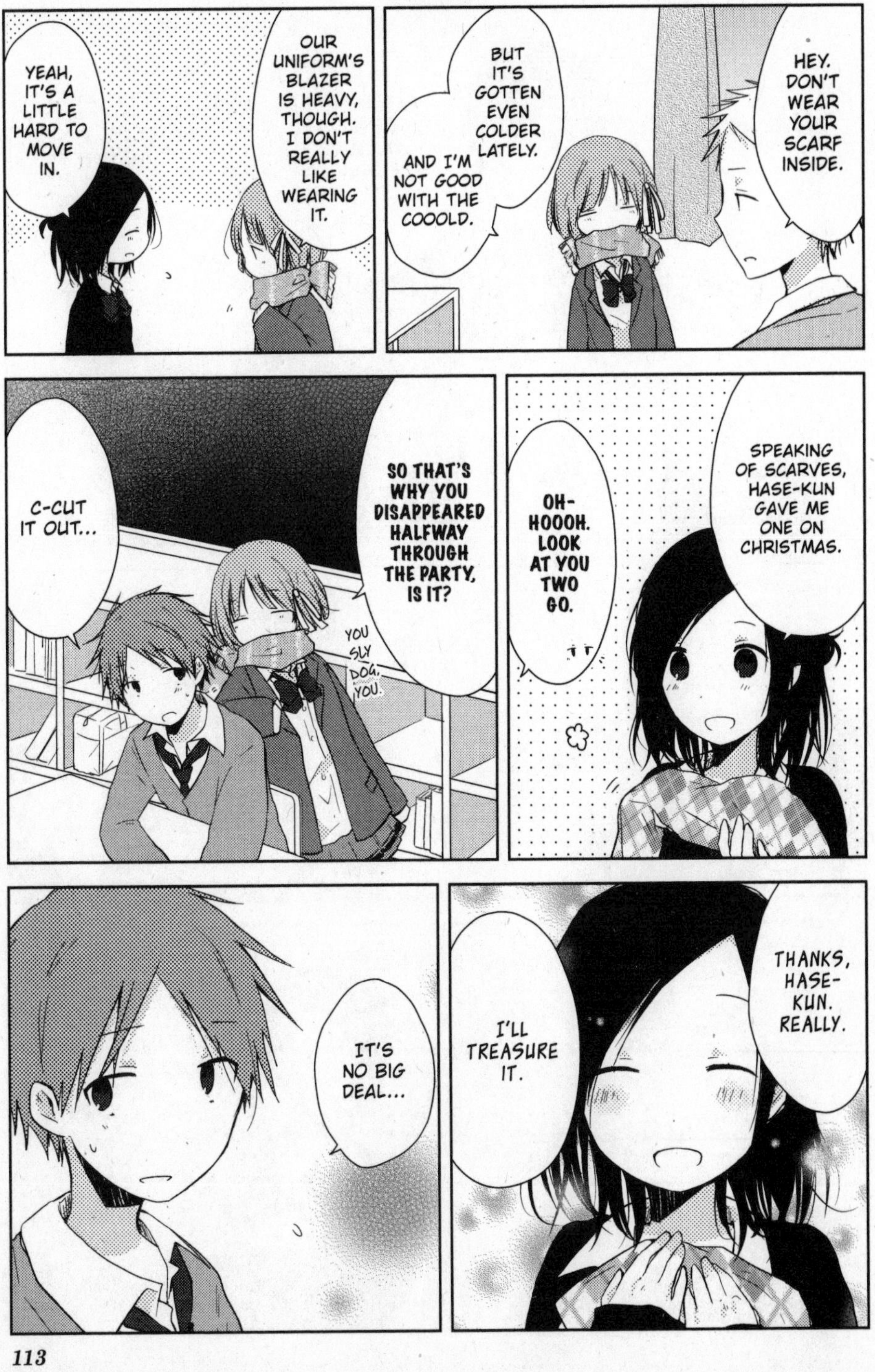
HEY. DON'T WEAR YOUR SCARF INSIDE.
BUT IT'S GOTTEN EVEN COLDER LATELY.
AND I'M NOT GOOD WITH THE COOOLD.
OUR UNIFORM'S BLAZER IS HEAVY, THOUGH. I DON'T REALLY LIKE WEARING IT.
YEAH, IT'S A LITTLE HARD TO MOVE IN.
SPEAKING OF SCARVES, HASE-KUN GAVE ME ONE ON CHRISTMAS.
OH-HOOOH. LOOK AT YOU TWO GO.
SO THAT'S WHY YOU DISAPPEARED HALFWAY THROUGH THE PARTY, IS IT?
YOU SLY DOG, YOU.
C-CUT IT OUT...
THANKS, HASE-KUN. REALLY.
I'LL TREASURE IT.
IT'S NO BIG DEAL...

ABOUT WINTER BREAK

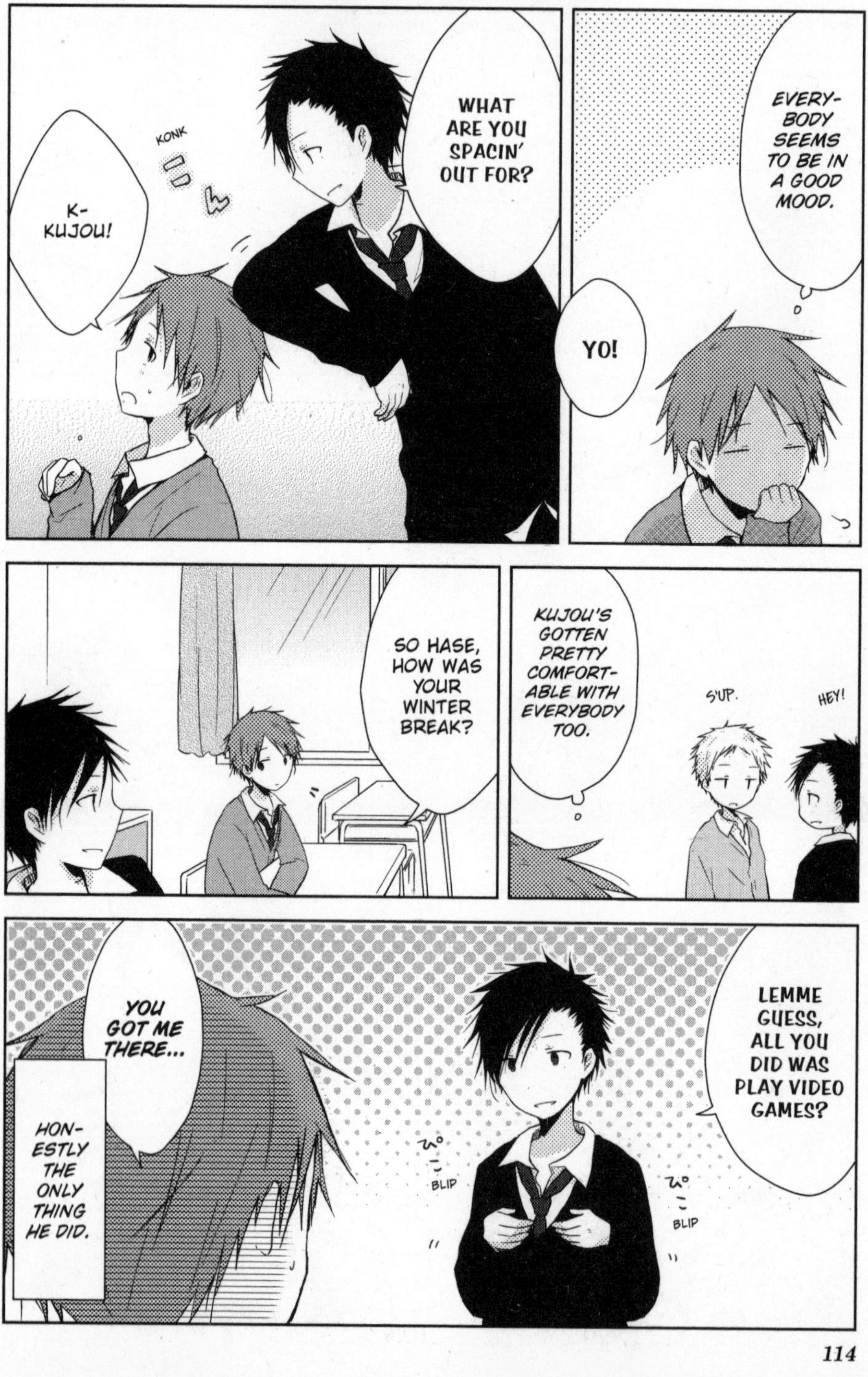
EVERY-BODY SEEMS TO BE IN A GOOD MOOD.
YO!
WHAT ARE YOU SPACIN' OUT FOR?
KONK
K-KUJOU!
KUJOU'S GOTTEN PRETTY COMFORTABLE WITH EVERYBODY TOO.
HEY!
S'UP.
SO HASE, HOW WAS YOUR WINTER BREAK?
LEMME GUESS, ALL YOU DID WAS PLAY VIDEO GAMES?
ぴこ
BLIP
ぴこ
BLIP
YOU GOT ME THERE...
HON-ESTLY THE ONLY THING HE DID.

SURPRISINGLY

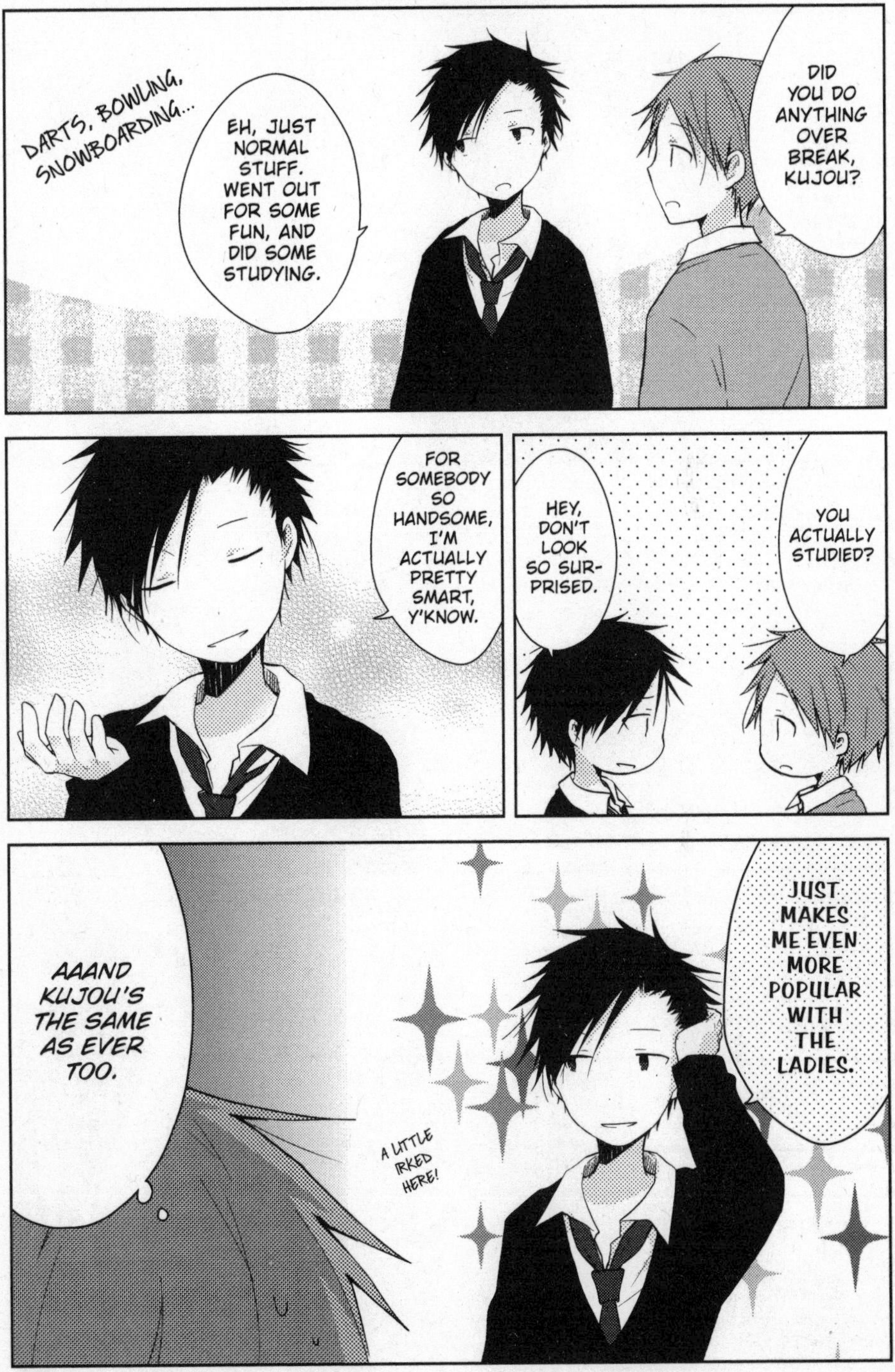
DID YOU DO ANYTHING OVER BREAK, KUJOU?
EH, JUST NORMAL STUFF. WENT OUT FOR SOME FUN, AND DID SOME STUDYING.
DARTS, BOWLING, SNOWBOARDING...
YOU ACTUALLY STUDIED?
HEY, DON'T LOOK SO SUR-PRISED.
FOR SOMEBODY SO HANDSOME, I'M ACTUALLY PRETTY SMART, Y'KNOW.
JUST MAKES ME EVEN MORE POPULAR WITH THE LADIES.
A LITTLE IRKED HERE!
AAAND KUJOU'S THE SAME AS EVER TOO.

CAN'T MEET YOUR EYES

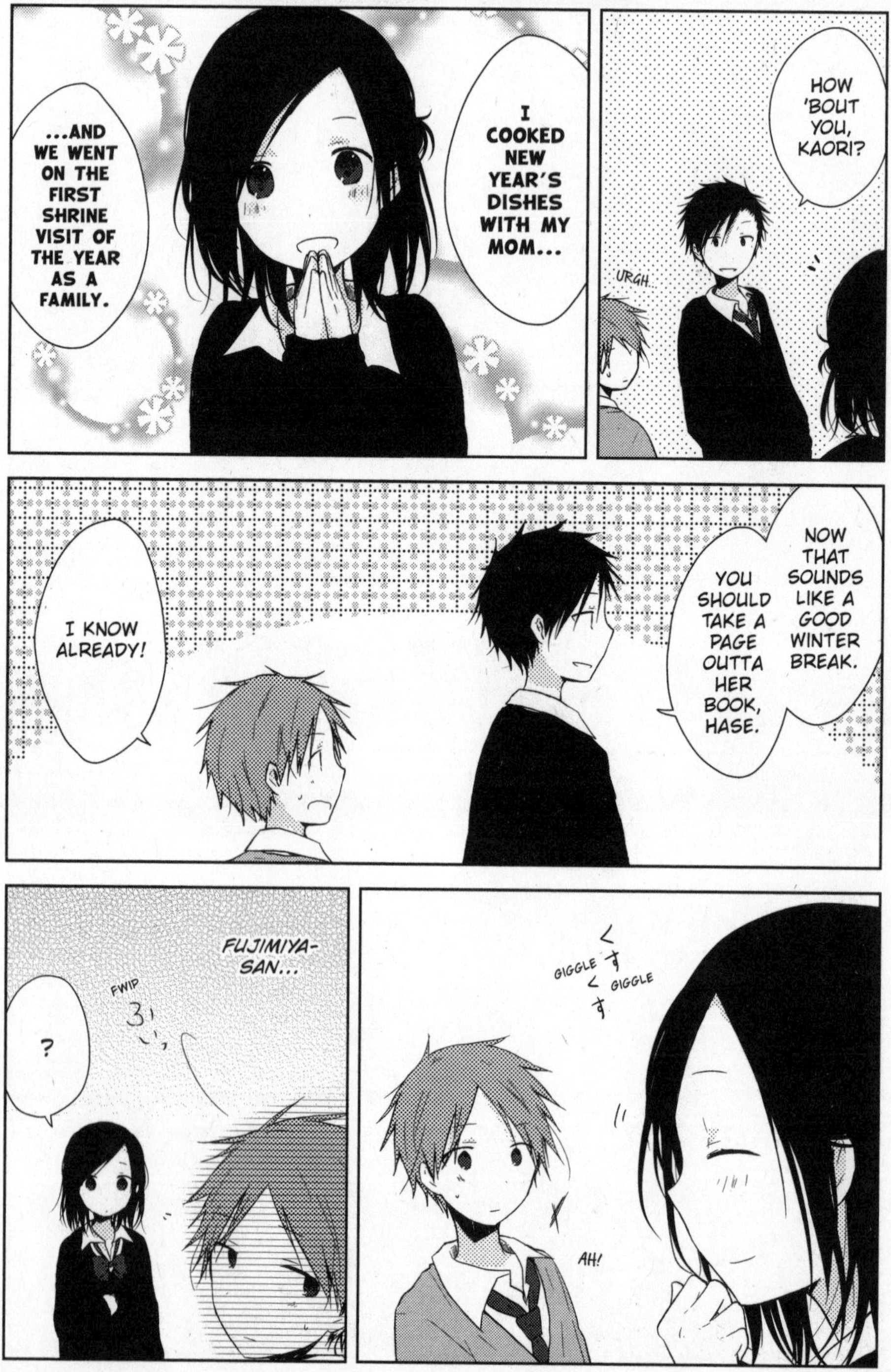
HOW 'BOUT YOU, KAORI?
URGH...
I COOKED NEW YEAR'S DISHES WITH MY MOM...
...AND WE WENT ON THE FIRST SHRINE VISIT OF THE YEAR AS A FAMILY.
NOW THAT SOUNDS LIKE A GOOD WINTER BREAK.
YOU SHOULD TAKE A PAGE OUTTA HER BOOK, HASE.
I KNOW ALREADY!
くすくす
GIGGLE GIGGLE
AH!
FUJIMIYA-SAN...
FWIP
?

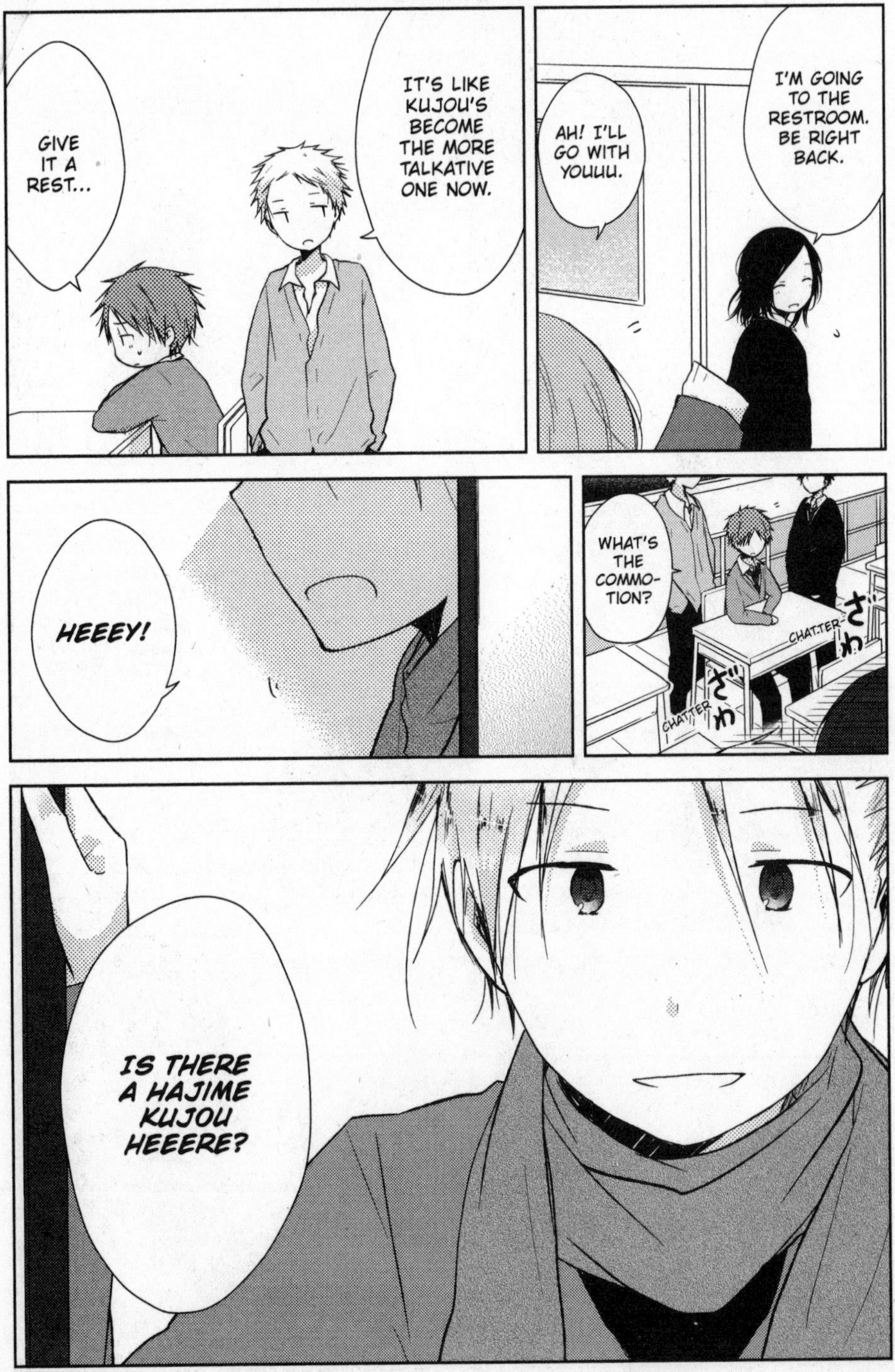
I'M GOING TO THE RESTROOM. BE RIGHT BACK.
AH! I'LL GO WITH YOUUU.
IT'S LIKE KUJOU'S BECOME THE MORE TALKATIVE ONE NOW.
GIVE IT A REST...
WHAT'S THE COMMO-TION?
ざわ CHATTER
ざわ CHATTER
HEEEY!
IS THERE A HAJIME KUJOU HEEERE?

THE BROTHER

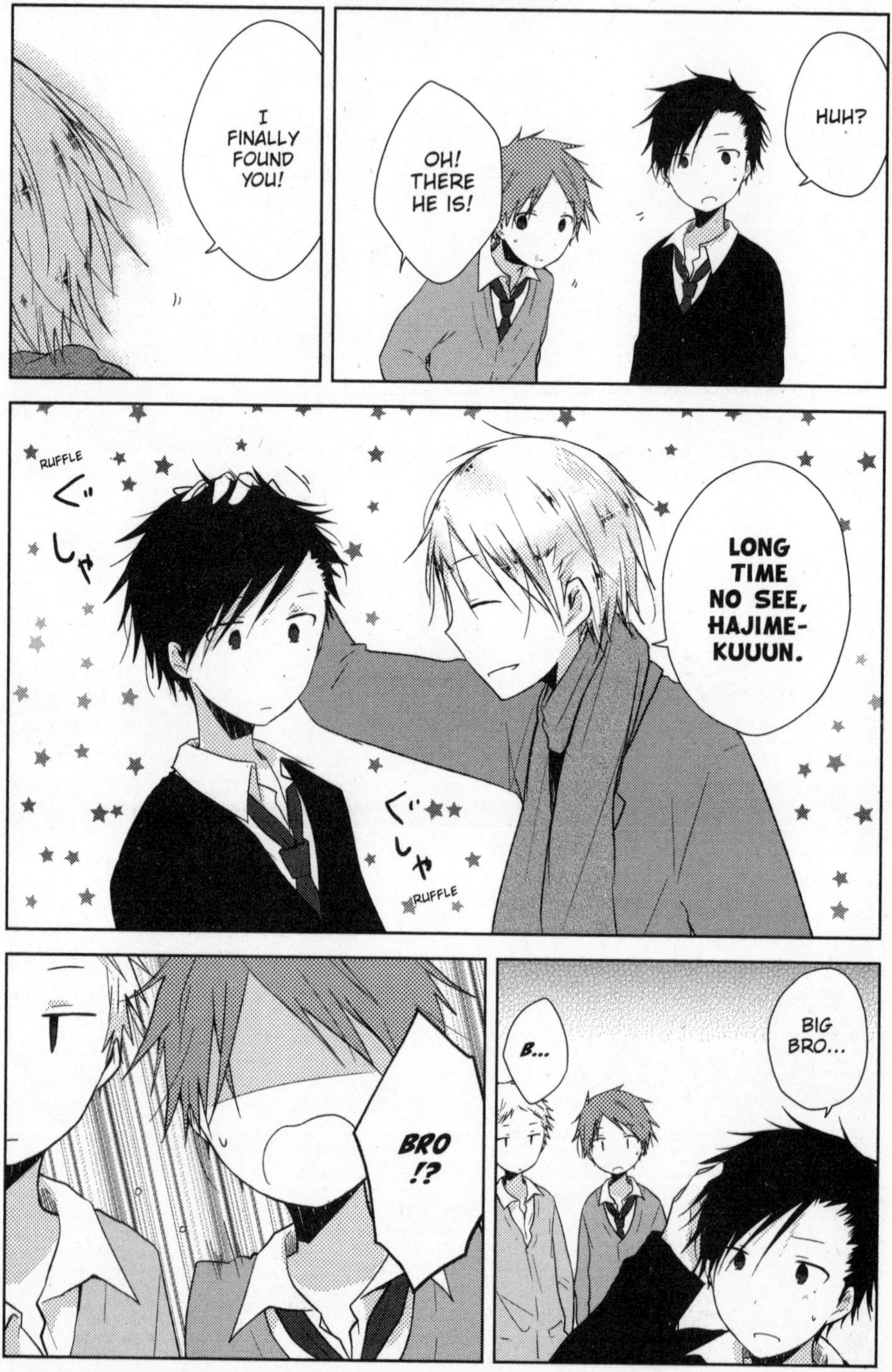
HUH?
OH! THERE HE IS!
I FINALLY FOUND YOU!
LONG TIME NO SEE, HAJIME-KUUUN.
ぐしゃ
RUFFLE
ぐしゃ
RUFFLE
BIG BRO...
B...
BRO!?

THAT KINDA GUY

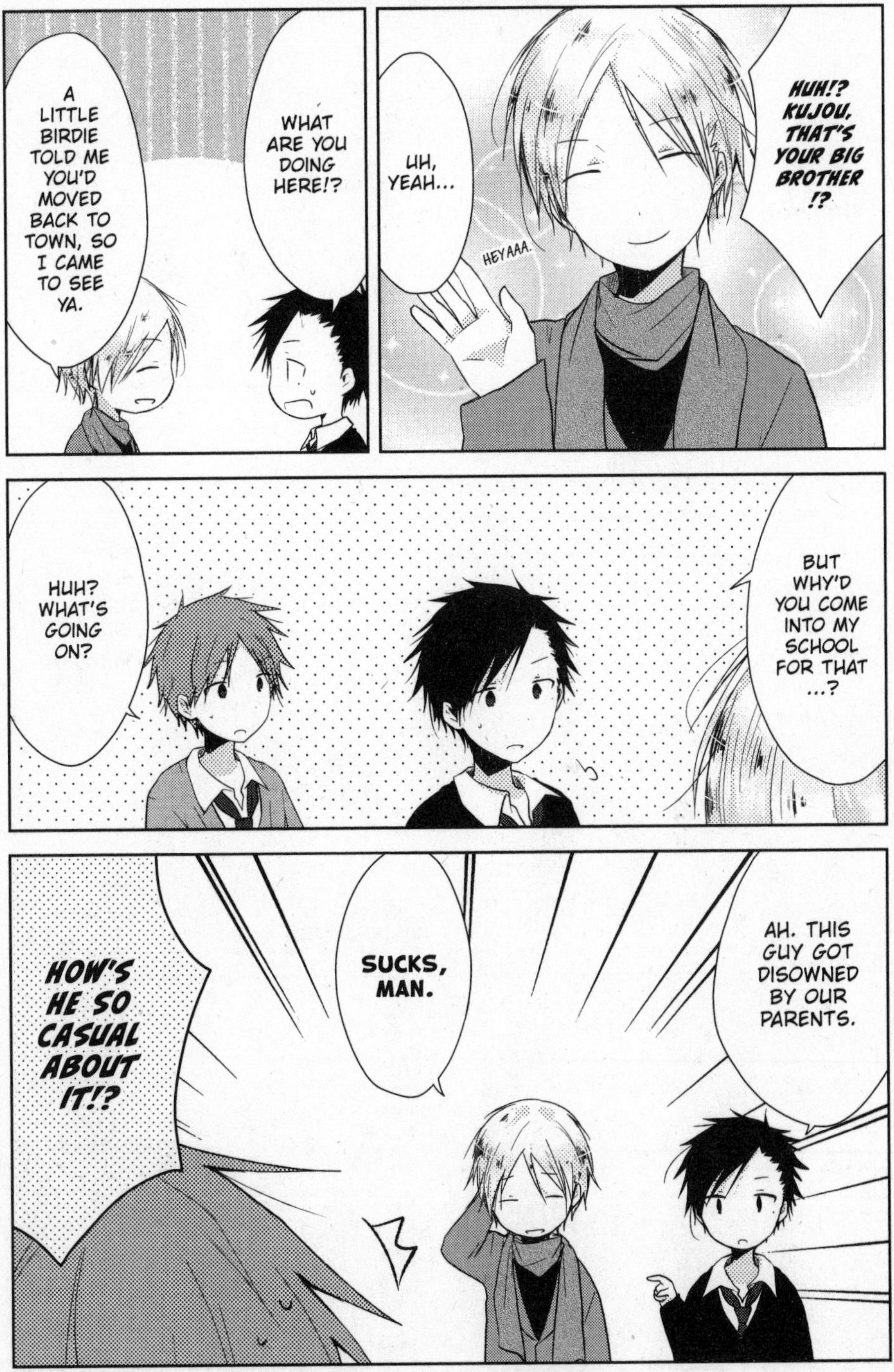
HUH!? KUJOU, THAT'S YOUR BIG BROTHER!?
UH, YEAH...
HEYAAA.
WHAT ARE YOU DOING HERE!?
A LITTLE BIRDIE TOLD ME YOU'D MOVED BACK TO TOWN, SO I CAME TO SEE YA.
BUT WHY'D YOU COME INTO MY SCHOOL FOR THAT...?
HUH? WHAT'S GOING ON?
AH. THIS GUY GOT DISOWNED BY OUR PARENTS.
SUCKS, MAN.
HOW'S HE SO CASUAL ABOUT IT!?

HAJIME & MITSURU

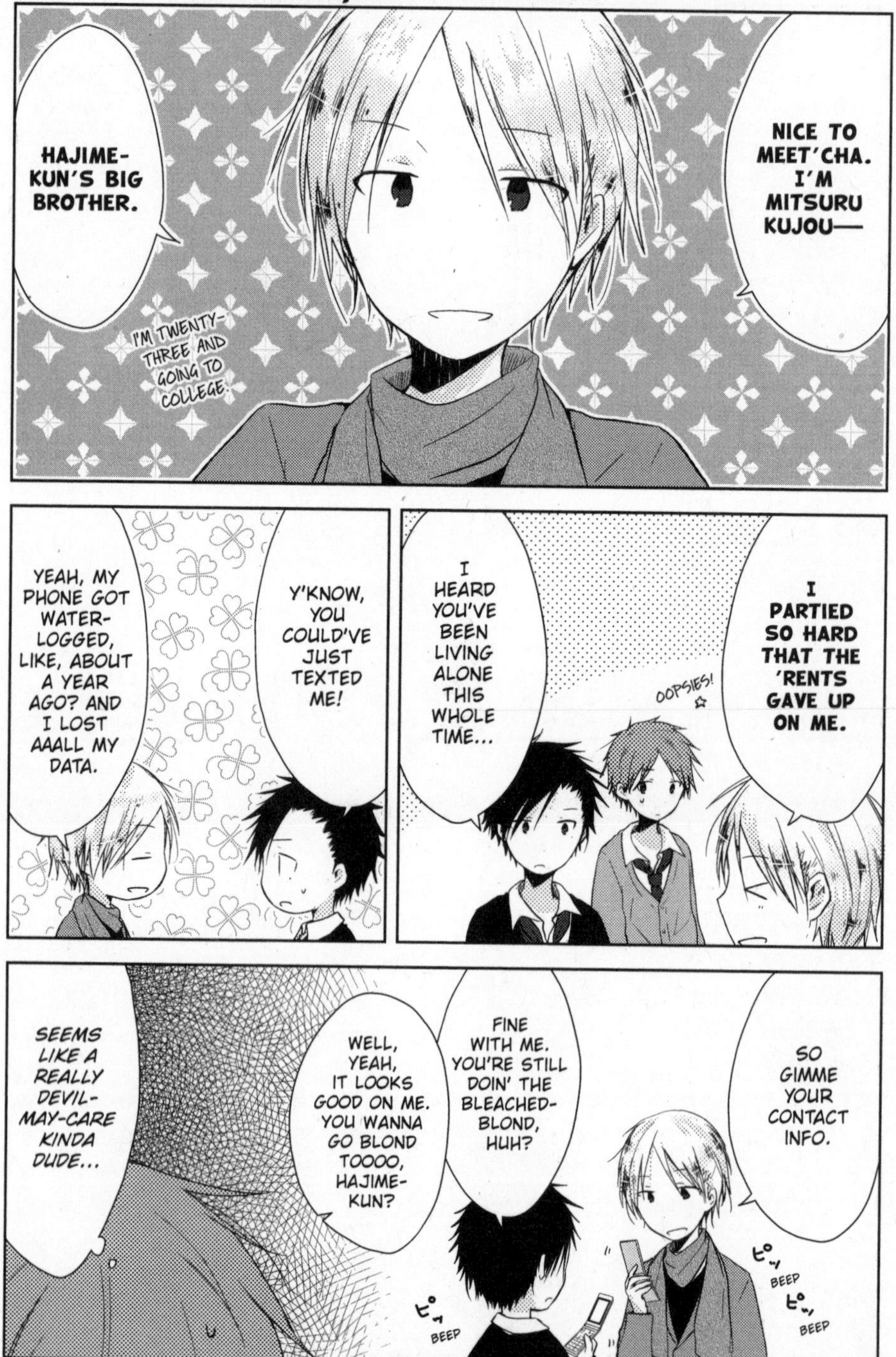
NICE TO MEET'CHA. I'M MITSURU KUJOU—
HAJIME-KUN'S BIG BROTHER.
I'M TWENTY-THREE AND GOING TO COLLEGE.
I PARTIED SO HARD THAT THE 'RENTS GAVE UP ON ME.
OOPSIES!
I HEARD YOU'VE BEEN LIVING ALONE THIS WHOLE TIME...
Y'KNOW, YOU COULD'VE JUST TEXTED ME!
YEAH, MY PHONE GOT WATER-LOGGED, LIKE, ABOUT A YEAR AGO? AND I LOST AAALL MY DATA.
SO GIMME YOUR CONTACT INFO.
ピッ BEEP
ピッ BEEP
FINE WITH ME. YOU'RE STILL DOIN' THE BLEACHED-BLOND, HUH?
WELL, YEAH, IT LOOKS GOOD ON ME. YOU WANNA GO BLOND TOOOO, HAJIME-KUN?
ピッ BEEP
SEEMS LIKE A REALLY DEVIL-MAY-CARE KINDA DUDE...

LIVING WELL

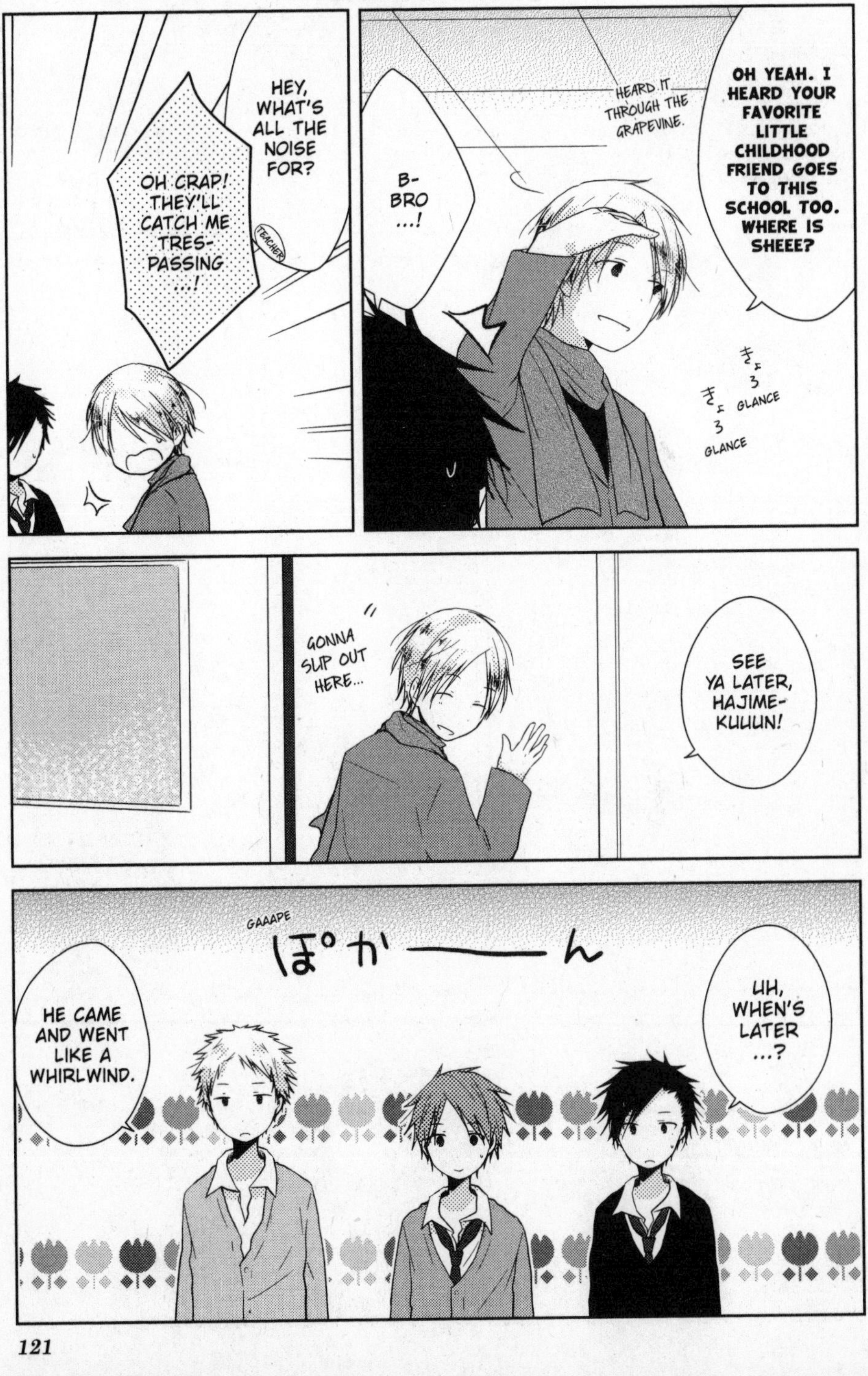
OH YEAH. I HEARD YOUR FAVORITE LITTLE CHILDHOOD FRIEND GOES TO THIS SCHOOL TOO. WHERE IS SHEEE?
HEARD IT THROUGH THE GRAPEVINE.
B-BRO ...!
きょろ GLANCE
きょろ GLANCE
HEY, WHAT'S ALL THE NOISE FOR?
TEACHER
OH CRAP! THEY'LL CATCH ME TRES-PASSING ...!
SEE YA LATER, HAJIME-KUUUN!
GONNA SLIP OUT HERE...
UH, WHEN'S LATER ...?
GAAAPE
ぽかーーん
HE CAME AND WENT LIKE A WHIRLWIND.

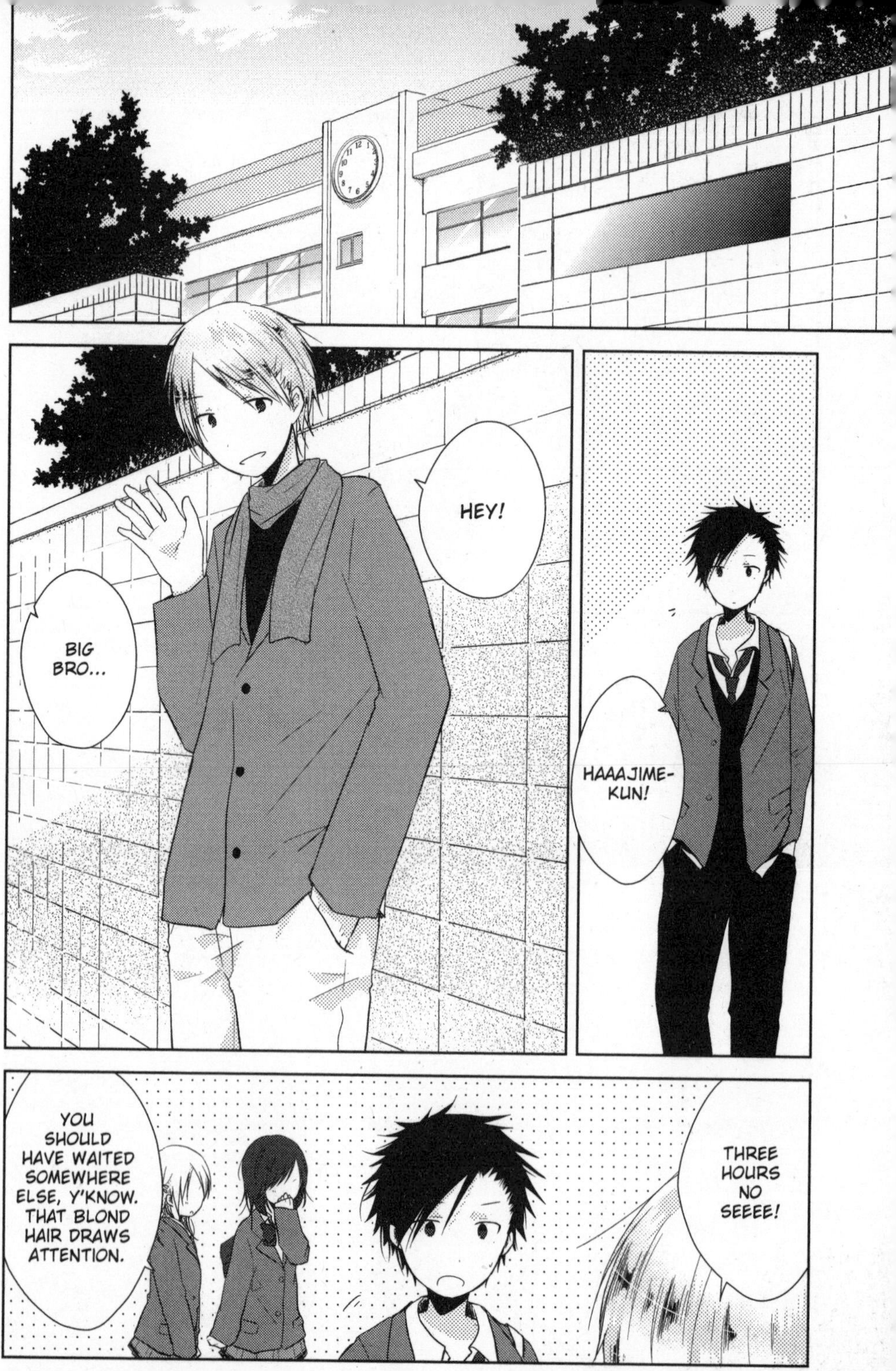
HAAAJIME-KUN!
HEY!
BIG BRO...
THREE HOURS NO SEEEE!
YOU SHOULD HAVE WAITED SOMEWHERE ELSE, Y'KNOW. THAT BLOND HAIR DRAWS ATTENTION.

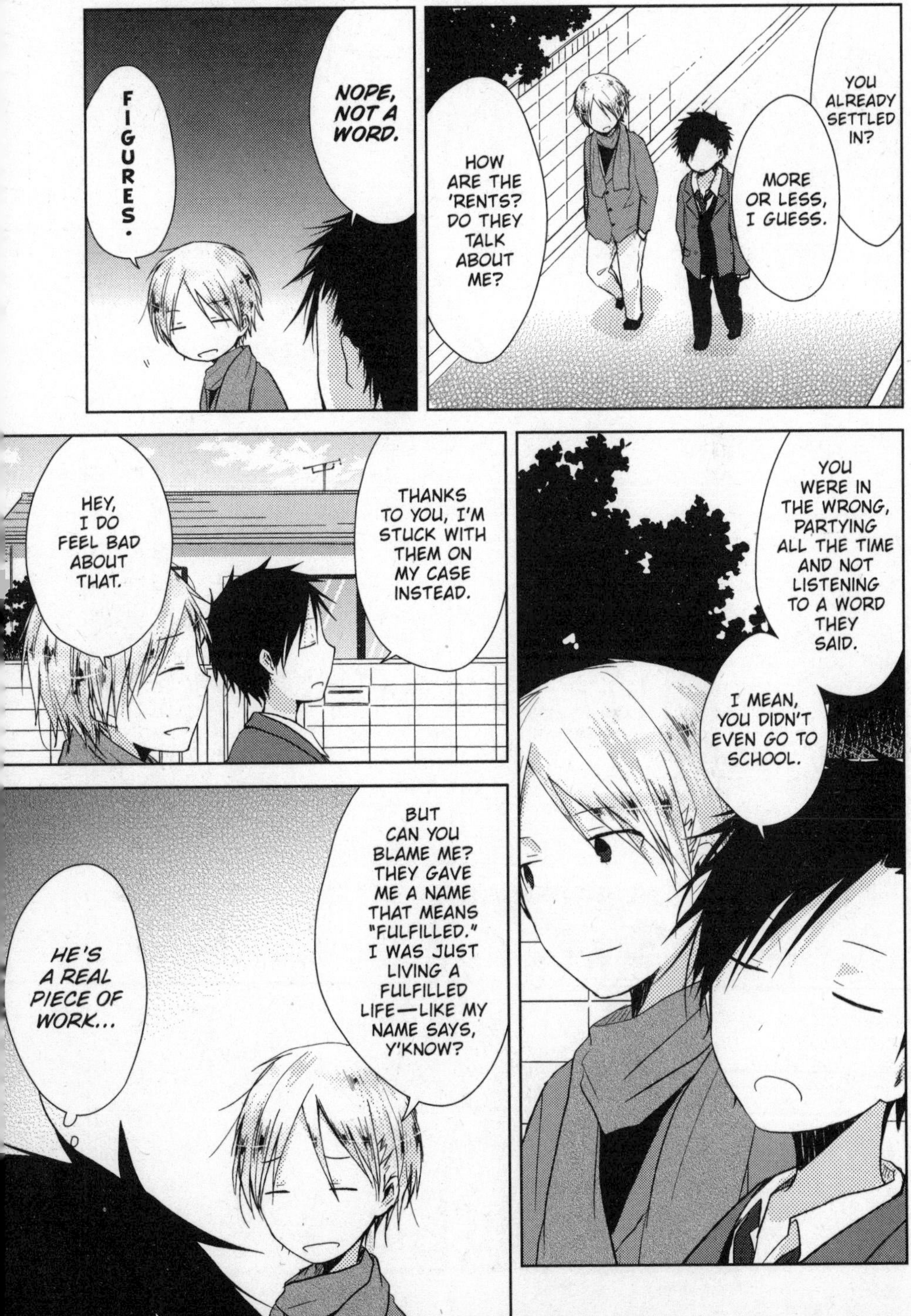
YOU ALREADY SETTLED IN?
MORE OR LESS, I GUESS.
HOW ARE THE 'RENTS? DO THEY TALK ABOUT ME?
NOPE, NOT A WORD.
FIGURES.
YOU WERE IN THE WRONG, PARTYING ALL THE TIME AND NOT LISTENING TO A WORD THEY SAID.
I MEAN, YOU DIDN'T EVEN GO TO SCHOOL.
THANKS TO YOU, I'M STUCK WITH THEM ON MY CASE INSTEAD.
HEY, I DO FEEL BAD ABOUT THAT.
BUT CAN YOU BLAME ME? THEY GAVE ME A NAME THAT MEANS "FULFILLED." I WAS JUST LIVING A FULFILLED LIFE—LIKE MY NAME SAYS, Y'KNOW?
HE'S A REAL PIECE OF WORK...

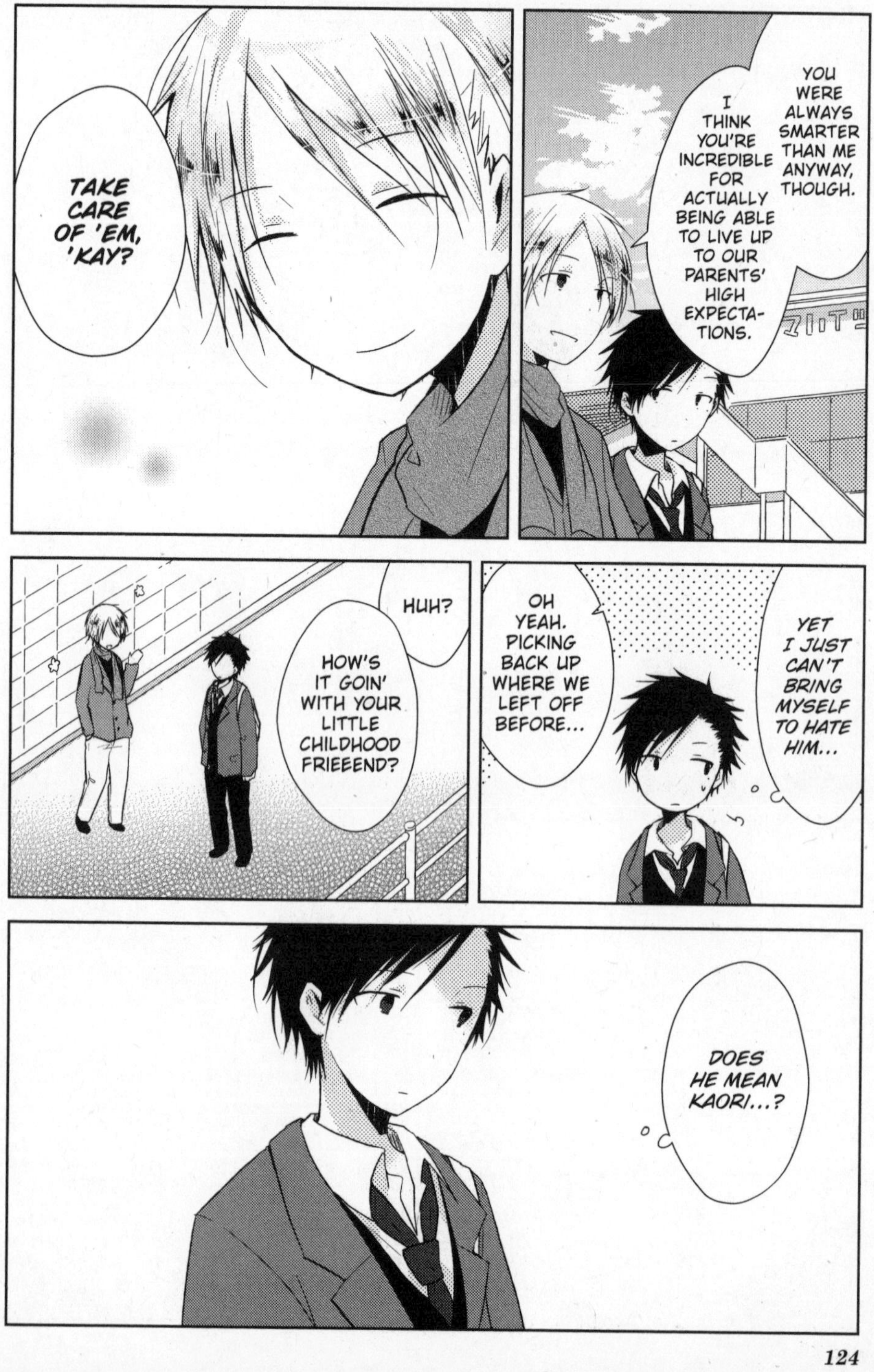
YOU WERE ALWAYS SMARTER THAN ME ANYWAY, THOUGH.
I THINK YOU'RE INCREDIBLE FOR ACTUALLY BEING ABLE TO LIVE UP TO OUR PARENTS' HIGH EXPECTATIONS.
TAKE CARE OF 'EM, 'KAY?
YET I JUST CAN'T BRING MYSELF TO HATE HIM...
OH YEAH. PICKING BACK UP WHERE WE LEFT OFF BEFORE...
HUH?
HOW'S IT GOIN' WITH YOUR LITTLE CHILDHOOD FRIEEEND?
DOES HE MEAN KAORI...?

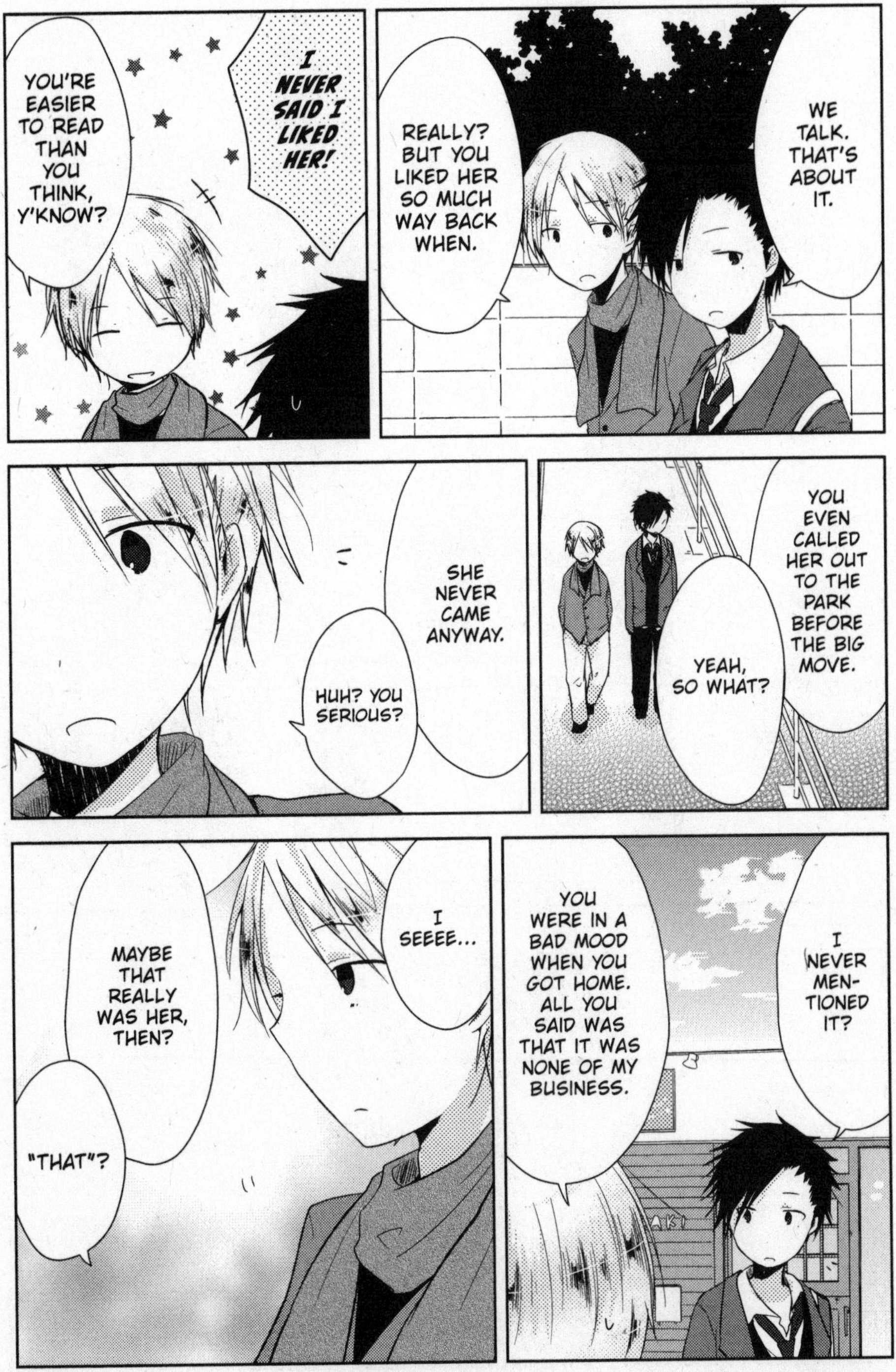
WE TALK. THAT'S ABOUT IT.
REALLY? BUT YOU LIKED HER SO MUCH WAY BACK WHEN.
I NEVER SAID I LIKED HER!
YOU'RE EASIER TO READ THAN YOU THINK, Y'KNOW?
YOU EVEN CALLED HER OUT TO THE PARK BEFORE THE BIG MOVE.
YEAH, SO WHAT?
SHE NEVER CAME ANYWAY.
HUH? YOU SERIOUS?
I NEVER MEN-TIONED IT?
YOU WERE IN A BAD MOOD WHEN YOU GOT HOME. ALL YOU SAID WAS THAT IT WAS NONE OF MY BUSINESS.
I SEEEE...
MAYBE THAT REALLY WAS HER, THEN?
"THAT"?

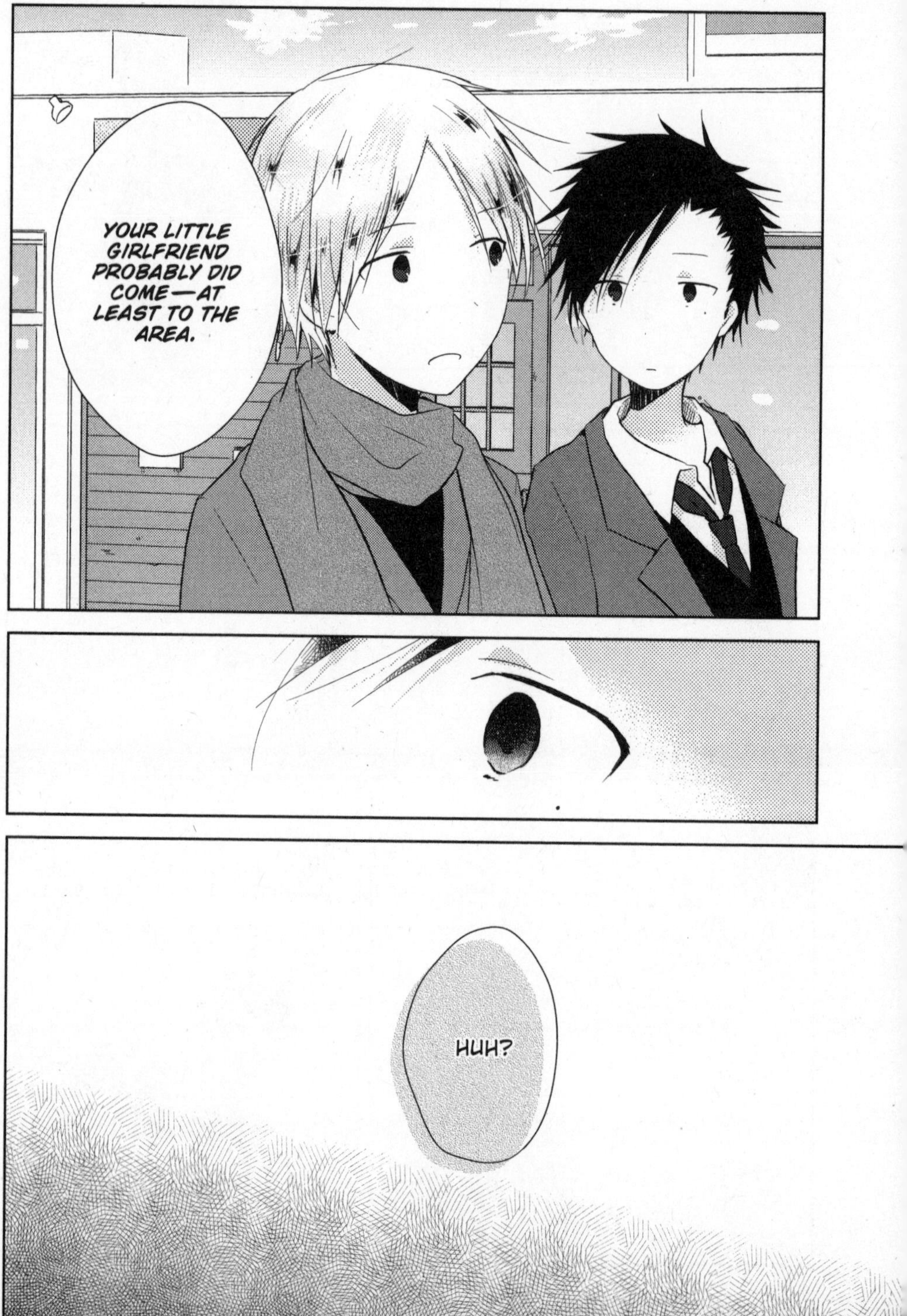
YOUR LITTLE GIRLFRIEND PROBABLY DID COME—AT LEAST TO THE AREA.
HUH?

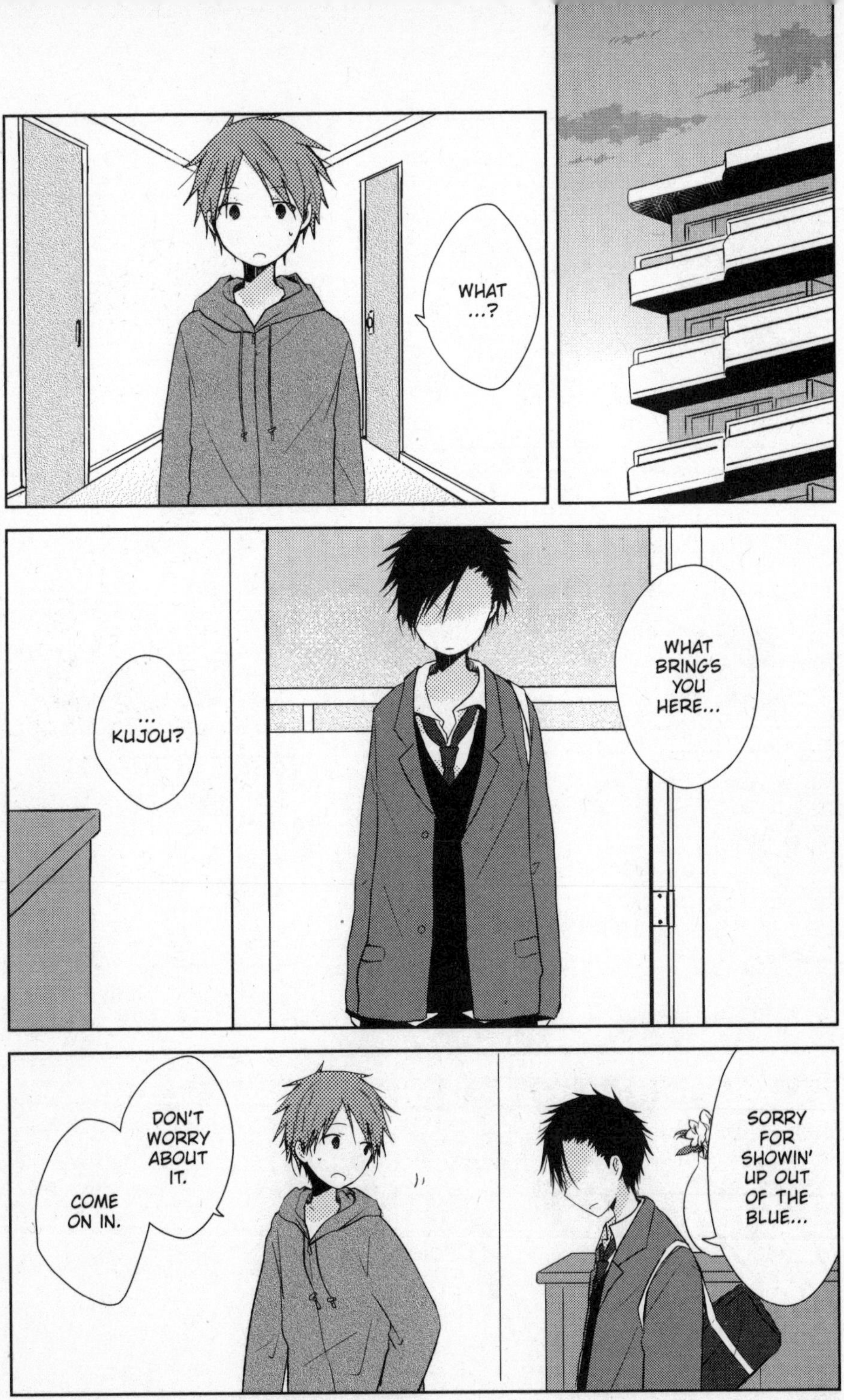
WHAT ...?
WHAT BRINGS YOU HERE...
... KUJOU?
SORRY FOR SHOWIN' UP OUT OF THE BLUE...
DON'T WORRY ABOUT IT.
COME ON IN.

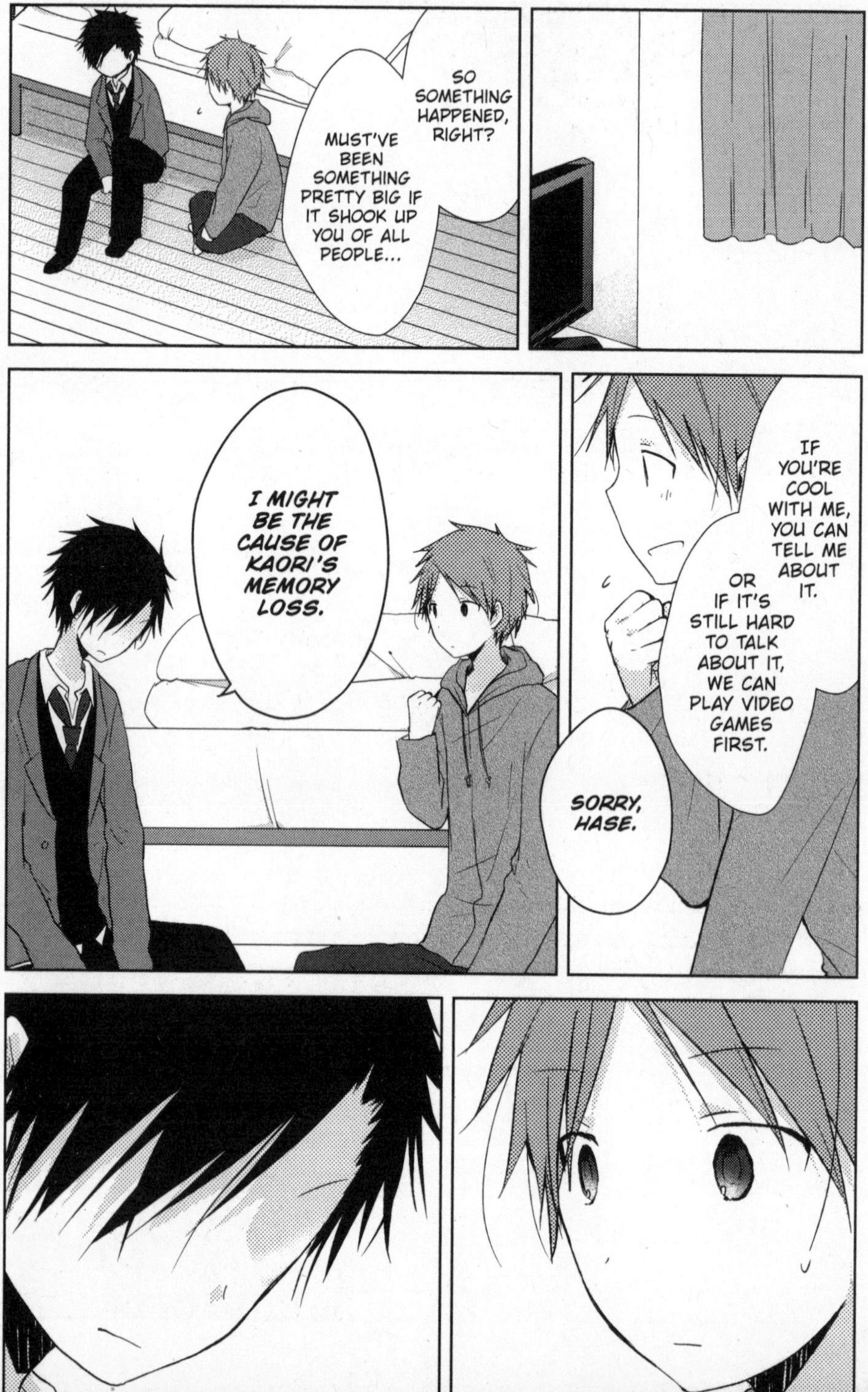
SO SOMETHING HAPPENED, RIGHT?
MUST'VE BEEN SOMETHING PRETTY BIG IF IT SHOOK UP YOU OF ALL PEOPLE...
IF YOU'RE COOL WITH ME, YOU CAN TELL ME ABOUT IT.
OR IF IT'S STILL HARD TO TALK ABOUT IT, WE CAN PLAY VIDEO GAMES FIRST.
SORRY, HASE.
I MIGHT BE THE CAUSE OF KAORI'S MEMORY LOSS.

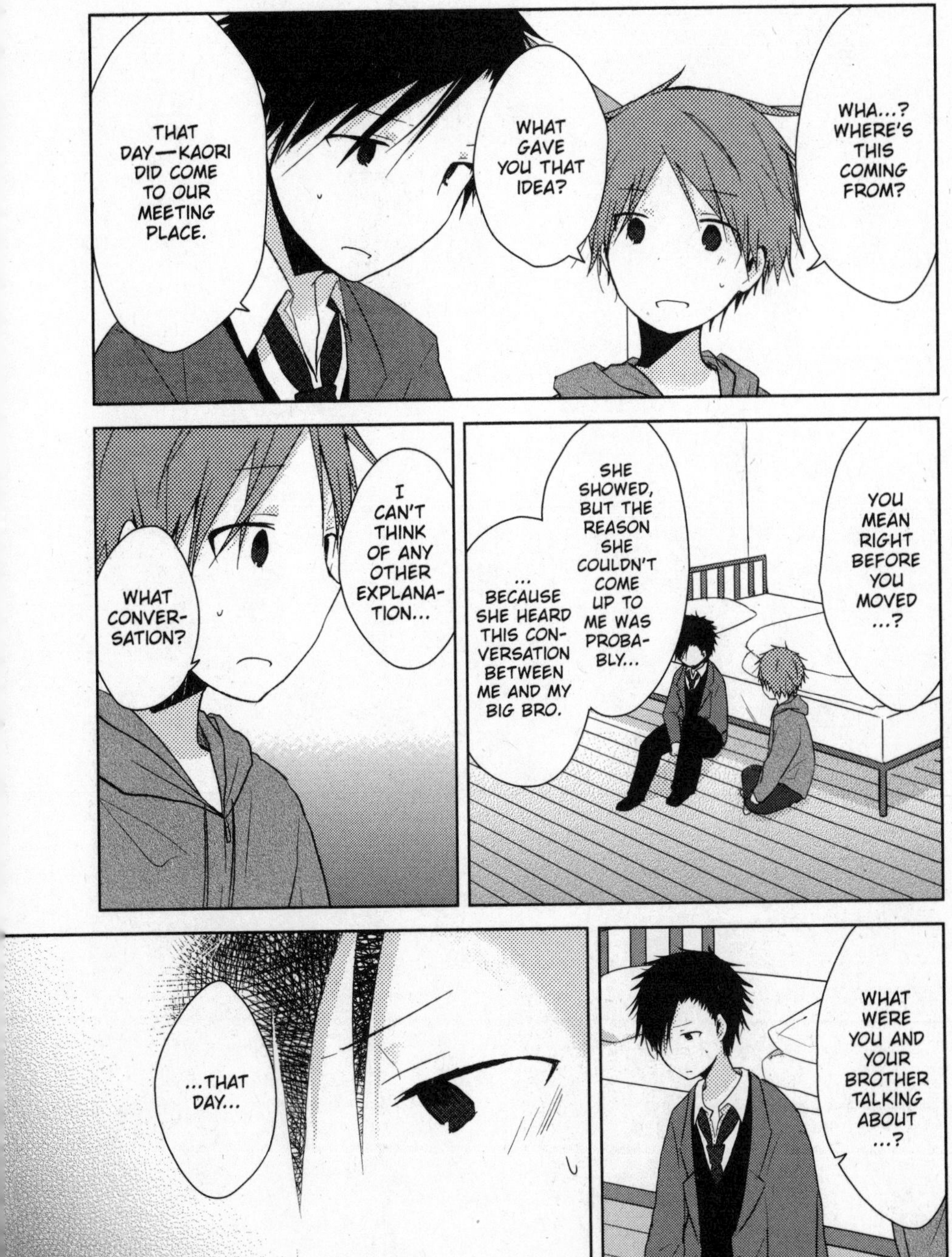
WHA...? WHERE'S THIS COMING FROM?
WHAT GAVE YOU THAT IDEA?
THAT DAY—KAORI DID COME TO OUR MEETING PLACE.
YOU MEAN RIGHT BEFORE YOU MOVED ...?
SHE SHOWED, BUT THE REASON SHE COULDN'T COME UP TO ME WAS PROBABLY...
... BECAUSE SHE HEARD THIS CONVERSATION BETWEEN ME AND MY BIG BRO.
I CAN'T THINK OF ANY OTHER EXPLANATION...
WHAT CONVERSATION?
WHAT WERE YOU AND YOUR BROTHER TALKING ABOUT ...?
...THAT DAY...

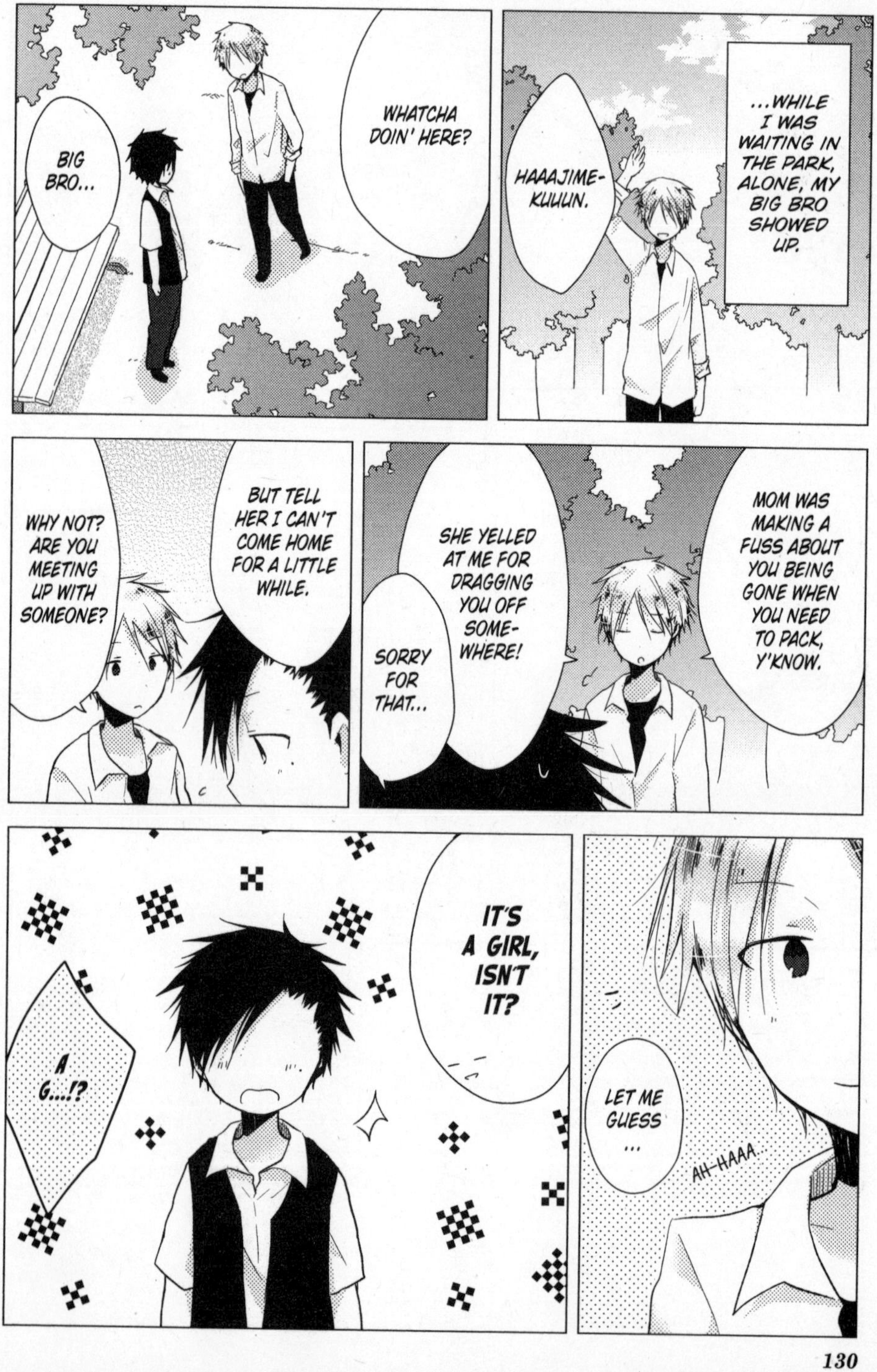
...WHILE I WAS WAITING IN THE PARK, ALONE, MY BIG BRO SHOWED UP.
HAAAJIME-KUUUN.
WHATCHA DOIN' HERE?
BIG BRO...
MOM WAS MAKING A FUSS ABOUT YOU BEING GONE WHEN YOU NEED TO PACK, Y'KNOW.
SHE YELLED AT ME FOR DRAGGING YOU OFF SOME-WHERE!
SORRY FOR THAT...
BUT TELL HER I CAN'T COME HOME FOR A LITTLE WHILE.
WHY NOT? ARE YOU MEETING UP WITH SOMEONE?
AH-HAAA...
LET ME GUESS...
IT'S A GIRL, ISN'T IT?
A G...!?

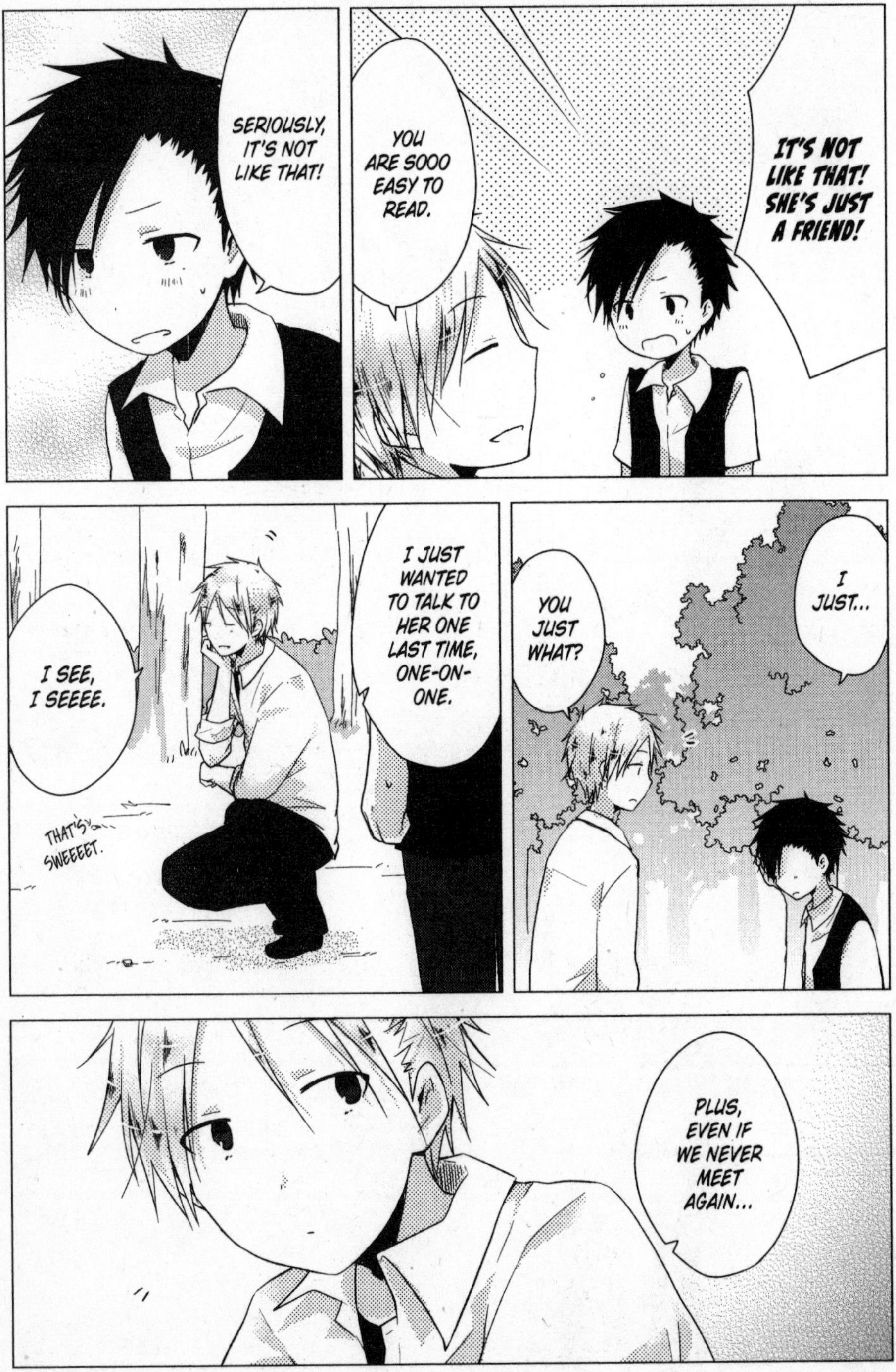
IT'S NOT LIKE THAT! SHE'S JUST A FRIEND!
YOU ARE SOOO EASY TO READ.
SERIOUSLY, IT'S NOT LIKE THAT!
I JUST...
YOU JUST WHAT?
I JUST WANTED TO TALK TO HER ONE LAST TIME, ONE-ON-ONE.
I SEE, I SEEEE.
THAT'S SWEEEET.
PLUS, EVEN IF WE NEVER MEET AGAIN...

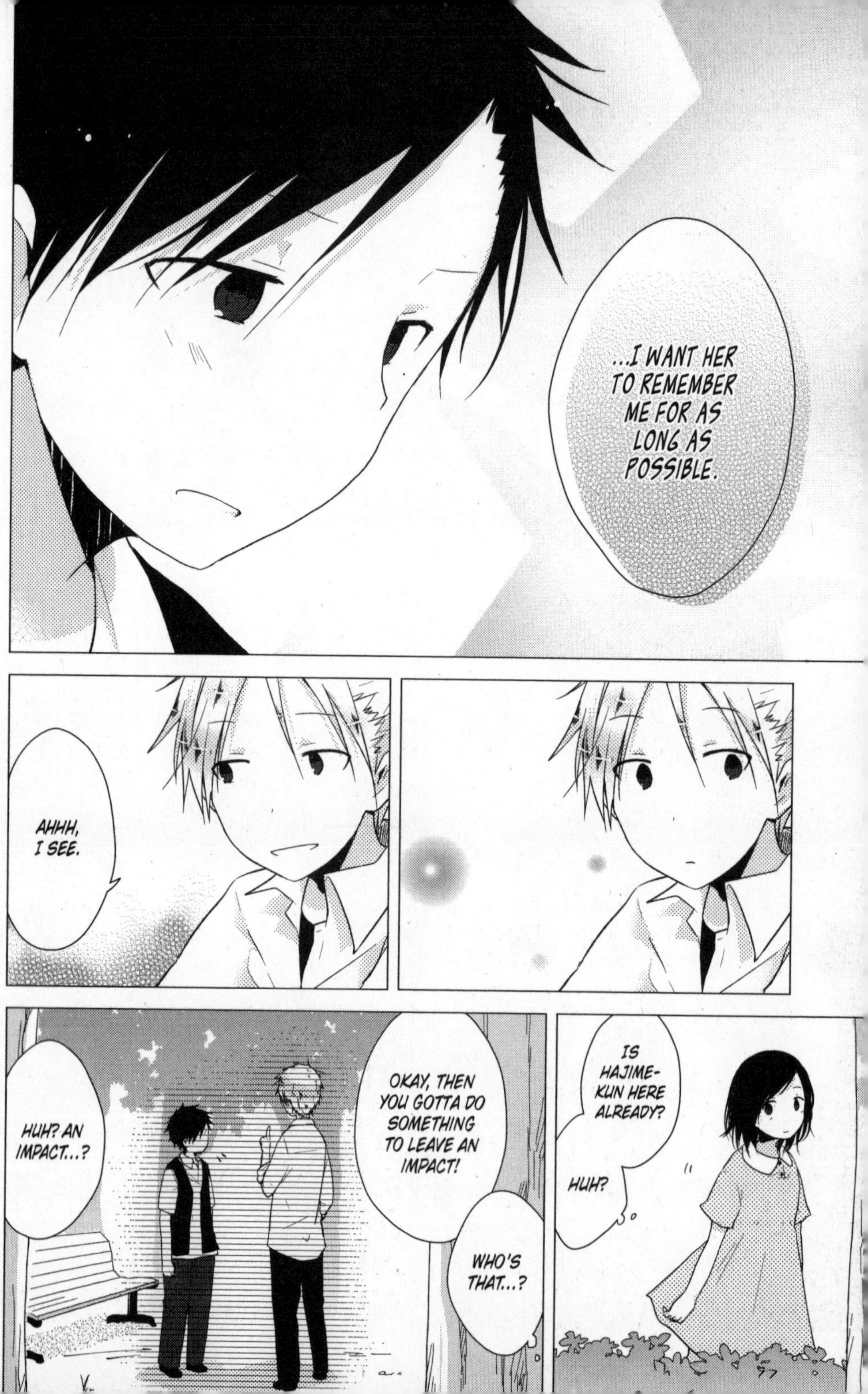
...I WANT HER TO REMEMBER ME FOR AS LONG AS POSSIBLE.
AHHH, I SEE.
IS HAJIME-KUN HERE ALREADY?
HUH?
OKAY, THEN YOU GOTTA DO SOMETHING TO LEAVE AN IMPACT!
WHO'S THAT...?
HUH? AN IMPACT...?

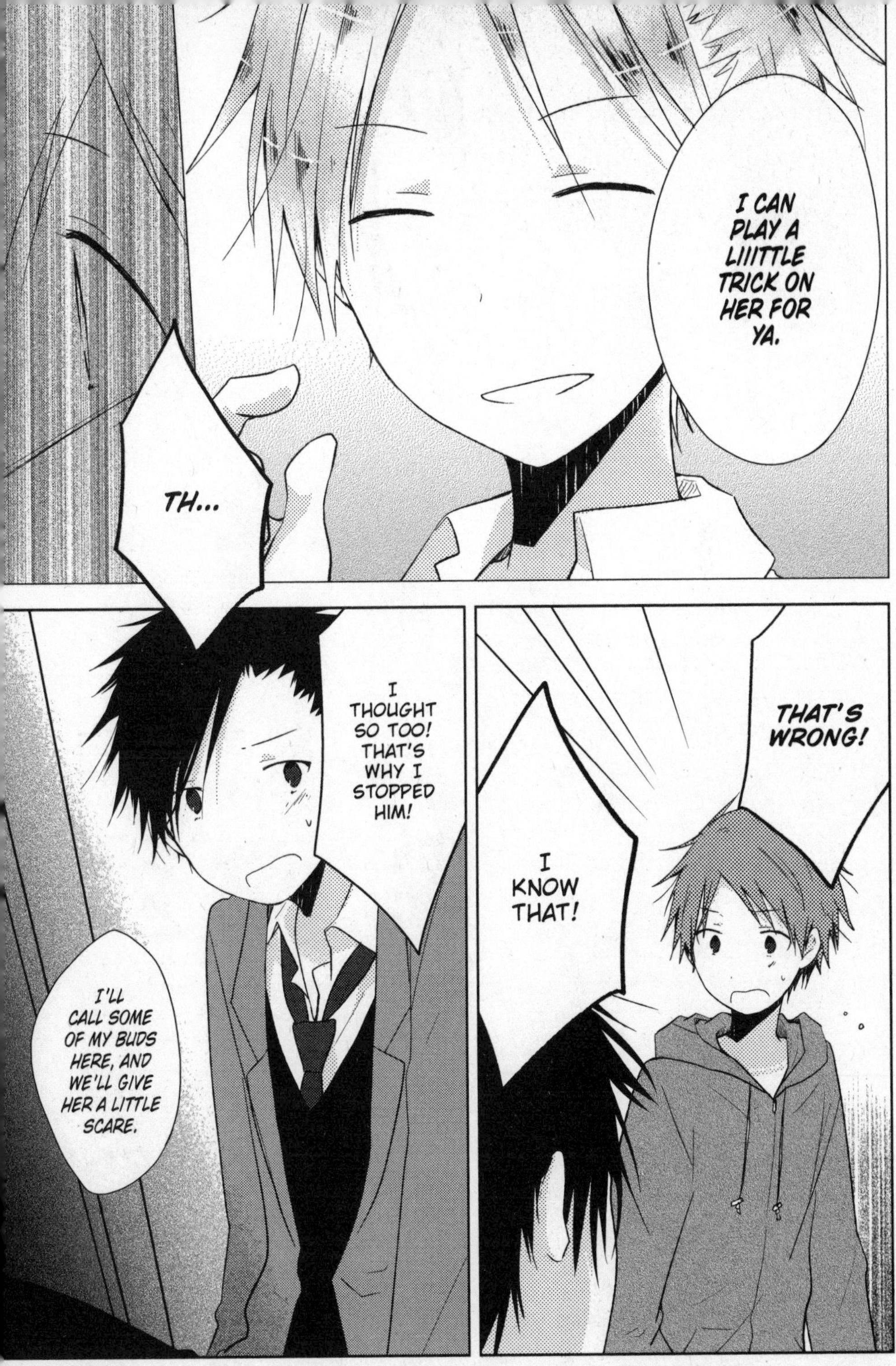
I CAN PLAY A LIIITTLE TRICK ON HER FOR YA.
TH...
THAT'S WRONG!
I KNOW THAT!
I THOUGHT SO TOO! THAT'S WHY I STOPPED HIM!
I'LL CALL SOME OF MY BUDS HERE, AND WE'LL GIVE HER A LITTLE SCARE.

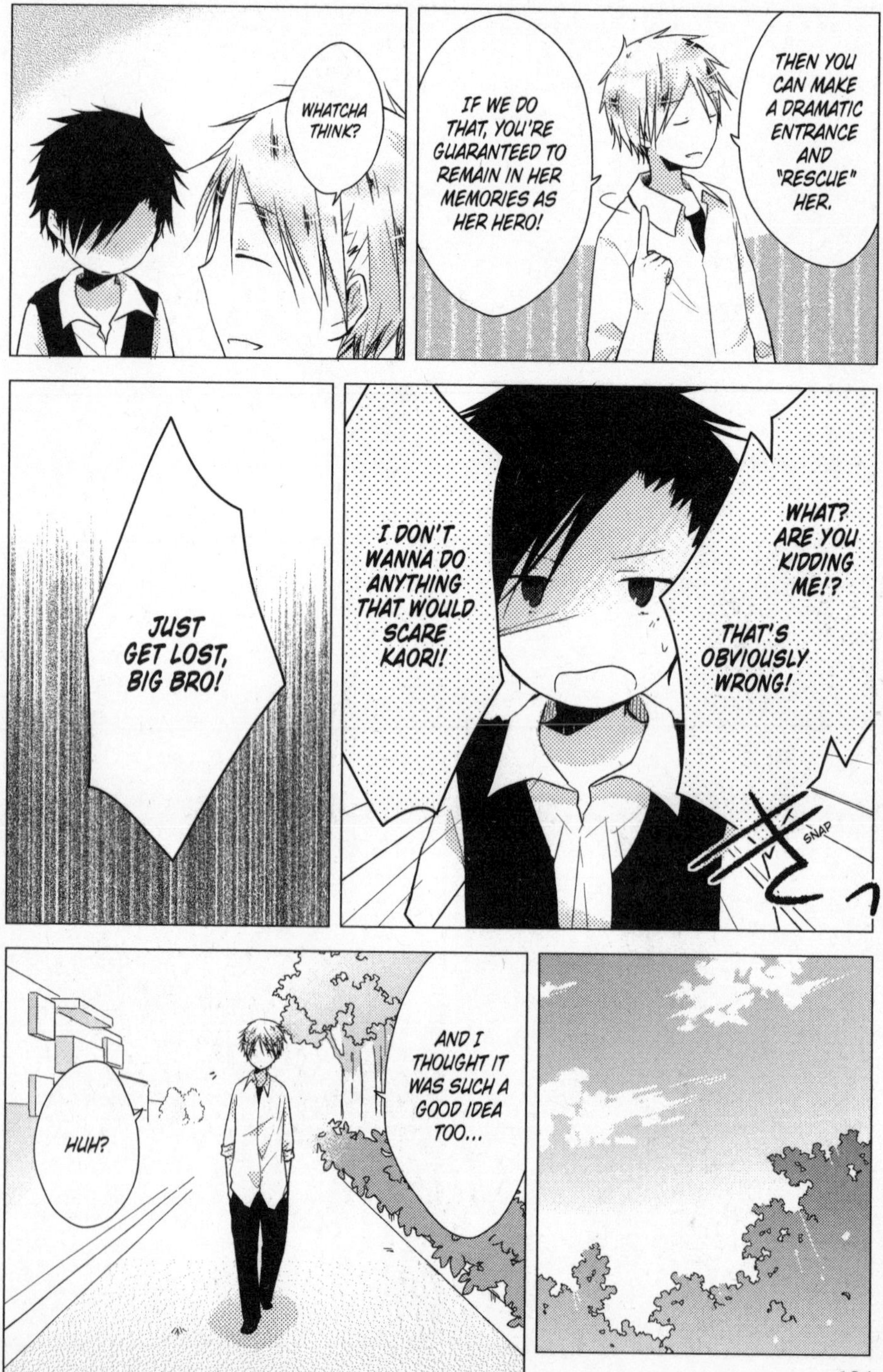
THEN YOU CAN MAKE A DRAMATIC ENTRANCE AND "RESCUE" HER.
IF WE DO THAT, YOU'RE GUARANTEED TO REMAIN IN HER MEMORIES AS HER HERO!
WHATCHA THINK?
WHAT? ARE YOU KIDDING ME!?
THAT'S OBVIOUSLY WRONG!
I DON'T WANNA DO ANYTHING THAT WOULD SCARE KAORI!
SNAP
JUST GET LOST, BIG BRO!
AND I THOUGHT IT WAS SUCH A GOOD IDEA TOO...
HUH?

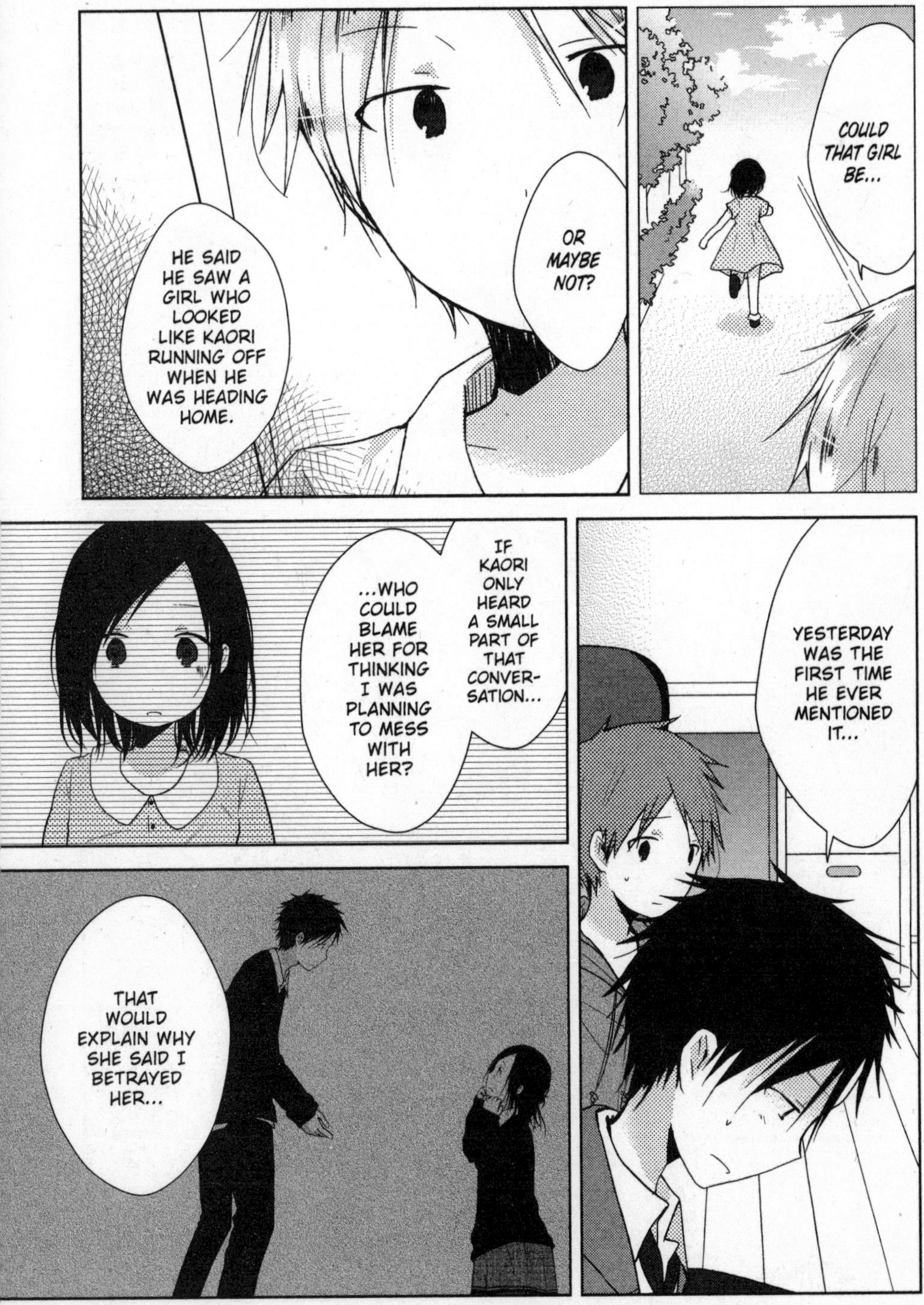
COULD THAT GIRL BE...
OR MAYBE NOT?
HE SAID HE SAW A GIRL WHO LOOKED LIKE KAORI RUNNING OFF WHEN HE WAS HEADING HOME.
YESTERDAY WAS THE FIRST TIME HE EVER MENTIONED IT...
IF KAORI ONLY HEARD A SMALL PART OF THAT CONVER-SATION...
...WHO COULD BLAME HER FOR THINKING I WAS PLANNING TO MESS WITH HER?
THAT WOULD EXPLAIN WHY SHE SAID I BETRAYED HER...

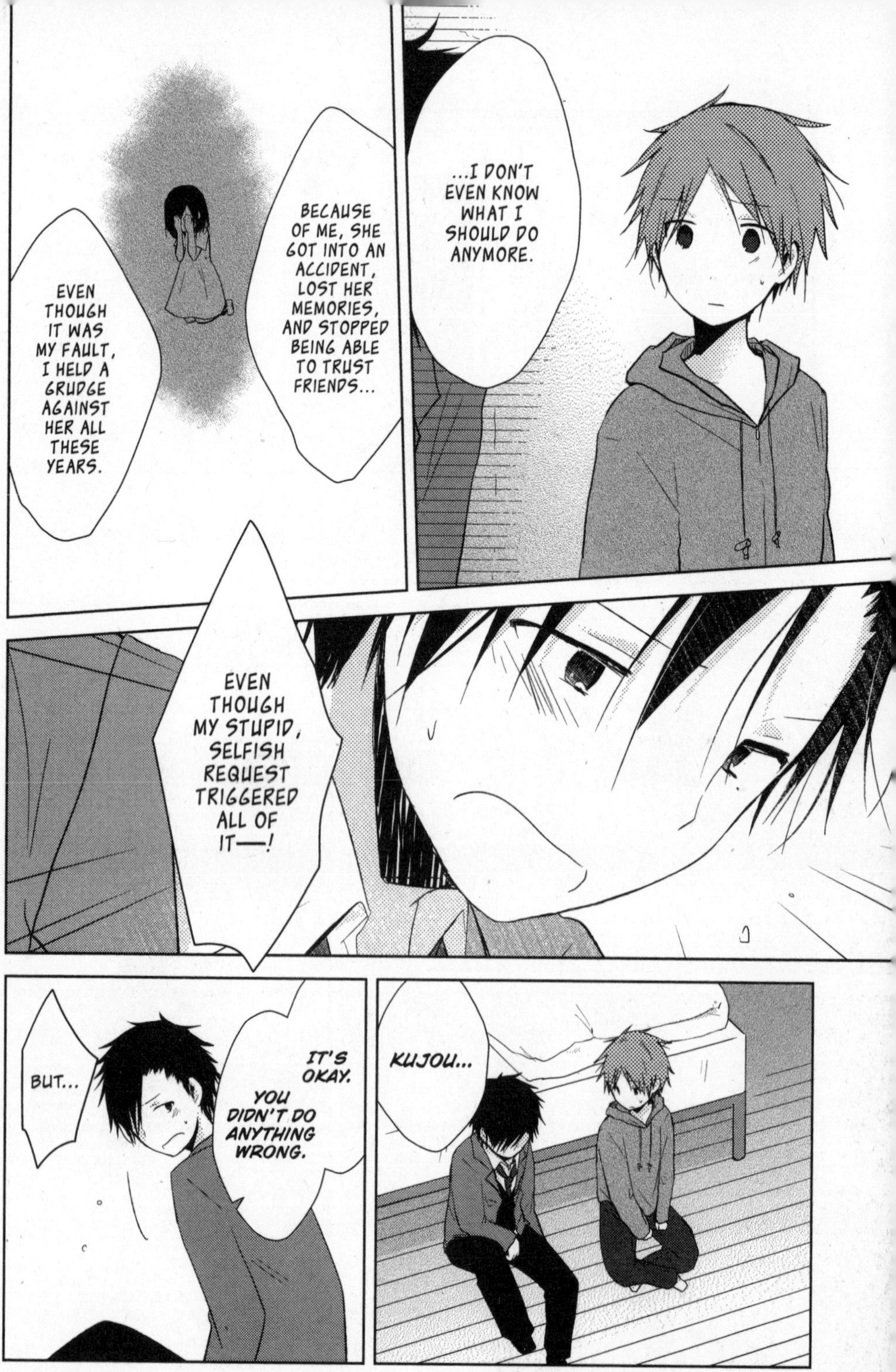
...I DON'T EVEN KNOW WHAT I SHOULD DO ANYMORE.
BECAUSE OF ME, SHE GOT INTO AN ACCIDENT, LOST HER MEMORIES, AND STOPPED BEING ABLE TO TRUST FRIENDS...
EVEN THOUGH IT WAS MY FAULT, I HELD A GRUDGE AGAINST HER ALL THESE YEARS.
EVEN THOUGH MY STUPID, SELFISH REQUEST TRIGGERED ALL OF IT—!
KUJOU...
IT'S OKAY.
YOU DIDN'T DO ANYTHING WRONG.
BUT...

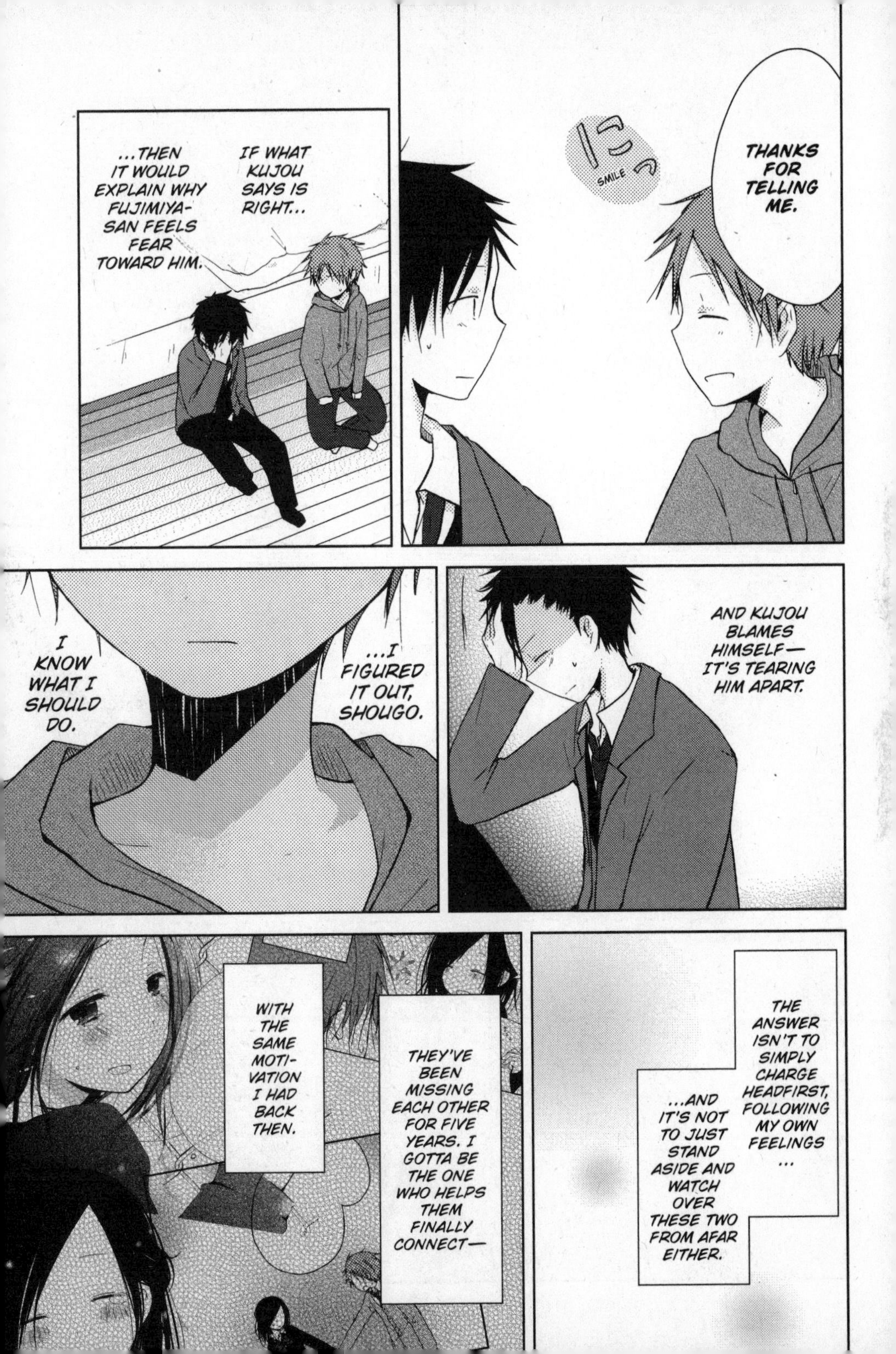

SMILE
THANKS FOR TELLING ME.
IF WHAT KUJOU SAYS IS RIGHT...
...THEN IT WOULD EXPLAIN WHY FUJIMIYA-SAN FEELS FEAR TOWARD HIM.
AND KUJOU BLAMES HIMSELF—IT'S TEARING HIM APART.
...I FIGURED IT OUT, SHOUGO.
I KNOW WHAT I SHOULD DO.
THE ANSWER ISN'T TO SIMPLY CHARGE HEADFIRST, FOLLOWING MY OWN FEELINGS...
...AND IT'S NOT TO JUST STAND ASIDE AND WATCH OVER THESE TWO FROM AFAR EITHER.
THEY'VE BEEN MISSING EACH OTHER FOR FIVE YEARS. I GOTTA BE THE ONE WHO HELPS THEM FINALLY CONNECT—
WITH THE SAME MOTIVATION I HAD BACK THEN.

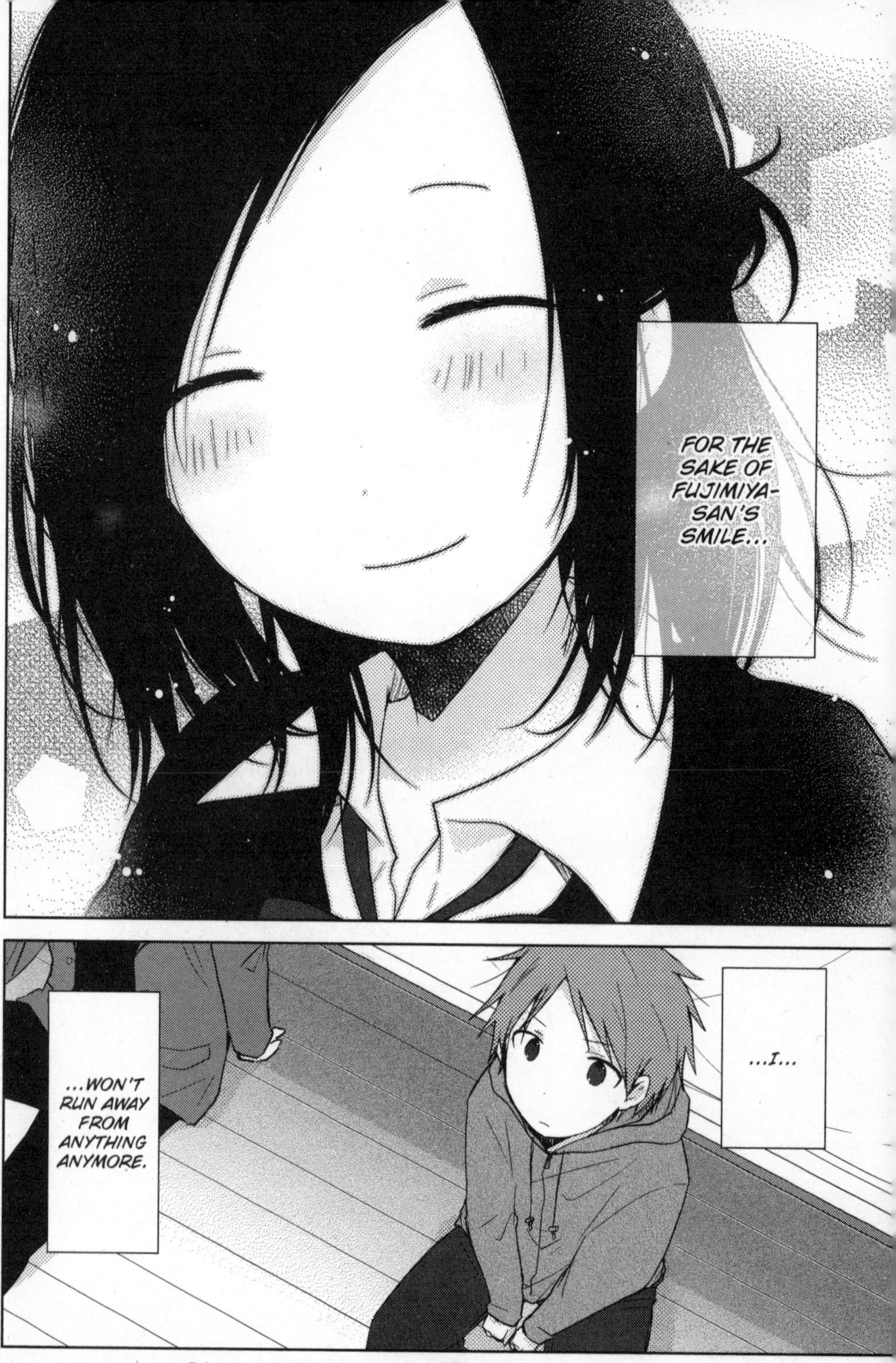
FOR THE SAKE OF FUJIMIYA-SAN'S SMILE...
...I...
...WON'T RUN AWAY FROM ANYTHING ANYMORE.

ONE WEEK FRIENDS 6 END

ONE
WEEK
FRIENDS

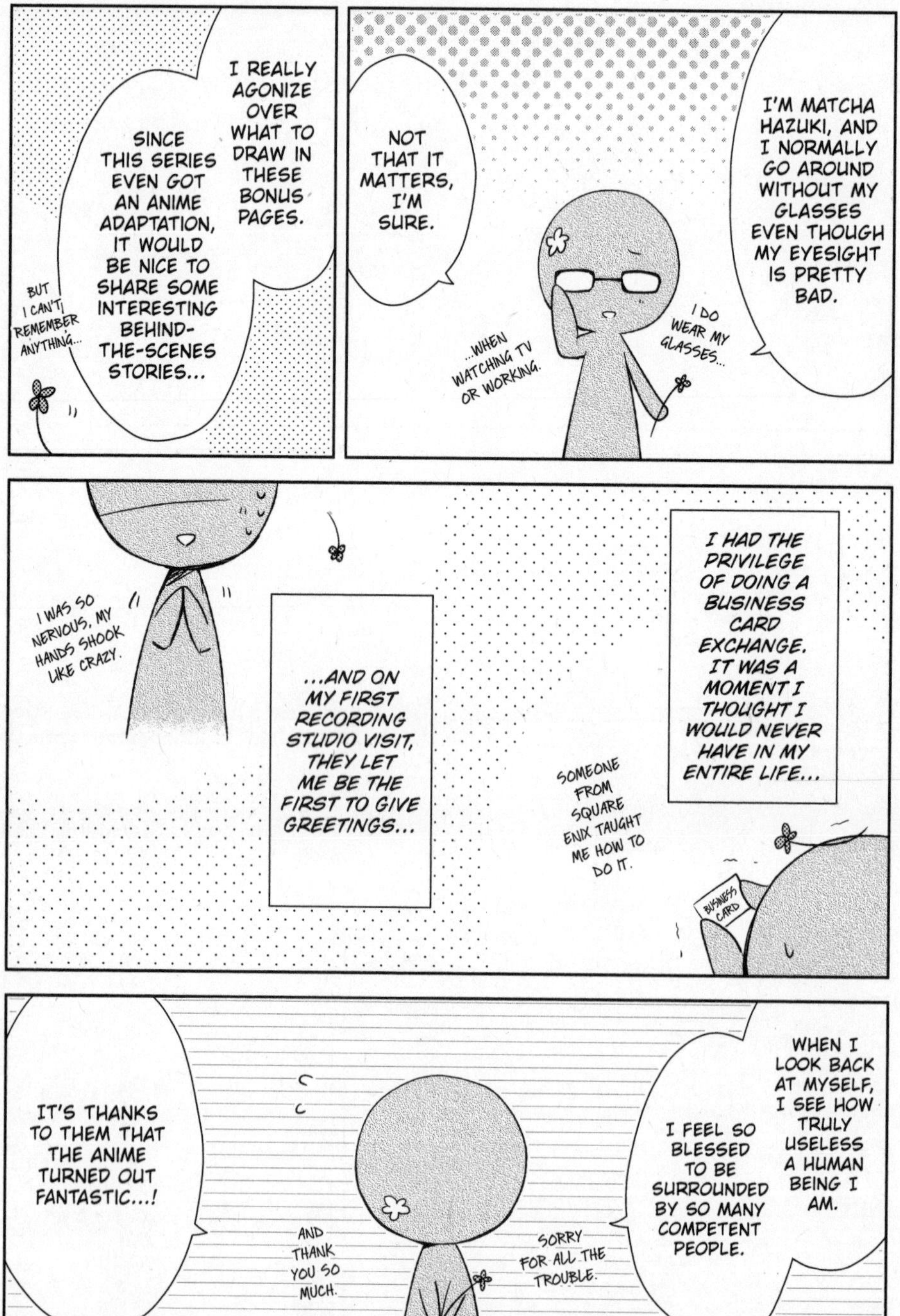
I'M MATCHA HAZUKI, AND I NORMALLY GO AROUND WITHOUT MY GLASSES EVEN THOUGH MY EYESIGHT IS PRETTY BAD.
I DO WEAR MY GLASSES...
...WHEN WATCHING TV OR WORKING.
NOT THAT IT MATTERS, I'M SURE.
I REALLY AGONIZE OVER WHAT TO DRAW IN THESE BONUS PAGES.
SINCE THIS SERIES EVEN GOT AN ANIME ADAPTATION, IT WOULD BE NICE TO SHARE SOME INTERESTING BEHIND-THE-SCENES STORIES...
BUT I CAN'T REMEMBER ANYTHING...
I HAD THE PRIVILEGE OF DOING A BUSINESS CARD EXCHANGE. IT WAS A MOMENT I THOUGHT I WOULD NEVER HAVE IN MY ENTIRE LIFE...
SOMEONE FROM SQUARE ENIX TAUGHT ME HOW TO DO IT.
BUSINESS CARD
...AND ON MY FIRST RECORDING STUDIO VISIT, THEY LET ME BE THE FIRST TO GIVE GREETINGS...
I WAS SO NERVOUS, MY HANDS SHOOK LIKE CRAZY.
WHEN I LOOK BACK AT MYSELF, I SEE HOW TRULY USELESS A HUMAN BEING I AM.
I FEEL SO BLESSED TO BE SURROUNDED BY SO MANY COMPETENT PEOPLE.
SORRY FOR ALL THE TROUBLE.
AND THANK YOU SO MUCH.
IT'S THANKS TO THEM THAT THE ANIME TURNED OUT FANTASTIC...!

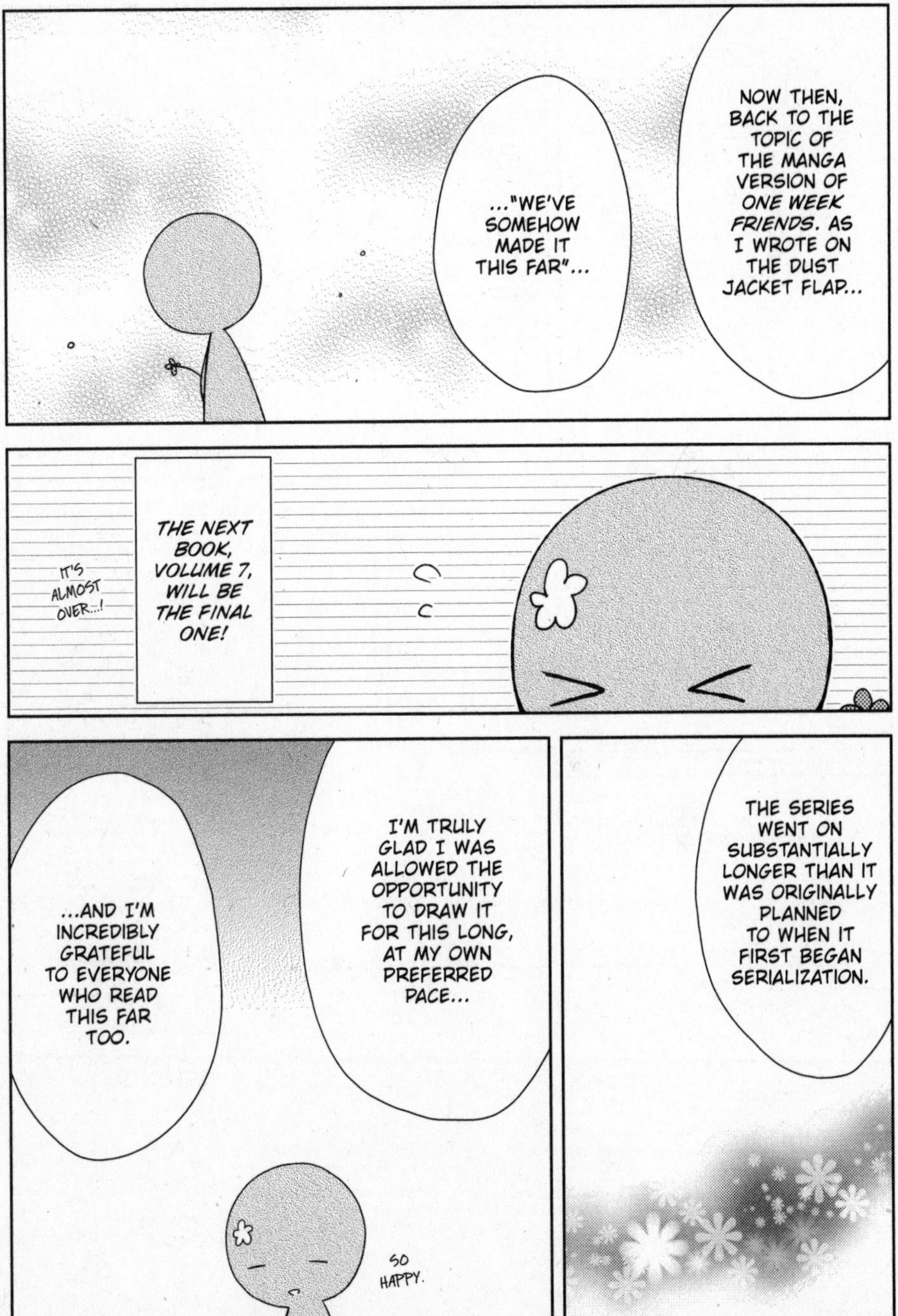
NOW THEN, BACK TO THE TOPIC OF THE MANGA VERSION OF *ONE WEEK FRIENDS*. AS I WROTE ON THE DUST JACKET FLAP...
..."WE'VE SOMEHOW MADE IT THIS FAR"...
THE NEXT BOOK, VOLUME 7, WILL BE THE FINAL ONE!
IT'S ALMOST OVER...!
THE SERIES WENT ON SUBSTANTIALLY LONGER THAN IT WAS ORIGINALLY PLANNED TO WHEN IT FIRST BEGAN SERIALIZATION.
I'M TRULY GLAD I WAS ALLOWED THE OPPORTUNITY TO DRAW IT FOR THIS LONG, AT MY OWN PREFERRED PACE...
...AND I'M INCREDIBLY GRATEFUL TO EVERYONE WHO READ THIS FAR TOO.
SO HAPPY.

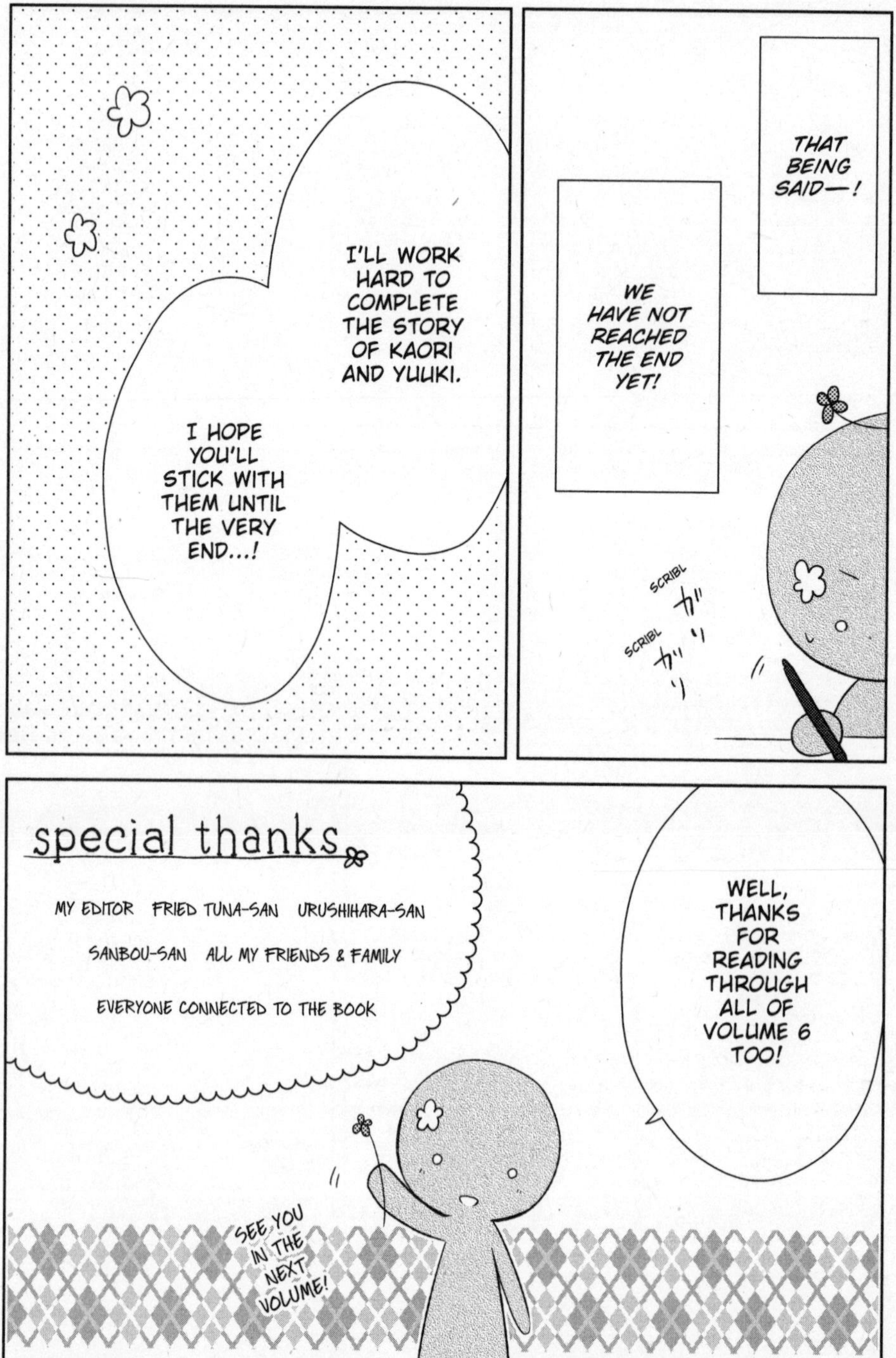
THAT BEING SAID—!
WE HAVE NOT REACHED THE END YET!
ガリ
SCRIBL
ガリ
SCRIBL
I'LL WORK HARD TO COMPLETE THE STORY OF KAORI AND YUUKI.
I HOPE YOU'LL STICK WITH THEM UNTIL THE VERY END...!
WELL, THANKS FOR READING THROUGH ALL OF VOLUME 6 TOO!
special thanks
MY EDITOR FRIED TUNA-SAN URUSHIHARA-SAN
SANBOU-SAN ALL MY FRIENDS & FAMILY
EVERYONE CONNECTED TO THE BOOK
SEE YOU IN THE NEXT VOLUME!

TRANSLATION NOTES

COMMON HONORIFICS

No honorific: Indicates familiarity or closeness; if used without permission or reason, addressing someone in this manner would constitute an insult.

-san: The Japanese equivalent of Mr./Mrs./Miss. If a situation calls for politeness, this is the fail-safe honorific.

-kun: Used most often when referring to boys, this indicates affection or familiarity. Occasionally used by older men among their peers, but it may also be used by anyone referring to a person of lower standing.

-chan: An affectionate honorific indicating familiarity used mostly in reference to girls; also used in reference to cute persons or animals of either gender.

-sensei: A respectful term for teachers, artists, or high-level professionals.

PAGE 20

Christmas is not really celebrated as a religious holiday in Japan, and people often spend it with their significant others or friends. If Yuuki's top priority is a romantic relationship with Kaori, you'd expect him to jump on the possibility of spending Christmas with her.

PAGE 26

In Japanese, the card game Concentration is called *Shinkiei Suijaku*, or literally, "Nervous Breakdown."

PAGE 47

Calling someone by their given name is usually reserved for the closest relationships—family, close friends, or a romantic partner. By asking Hajime to use her given name, Shiho is probably enjoying the fantasy of having the attention of a younger man.

PAGE 116

In Japan, a set of special dishes called *osechi* are cooked for the New Year's celebrations. Each dish is symbolic. Another part of the Japanese New Year is *hatsumoude*, the year's first visit to a Shinto shrine (or Buddhist temple), usually made within the first few days of the year.

PAGE 120

Bleached-blond hair is commonly associated with youth delinquency in Japan, so one might suspect Mitsuru is trouble immediately based on his appearance.

PAGE 141

The Japanese version of *One Week Friends* has a dust jacket, and on the flap of this volume, the author wrote a short note, which says: "We're at volume 6—times flies. With the full realization of the difficulties of making something from my imagination into a manga, we've somehow made it this far. Somewhat unfortunate that we've gotten to this point already...I hope you enjoy this volume!"

SO LET'S BECOME FRIENDS ALL OVER AGAIN!

THE PAIR'S MEMORIES, GOING ROUND AND ROUND. THE PAIR'S RECORDS, IN WRITING BOUND.

WHAT DID I WANT FUJIMIYA-SAN AND I TO BE?

HASE-KUN. I KNOW YOU.

I WON'T LET YOU BE ALONE!

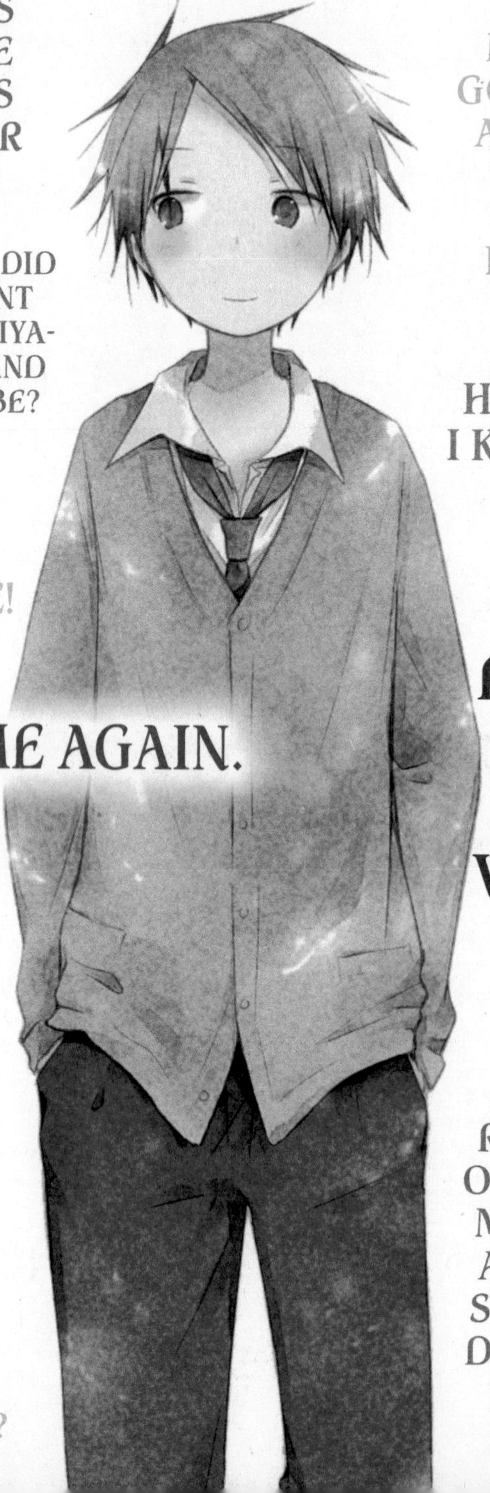

WITH ME AGAIN.

ONE WEEK FRIENDS 7, THE FINAL VOLUME.

I'LL ASK YOU AS MANY TIMES AS I HAVE TO.

FOR STARTERS, IT'S MORE LIKE YOU NOTICE YOU'RE FRIENDS AFTER THE FACT, RIGHT?

WE'LL REPEAT OUR ONE WEEK. AS MANY TIMES AS IT TAKES. SO THAT ONE DAY, WE'LL BE FRIENDS.

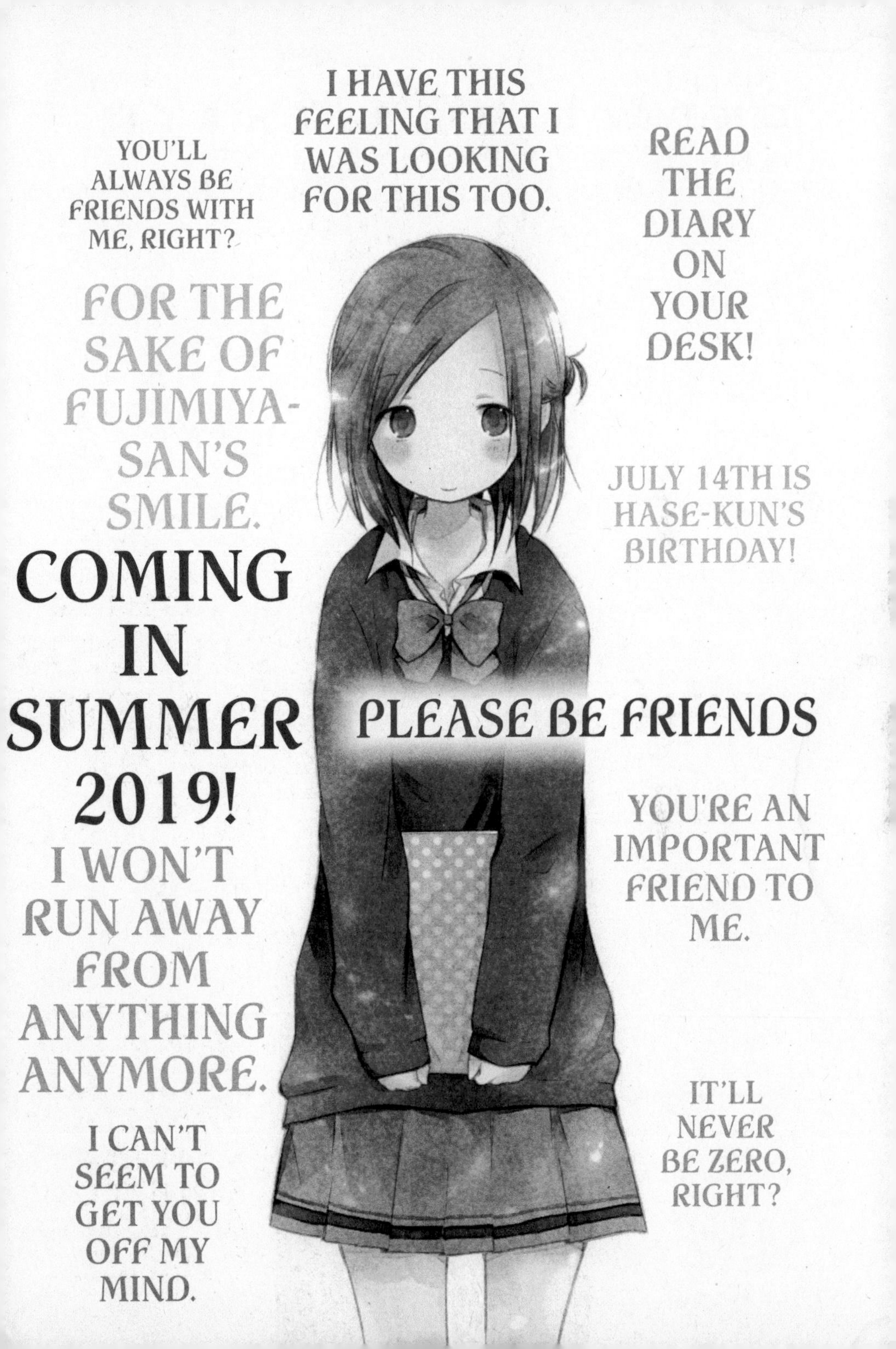
YOU'LL ALWAYS BE FRIENDS WITH ME, RIGHT?
I HAVE THIS FEELING THAT I WAS LOOKING FOR THIS TOO.
READ THE DIARY ON YOUR DESK!
FOR THE SAKE OF FUJIMIYA-SAN'S SMILE.
JULY 14TH IS HASE-KUN'S BIRTHDAY!
COMING IN SUMMER 2019!
PLEASE BE FRIENDS
I WON'T RUN AWAY FROM ANYTHING ANYMORE.
YOU'RE AN IMPORTANT FRIEND TO ME.
I CAN'T SEEM TO GET YOU OFF MY MIND.
IT'LL NEVER BE ZERO, RIGHT?

ONE WEEK FRIENDS 6

MATCHA HAZUKI

Translation/Adaptation: Amanda Haley

Lettering: Bianca Pistillo

ONE WEEK FRIENDS Volume 6 ©2014 Matcha Hazuki/ SQUARE ENIX CO., LTD. First published in Japan in 2014 by SQUARE ENIX CO., LTD. English translation rights arranged with SQUARE ENIX CO., LTD. and Yen Press, LLC through Tuttle-Mori Agency, Inc.

English translation © 2019 by SQUARE ENIX CO., LTD.

Yen Press
1290 Avenue of the Americas
New York, NY 10104

Visit us at yenpress.com
facebook.com/yenpress
twitter.com/yenpress
yenpress.tumblr.com
instagram.com/yenpress

First Yen Press Edition: March 2019

Yen Press is an imprint of Yen Press, LLC.
The Yen Press name and logo are trademarks of Yen Press, LLC.

The publisher is not responsible for websites (or their content) that are not owned by the publisher.

Library of Congress Control Number: 2017954140

ISBNs: 978-0-316-44749-2 (paperback)
       978-0-316-44750-8 (ebook)

10 9 8 7 6 5 4 3 2 1

WOR

Printed in the United States of America

THANKS SO MUCH FOR EVERYTHING!

US $15.00   CAN $19.50

ISBN 978-0-316-44749-2

Rebuilding her friendship with Hajime is what would make Kaori happiest...or at least, that's what Yuuki's convinced himself of. If it may help get her memory back, there's no chance Yuuki will stand in the way. But the sudden switch from his usual enthusiasm leads his friends to notice something is off...and more than that, Kaori comes to realize that she can't seem to get Yuuki off her mind...

ONE WEEK
FRIENDS